Forge Books by Michael A. Smith

Jeremiah: Terrorist Prophet
New America
The Inheritors

NEW
AMERICA

Michael A. Smith

A TOM DOHERTY ASSOCIATES BOOK
NEW YORK

This is a work of fiction. All the characters and events portrayed in this book are either products of the author's imagination or are used fictitiously.

NEW AMERICA

A Forge Book
Published by Tom Doherty Associates, LLC
175 Fifth Avenue
New York, NY 10010

www.tor.com

Forge® is a registered trademark of Tom Doherty Associates, LLC.

ISBN: 0-812-56669-6
Library of Congress Catalog Card Number: 98-47003

First edition: April 1999
First mass market edition: June 2000

Printed in the United States of America

0 9 8 7 6 5 4 3 2 1

To my wife, Patricia,
for her unfailing love and support

Thus says the LORD:
"Behold, a people is coming from
the north country,
a great nation is stirring from
the farthest parts of the earth."
—Jeremiah 6:22

God sent Moses to Lead his People
out of Egypt, and
God has sent Jeremiah the Second
to Lead the Chosen People
to New America.
—2 Jeremiah 6:1

1

As Laura brought the coffee mug to her lips, an indistinct shape ran into her peripheral vision. Looking out the kitchen windows, she saw a burly man dressed in black rushing up the hill toward the house. As his legs pumped and his arms churned, a gun grasped tightly in his right hand jerked about wildly.

Laura jumped up, dropping the heavy earthenware mug. It bounced on the table and spewed hot coffee toward her husband, Steve, who threw aside the morning newspaper as he scooted back in his chair.

"What's wrong!" he yelled.

Speechless, Laura could only point.

Steve looked in the direction of her finger. "Goddammit!"

As the man leaped onto the front porch, Steve jerked open a kitchen cabinet drawer, and took out a black 9-mm Sig-Sauer.

Through the east window, Laura watched the trespasser kick the front door, the sole of his heavy boot landing with such force the wall vibrated. But the door held.

"Where are the guards?" Laura screamed. "Where's Maria?"

"Stay here," Steve commanded, as he rushed out of the kitchen toward the front hallway.

Laura felt rooted to the floor of the kitchen nook as the nightmare unfolded in slow motion. One of their bodyguards, Shawntel, ran into view. Through the open window, she heard him shout at the gunman, "Stop, or I'll shoot!"

The armed invader whirled around and shot first, causing Shawntel to collapse on the front lawn. The gunman resumed his assault on the door, which suddenly gave way with the sound of wood cracking. The man charged into the house.

Gunfire erupted. One shot, loud and deadly, followed by two shots so rapid their sounds nearly blended. An awful silence then prevailed, causing Laura to almost quit breathing. Her heart pounded furiously and her temples throbbed. Someone walked heavily toward the kitchen.

Suddenly, he came into view and Laura let out her breath. She ran into Steve's arms.

"It's all right," he said, his voice husky with emotion.

Clinging fiercely to her husband, Laura looked over his shoulder at the intruder lying in the entryway, half in the house, half on the porch. The smell of exploded gunpowder hung heavy in the air.

"Is he dead?" Laura asked.

"I think so."

At that point, Maria burst into the house, both hands wrapped around a handgun pointed at the man Steve had shot. Her eyes darted wildly from the fallen intruder to Steve and Laura. "I'm sorry," she said.

Is that all you have to say? Laura wondered, as Steve broke away from their embrace, picked up a phone, and dialed 911.

An hour later, Laura stood near the living room fireplace as Steve and Maria Inglesias, head of their private security detail, pieced together the story for the county sheriff, Bo Hendricks. His deputies swarmed over the house and grounds of Steve and Laura's northern Virginia farm.

Steve sat on the edge of a sofa, the Sig-Sauer lying ominously on the coffee table in front of him. Maria stood beside Hendricks, who sat on a chair across from Steve.

Laura's hands shook as she hugged herself against a pervasive chill, even though she wore a yellow sweater over a white blouse and jeans. She glanced anxiously at Steve, who occasionally looked toward the entryway where the dead intruder lay, covered by a blanket. The sickeningly sweet smell of spilled blood caused Laura to choke back vomit rising in her throat.

"Three men got out of a car parked alongside the highway and climbed the fence," Maria explained. She wore a dark blue windbreaker with yellow FBI lettering on the back. Shortly after he retired three years ago, Steve had given it to her as a present. "They ran toward the pond, and two of my guys went to head 'em off."

"This one must have come from the southwest edge of the property," Steve said, nodding toward the body. "Shawntel saw him first and took out after him."

"How is he?" Laura asked, referring to the wounded bodyguard who had been taken away by ambulance to the hospital east of Leesburg.

"It's a serious wound, but he'll survive," Steve answered.

Laura cast an accusatory look at Maria, who responded defensively, "I was down by the front gate. Someone buzzed the house and said there was a delivery."

"It was an elaborate ruse, Laura," Steve suggested, "so he could get close to us."

Laura looked helplessly about the room, then shrugged her apology to Maria, who'd become a close friend over the past four years.

Hendricks said, "Don't worry, we'll find out who this guy is." The sheriff was bald and so thin his uniform appeared to be draped over a clotheshorse.

"He's one of *them*," Laura said, sounding indignant and fearful at the same time. *Isn't that obvious to everyone?* The dead man was one of the disciples of Jeremiah, the Terrorist Prophet. One of thousands of his acolytes who'd made the pilgrimage over the past three-and-a-half years to their farm located in the foothills of the Appalachians; specifically, to the small pond in the northwest pasture where Jeremiah had mysteriously escaped the FBI in 1995, after threatening to detonate an atomic bomb located in the back of a van parked in front of their house.

"Laura's probably right," Hendricks said, pursing his

lips. "This business certainly has taken a new turn."

"Yeah," Steve agreed. "Usually they just throw some flowers in the pond, pray, or stand around and gawk."

"They've thrown eggs and rotten fruit at the house before," Laura objected sarcastically, "and shouted threats at us." Laura fixed the sheriff with a withering stare. "It wouldn't have happened if we'd been able to electrify the fence."

"Laura, you know I supported you on that," Hendricks said, wearily. "And so did the local district judge. It was the appellate court that said no."

Laura mimicked the essence of the ruling: "Our property rights don't include *'endangering the lives of innocent people expressing religious convictions.'* What crap! I hope those judges are ashamed of themselves now."

Laura swiped the hair off her face, took a cigarette out of a pack lying on the mantel, and lit up. She remembered the quaint fence of hand-stacked stones that had once outlined the front of the property and had been joined to a traditional white post-and-board fence around the horse pasture. Then came the chain-link fence topped with razor wire, but *they'd* cut through that, or found ways to climb over the top.

Hendricks coughed and stood, hitching up the pants of his dark green uniform. "When my report's typed up, I'll ask you all to review the findings and sign it, if you agree." He tried to console them. "It seems an open-and-shut case to me. An armed intruder intent on mayhem. You were perfectly justified in using deadly force, Steve."

Laura disdainfully blew a plume of smoke into the air.

Later, when everyone was gone from the house except her and Steve, Laura once again stood in the kitchen. She looked through the windows down the driveway toward the road; the direction from which the gunman had come. April showers indeed had brought May flowers. Delicate white blossoms decorated the perfectly shaped pear trees flanking the driveway. The forsythia bushes near the front gate sported bright yellow buttons. In the woods across the road, the angular dogwood trees blazed with pink and white flowers. It was the season of renewal. Even the mare in their barn was about to foal.

Laura caught a glimpse of her own reflection in the window, causing instant self-analysis. Even at thirty-eight, she had much of the beauty pageant loveliness that had carried her to the top of the television news business. Her shoulder-length hair was naturally blonde and she hadn't gained a pound in retirement, despite her teasing threats to Steve to grow fat as a result of repeated pregnancies. But there was no baby. *The big disappointment.* Even worse than the invasion of their home and privacy.

Steve walked up behind her. "What are you thinking about?"

"Nothing," she lied, pouring him a cup of coffee from an urn sitting on a hot plate. *Maybe this time we'll get to finish it,* she thought, sitting at the table.

Steve joined her. "Be truthful."

As she looked up at him, Laura became aware for the first time that day that Steve was dressed as if going to work—a white shirt, dark wool-blend trousers, dress shoes. She doubted anyone could tell he had recently been in a life-and-death struggle.

"I was thinking of the night you first moved in here," she admitted.

"I remember that red teddy you wore."

"It wasn't really edible." *Our usual banter is nice,* Laura thought, *even if awkward given the situation.* "You remember what I said."

"You said you couldn't ever imagine leaving here, or anything coming between us," Steve replied.

"Yeah," Laura said, her chagrin obvious. At the time, nearly four years ago, Steve had been an FBI agent—head of the bureau's counterterrorism unit, in fact. He'd been assigned to protect her after Jeremiah decided to use Laura as his mouthpiece; rather, to use *American Chronicle,* the twice-weekly newsmagazine show she'd hosted then, as the channel for broadcasting to the nation his twisted philosophy. "Now I can imagine leaving."

Steve nodded. "I understand, but I'm not sure that's necessary. We just have to find a new strategy."

"We had a strategy? Beyond just reacting to whatever his followers decided to do to us?"

"Yeah. The fence was a strategy. An imperfect strategy, but the best we could do when it appeared they only wanted to harass us."

"Now he wants to kill us."

Steve smiled. "Not us, Laura. Me. He'd never kill you; you know that. He has an obsession with you. Always has had."

Laura shivered, remembering Jeremiah's words whispered in her ear during the standoff down by the lake: *"Dear Laura, I'm sorry I had to bring you this far. But don't fear, you won't be killed. You can't be. Our son someday will lead New America! It's prophesied. In this war between good and evil, Laura, don't mistake the first battle for the last."*

"Who shot first?" Laura asked, nodding toward the front hallway.

"He did."

"Were you afraid?"

"Sure. Afraid he'd kill me and I'd never see you again."

"Oh, baby," Laura said, climbing onto Steve's lap, peppering his face with kisses; tasting the salt from her renewed tears. She didn't doubt he'd been afraid, just that his idea of fear was different from hers. She'd have been paralyzed; Steve meant his senses and reactions had been sharpened.

"What's changed all of a sudden?" she asked.

Steve sighed. "I don't know, Laura. We've always known Jeremiah was out there. Hiding. Waiting. Watching his followers flood into the Dakotas. Now he's ready to start the next phase of his campaign, whatever that is."

Laura felt like a coward for asking. "Steve, would it seem like I was running away if I went home to Texas for a few days? I really want to see my mom and dad."

Steve gently stroked her cheek. "Sounds like a good idea, sweetie."

"Will you come with me?"

"Let me do a few things around here, and I'll join you in a couple of days. Take Maria with you. You'll be fine."

2

Evening commuters filed off the bus, including Robert Dean, who lingered at the side of the road, waiting for several friends who'd sat in back. At this time of day, commuter buses clogged state highway 83, which connected Pierre and Bismarck, the capitals of the Dakotas, although everyone Robert knew now referred to the entire area as "New America." Nearly six million people had heeded the Prophet's call so far and migrated into the four-state area.

Robert stood near the bus shelter, his hands shoved into his pants pockets, as he rocked idly from heel to toe and looked out over the countryside—rolling hills covered with long, green prairie grasses sprinkled with tiny yellow, purple, and pink flowers.

"So, Robert, what was the condom count down at the shit factory today?" interrupted Winston Margolis, one of Robert's fellow commuters and a physical therapist at the nearby sprawling Science Center.

Robert laughed politely at the tired old joke about his job at the local sewage treatment plant. Truth was, most people had no idea what their neighbors flushed down the toilet. Still, Margolis's comments rankled a bit, since Robert considered his work to be socially necessary and important, as defined by *Second Jeremiah.*

Robert changed the subject by gesturing toward laborers

working on the highway even during rush hour. "I hear it will be six lanes wide by next summer."

"Think about what a mess it would be if we all had our own cars up here," Margolis responded.

Personal cars were seldom seen in New America because they had been described by the Prophet in *Second Jeremiah* as being related to excessive pride and rampant individualism, both sins.

"Automobiles pollute the environment," Robert said. "They deplete the oil reserves of Third World countries, ensuring that native populations will be eventually impoverished and that America could always be sucked into a war over oil."

Margolis playfully put up both hands to stop Robert's recitation. "I know, I know. Cars are a symbol of racism and imperialism. I read the book. Still, you've got to admit, Robert, it would be nice to hop in your own buggy now and then and take off by yourself."

That's how social disorder started, Robert thought, *when everyone began thinking only of their selfish needs.* Robert vividly remembered his commute on the highways surrounding Saint Louis. Hundreds of frustrated, enraged road warriors manipulating two-ton killing machines across multiple lanes of traffic in some insane game of competition and intimidation.

Robert didn't mind riding the bus to and from his job at the new sewage treatment plant, where he was chief engineer. The atmosphere inside the bus promoted a sense of community. The ride allowed him time to read, relax, and think positive thoughts.

Robert walked with the other commuters down the main street of Anathoth, named after a village in ancient Judah that was the birthplace of the Old Testament Jeremiah. The early Jeremiah had envisioned a purged and rejuvenated Davidic kingdom. *It's been a long-time coming,* Robert thought, *and on the other side of the earth, New America, inspired by Jeremiah the Second.*

Those in the outside world might see Anathoth as a large trailer court, with all the unfortunate connotations of that phrase, but Robert understood that a community experiencing such rapid growth—nearly forty thousand newcomers in the last two years alone—had to rely temporarily on "manufactured housing." They'd build permanent homes when time allowed. Now they were busy building a nation.

Most of the roads in Anathoth remained unpaved. With residents walking wherever they went, and kids constantly running about, a dust cloud hung permanently above the settlement. *It must have been this way when these rolling prairies were covered with migrating herds of buffalo,* Robert thought. He fervently hoped New America wouldn't go the way of the buffalo.

Robert smiled as he saw a towhead running toward him. Douglas, his eight-year-old son, who the neighborhood kids affectionately called Douggie.

"Douglas!" Robert said, as the boy ran right into his arms. Robert hoisted him into the air, and then Douglas sat in the crook of his father's strong, right arm. Annie, his wife, and Patty, their eleven-year-old daughter, stood up the road a ways, at the entrance to their cul-de-sac.

"What did you learn today?" Robert asked Douglas.

"More math. I can do all my multiplication tables up to ten."

"Great. Remember, math and science are keys to knowledge. And mankind's purpose in the world is accumulation of knowledge."

"So sayeth the Prophet!" Douglas recited, flashing a broad smile marred by several missing teeth.

As Robert and Douglas came abreast of the two women in the family, Annie said, "Hi, honey, how was your day?"

"Great. Patty, Douglas was telling me about his math exercises. What did you learn today?"

"I learned there's a lot of smut on the Internet," Patty said, breathlessly, as she sneaked a sideways look at her mother.

"Some things you can't get away from, even up here," Annie explained, arching her eyebrows critically. "On the other hand, I believe someone was supposed to be searching cyberspace for information on photography, not pornography."

When the Dean family reached their single-wide, Robert

reached out and opened the door for his family. He beamed at his wife, son, and daughter. "I just can't get over it. No locks on the door! And we don't have to worry about anyone breaking in." Anathoth truly was the "dream" Jeremiah had spoken about so often. They lived here without fear.

After dinner, Robert helped Annie with the
dishes, while the kids went outside to play before it got dark. Robert feared Annie would once again bring up the subject of money. It was all they talked about lately when they were alone.

She didn't disappoint him. "Are they still talking about implementing wage equality at the plant?"

"Eventually, it'll happen," Robert replied. It was in the book. *Second Jeremiah*, chapter 4. Wealth could only be created by physical and intellectual labor, usually collective labor. No man should own the product of another man's labor, which he willingly donated to the state in return for being part of a community and enjoying the benefits of a shared philosophy. All labor in socially necessary work was therefore equal. Wage equality would be achieved through a sophisticated computer-run barter system still in the conception stage. The Wealth Exchange.

"I just worry about how we'll make out if you don't get your wage differential," Annie repeated. Concern, even fright, was written on her face.

Robert shrugged. He currently received a higher salary than unskilled labor at the treatment plant because he had a college degree in engineering. Despite rumors about a new currency, New American wages were paid in old American dollars.

"It's one of the reasons we were able to move here," Annie noted, pointedly.

"Yes, but we also knew there'd eventually be a transition to a fairer reward system," Robert gently reminded her. He considered himself lucky to have such a worthwhile job, even though it might be a joke to some of his neighbors. Some people, he knew, were *assigned* necessary jobs. Everyone worked. It's what had to be done to allow New

America to survive and prosper. In Robert's mind, state economic planning made more sense than workers having to choose among jobs made available in a marketplace manipulated by shadowy Wall Street figures for the sole purpose of *profit*. Planning allowed implementation of social goals. For example, several clothing and shoe factories had been established in New America so they wouldn't be dependent on foreign workers to clothe them.

Annie rose and began clearing the table. "It's just that I don't understand how it will work. Right now, we need money to live. If we're going to have another baby, we'll need a bigger place. You know how long the waiting list is for a double-wide? Will we ever be able to afford to build a real home here?"

Robert took his wife in his arms. "It'll work out, Annie. Look at all the wonderful things that are happening in New America. Take the kids. We get to school them at home, and in the neighborhood teaching co-op. Isn't that working out?"

"I agree, it's wonderful, Robert."

"You and the other wives can teach the basics and the Bible. We don't have to worry about what will happen to our kids in public schools. We don't have to worry about them being assaulted, or pressured into sex and drug use, or having to listen to all kinds of evil ideas."

"You're right," Annie agreed, although still shaking her head.

Robert rubbed her back. "You just have to have faith, Annie. With faith, everything will work out."

"I know, I know," she said, but he felt hot tears running down the side of her face. He pressed her slender frame close to him, so he could feel her stomach. Was a seed already planted there?

Later, Robert walked alone in the neighborhood, wanting to enjoy a few minutes of solitude and the wonderful spring weather. They'd moved here a year ago last February, when the wind chill yielded temperatures the equivalent of twenty below. Still, he loved life in Anathoth. The "big sky" above the prairie seemed to indicate there was room here for everything under the heavens.

Anathoth was largely contained within an outer ring road. Inside the circle, two intersecting straight roads formed a cross. Within each quadrant were figure-eight roads providing access to many tear-shaped cul-de-sacs, like the one Robert and his family lived in. Someone had told him that from the air the design resembled a giant pendant, combining elements of the Christian cross and the ROSE flag carried by the New America National Guard.

Robert didn't like to think of the military. He hadn't even approved of Jeremiah's use of terrorism to attract followers, although Robert would never tell that to anyone else. He had come here just to lead a different lifestyle, based on God's revelations to Jeremiah. Fairness, equality, justice, a high moral purpose; that's what Robert wanted, whether the Prophet was alive or not.

As he walked on a makeshift dirt path linking two cul-de-sacs, Robert heard a commotion behind some bushes. He peered through an opening and saw three men wrestling another to the ground.

"What's going on!" Robert demanded.

"We caught this degenerate exposing himself to some kids!" replied Sgt. Vincent Dale, who wore the distinctive uniform of the New America State Police: campaign hat, taupe-colored shirt, jodhpurs, and knee-high, black leather boots. Every community in New America had a resident policeman who enforced the Social Contract set forth in *Second Jeremiah*.

"It's all a lie," the accused flasher protested.

The man had a day or two's growth of dark beard and his hair was uncombed and matted. He wore baggy, light-gray pants that were clearly stained. *Has he been masturbating?* Robert wondered. *My God, were the social diseases of Saint Louis and old America infecting Anathoth?*

"Two people saw you!" Sergeant Dale said, shoving the handcuffed man forward. "The rest of you come with me. Everyone needs to witness this."

The policeman pushed the man down several streets toward the community stocks. As news of the crime spread, the procession increased in number. Robert watched as some began to kick and hit the accused. One woman repeatedly lashed him with a large switch that appeared to be a branch from a sapling, although precious few trees grew on the prairie.

Near a community hall still under construction, Sergeant Dale uncuffed the man and forced him into one of the stocks, which closed like a vice around his hands and neck, causing the prisoner to bend at nearly a ninety-degree angle from his waist. Five other members of the community were similarly incarcerated.

The alleged exhibitionist continued to loudly protest his innocence. "I didn't do nothin'!"

"That's not what the kids say!"

"They're lying! Those goddammed kids lie all the time."

"A woman saw you," Sergeant Dale snarled.

"She's a bitch! She hates me 'cause she says I stole a lawnmower from her yard."

"So you're a thief, too!"

"No, she's lying 'bout everything."

"You're not fooling anyone," another voice boomed from the crowd. "There's no presumption of innocence here. *Second Jeremiah* 5:12."

The man in the stocks replied angrily, "Ain't suppose to be any taxes in New America. Same chapter, verse 8. No representative government, either, but the so-called leaders of this community have been 'round to my place telling me who to vote for. Asking for donations so we can put up this so-called community center. What's the difference between taxes and somebody forcing you to make a donation?"

Robert looked around, surprised at how large the crowd had grown. Many people shouted out responses:

"Rome wasn't built in a day!"

"You should be happy to help this Christian city grow!"

"Go back to wherever you came from!"

Robert agreed with most of what was said. The accused man's remarks bothered him, though. *Second Jeremiah* decried representative government and advocated a direct democracy, presumably to be conducted over the Internet. Yet New Americans were still asked to go to the polls and elect city and county officials, members of the state legislature, and members of Congress. The official justification put out over the state news network was that New Americans had to have their own kind in elective office to protect every-one's rights. Direct democracy would come later.

Sergeant Dale disappeared into the crowd and reemerged moments later with a man Robert recognized as the com-munity tattooist. Those put in the public stocks for a serious infraction had a numbered code tattooed on their body. In the case of this pervert, it would be across his forehead.

The tattooist efficiently went about his work with needles and ink and a satisfied murmur rippled through the crowd.

"I don't have any problem with you locking up a per-vert," a woman shouted to the crowd, "but what about my boy!" The woman pointed to a teenager in the stocks. He had a distinctive appearance Robert seldom saw in Ana-thoth, or anywhere else in New America, for that matter. The boy's hair was close-cropped two inches above his ears, then long and braided. He had a barbed-wire tattoo around his upper arm. He wore a T-shirt on which several obscenities were imprinted. The boy's jeans rode so low on his hips that the top half of his boxer shorts could be seen. However, the effect of this in-your-face outfit was offset by the prisoner's near state of collapse. His body sagged so much that Robert feared he might strangle in the stocks.

"What's Rex here for?" his mother asked again. She had close-cropped blonde hair and black semicircles under her eyes. Robert saw she smoked a cigarette in clear violation of a prohibition set forth in *Second Jeremiah*.

"I'll tell you why. It's because you people don't like him. Don't like his haircut, don't like the way he dresses, don't like his music." She released pent-up energy by jabbing at the heavens with the two fingers holding the cigarette. "This place is like Nazi Germany!"

A woman stepped out of the crowd, her face equally twisted in anger, "That's right, Mary Ann, we don't like Rex! Everyone knows all about him. He's a wannabe street thug who smokes, curses, and bullies other kids."

"People have caught him with alcohol."

"He steals!" someone else shouted out.

"Fuck all of you!" Mary Ann retorted, and an ugly buzz swept through the crowd.

"Go back to LA!"

"Believe me, we're outta here," Mary Ann shouted, defiantly. "Just as soon as you let Rex go."

"Good riddance," said a man standing beside Robert. "I know your husband, Mary Ann. You two came up here just for the construction work. To make big money, quick. You never shared our values, but you thought you'd flaunt yours in our faces. We came here to get away from trash like you and your boy."

As Mary Ann again cursed her adversaries, Robert watched another woman open her personal copy of *Second Jeremiah*, and read in a loud, singsong voice, " 'The life of cleanliness, orderliness, self-sacrifice, dignity, prayer, and reflection is much beloved by the LORD; the loud, boisterous, disorderly, and obnoxious are a grievous vexation to the LORD.' "

Mary Ann gave the crowd the finger, prompting Sergeant Dale to walk over and slap her face. "I think you can join your son for a day or two." He began to wrestle her toward an empty stock.

"Wait a minute!" a man called out, and Robert looked in his direction, as did all others in the assemblage. The man stood on a small hill located behind the stocks. He was dressed in black, as was the custom among many community leaders, most of whom had emerged by the force of their personality. This man looked vaguely familiar, although Robert couldn't place him. Certainly, he projected a commanding presence.

Equally intriguing to Robert were the three individuals standing beside the man in black. They looked to be a television news crew: two men and a beautiful young woman. Robert looked more closely at a camera held by one of the men and made out the words: "MIDWEST NEWS SERVICE."

"Outside media agitators" weren't allowed in New

America, but Robert noticed that Sergeant Dale hadn't made an effort to run off this crew.

The man dressed in black walked to a spot in front of the stocks, where he faced the crowd. "I've been listening to all this and it makes my heart ache," he said. "I hoped I'd left all this behind. People breaking the law without any fear of consequences. Inadequate punishments that don't really deter criminals. Greed. Endless bickering, with a thousand points of view represented, but no consensus ever achieved. No firm philosophical ground, just moral quicksand. You know when it was I committed myself to Jeremiah and the concept of New America?" He paused, although not really waiting for an answer to his rhetorical question. "It was when Jeremiah said people had a choice between good and evil. They weren't compelled to do evil by Satan, or society, or their genes, or anyone else. It was a *choice* they made.

"Jeremiah said good people should separate themselves into a new land. That's what we did. That's why we're here in New America. We're building the good life. We've chosen it freely. As for the many who won't make that commitment and choice, remember what the Prophet said, 'Obey or die!' "

Robert saw many in the crowd nod vigorously.

The man looked over his shoulder at those in the stocks, then back at the crowd. "I say let this woman and her boy get on the road to Los Angeles right now. He can get back into his old gang, selling dope and shooting innocent people. His mom and dad can sit isolated in their small apartment, smoking and boozing it up, and worrying about money."

Robert shoved his hands in his pockets and looked at the ground in shame for his wife's worries.

"As for the scum who exposed himself to children, we know what he's likely to do next. Cast him out also. If you see him again anywhere in New America, with the mark of a Sodomite on his forehead, kill him." The man paused, smiled, and then melted into the crowd.

Robert watched Sergeant Dale unlock the stocks and free Rex, as well as the man accused of exposing himself. The policeman talked briefly to all three violators, who then hustled away. All the while, the camera crew continued filming.

Some in the crowd began returning to their homes, but Robert edged closer to the news crew. He couldn't help but stare at the young woman with the microphone. She was more beautiful than anyone he'd seen in a long time. Blonde, busty, wearing a short, tight skirt that barely covered her beautiful, long legs.

As the camera continued to roll, Robert listened to part of her stand-up report. "This is Julie Burton reporting from Anathoth, in New America, giving many of our viewers their first look at justice, New America style, which seems like a throwback to colonial times. There was an extraordinary scene here today . . ."

As Robert walked home at sunset, he thought

about the last man's speech to the crowd: obey or die. Robert had come to fervently believe in that philosophy. He knew it seemed harsh back in Saint Louis, where many people, including some of his relatives, thought everyone in New America was a nut or racist. They just didn't understand the beauty of social order and shared values.

But Robert knew that real evil involved breaking the expanded commandments the Lord gave to Jeremiah the Second, which were referred to in New America as the Social Contract, 2 Jeremiah 2: 6–26.

Why is it so hard for people to do good? he wondered. You just did it. But for the last two thousand years, most people did just exactly as they pleased, motivated by selfishness or their obsession with power and greed. *They won't even obey God's word, let alone man's law.* Unless the punishment was so severe that fear compelled them *not* to do evil. It was harsh, but it was true. Robert would have preferred that people do the right thing because it was the right thing to do. But they wouldn't, and the Prophet had come up with a better way: obey or die.

All it will take to make New America a utopia is committed, hard-working, righteous people who choose to do good, Robert thought. He was committed to being one of the chosen few. The last thing he wanted was to return to Saint Louis.

3

Relaxed, happy, safe. That's how Laura felt as she sat poolside at her parents' house in the west Texas hill country, between the Pedernales and Colorado Rivers.

She sat with her eyes closed, imagining she was one of the hawks soaring high above the hacienda-style ranch where she had been born and raised. She remembered every chink in the house's white stucco finish and knew where a whole section of red roof tiles had been replaced following a storm when she was a sophomore in high school. She envisioned every nook and cranny inside the house, which sat well back from the road, shaded by oak, box elder, and pecan trees. As a girl, Laura at one time or another had climbed all of them, imagining then, as now, that she was above it all.

As a child, Laura had roamed the nearby hills on horseback, exploring plateaus and canyons. Once, she'd swam naked in a lake lined with cypress trees. Horses, cattle, deer, quail, and armadillos outnumbered people. It was a place where she could be free from fear.

The pool was nestled into a U-shaped area created by the front of the house and its two parallel wings. A stone and wrought iron wall connected the two wings and enclosed the compound. Beyond the wall was a greenhouse where Laura's mother lovingly raised all varieties of plants and flowers. Surrounding the house were a thousand acres of fenced pasture where cattle grazed, as it seemed they always had.

Wearing a floppy, broad-brimmed hat and white bikini, Laura sipped on a mint julep and thought for the longest time about absolutely nothing. When her skin began tingling from the effects of the hot summer sun, Laura lathered herself with sunscreen.

She glanced over at Maria, who sat beside her on a lounge chair with its back up. Maria was alert, watchful. Laura's bodyguard wore a one-piece black bathing suit that complimented her dark hair and olive skin. Maria drank from a glass of iced tea that sat on a table beside a nasty-looking Beretta.

"Wouldn't you rather have a mint julep?" Laura asked, feeling guilty that Maria was on the job.

"Booze takes away my edge," Maria replied, swinging around to sit sideways on her chaise longue, so she could look directly at Laura. "You go ahead and knock yourself out, though."

"We're perfectly safe here," Laura said, with as much conviction as she could muster. With all the evasive measures they'd taken in leaving the Washington, D.C., metro area, including flying out on a private jet, no one could have possibly followed them here. Steve had arranged for two additional security guards to patrol the ranch grounds.

Over the past four years, Laura had developed an easy relationship with Maria. The bodyguard maintained her sculpted physique through a routine of running and weight lifting. She sometimes practiced her martial arts skills with Steve, who'd told Laura that Maria also was a crack shot with the nine millimeter and other weapons.

It occurred to Laura how much happier she'd be if she was in better shape; if she were happier, maybe she could get pregnant.

Laura watched as Maria frowned and looked around, not so much at their surroundings, but as if to take in a broader perspective. "This trip has brought back a lot of memories," the bodyguard said.

"You were raised in El Paso, right?" Laura asked.

"Talk about the end of the earth!" Maria spat. "When I

was fifteen, we moved to Corpus Christi. I was really excited when we drove down Ocean Drive past all the beautiful homes lining the bay. But I got a dose of reality when we arrived at our shack in the Hispanic ghetto. We were still spics, greasers, beaners. Take your pick of labels. I've been called all of 'em."

Laura remained silent, embarrassed, not knowing what to say. She'd grown up happy, benefiting from a lifestyle of wealth and privilege.

Maria inhaled deeply and blew out a long breath. "I'm sorry. Just some latent resentments."

Laura reached over and squeezed her bodyguard's hand, hoping to acknowledge the hurt a beautiful, smart young girl like Maria must have felt at being the object of discrimination. *Maria could have let such prejudices warp her personality and push her into antisocial action,* Laura thought.

" 'Course, there was a bright side, too," Maria continued, standing and shaking out her cramped leg muscles. "My dad was a maintenance man at a hotel on the bay. When I drove down to pick him up one afternoon, we gave this young waiter a ride home."

Laura's eyes brightened. "José!"

"Yeah," Maria said. "He was hot! Three years older than me. A college student from San Antonio, working a summer job."

The University of Texas had a branch campus in San Antonio, Laura remembered. She'd attended two years at the main campus in Austin before taking her first television broadcast job as "the weather girl" at NBC's Kansas City affiliate. Ironically, Jeremiah had killed José at a Kansas City hotel airport nearly four years ago. In turn, Steve nearly killed Jeremiah. God, how Laura wished it had ended there!

Unlike Maria, Laura had nothing but good memories of her childhood, which truly had been a fairy-tale existence, complete with storybook parents—her beautiful mother, who'd been Miss Texas four years before Laura was born, and her handsome father, an oil and cattle baron, state senator, and once ambassador to Panama. She still had good relationships with her older brother, Bill, a businessman in Dallas, as well as her younger sister, Cathy, who was married to a doctor and lived in Houston. Both had promised to come visit this weekend, giving Laura four precious days alone with her parents.

At that moment, they came out of the house, with Laura's mother, Barbara, leading the way. Her father, Wyatt, who'd suffered a stroke a year ago, lagged behind, walking with a cane.

Her mother still looked like a reigning beauty queen. Not one silver-tinted hair was out of place, and her face had few lines. Bright and cheerful as usual, she wore crisp, cuffed white shorts and a sleeveless blouse that resembled an abstract painting, featuring all the colors on the palette.

Laura had followed in her mother's footsteps, having been named Miss Texas in 1978 and fourth runner-up in the Miss America contest. That had led to the job in Kansas City, where Laura Delaney was "discovered" and began her career in broadcast journalism, first with NBC and later with the United Broadcasting Corporation.

"More mint juleps," Barbara announced, holding forth an iced pitcher dripping with condensation.

"More booze," Wyatt proclaimed, slurring his words. He wore his usual uniform of jeans and a patterned western shirt with fake pearl snap buttons that Laura swore was at least thirty years old.

Laura rose and took the pitcher from her mother.

"Pour me one, girl," her father said. The stroke had mainly affected the right side of his face, giving him a squinty-eyed, wild appearance, exaggerated by gray hair that stood on end, as if electrified.

Laura couldn't help but tease him. "I thought the doctor said you weren't supposed to drink, Daddy?"

"He don't know shit!" Wyatt answered, rising to the bait.

"Your father, of course, has a medical degree," Barbara observed drolly, giving Laura a sudden insight into her relationship with Steve. She'd learned how to handle men from her mother.

All in all, my parents seem the same, Laura thought, *even though they are both well into their sixties.* She put an arm around each aging parent and steered them toward a patio table shaded by an umbrella. She prayed silently and unrealistically that neither of them would ever die. Lately, Laura had developed a great fear of being left alone in the world.

"Come join us, Maria," Wyatt said, "unless you want to take a dip. You can skinny dip here, ya know. Nobody can see you."

"Wyatt, for God's sake!"

"What?" he stuttered. "What'd I say?"

The statuesque bodyguard sauntered over to the table, smiled at Wyatt, and raised one eyebrow seductively.

"Jesus, don't encourage him." Laura laughed.

Laura and her parents each had a glass of the syrupy bourbon, although Maria stuck with her iced tea.

"I've got an idea about how to deal with those shit heads who trespass on your farm, Laura," her father said, parceling out each word carefully and slowly.

"Wyatt, we don't need to talk about that."

He ignored his wife's gentle rebuke. "You remember the annual rattlesnake hunt, Laura? I'll have the boys put about a hun'erd rattlers in a big crate and ship it up there to Virginny. You dump 'em in the pasture, and I'll guarantee those folks'll stay off your land!"

"Great idea, Daddy. Don't know why we didn't think of it before."

As her mother announced plans to visit neighbors and relatives the next morning, Laura watched her father light up a cigar and fill the air with a heavy blue smoke.

After a late dinner of thick steaks and two bottles of California merlot, Laura was exhausted by too much sun and alcohol. At nine o'clock, she headed toward her bedroom in the west wing of the house. Maria would be sleeping next door, in Cathy's old room.

Laura carelessly shed all her clothes and collapsed into bed, covering herself partly with a sheet. Before drifting off to sleep, she thought about how much fun it would be when her husband, brother, and sister came to visit. She felt like a child whose wishes were about to come true.

But Laura's dreams were very mature, as she lay on her stomach, imagining Steve was astride her, rubbing her shoulders and back, her buttocks, her thighs—between her thighs. She spread her legs to accommodate him and, then, her dream world and reality merged as Laura realized that *someone else was in her bed!*

She flipped onto her back, and even in the dark she recognized him. Laura tried to scream, but he clamped his hand over her mouth and lay on her stomach, pinning her down with his weight.

"Laura, it's been such a long time," Jeremiah whispered in her ear.

She struggled, but to no avail. He was too strong.

"That's it, relax," he whispered in her ear.

Her eyes bulged, giving Laura a distorted view of the room beyond his head. All she could see was his face—the slender nose, the tightly curled blond hair now flecked with gray. The vacuous, faded blue eyes.

He used a knee to force open her legs, and Laura responded by biting down hard on his hand. She bit into muscle and bone, hoping something would break. Although he had a grip on one arm, Laura dug the fingernails of her free hand into Jeremiah's back until she felt blood running.

Jeremiah didn't seem to notice her efforts to wound him as he entered her, causing a hot, searing pain that made Laura involuntarily give up her struggle, close her eyes, and arch her neck. *Where is Maria? Did Jeremiah kill her?*

"That's it," Jeremiah said, his breath labored. "Just lie back and enjoy yourself."

That comment reinvigorated Laura, who freed her other arm and began flaying about with both fists, hitting his back, trying unsuccessfully to knock the phone off the nightstand. She also used her heels like hammers on the back of his calves.

"That's good," Jeremiah responded. "Keep bucking, Laura! I like it. You're everything I've dreamed about."

She temporarily exhausted herself, and Jeremiah took that opportunity to gag her with a pillowcase. He pinned her wrists to the bed and continued to pound away at her.

Laura's head lolled from side to side as she drifted into a state of semiconsciousness escape.

Finally, he finished and rolled off. Jeremiah forced Laura to turn on her side and covered her body with an arm and a leg, to prevent her from escaping. Laura smelled his sweat and sour breath, as well as the semen leaking from her body.

"Was it as good for you as it was for me, Laura? I hope so. You'd better get used to it because you're coming with me back to New America."

She screamed, *No, no!* but it came out as unintelligible grunts, causing Jeremiah to tighten the pillowcase gag. "Don't accidentally smother yourself, Laura. You listen quietly and I'll tell you everything that's happened to me over the past three-and-a-half years. Bring you up to date. I know you're interested; otherwise why would you have come here alone, without Steve? My people have been watching and waiting for the right moment for us to get together. How nice of you to accommodate me. Nothing happens without a purpose, you know."

Laura heeded his warning about the gag. When she quit struggling, he relaxed his hold on the pillowcase, allowing her to breathe easier.

"I know Steve and the FBI were stunned and baffled when they discovered the air lock and drainage pipe near the bottom of the pond," Jeremiah said. "The Lord always provides for those doing his work. Anyway, after I crawled out the end of the pipe where it empties into the creek, my supporters were waiting.

"I hid out in Winchester for a while until arrangements were made to transport me to Canada. Then it was on to China, where the Americans couldn't touch me."

Laura tried to see him out of the corner of her eye. *This can't be happening,* she told herself. *It's a nightmare.*

"For the last year and a half, I've been operating secretly in New America, making preparations for my official coming out," Jeremiah said, softly. "Which will occur soon. Remember the prophecy, Laura? There's a big battle coming in the year three that will result in New America's independence, so sayeth the Lord to me in *The Book of*

Second Jeremiah." He kissed her cheek. "Also, you remember what I told you at your farm nearly four years ago. The Lord has prophesied a new leader for New America in the year twenty-seven. That will be our son. If we didn't conceive him tonight, Laura, we'll try, try again. It's the New American way!"

Jeremiah leaned over Laura, snatched a piece of rope from the floor and tied her hands behind her back. Laura watched him get dressed in the dark, and she felt embarrassed, lying naked in bed. Then she summoned all her courage and rolled off the bed, fearlessly aiming her head at the nightstand. She felt a sharp pain in her neck as she connected with the target. Laura fell to the floor with a loud thump as the nightstand came crashing down, flinging the telephone against a chest of drawers. Its internal bell rang once.

Jeremiah grabbed Laura by one arm and jerked her to a standing position, before shoving her violently back onto the bed. "You'll regret that," he hissed, and indeed she was immediately sorry. What if her parents did come to her rescue? They were no match for him! Even in the moonlight filtering through an open window, she could see the well-defined muscles of his body.

Laura heard footsteps in the hallway and guessed it was her mother. Even though her parents' bedroom was in the opposite wing of the house, many years ago her dad had installed a security system that included sound sensors that conveyed noises from throughout the house to a master console in their bedroom. Wyatt had felt it was necessary, given his wealth and celebrity at the time.

Laura tried to scream a warning, but the gag muffled her voice.

When the door to her room opened, however, it was her father she saw leaning on his cane and pointing a revolver with his left hand. He looked briefly at Laura and she obligingly rolled off the other side of the bed onto the floor next to the wall, so her father would have a safe field of fire.

But Jeremiah slammed the door shut, holding it with his right hand as he reached out and opened the top drawer of the nearby dresser to get a handhold. Before he could drag the dresser against the door, her father fired two bullets through it, causing Jeremiah to jump aside and press himself against the wall. Laura was jubilant. *Her precious, loving, stroke-impaired father—no shrinking violet was he in the face of danger!*

As the door opened again, Laura sat up and looked over the top of the bed at Jeremiah, so her father knew where the terrorist was. But Jeremiah quickly shoved the entire chest of drawers along the wall, closing and blocking the door.

Laura pulled her knees to her chest, straining mightily to slip her bound hands over her butt and ankles. She succeeded just as Jeremiah reached for her. Laura lashed out with a well-placed kick, catching him between the legs. He doubled over in pain and backed away toward an open window.

Laura scrambled to her feet, jumped over the bed, and pushed aside the dresser. She opened the door and pulled the gag from her mouth. "Shoot the sonofabitch!" she yelled at her father, who squeezed through the opening, took aim, and fired once at Jeremiah.

The terrorist dove headfirst out an open window. Wyatt hobbled to the window, firing three more shots into the night.

"Are you all right?" her father stammered.

"Yes," Laura said. Naked, but too engrossed to be self-conscious, she held out her bound hands and her father helped her untie the rope.

Her mother appeared suddenly, gasped at the scene, and picked up the telephone. As she dialed 911, Laura stepped into the hallway and cautiously opened the door to the adjoining bedroom, expecting the worst. She flipped on the light switch. Maria lay on her bed, bound and gagged. Laura stepped into the room and shut the door, so her parents couldn't see in.

Maria wasn't dead, she was naked and drenched in sweat. "I'm sorry, Laura," Maria moaned, as Laura took out the gag and began to untie her. "I don't know how he got into my room!"

"Did he rape you?" Laura asked, horrified.

Maria bit her lip and looked away as she nodded once. Then she looked back at Laura, in the same appraising way. "You, too?"

Laura didn't answer. She backed across the room and leaned against the door, which vibrated from her father's insistent pounding and garbled questions. Laura slid down the door and sat on the floor, covering her mouth with her hands to muffle the sobbing she couldn't control.

But her head jerked up when her mother announced, "Someone's lying in the yard!"

Laura jumped up and rushed to the bedroom window, as the door opened and her parents entered. Maria hurriedly put on her pajamas, while Laura leaned halfway out the window, squinting into the darkness.

"One of the guards is standing over a body," Laura said, looking back at the others.

Still holding the handgun, Wyatt did a dance around his cane. "I got the sonofabitch!" he crowed. "Shot him fuckin' dead!"

4

As the jetliner made its approach to the Sioux Falls airport, Hans Dietrich Hoffman looked out the window at the hometown of Trent Dillman, aka Jeremiah the Terrorist Prophet. An influx of New Americans into the South Dakota city over the past three years had tripled its population to approximately three hundred thousand.

Hoffman's educated eye noted a half-dozen F-16s sitting on a tarmac adjacent to the airport—fighter jets of the South Dakota Air National Guard that were now under the direct control of Gov. Davey Schropa, Jeremiah's boyhood friend, who had suddenly become a successful politician.

Walking into the small airport terminal, Hoffman scarcely broke stride as he spotted a black-suited chauffeur holding a sign that read: HOFFMAN. That alias hadn't yet been compromised.

"You Duncan?" Hoffman asked.

"Yeah. You check your bags?"

"Yeah," parroted Hoffman, handing over the claim stubs to the driver who, in reality, he knew to be an undercover FBI agent.

"It's the black BMW out front," Duncan said.

Hoffman watched the "chauffeur" walk over and stand near the baggage carousel. Short and wiry, with a cocky bearing, Duncan took off his cap and ran a hand over his bald head, a contrast to his dark beard stubble.

Hoffman walked outside and waited, confident that his

appearance and Americanisms made him indistinguishable
from any other visiting businessman.

A half-mile southeast of the airport, Hoffman saw a state
prison, similar to the federal penitentiary at Leavenworth,
where Jeremiah had poisoned the water system, killing
nearly 230 inmates. Hoffman hoped to be instrumental in
sending the terrorist to jail, but he suspected Jeremiah
wouldn't be taken alive. Prison for him would be a death
sentence anyway.

Duncan loaded Hoffman's luggage into the trunk, got
behind the wheel, and drove north several miles to an on-
ramp leading to Interstate 29. "We're taking a roundabout
route to Pierre, the state capital," Duncan explained, talking
into the rearview mirror as he adjusted it. "They want me
to give you a look-see at a cross section of the state, so
you'll get an idea of what's been happenin' up here in
South Dakota-cum-New America."

Hoffman chuckled. "What's your cover?"

Duncan pulled an ID wallet out of his jacket pocket and
held it up for Hoffman's view. "Sergeant, State Police."

"Very impressive."

"I'm stationed in the barracks at Pierre, not far from the
National Guard post where you'll report. They always detail someone to pick up VIP's, including newly arriving
military officers, so I made a few subtle moves to get this
job," Duncan explained. "Money passed hands, if you know
what I mean."

"Gotcha."

Duncan glanced at Hoffman's image in the rearview mirror. "What can you tell me about yourself?"

Hoffman understood. He and Duncan would be working
close together and might have to trust each other with their
lives.

"After graduating from the University of Heidelberg, I
did a tour of duty in the Bundeswehr," Hoffman said. "Artillery officer. Now I'm a magazine journalist." Duncan already knew he'd worked for the American Central
Intelligence Agency the past fifteen years.

Since the CIA was prohibited by law from conducting
covert operations within the United States, Hoffman was

"on loan" to American Patriots, a private organization created in 1995 by Arnold Wescott, a former top aide to Pres. Bob Carpenter. Wescott, now deceased, had used the organization as a vehicle to raise reward money for the capture of Jeremiah. Now the business-oriented, conservative organization served occasionally as an FBI contractor. Hoffman knew there was speculation American Patriots might be converted to a third U.S. political party, given the right circumstances.

"You knew Dorfler and his daughter," Duncan said.

Hoffman nodded. "I was with a U.S. Army unit when they interrogated Katrina Dorfler near Nuremberg. Trying to find out where her father was, but she didn't really know anything." Her father had fled Germany only to be cornered in Quebec City by Steve Wallace and a CIA team. There, the German neo-Nazi, Trent Dillman's uncle and the mastermind behind the plot to establish New America, committed suicide by taking a cyanide pill.

"She's in New America, you know."

"Yeah." That was another reason they'd picked him for this assignment, Hoffman knew. If he could spot Katrina, he might find her first cousin and sometimes lover, Jeremiah. The terrorist had been spotted several months ago in New America.

Hoffman looked out the window at the bucolic scenery, which reminded him of parts of Germany—rolling hills of fertile ground planted with endless acres of alfalfa, soybeans, and corn. Miles and miles of corn. He recalled an American ditty about a good corn crop being "knee-high by the fourth of July," which was only a few weeks away. The last American Independence Day of the century, if you thought that the new millennium began January 1, 2000. Everything in life was really open to question, he knew.

"There's a storm rolling in from the west," Duncan observed.

Hoffman looked out at the sky. Dark angry storm clouds pushed towering white cumulus clouds ahead of them. Where they'd collided, the sky became a multicolored painting—azure blue at the top, dark gray in the middle, and pink at the bottom, where light from the hidden sun filtered through. Powerful lightning strikes generated secondary tentacles and a delayed boom that caused farm animals feeding in the fields to begin moving toward the protection of barns. The wind picked up, blowing through the evergreen windbreaks and causing seed tufts from the cottonwood trees to soar high into the air. Then the rain came.

After about a half hour of driving north, Duncan turned east, away from the fertile eastern river valleys, and headed west on a two-lane highway into the interior of the state. Within twenty miles, the terrain changed subtly, as an occasional area of rolling range land appeared, covered with the ubiquitous prairie grasses. They passed many small lakes fed by underground aquifers and more fields of wheat and oats. On the otherwise flat prairie, the farm houses were especially noticeable because of their carefully cultivated trees. It was the South Dakota Hoffman had read about in Ole Rolvaag's books. Many western Europeans, including thousands of Germans, had immigrated to the Dakotas during the last century.

But there also was something new in east-central South Dakota—evidence of New America. Large mobile home parks had sprouted on the open range. Hoffman knew enough about American history to draw a parallel with the westward migration of the nineteenth century, when settlers in covered wagons circled together for protection from the elements and their many enemies.

"The reason for all the mobile homes is that it's the most practical way for them to cope with the tremendous population growth," Duncan explained.

Although the legitimate news media was severely harassed in South Dakota and often prevented from doing their job, they had amply documented the migration of "old Americans" to the area called New America, and Hoffman—at the direction of his superiors—had become a serious student of the phenomenon. Still, he wanted Duncan's first-hand observations.

"Who are all these people?"

"Oh, you've got your religious extremists who want to live in a theocracy where God's law rules. As interpreted by Jeremiah, of course. There's a fair number of white supremacists. There're no racial problems in New America because everyone here's white."

Like all Germans grounded in history, Hoffman couldn't help but think of Hitler and his racial policies.

"There's a lot of law-and-order advocates up here. Antigovernment folks. Even some socialists attracted to Jeremiah's idea of wage equality. But most of them, in my opinion, are just run-of-the-mill types who've been snowed by Jeremiah's BS about a society built on high moral principle, dedicated to advancing knowledge and understanding the mind of God."

"Good folks led astray, huh?"

"Don't get me wrong; they do what they're told. They vote as a bloc and have taken over every unit of government from the local to the federal. Hell, I understand the next federal census probably will increase South Dakota's representation in Congress from one to six, as well as two senators. Same thing's happening in North Dakota, Wyoming, and Montana, although not as fast."

"Not bad for folks who hate Washington."

"Yeah, and at the local and state level, they're channeling tax dollars and federal grant money into housing subsidies, new water and sewage treatment plants, power plants, roads. Whole new cities just appear overnight. The service industry is booming. Restaurants, drug stores, hotels, grocery stores, that kind of stuff. And there're a surprising number of new shoe and clothing factories. New Americans are adamant about being self-sufficient." He looked in the rearview mirror and sneered. "Of course, there's a thriving cottage industry devoted to the publication of religious texts. You know, the Bible, plus *Second Jeremiah!*"

Hoffman grinned and shook his head. "I understand there've been a few clashes between the new settlers and the permanent residents," he said.

"About a week ago there was a pitched battle in Aberdeen, and Governor Schropa had to call in the National Guard to restore order. I don't know what set it off specifically, but it's economic in nature. The New Americans are younger, wealthier. They've sold homes and businesses elsewhere, and arrived here with lots of cash. South Dakota had an aging population anyway. Most of the young people have traditionally moved away in search of jobs. So in the beginning, it was easy for the newcomers to buy up businesses and much of the land. That's when the rub began."

"What do you mean?"

"Without land, the New Americans couldn't take hold. Believe it or not, in the beginning land here sold for as little as three hundred dollars an acre. When the locals found out what was happening, they banded together and quit selling. Then the New Americans bought land through front organizations, like real estate development firms and banks. When they took over the state legislature, they changed a bunch of laws making it easier for them to foreclose on land or simply squat on it. Especially range land. Now the courts are clogged with cases of New American 'squatters' occupying land they claim was unused. Who's gonna eject them? They control the legislature, the courts, and the police." Duncan shrugged. "It's all semilegal."

"The federal government can't stop people from exercising their constitutional rights," Hoffman said, playing the devil's advocate. "They can live where they want, believe what they want, vote for their own kind, and patronize their own businesses."

"Of course, this so-called New America revolution wouldn't amount to anything if they didn't revitalize the economic base," Duncan said, as he braked for a stop sign at a rural intersection. "Agriculture used to be the economic engine here, but the new regime is diversifying the economy, bringing in lots of new, high-tech businesses. There's a new computer chip factory at Mitchell, for example. A new automobile plant at Huron."

"Which car company?" Hoffman inquired.

"The Bavarian Motor Works, of course. Most of the cars are sold out-of-state, but the revenue stays here."

Hoffman nodded grimly. Walter Dorfler had once been an executive at BMW in Munich. New America wasn't just attracting immigrants and investors from other American states, but many foreign countries as well.

"You heard about the New America Economic Development Corporation? Rupert Carlson?" Duncan asked.

"The U.S. senator? Sure."

"Carlson was a former futures trader suspected of having links to Walter Dorfler and, probably, Jeremiah. He formed the Twin Cities Stock Exchange, which began operation immediately after Jeremiah dynamited the New York Stock Exchange in 1995.

"Carlson was investigated by the FBI, but no charges would stick. He formed the economic development corporation and then campaigned for a senate seat as an independent, easily winning election with total support from the new settlers in South Dakota."

"So what's this development corporation do?"

"Money flows into it, a lot of it from overseas. The money then gets channeled through banks and other front organizations that buy businesses and land from people who don't even know who they're selling to."

Thereafter, they traveled in silence, as Hoffman looked out the car window at a land in transition. He wondered if people in other parts of the United States—and the world—knew how much open space there was in America's upper Midwest. On this incredibly productive land, a single farmer could raise enough food to feed a hundred people. But it could be diverted to other uses also.

The population can easily swell into the tens of millions, he thought. *North and South Dakota together are larger than Germany, which has a population of more than eighty million. New America already is nearly as populous as Israel, and about the same size as Quebec to the north— another area with separatist ambitions.*

Nearly six hours after leaving the Sioux Falls airport, Duncan drove through the town of Gettysburg, so named because it was originally founded by Union Civil War veterans taking advantage of free land available as a result of the Homestead Act. Then they arrived at a junction with a north-south highway becoming known as the "eighty-three corridor."

"Nearly half of the New Americans living in the Dakotas

live along this state highway connecting Bismarck and Pierre," Duncan said, referring to the two state capitals. "Lots of new cities, like Anathoth up the road. Must be fifty-thousand people living there now."

"There're more cars on this highway," Hoffman said.

"Tourists, mainly," Duncan said. "Here to visit the Badlands, the Black Hills, Mount Rushmore, or just to see what's goin' on in New America."

Traffic soon slowed to a crawl.

"We're coming up on a highway checkpoint," Duncan told his passenger. "The state police are searching cars, checking ID."

"What are they looking for?" Hoffman asked.

"Contraband, which includes drugs, tobacco, alcohol, firearms, and subversive literature," Duncan replied, "and anything else banned by *Second Jeremiah*. Enforcing the 'Social Contract' has been a big problem. Many of the construction workers are here for the pay, not to stay. A lot of them are single, or without their wives, and the state police are having a helluva time keeping out the drugs, booze, and camp followers."

"Will we have any trouble?"

"I don't think so. My ID and papers already have passed scrutiny, and I assume yours are the best in the world. On the other hand, I know for a fact that the state police are also looking for infiltrators." Duncan craned his neck to look into the backseat. "The number of these checkpoints has doubled in recent weeks."

"Why?"

Duncan shrugged. "Something's in the wind."

"Such as?"

"I don't know, but the state National Guard you're coming to join probably now numbers more than a hundred thousand well-trained, well-equipped soldiers, not including five thousand state policemen like me."

Hoffman was incredulous. "You don't think they'd try to use this force against the United States?"

"It seems nuts, I admit, but not out of the question. Doesn't all of this seem a little surreal to you anyway?"

Hoffman slumped back in his seat. "Yeah."

Two uniformed state policeman were stopping southbound traffic. Two more cops armed with submachine guns sat in a car parked on the shoulder.

Duncan handed their papers to one policeman, while the other one studied Hoffman through the car window. Just as Hoffman began to squirm and think something was wrong, they got their papers back and were waved on.

As they neared a junction with state highway 14, Duncan pulled off at a scenic overview located on a high hill. "Here's the crown jewel of New America," he said, "the Science Center."

They got out of the car to stretch their legs. Duncan threw his black suit coat into the car and rolled up his shirtsleeves to reveal thick, hairy forearms.

Acres of blooming sweet clover had turned the surrounding range land chartreuse. Hoffman walked to an area containing several informational signs and read about the Science Center, which loomed in the distance.

It resembled a wagon wheel, with a thirty-five-story Saint Jeremiah Hospital serving as the hub. The silver steel-and-glass hospital appeared on the windswept prairie as a monolith embedded in the earth. A half-dozen two- and three-story "spokes" housed additional treatment facilities, including a rehabilitation unit, numerous research centers, laboratories, and, of course, New America University. Under construction for nearly four years, the center was 80 percent completed. Ultimately, the five-thousand-acre, ten-million-square-foot complex would be three times larger than the Pentagon in Washington, D.C.

"Washington's worried about a lot of things," Duncan said. "The migration up here, the shifting political balance, the possibility of secession, the foreign economic influence, the ever-present state police, the expanding National Guard, but I think they've underestimated the importance of this place." Duncan jerked a thumb over his shoulder toward the Science Center.

"How so?" Hoffman asked, popping a fresh stick of gum into his mouth.

"Saint Jeremiah's is a cash cow, even surpassing the Mayo Clinic as the premiere health center in the United

States. They specialize in tending to rich, important foreigners, which also enhances New America's prestige and
influence abroad. But what I think is even more important
is that this place is attracting a tremendous number of talented scientists."

"Really?"

"Yeah. Jeremiah always was the nerd terrorist, using the
Internet as his primary means of communication, especially
for *The Book of Second Jeremiah*. You remember how he
praised scientists and educators and predicted they'd be the
true superstars in his new society."

Hoffman picked up on Duncan's line of thought. "He
predicted New American scientists would make revolutionary discoveries in computers and genetics."

Duncan nodded. "And this place is a magnet for those
folks. They come from all over the world. There's no end
to scholarship and research money, and the science labs are
state-of-the-art."

"How many people work here?" Hoffman asked.

"Forty thousand. It's by far and away the largest em-
ployer in New America."

Hoffman pondered the giant complex in the distance. He
thought about the history of his homeland. "You know,
Hitler and the Nazis made technological superiority a priority. Their rocket program was way ahead of the times."

"Tell me about it. NASA was still picking Wernher von
Braun's mind way into the seventies," Duncan observed.

"Germany put jet-propelled aircraft into the skies at the
end of World War II," Hoffman continued. "They just
didn't have enough planes to make a difference." He looked
directly at Duncan. "Think of what might have happened
if the insane racial policies of the fascists in Germany and
Italy hadn't driven off scientific geniuses in the Jewish
community, like Einstein, Fermi, the Oppenheimers."

Duncan completed the thought. "Germany might have
developed the atomic bomb first and changed the course of
world history. Like I said, this may be the real danger of
this place. Anyway, let's get you settled at our apartment
in Pierre."

"Apartment?"

Duncan nodded. "It's really yours. One of the perks of an artillery officer. Most of the time we'll be staying in our barracks, but it's someplace we can meet and plot."

Hoffman cleaned his glasses with a handerchief. "Great. I have a feeling I'll need a safe place to relax."

"Tomorrow morning, you report to your duty post."

"Where's that?"

"When you get there, you're gonna think it's on Mars."

5

Laura lay on the white table, staring at the white light shining from a hole in the white ceiling, until she became slightly disoriented. She put her chin on her chest, so she could look between her legs, which were spread wide and draped with a white cloth. Wearing a white medical smock, Dr. Helen Cureton, her gynecologist, was doing an internal exam. Although everything in the room was sterile and sparkling clean, Laura felt dirty.

"You're in great shape, Laura," the doctor concluded, standing and peeling the latex gloves off her hands. "And you're preggers according to the lab tests! Congratulations. I told you it'd happen."

Laura lifted her feet out of the stirrups and swung around to sit sideways on the examination table, her legs dangling over the edge. She stared at the floor, dreading the necessary conversation.

"You can get dressed now," Helen said. "You're kind of solemn, Laura, given this joyous occasion." The doctor arched her eyebrows. "All tired out from the hard work of becoming a mother?"

Ordinarily, Laura would have laughed at the sly reference. She'd selected Helen as her gynecologist in part because of the doctor's sense of humor. But Laura only felt sick to her stomach, and it wasn't due to morning sickness. After she and Steve had tried unsuccessfully to conceive for several years, Laura began taking a fertility drug six months ago. Now she felt guilty about that decision, especially if it had aided her pregnancy by Jeremiah.

"I'm not certain the baby is Steve's," Laura admitted, tears forming in her eyes.

"Jesus!" Helen replied, sitting in the only chair available in the small room.

"I was raped about a month ago," Laura explained, reluctantly. "I don't want anyone else to know." Being a celebrity had made Laura suspicious even of her friends.

"What's said here stays here, Laura. Do you know the man who attacked you?"

"All I want to do now is make certain who the baby's father is, or isn't."

Helen bobbed her head in agreement. "We can do a Chorionic Villi sample test in about three weeks. It's a way of extracting fetal fluid from the placenta. The cells are cultured for about a week until a DNA sample can be obtained. Then we compare it to Steve's. It will rule him out or in." The doctor hesitated. "We should do some other tests today for venereal disease."

Laura spoke softly. "I had all that done at a hospital shortly after *it* happened, and they said the tests were negative for the standard stuff—syphilis, gonorrhea, hepatitis. They said it would be some time before HIV would show up, if I was infected." The physician in Austin was a trusted family friend, but Laura knew someone could have seen her visiting his office. The local sheriff, his deputies, and the surviving bodyguard knew of the break-in. They'd gossip.

Laura knew some enterprising reporter could unearth the whole mess; maybe even get hold of confidential physician records and lab test results. Such revelations wouldn't do anything to bring Jeremiah to justice, but they were "news" as traditionally defined. *The former TV news star and the terrorist.* Laura wasn't comfortable being on the other side of the camera.

"The dormancy period for HIV could be several years," Helen said, pausing. "Have you told Steve?"

"No, but we haven't had sex since, you know, *it* happened."

Dr. Cureton looked shocked. "Laura, for god's sake, you have to tell him! He has a right to know. You should consider counseling. Maybe Steve, too. I'll refer you to someone. Will you go?"

Laura shrugged noncommittally as she climbed off the table, took off the backless gown, and began getting dressed.

Maria had waited for Laura in the doctor's outer office. As they left the building and walked silently toward the Land Rover, both instinctively looked about the parking lot; assessing various people, gauging the possibility of danger.

Once behind the wheel, Maria turned to Laura. "So? What's the doc say this time?"

"I'm pregnant," Laura confided, her voice barely a whisper. She'd considered not telling Maria. Her bodyguard, friend, and sister rape victim might be tempted to sell the tabloids this story for the right amount of money.

"It could be Steve's," Maria said, as she maneuvered the truck out of the parking lot.

"Helen will do a test to determine that." Laura looked inquisitively at Maria. "Did you have a VD test? Pregnancy test?"

Maria glanced at Laura, and then focused both eyes on the road. "I'm not pregnant, believe me. I take birth control pills. As for VD"—Maria gave forth a deprecating half-laugh—"that's unlikely, since we know who did it. I mean, I don't think *he* has VD. Certainly not HIV. He's a little too virile for that. Too big."

This uninvited confidence horrified Laura. Also, she thought she detected the hint of a smile playing at the corners of Maria's mouth. The bodyguard quickly averted her face, honking at another driver who cut too quickly in front of them.

"The main thing is you're going to have a child," Maria said, after a silence of several miles. "You're going to be a mother, like you wanted. I'm Catholic. A life is innocent at conception, until birth. You know what I mean?"

"Are you nuts?" Laura lashed out. "This is the devil's seed in me. How can you feel that way?"

"I just meant . . ."

Laura cut her off. "You'd feel differently if *you* were pregnant."

Both were silent the rest of the ride home.

When they arrived at the farm, Laura went upstairs to her bedroom on the second floor, thinking she might take a nap. But she lay wide-eyed on the bed for fifteen minutes before rising abruptly and walking down the hallway to the adjoining room—the nursery.

She and Steve hadn't done much work in the room, having decided to delay repainting the walls until they knew she was pregnant and the gender of the baby was established. Then they'd know whether to paint the walls pink or light blue.

The only item of furniture Laura had purchased was a baby bed, not wanting to fully furnish the room and usurp the baby-shower prerogatives of her family and friends. But Laura wanted to make certain the bed was safe, with narrow spaces between the vertical wood slats, so the baby's head couldn't get lodged between them, causing injury or death.

She looked about, envisioning the rest of the furniture that would be added later: a chest of drawers, a changing table, organizer, a rocker. She hadn't decided on an overall color scheme for the room. Maybe a combination of blue, pink, white, and green, she thought. Or a calico print would be nice. Perhaps even a stripe and floral print, or a patchwork design. Of course, it could be an animal motif, too.

She wanted a sound video monitor mounted on the wall, so she could always see and hear the baby; so she'd be able to save the baby—her and Steve's baby—from any life-threatening eventuality, such as sudden infant death syndrome. Or an intruder bent on mayhem.

As Laura closed the door to the room, she knew now for a fact that the best of safeguards were sometimes inadequate to protect a person from every evil threat.

*   *   *

Steve came home late, saying he'd been "downtown"—meaning the District of Columbia—on business. *He's probably been at the FBI,* Laura thought, *discreetly trying to find out what his former colleagues know about Jeremiah's whereabouts.* Laura knew, he'd told her. The terrorist was in New America, making preparations for his coming out.

The bastard wasn't dead. The body lying on the ground outside her parents' ranch had been one of the bodyguards whose neck had been broken.

She and Steve sat on each side of a corner of the long, mahogany dining room table, eating a fried chicken dinner prepared by Gladys Schuyler, their property manager's wife.

"So how was your day?" Steve asked.

"Okay. How about you?"

As he started to speak, Laura put a cautionary hand on his arm. They both watched Maria come down the stairs and exit out the front door, presumably to check the grounds and confer with the guards, who were now in a state of high alert.

"What's the matter?" Steve asked.

Laura shook her head. "Sometimes I wonder if our conversations are totally private."

"One day last week, when you and Maria were gone, I had some friends come out and sweep the house and the property for bugs, cameras, and whatever. The place is clean."

"Why'd you do that?"

"I think it's obvious after what happened in Austin."

"We need to talk about that."

"I agree, but first I want to tell you something." He stared intently at Laura, causing her to frown. She feared he was getting a good, long, last look.

"What?"

"I love you, Laura, no matter what. Remember? For richer, for poorer, in sickness and in health, 'til death due us part."

Laura smiled, despite the gravity of the subject they were about to discuss. "Did you make that up?"

"Yeah. Catchy, ain't it?"

She looked lovingly at her husband, the hunk. Star baseball player in college, FBI agent, partner-for-life, she hoped. "Let's go for a walk," Laura suggested.

At 8:30 P.M. the sun had disappeared over the mountains and left only a reddish glow as a reminder of the hot, summer day. The humidity made the air almost too heavy to breathe.

As they neared the fence and gate leading to the north pasture, a man stepped from behind a tree.

"Hi, folks," said Quentin, another of their bodyguards. He held an assault rifle by the stock, so the barrel pointed at the sky. "Going for a walk?"

"Yeah," Steve replied.

As they walked toward the northeast pasture, away from the pond, it comforted Laura knowing that Quentin was shadowing them, ready to gun down an attacker, although no one had trespassed on their property since—Austin.

They walked for several minutes before she got up the courage to tell the truth. "He raped me in Austin." Laura drew in her breath, awaiting Steve's response.

"I was afraid of that," he said.

"What do you mean?" she asked, hoping her question didn't sound hostile.

Steve explained. "I used to be a federal cop, remember. I see dark designs everywhere."

Steve had flown to Austin as soon as she'd called and told him Jeremiah had broken into the ranch and tried to abduct her.

"Your dad and mom are great people," Steve said, "but they're not very good liars."

"They were just trying to protect me."

"I know. I'm not blaming anyone. What happened to you is horrible."

"It's even worse. I'm pregnant."

He never broke stride. "Is it ours or his?"

"I won't find out for several weeks."

Steve picked her up off her feet, one arm under her

knees, the other under her arms. He kissed her and said, "You didn't need to keep this terrible secret to yourself for so long." Laura hung on tightly and buried her face in Steve's neck, as he walked effortlessly across the pasture.

On the crest of a small hill he knelt and sat Laura down in the grass, reclining beside her.

"I was afraid you'd reject me!" she blurted. "I feel so dirty, guilty."

"You're totally blameless," Steve replied.

"If the baby is his, I'll abort it!"

"I'll support you, whatever your decision."

"I'll never have it, that's for certain!"

"Maybe we'll be lucky and it will be our baby."

Back at the house, they immediately went to their

bedroom. Laura poured a generous portion of brandy into a glass, gulped it down, and went into the bathroom, where she quickly undressed and got into the shower. Despite the July heat outside, she felt chilled to the bone and made the water as hot as possible.

Suddenly, Steve stepped into the shower. He had a throbbing erection.

"Want some company? God, you're beautiful."

"I haven't made love to you . . ."

". . . damn near forever, it seems!"

". . . because I don't know about HIV!"

Laura watched a frown form on Steve's brow, as he considered this sobering new information.

"How long before you know?"

"As long as a year."

"Oh."

Laura looked from his face to his erection, wondering if it would fall, too. What had she expected? For him to say the hell with it and plunge ahead? A part of her would have liked that, but not at the cost of possibly passing on to him a fatal virus.

"At least wear a condom until we know," she said.

They washed, toweled themselves dry, and moved into the bedroom. *Steve doesn't seem to know what to do,* Laura thought, *and he isn't exactly ready now, as I'd feared.*

Nevertheless, she'd considered this eventuality. A week ago she'd gone into a pharmacy and self-consciously purchased condoms, feeling like a coed again.

She took one out of the nightstand drawer and tore off the foil wrapping. She held up the red condom for him to see, and said, "I got a great idea about how to put this on."

Her trick had the intended consequence, but the resulting lovemaking wasn't entirely successful. Ordinarily an enthusiastic partner who liked to make a lot of noise, Laura didn't want to appear too carefree, as if the rape was inconsequential. That she'd already forgotten about it.

So she attempted to create a romantic mood, aimed primarily at pleasing her husband. In the end, she didn't have an orgasm and worried that Steve would now think he was inadequate. Worse, that she had somehow been "ruined" by Jeremiah.

Laura felt her sanity slipping away. Maybe her doctor was right about her seeing a shrink. She got out of bed, refilled the snifter with brandy, and sat near the footboard, wrapped in a sheet.

"I'm sorry," she said.

"Don't be, Laura. Look, we've both had lovers and spouses and friends and enemies. They all may have made some mark on us, but none of them stained us permanently, especially with a stain of shame or dishonor that we pass on to others."

As she'd hoped, the brandy helped her regain a measure of her former playfulness. "You're such a stud that I always forget how smart you are."

"Well, what I are is in here," he said, lightheartedly, pointing to his eyes. "It ain't got nothing to do with the water and other crap floating around in my body. It's something beyond the flesh."

Laura crawled toward Steve, brandy slopping out of her glass onto the bed. She slipped into his waiting arms and said, "I hope *it* survives this body, whatever it is."

"Me, too."

They rocked together for several minutes, until Laura felt Steve tense and draw back.

"What's the matter?"

He cocked his head, as if he'd heard something. He held a finger to his lips, got out of bed, picked up his gun from the nightstand, and walked quietly to the door. He jerked it open, sticking the gun barrel into the hallway.

Laura could see Maria Inglesias leaning against the far wall, her arms folded. The bodyguard looked at Steve's gun and then his naked body. An apologetic look came over her face and she started to say something. Then she turned and walked away rapidly.

"What was she doing out there?" Laura asked, when Steve returned to bed.

"I don't know," he replied, flopping down on his back. He locked his fingers behind his head and stared reflectively at the ceiling.

Laura sat cross-legged on the bed. "It'll never be the same again, will it?"

He turned his head toward her. "No."

Laura was too fearful of the answer to ask Steve exactly what he meant.

6

Jeremiah watched units of the New American Army prepare for a major military exercise. On a blistering day in late July, he stood with the army's top brass on the deck of an elevated, roofed observation tower, where they had a commanding view of a simulated battlefield located between the southwest corner of the Cheyenne River Indian Reservation and the Badlands.

State police units guarded the perimeter of the military reservation, although Jeremiah knew there was little chance unauthorized observers would wander into the area. No incorporated towns existed within a twenty-mile radius of the camp and fewer than twelve hundred people lived nearby.

As usual, he wore black clothing and dark sunglasses because black was the intimidating color of death. His officers wore camouflage battlefield uniforms and stood a slight distance away, as if not to encroach upon his "space." Many of the soldiers running and sweating on the training field below occasionally sneaked a glance at the observation tower, trying to guess his identity.

"What are we doing here today, General?" Jeremiah asked the officer with three Silver Stars on each collar wing.

"The battalion in the field will assault a reproduction of a heavily guarded facility similar to the target," Lt. Gen. Benjamin Arnot replied.

"Very good."

"There's a makeshift checkpoint and guard post in the foreground, as you can see," the general continued, using a riding crop to direct Jeremiah's view. "Beyond that, we have three closely grouped buildings, which are the primary objectives. All were constructed to actual size."

Jeremiah trained his binoculars on the roofless facades. Interior rooms were cordoned off with rope, or tape, although several had real walls, and one a steel-reinforced door. New American soldiers wearing white jumpsuits played the role of defenders.

"The assaulting infantry normally would be armed with standard-issue M-16s," General Arnot said, "although for this exercise attackers and defenders are using weapons that fire paint pellets, so we can approximate casualties. The Fourth Platoon of each attacking company will set up mortars and heavy machine-gun emplacements around the perimeter. They are also armed with antitank and antiaircraft missiles. Another platoon will simulate a water approach. The engineers will use live explosives, so casualties in this training session are not out of the question."

Jeremiah lowered the field glasses and said, "Let loose the dogs, General."

He was pleased that the attacking troops had abandoned the subterfuge of being units of the South Dakota National Guard. A cloth badge sewn on the breast pocket of their battlefield uniforms read: NEW AMERICA ARMY. A shoulder patch reproduced the "ROSE" flag carried by unit standard bearers. On a red background was centered a black-and-white circular design with a word in each of four quadrants: Reverence, Obedience, Strength, Equality.

Jeremiah watched intensely as the practice attack began with excited human voices shouting commands. Forty-five minutes later, the air was filled with dust and smoke, and the attacking troops had captured their targets.

Later, inside one of several air-conditioned Quonset huts erected in the training area, Jeremiah hosted a modest reception for his officers and invited guests. Sandwiches, snack food, soft drinks, and iced tea were served.

General Arnot accompanied Jeremiah as the Prophet worked the room like a politician, shaking hands, making small talk, and impressing his officer corps and guests with a comprehensive memory for names and events.

"Here we have a new artillery officer," General Arnot said. "Capt. Hans Dietrich Hoffman, from Germany."

"It's a great honor, sir," Hoffman said, saluting.

"Wo ist Ihr Haus in Deutschland?" Jeremiah asked, thinking to test Hoffman's German.

"Stuttgart, sir."

"Gab es einmal eine Kriegsakademie in der Stadt, ich glauben." Surely Hoffman knew about the former military academy in his own hometown.

"Ja. Die jungsteren Sohne verwendeten das Schlossplatz als Paradeboden, tatsächlich."

Hoffman had passed the easy tests. "Wie kommen Sie, unsere Auslesegruppe, Kapitän zu verbinden?"

General Arnot answered his leader's question. "Captain Hoffman was recommended to us by Herr Ludwig Hempel."

"I served with Colonel Hempel as an officer of artillery in the Bundeswehr," Hoffman elaborated.

"Ah, yes, I remember Hempel," Jeremiah replied. "Your artillery skills will be put to good use, I can assure you, Captain Hoffman."

As they walked away, Jeremiah said to Arnot, "I hope we're doing thorough background checks on all these people. There're bound to be spies among them."

"It's a diverse group, all right," Arnot said, as he surveyed the room. "Lots of foreigners. But we require multiple recommendations, including at least one from people I know, or who are known to senior commanders I trust implicitly. Of course, the officers you recommended are beyond reproach. Personally, I don't mind the Germans, other Europeans, the South Africans. But the Asians and the Arabs"—the general shook his head distastefully—"Commies, Islamic fundamentalists. We'll just have to fight them someday."

Jeremiah chuckled. "Hopefully not for a long time, General. Right now, we couldn't do without these mercenaries,

especially since you were unable to persuade enough of
your fellow officers in the U.S. Army to come over to our
side." He enjoyed needling Arnot.

"They'll be sorry later."

"Let's hope so."

These officers will do fine, Jeremiah thought, *since they
possess the two primary prerequisites: they are experienced
combat soldiers and expendable.* Many undoubtably were
psychopaths, although these professional soldiers were far
from naïve. Whether attracted to this latest impending conflict by money or simple blood lust, they knew the risks
and willingly gambled on their chance of survival.

Political, religious, or philosophical beliefs motivated
others, he knew. They hated the United States for one reason or another. To them, America would always be "the
evil empire." Jeremiah agreed wholeheartedly.

"You know the only reason the Russians and the Chinese
observers are here offering help is so they can field test
new military tactics and ordnance," Arnot said.

"And what's wrong with that?"

"When they've helped weaken the United States, they'll
turn on us."

"There's an old Chinese proverb that says that he who
hands his enemy a weapon also hands over his destiny.
Now, excuse me, General Arnot. Speaking of the Chinese,
I'm scheduled to meet with Li Gongquin. You and I need
to get together later to finalize our plans."

While making his way across the room toward an end
office, Jeremiah stopped briefly and chatted with two other
guests who were not military men. One was Karl Monroe,
a black postal worker from Philadelphia. Karl's brother,
Vernon, had been a die-hard Communist Jeremiah had met
in Japan when Vernon was stationed there with the U.S.
Army and Jeremiah was seeking converts. Jeremiah was not
an admirer of black culture worldwide, but he and Vernon
became friends, bound together by their common belief that
African Americans should have their own nation on the
North American continent.

"How are your efforts going, Karl?" Jeremiah asked.

Monroe, a huge man who towered over all others in the

room, said, "I'm still recruiting cells of guerrilla fighters in most of the northeastern cities. They'll take up the gun when the moment's right."

Jeremiah nodded. "Let's talk later. I may have a new weapon for you."

"I'll be around."

Jeremiah didn't hold much hope of a significant black uprising in the United States, largely because they lacked a charismatic leader, like Vernon, whom Steve Wallace had killed in Seattle in 1995. On the other hand, if even a small band of black rebels had biological weapons, they could create havoc in the large, East Coast cities.

Jeremiah spoke briefly with Carlos Fuentes, a high-ranking member of the Tijuana cartel, which controlled the drug traffic coming into the United States at the busy border crossing south of San Diego. It was a $10-billion-a-year business.

"My people and your people have set up three new clandestine drug laboratories," said Fuentes, a handsome, well-dressed man. "You have a lot of talented chemists up here. I'll think we'll do well."

Jeremiah had decided that narco dollars derived from the sale of laboratory-manufactured drugs could be an important source of funding for New America's military, which cost a staggering amount of money. *Second Jeremiah* forbid drug use, of course, but the one anointed by the Lord had the latitude to bend the rules. Especially in these critical times. *All's fair in love and war.* Jeremiah grinned, once again reminded of lovely, luscious Laura Delaney.

"Were you impressed with the military exercise?" Jeremiah asked the Mexican.

"Very much so."

"We'll make our move soon," Jeremiah said, only slightly concerned about information leaks. No one would believe what he had in mind anyway. "It could be an opportunity for you. You already control a paramilitary organization with significant financial resources. You could take back the Southeast."

"I can't make that decision myself, Jeremiah."

Jeremiah nodded. The one-time Spanish talent for military conquest had been bred out of them in Mexico, when their racial gene pool was diluted. Now they were interested only in profits, not politics or history or destiny.

Jeremiah and Li Gongquin, the unofficial emissary of the Chinese government, met in the lone office at one end of the Quonset hut. With no lack of willing sponsors—indeed, Jeremiah had been assiduously courted by many governments—he preferred to deal mainly with the Chinese, even though Walter Dorfler had always dealt with the Russians.

But Russia was in a state of internal chaos and weak economically. They had readily abandoned communism for a form of ersatz capitalism, whereas the Chinese still kept the faith, in a manner of speaking.

China, the sleeping giant of Asia, had been transforming itself for decades. Having just spent nearly a year there, Jeremiah had seen the results first-hand. With a booming economy and its nationalistic fervor at fever pitch, China had moved beyond past introspective periods occasioned by imperialism, poverty, and isolation, and the effects of Confucianism, Taoism, Maoism, and communism.

Now China simply wanted to be a world economic and military power. Fortunately for him, China's history and traditions had instilled in its leaders a paranoia often translated into jingoism and a foreign policy based on intrigue, endless posturing, and feigning. China's main nemesis was the United States. He and the Chinese had much in common and were therefore willing to make use of each other.

"I'll soon need the specialized weapons we've spoken of in the past," Jeremiah said to Li. "The big artillery guns, the chemical ordnance, the tactical nuclear weapons."

"They're stockpiled in Canada and can be delivered whenever you desire," Li said, inclining his head politely. A slight, balding man who always wore a baggy, dark suit and open-collar white shirt, Li was a scientist by training, a diplomat by choice.

"Good. I've been thinking again about biological agents. Something that could be put into the water supply. Like the

E. coli botulism agent I used at Leavenworth, except more deadly. The kill rate there was terribly disappointing."

"Perhaps, but the effect on the public was immense," Li responded, holding a cigarette between his fingers as if it were a delicate instrument. "We've talked about this before, Jeremiah. The wise tactician forces the enemy to the bargaining table and wins there through guile what could only be won on the battlefield at enormous costs in matériel and men." He paused deliberately. "Especially when one's resources are limited."

Jeremiah forced a smile. He didn't like being lectured to, but he couldn't afford to offend the Chinese. Besides, Li was right, of course. As was General Arnot. The Chinese were playing both ends against the middle; allies now, enemies likely later. But Jeremiah remained gracious. "Without your government's help, Li, we could not succeed."

As Jeremiah waited for his next appointment, he considered how his tactics indeed had changed over the past four years. Originally, he had only hoped to establish a small guerrilla movement in the Midwest. When his plans were foiled at Laura's ranch, he'd been forced to lie low, trying to come up with another scheme.

He'd been stunned at the fervor of his converts and their success in establishing New America in the Dakotas. It was a by-product of the unexpected appeal of *The Book of Second Jeremiah,* as well as a growing dissatisfaction with American society. Accordingly, Jeremiah's goals suddenly were enlarged, and his tactics changed correspondingly. Life was good when one's expectations were exceeded by reality. It was additional evidence that God approved of his efforts. Jeremiah chuckled.

Finally alone with his military commander, Jeremiah recalled that Walter Dorfler first met General Arnot in Grafenwoehr, Germany, when Arnot was a brigadier general in charge of the U.S. Seventh Army Training Command. Thereafter, the two became hunting companions and eventually friends. The outspoken American general attended several private meetings, where various career opportunities were brought to his attention.

At first, Arnot seemed an unlikely recruit, given his distinguished military service record. The general had won a Silver Star and two Purple Hearts during combat in Vietnam in the sixties. Nevertheless, the outspoken warrior had sabotaged his career with his mouth, as he sounded off over the years against godless Communists, liberal pinkos, fags, dinks, "towel heads," and anyone else he thought posed even a minor threat to the America he loved. Jeremiah had pointed out to the general that his ideal society had taken root on America's high plains—a white, Christian, conservative, law and order New America.

In a peacetime army, where political skills counted for as much as tactical skills, General Arnot's career had topped out at the relatively young age of fifty. He'd have been cast on the scrap heap, Jeremiah knew, without this second chance. *Of course, that could be said of most of my officers,* Jeremiah thought, *as well as tens of thousand of potential New America supporters maintained on computer files. Discontent breeds revolutionaries,* he knew.

"So, how many battle-ready troops do we have, General?" Jeremiah asked.

"Six divisions," Arnot replied, whacking the table twice with a riding crop.

Jeremiah wondered about the gray-haired, barrel-chested man, with a pasty face and flat nose that had absorbed too many punches during an amateur boxing career. *Does he really think he's a modern-day cavalry officer?*

"Roughly a hundred and twenty thousand men?"

Arnot nodded. "With maybe another ten thousand in reserve."

"How are we keeping this all secret?" Jeremiah asked.

"We have a dozen training camps similar to this in surrounding states," Arnot replied, "as well as in some remote areas of Canada. We never put more than a regiment in the field at one time. It's not that much of a disadvantage to separately train the various pieces and bring them together for the real assault. It happens all the time in the U.S. military."

"What about security?" Jeremiah asked.

"All our training areas are heavily guarded to prevent infiltration, and we conduct training, as we did today, only when the U.S.'s spy satellites are over other parts of the world." The general laughed appreciably. "You really have some very sophisticated computer people in your employ, you know!"

Jeremiah agreed, thinking how this was one tiny aspect of the complicated plan put in motion by Walter Dorfler nearly twenty years ago. Some of the world's finest scientific talent—especially computer programmers and researchers in chemistry, physics, and genetics—had been cultivated since they were youths: first by mail and then over the Internet. Now they were flocking to the Science Center, attracted by money and visions of being superstars in a science-centered society.

"We're ostensibly part of the South Dakota National Guard, or so Governor Schropa continues to tell everyone," Arnot continued, "but we're not really fooling anyone of importance." The general smiled slyly.

Jeremiah understood. People like Atty. Gen. Peter Thompson and others at the Pentagon suspected something was in the works. But those with the power to act, including President Carpenter, had vacillated and wasted precious time, as he'd calculated. It was strikingly similar to the way in which the Western democracies had ignored Hitler's rise to power in the thirties. *Those who cannot remember the past are condemned to repeat it,* Jeremiah thought.

"And the necessary equipment?"

"We've appropriated from the National Guard here and in several surrounding states much equipment, vehicles, and aircraft," Arnot replied. "We'll seize more once the campaign begins in earnest. Of course, we're relying on our foreign friends to supply us with the critical weapons, all of which are easily disassembled and smuggled by truck into the nation. We'll be short on armor, but that's not critical to our plan."

"How soon are you prepared to implement the plan?" Jeremiah asked.

Arnot's arrogance was palpable. "Two weeks' notice; that's all I need."

Jeremiah arched an eyebrow. "You're convinced we're ready?"

"Yes," Arnot replied. "Given the limited objectives we hope to accomplish." The general rose from his seat at the folding table, stroking his thigh lightly with the crop as he walked restlessly to the one window at the end of the hut. "The military forces of the United States are not ready for us. They're like the French in thirty-nine and forty. They're ready to fight yesterday's war."

"I like that analogy, General," Jeremiah said.

"The United States has a million-and-a-half men on active duty in the various services," Arnot said, continuing his lecture. "Another two million in the guard and reserves. Overall, it's the best-equipped, most efficient military in the world, bar none." He turned, pointing the riding crop at Jeremiah. "And while some armies, most notably our Russian and Chinese friends, maybe even the Vietnamese, could put up a good fight against U.S. troops on the ground, no one is even in the same league with America in terms of naval forces and airpower, let alone the sophisticated electronic battlefield equipment that was demonstrated in Desert Storm and elsewhere."

Jeremiah cringed in mock fear. "You make them sound invincible!"

"They could overrun New America in a couple of hours," Arnot conceded. "But they're looking outward for their threat, and their commanders are cautious. We saw that in Desert Storm. They waited months to prepare to do battle with an Iraqi army only three times larger than ours. And the Iraqis had no stomach for the fight. Our troops are better trained and motivated, our equipment and tactics superior. They ain't ready for my version of blitzkrieg!"

Jeremiah knew he'd have to kill the general after his usefulness was exhausted, which would be soon. Arnot was not only a military genius—with appropriate guidance, of course—but also an egomaniac who, once having humiliated those who'd humiliated him, would want to step up another rung on the ladder.

"Show me the targets again," Jeremiah said, standing.

General Arnot opened a map case and placed maps on the table, one atop another and once again explained the significance of each target, the plan of attack, military and psychological impact, and variables that could influence the outcome. "Once we've secured these objectives, as we demonstrated today we can do within only a few hours, we will switch to a defensive mode, daring them to attack us."

"If all goes as planned, General, we'll take over much of the Midwest, although I plan to demand even broader boundaries."

General Arnot whacked the table with his riding crop. "It's an outrageous plan!"

"It's based on America's historical reluctance to fight and suffer massive casualties," Jeremiah explained. "As you know, General, in World War II, less than three hundred thousand Americans were killed in battle. The Russians and Germans probably suffered casualties totaling thirty million, including soldiers and civilians. Americans have no experience with death and destruction at that level. Based on the Vietnam experience, and various other U.S. interventions since then, I don't think the government or public have the stomach for it."

General Arnot's face appeared hard as stone. "Neither do I."

"When faced with the possibility of a massively destructive civil war, I believe most Americans will pressure their government to grant independence to New America. In fact, this federal union always has been fragile. Many areas of the country will seize this opportunity to press their own secessionist goals."

The general drew himself up proudly. "I'm originally from South Carolina."

"Then you understand why my plan might work," Jeremiah said.

Soon I'll be in a superior negotiating position, he thought, *much better than that day at Laura's ranch.* It was a good, simple plan, although not really like Arnot's reference to the Nazi blitzkrieg, in which armored columns simply drove over defending French bunkers on the Maginot Line, moving so fast as to neutralize the French artillery. The Germans had been out to win battles quickly. Jeremiah planned to lose most of the military conflicts he initiated, but lose in such a way as to win the public relations battle, a prerequisite for all modern-day wars. Jeremiah imagined he would soon be recognized as a brilliant military tactician, adding to his mythology.

He smiled at Arnot. "Let's establish D day, then."

7

Steve drove from the farm east on Interstate 66 until he reached the Vienna metro stop, where he boarded an orange line train that traveled east through the remaining Virginia suburbs and then under the Potomac River into the District of Columbia. After the train went underground, the interior lights popped on and Steve was startled by his reflection in the dark window. He stared at a sad, frustrated man. What had happened recently to his and Laura's lives was incomprehensible.

Forty minutes later, the train reached the Capitol South station, where the escalator leading above ground was long and steeply inclined.

He jaywalked across First Street and walked north past many of the institutions of federal government, including the Cannon House Office Building, the old and new Library of Congress Buildings, and on his left, the U.S. Capitol Building.

On this hot, sticky day, with the temperature already in the midnineties at 10:00 A.M., Steve wore a lightweight, dark blue summer suit, a common uniform among the staff aides and lobbyists walking the streets in and about the Capitol complex. Congress would adjourn shortly and not come back into session until after Labor Day. As he neared East Capitol Street, Steve encountered an abortion rights demonstration in front of the Supreme Court Building. A tightly bunched crowd waved placards and listened to a speaker talking into a bullhorn. A squad of Capitol Hill cops stood by as television camera crews filmed the action.

The police directed most visitors to the Maryland Street entrance. When Steve showed a pass signed by Atty. Gen. Peter Thompson, he was allowed to walk up the marble steps of the west entrance, past the huge columns supporting the portico, through the massive bronze doors into the first-floor hallway. After passing through a metal detector, he walked down the hallway and handed his pass to one of several gatekeepers, who then ushered him into the inner sanctum.

In all his years in Washington, Steve had been in the main courtroom only once before. Behind the Doric columns that outlined the room were massive maroon drapes trimmed in gold. The frieze near the top of the huge ceiling contained sculptures of the great lawgivers of history. The cool, musty air smelled of old constitutional arguments.

Steve walked past the public benches in the back of the room through a bronze gate and railing to the area of reserved seating. Thompson, once deputy director of the FBI, and Steve's boss, waved him over.

Steve sat down, smiled at his old friend, and whispered, "What's going on?"

"A case involving developments in South Dakota," Thompson said. "We can get out of here in a few minutes, after I see how it's going."

The nine justices sat behind an elevated, concave bench located at the front of the room and flanked on either end by American flags. Behind the bench, a clock suspended from the ceiling served as a not-so-subtle reminder to the lawyers that their arguments should be succinct.

Steve recognized all the justices from their photographs, including the chief justice sitting at the center of the bench. They all looked old and put-upon. Summer sessions of the high court were rare. One testy judge grilled a government lawyer standing at the lectern in front of the bench.

Steve gleaned from the interchange that the case had something to do with bank loans in South Dakota. He recognized the assistant attorney general presenting the government's position.

Thompson whispered to Steve, "Let's get out of here."

Outside, the demonstrators had dispersed. Steve and Peter stood briefly under the west portico, relishing the shade. A policeman recognized Thompson and tipped his hat respectfully. A handsome man with naturally wavy, brown hair and a perpetual tan, Thompson was, as usual, a model of sartorial splendor. He wore an exquisitely tailored blue, pin-striped, double-breasted suit and a patterned silk tie covering a gleaming white shirt. His cuff links reproduced the presidential seal.

"Is there something about this court case that's of interest to me?" Steve asked.

Looking off in the direction of the Capitol, Thompson replied, "This is an important Fifth Amendment case, Steve, and I needed to be present largely for political reasons. Show the flag. Some constitutional scholars contend that nothing is so sacred as the government's role in protecting property rights."

"I assume it involves New America?"

"South Dakota," Thompson corrected, nevertheless flashing a grin. "There's been no bigger bone of contention out there over the last three years than how the new settlers could acquire all the land they needed for their homes and businesses. At first, of course, they just bought it. But when it became obvious they intended to form a secessionist colony, the locals quit selling them land."

"And Jeremiah's followers wouldn't accept that?" Steve guessed.

"Of course not. After his disciples took over the legislature and state courts, they began a counterattack. They passed legislation revoking previous public land grants, alleging they were fraudulently granted in the first place. They increased the state's powers of eminent domain. Local zoning commissions arbitrarily changed their classifications, making it impossible for established businesses to operate."

Thompson sighed, as if wearied by this recitation of perfidy. "Their main thrust, however, was to rewrite mortgage contract law, so it was easier for banks and lending institutions to foreclose on land."

"You mean banks that had been taken over by New Americans?"

"Precisely. The state legislature helped by greatly increasing property and inheritance taxes. It's all patently unconstitutional in a host of areas, and we'll easily win this case and others like it."

"You don't seem happy, though."

Thompson took Steve's arm and steered him toward the stairs. "Let's walk awhile."

They crossed the street toward the pebbled walk running along the north side of the Capitol. They passed through several "concrete flowerpots" designed to prevent a mad bomber from driving a truck onto the Capitol lawn.

Thompson sat on a park bench located between two towering trees, one an elm, the other a hybrid oak. They had a splendid view of the east Capitol lawn; and no one could overhear their conversation. Somewhere nearby, Steve knew, electronic sensing equipment was operating to detect and defeat long-range snooping devices.

"This case today is just the first in an almost endless parade of constitutional issues involving New America," Thompson said, abandoning his own insistence on the state's proper 'name. "They won't be decided under my watch, nor the next attorney general's, or maybe even the one after him."

"That is discouraging."

"Every major constitutional issue of the last two hundred years is being revived by what's going on in New America slash South Dakota. Next will be a host of cases concerning the Bill of Rights, the due process clause of the Fourteenth Amendment, the right to privacy, immigration policy, state police powers. Now there's a can of worms." The attorney general shook his head in frustration. "Imagine this scenario, if you will, Steve. New America is turning the Constitution on its head, but people in other states, including elected officials, think this exercise may have some value."

Steve frowned. "I don't understand."

"Many people legitimately think the federal government has too many regulatory powers vis-à-vis the states," Thompson explained. "The attorneys general in many other states think these constitutional challenges coming out of New America might indirectly strengthen state and local governments."

"How?"

"They hope the court will carve out a middle ground."

"Then they don't understand what's really at stake."

Thompson agreed. "Self-interest is always myopic."

"A terrorist kills a couple of thousand people, and sidewalk vendors begin selling hats and T-shirts bearing his image and words," Steve said, mentioning one example of Thompson's rule. "The Florida hotel where Jeremiah killed over four hundred lobbyists and congressmen is booked into the next century. The New York Stock Exchange has been rebuilt, and the Dow is consistently over the nine thousand mark."

"That's America."

Steve didn't mention that Pres. Bob Carpenter had been reelected in 1996 in large part because of his adroit handling of Jeremiah's first campaign. Or that Peter had been rewarded with his current post for preventing the terrorist from exploding an atomic bomb at Laura's farm. Now Thompson was considered among a handful of politicians given a chance of moving into the White House after next year's presidential election.

Only Laura and I continue to suffer, Steve thought, *singled out for never-ending harassment by Jeremiah and his followers—for what reason? Because he'd disrupted Jeremiah's plans, forced Walter Dorfler to commit suicide, and nearly killed Jeremiah himself on several occasions? Or was it just the terrorist's obsession with Laura?* Steve tried to relax and control his twitching facial muscles.

As he and Thompson resumed walking around the north side of the Capitol, Steve noticed a sports utility vehicle shadowing them on Constitution Avenue. Behind the shaded windows undoubtedly were a couple of FBI agents assigned to protect Peter, who could be considered a top target of New American assassins.

"You a fight fan?" Thompson asked, as they walked by a security booth manned by two guards.

"You mean boxing?"

"Yeah. I'm not an expert, mind you, but it seems to me there are two fundamental styles: sluggers and boxers. Boxers are technicians. Patient and cunning. Always looking for the right opening. They rely on jabs and body blows. You know the old saying, 'Kill the body and the head dies.' "

Steve had a hard time thinking of Peter in the ring. His well-defined facial features, including a slender nose, would surely give way under a series of blows.

"Then there's the guy who just storms across the ring and tries to tear off his opponent's head," Thompson said, uncharacteristically punching the air with a right hand. "Like a young Mike Tyson. One big, crushing blow and your opponent is lying on his back, listening to the birdies sing."

Steve took off his jacket and slung it over his shoulder, waiting patiently for the conclusion. Did it have something to do with Jeremiah and his assault on Laura?

Thompson gestured over his shoulder. "Perhaps it's a crude comparison, but what's going on back there at the court is boxing. Over the next decade or so, we plan to counterpunch New America into submission, although there's bound to be some constitutional compromises before the final bell rings."

Steve bobbed his head in acknowledgment.

"As a lawyer, and the nation's chief legal officer, I'm supposed to be a boxer by nature, Steve. In this case, however, I believe in one crushing, roundhouse right."

They stopped at the northwest corner of the west lawn, under the shade of another large tree. Several joggers ran by. A work crew placed mulch around several bushes.

"What's all this got to do with anything concerning me?" Steve asked.

Thompson looked around to make certain no one was targeting them for attention. "If we somehow could take

Jeremiah out with one swift, fatal blow, New America might just dry up and blow away, like a prairie tumbleweed."

Steve wasn't convinced. "They've done pretty well up there, even with him in the background."

Thompson disagreed. "It'd be a harmless experiment if he were really dead."

Steve squared away in front of his former boss and looked down on him from a greater height. "No one in their right mind believed he was dead these last four years. Why didn't you or someone else in the government kill him long ago? You had the resources."

Thompson didn't flinch from the indirect criticism. "Lots of reasons. We're a democratic, constitutional society, Steve. Bound by laws, custom, and ethics. We don't kill lawbreakers. We hunt them down, arrest them, accord them their rights, put them on trial before a jury of their peers. Imprison them, rehabilitate them."

Steve snorted his disgust.

"He had the unofficial protection of the Chinese government," Thompson continued. "If we had assassinated Jeremiah while he was in Beijing, there would have been an international crisis. Besides, that's the president's call."

"He's been sitting on his hands for nearly four years."

"True, and I've been critical of him to his face, which he doesn't like, believe me. On the other hand, I understand his dilemma. We don't assassinate tyrants or despots who declare themselves to be heads of state. It's a bad precedent. Besides, what excuse could the president use to send federal forces into South Dakota?"

"A dozen outstanding warrants for Jeremiah's arrest?"

"Yes, but Jeremiah has an army and state police apparatus. I don't have enough FBI agents to stand up to them. Only the military can do that job, and that's a delicate political decision. The president would alienate millions of Americans if he used federal troops against a state government, even one that's spun out of control."

Steve nodded reluctantly. He'd been an FBI agent during the conflicts at Ruby Ridge and Waco, and those were small confrontations compared to what would be involved in dislodging Jeremiah and his supporters.

"Carpenter's a good guy in most ways," Thompson said about the president, "but he has a blind spot about Jeremiah for some reason. He thinks Jeremiah's just another nut. A minor player who'll fade from the scene eventually. The president is nearing the end of his second term. He's worried about his place in history. He's all wrapped up in trying to push national health care legislation through Congress as his crowning achievement."

"He'd better watch out, or he'll be remembered as the guy who let the fox into the chicken house."

"Exactly. But he doesn't listen to you, or me. In fact, I'm probably on my way out at any time."

"You gonna run for president?"

The attorney general shrugged. "That's another discussion. Let's keep to the topic. We have many assets in New America. Jeremiah's up to something. He was spotted recently by one of our spies at a military training exercise."

And he's been in Texas, too, Steve thought. "What's he up to? Surely he wouldn't be so crazy as to use military force against the United States?"

"I don't know. Maybe it's defensive; maybe he's got other plans. We haven't been able to find out. One thing's for certain, his little army is being subsidized to the tune of billions of dollars per year."

"Who besides the Chinese?"

"Middle East Islamic nations. Even the impoverished Russians, who'd like to see the same thing happen to the United States that happened to the old Soviet Union. Elements within Germany and Japan that harbor deep resentments against us. They all think of us as the bully on the block, and they're willing to give Jeremiah money to see if he can give us a bloody nose. It's just another version of the worldwide political, diplomatic, and military chess game."

Then what's the difference between Jeremiah and the so-called legitimate states that support him? Steve wondered.

"How's Laura holding up?" Thompson asked suddenly.

"She's badly shaken." He wasn't about to bring up the

rape, not even with a long-time friend like Peter. They would always deny that rumor. Still, Steve knew the resources at Peter's command. The attorney general knew about the break-in, and he could make an educated guess about the rest of it.

"Let's head over to the cafeteria in the National Gallery of Art," Thompson said. "We'll grab a sandwich, talk some more, and then I need to get back to the office. This walk constitutes my daily exercise."

They walked along that portion of Pennsylvania Avenue that had been converted to a VIP parking lot. On their left was Union Square, where a statue of Ulysses Grant overlooked a large reflecting pool.

"Let's cut to the chase, Peter. What's this all mean, and how do I figure in? Why'd you ask me to come up here?"

The attorney general took a deep breath. "Like I said, it would take a massive force and effort to capture Jeremiah, and the president doesn't want to make that political decision at this time. As I already said, the court battles with New America will go on endlessly. Frankly, I fear the consequences of capturing Jeremiah and putting him in jail. He'd just become a martyr and rallying symbol for his followers. I might point out that Hitler became even more famous while he was in jail, which is where he wrote *Mein Kampf*."

Jeremiah already wrote The Book of Second Jeremiah, Steve thought. Would it soon be only a dusty tome, or would it be a revolutionary document far into the future?

They hurried across Third Street and walked on the mall running between the various Smithsonian Museums.

Standing in the shade of a tree, Thompson said, "It's my legal opinion that as attorney general I have the authority to contract with private organizations to carry out Justice Department objectives."

Steve was skeptical. "That depends on what's done, and who does it."

The attorney general shrugged. "The law is a complicated thing, Steve. So is life. Many times we have only a Hobson's choice. All I know is that if you want to kill a rat, you send in a cat."

Covert action team! Steve thought. *Jesus, they had walked a long ways downhill from the Supreme Court. Now he fully understood the boxing analogy.*

"And you want me on this team?"

Thompson never flinched. "I thought you'd want to go."

Steve finished his friend's thought: *No one has the motivation you have to want Jeremiah dead.* He took a closer look at Peter, as if seeing him for the first time. His former boss was cool under fire, figuratively and literally. Maybe too cool, too goal-driven, too obsessive. Peter believed in action, however. Define the problem, choose a solution, implement it. A good attribute for an FBI agent could be a liability for a politician. Ambition might also be clouding his friend's judgment. On the other hand, Steve badly wanted Jeremiah dead. Who was he to criticize?

"No one's hunted him up close and personal like you, Steve. Your experience is unmatched."

That might be true, Steve thought, but he was also getting old and wasn't in the kind of physical shape necessary for such an operation. Further, his state of mind—the unobjective hatred he felt for Jeremiah—could be a liability on a paramilitary exercise.

"There's another reason," Thompson said, resuming his stroll toward the National Gallery of Art west building. "My sources tell me Katrina Dorfler is in New America."

Jeremiah's cousin and teenage lover.

"She might be easier to find than him. She might lead you right to the snake's den."

And what a story I'd have to tell Katrina, Steve thought. *So that's what this is about? If she knew Jeremiah still had an obsession with Laura, that he'd raped her, in fact, Katrina might give up the terrorist.*

"Who's running the team?"

"People I trust."

Rogue agents, mercenaries. The American Patriots. Maybe even the military. Hell, they'd freelanced in every other nation on earth, killing enemies of the United States, even if such activities were officially denied. Why not within the United States in this extraordinary time?

"You want me to rush across the ring and tear his head off?"

Thompson held open the door to the museum and said, uncharacteristically, "Drive a stake through the fucker's heart and bury him in an unmarked grave."

Later, as Steve walked on the mall toward the Smithsonian metro stop, he encountered one of the many homeless people who lived on the streets of the nation's capital.

The guy stood under a tree, wearing a heavy coat in the middle of summer. His skin was brown, not from the sun, but from encrusted body oils.

"You got some spare change, buddy? I'll trade you a secret for it."

Steve fished a dollar bill out of his pocket and handed it to the bum.

"Radio waves," the homeless man said, imparting a confidence. "That's how they control our minds."

As Steve walked away, he thought, *No, there are much more sophisticated and amazing ways.*

8

The young woman walking toward them cast a spell on Sgt. Ralph Duncan. *It might not be love at first sight,* he thought, *but what a sight!*

The tall, gorgeous brunette wore a big smile and little else except knee-high, black leather boots, and a matching bikini bottom outlined in silver studs. A very creative artist had used body paint to turn this classic beauty into a walking American flag. Tiny white stars were splashed across her blue face. Vertical red-and-white stripes covered her upper body, including her pert, bare breasts.

Duncan suppressed a desire to come to attention and salute as the "flag" strutted by. He looked over his shoulder and saw her go into the Pyramid Beer Gardens on Main Street in Sturgis, South Dakota. It was the first day of the annual Bike Week bash, and Duncan would have given anything to be able to take off his state policeman's uniform and join in the fun.

"This is a disgusting, disposable group of people," snarled Lt. Lars Magnum, second-in-command of the Belle Fourche State Police barracks. Today the beefy policeman with a widely-known drinking problem was Duncan's commanding officer.

"Absolutely, sir!" Duncan said, his admiration of America's enduring symbol now replaced by fear of an approaching group of large, hairy men. All wore boots, jeans, and black T-shirts imprinted with the Harley-Davidson emblem.

The bikers directed looks of hostility and contempt at the two policemen, and Duncan felt as naked as the flag beauty, even though he carried a baton and sidearm.

As the men passed by, Lieutenant Magnum snickered. "They're about to get theirs and don't even know it."

"Yes, sir," Duncan replied, trying to remember why he'd volunteered to be an FBI undercover agent and thinking of ways he could get out of town before all hell broke loose. Duncan didn't know what was going to happen specifically, but he feared the worse. He had been given no advance notice of today's assignment, so he hadn't been able to personally contact Washington. On the other hand, this crisis had been brewing for weeks, and the big shots back East should have guessed by now that the New America State Police would try to break up this annual motorcycle rally.

"Sergeant, this is a historic day," Lieutenant Magnum said, righteously. "Today we strike a blow against evil. Jeremiah would be proud."

"Yes, sir," Duncan said, although he had little respect for the strutting fascist beside him.

As they neared the end of the business district, the lieutenant stopped and looked back on Main Street, lined on both sides and down the middle with motorcycles, primarily vintage Harleys, including a fair number of classic Knuckleheads, Shovelheads, and Panheads. During their stroll, Duncan feared they might knock one over, starting a chain reaction that would end with them being beaten senseless.

"I think we've accomplished our mission," Lieutenant Magnum announced. "I didn't see any weapons or anything else that would cause us to alter our plans. Did you, Sergeant?"

"No, sir."

"Well, then, let's get back to the staging area and report the results of our reconnaissance."

Duncan suppressed a desire to go back to the beer garden and tell "the flag" to get out of town. He had the perfect hideout: his and Hoffman's apartment in Pierre. But "duty" called.

*   *   *

As Duncan walked about the encampment in the Black Hills that flank Sturgis on the south and west, he thought it resembled a Boy Scout jamboree, with all the tents and campfires. Except these units of the state police and National Guard bivouacked in several isolated mountain meadows were armed to the teeth with real weapons. They had blocked off various roads leading from the hills into town and could be observed only from the air.

Conversations and laughter carried far on the cool night air, although the camp was generally quiet. Everyone had been informed that state police commander, Brig. Gen. Carter Simpson, would address the troops at 9:00 P.M.

Duncan had scouted this particular encampment enough to estimate it held at least two thousand state policeman, and he knew from listening to various scuttlebutt that there could be as many as three regiments of the National Guard nearby. Many of his fellow policeman reported seeing towed artillery and armored personnel carriers on nearby mountain roads, and Duncan had no reason to doubt them.

The wiry undercover agent walked into the woods far enough so that he couldn't be seen standing behind a blue spruce. Duncan unzipped his pants and was prepared to start urinating if anyone came close to his location. At a prearranged time, he tuned the two-way radio to a particular frequency and used the off-on button to tap out a Morse code message that would be picked up locally and retransmitted.

His message was simple: "Troops in Black Hills prepared to attack bikers in Sturgis." He signed off with his code name.

Duncan returned to his tent and put on a jacket. An August cold front caused the nighttime temperature to dip into the fifties. He joined fellow members from the Pierre and Belle Fourche barracks gathered around a large television screen. Similar screens had been set up throughout the encampment, and all were connected to a large satellite dish mounted on the back of a truck. The closed-circuit telecast would be bounced off a foreign satellite.

Brigadier General Simpson suddenly appeared on screen, broadcasting from the Capitol rotunda in Pierre. The general was in full uniform and looked confident and fierce.

"I want to talk to you men this evening about the so-called Sturgis Rally and Races," General Simpson said. "They began in 1940, but this will be the last year our nation and the innocent residents of Sturgis are subjected to an invasion by outside agitators and scum whose only purpose is to turn this quiet city into a modern-day Sodom and Gomorrah.

"That is not an exaggeration! As those of you know who've been in Sturgis today, the unnatural practice of sodomy is commonplace on the streets, in the bars and back alleys, along with every other kind of immorality imaginable. Let's call it what it is. Bike Week is a celebration of drunkenness, debauchery, and outright evil. The only race here is to see who will get to hell the fastest."

Duncan forced himself to laugh along with his fellow state policemen at the general's sense of humor.

"Let me quote just one verse from the Prophet's book," General Simpson continued. "*Second Jeremiah* 1:6: 'America is awash in a sea of vulgarity, promiscuity, and violence!' Doesn't that say it all? This rally mocks the values of New America. It's a stick shoved in our eye by those who think they're free to do anything they want, even ignore the word of God. There's not a single commandment that won't be broken tonight in Sturgis. It happens year after year. Where did people in old America get the idea that allowing such evil is somehow essential to the practice of democracy?"

Duncan watched General Simpson's face screw up in anger as he paced back and forth on the rotunda's tile floor, in front of bronze sculptures representing Integrity, Wisdom, Courage, and Vision. "New America radio and television stations have been broadcasting warnings to these bikers for weeks, urging them to stay away. But did they listen? No!"

On this point, Duncan knew the general was right. The bikers had enthusiastically taken up New America's challenge, of course. Biker publications and the national grapevine characterized them as "freedom riders," compelled to exercise their constitutional rights of freedom of assembly and freedom of speech. American flags tattooed on muscular arms and plump breasts and sewn onto the back of jeans carried a whole new meaning this year.

And they'd come to New America. Duncan shook his head sadly as he remembered manning several roadblocks set up to intercept the bikers. In the minds of this largely male crowd, the ultimate expression of freedom was to thunder along the highways and byways of America on their modern-day chariots, with the wind in their faces and a long-legged chick clinging to their backs.

The state police had beaten them up, cuffed them, and hauled them away in the back of military transports to hastily erected, outdoor jail camps. But if Washington thought the bikers had given up, they were wrong.

"There've been up to a half-million biker scum who've invaded Sturgis in the past, but there're less than fifty thousand there right now," General Simpson said, smiling proudly. "They're the hard-core, and they need to be taught a lesson. They need to learn that in New America we'll use whatever means possible to maintain and preserve social order and prevent an erosion of public morals. I've even extended a special invitation to the national news media, including Julie Burton of the Midwest News Service, who filmed that snotty report about the community stocks in the Christian city of Anathoth. Maybe when the old Americans see first-hand how we preserve a moral environment in New America, they'll want to come join us."

Those standing around Duncan cheered as the general's image faded from the screen. Soon, officers told them to bed down and prepare for an early rising. Duncan was unable to sleep, however, as he lay awake dreading the dawn. He considered slipping out of the camp in the middle of the night, but someone had to document what was going to happen tomorrow.

The campaign began near sun-up on the second day of the rally. Duncan and his squad, as well as two other squads under the command of Lieutenant Magnum, rode in several M-35 two-and-a-half-ton trucks to a residential area on the edge of town.

Of the bikers who'd made it to Sturgis, few stayed in motels and hotels, largely because there weren't enough rooms for rent in the small city, or even the western half of the state. As in the past, most stayed in makeshift campgrounds or slept in sleeping bags on the ground beside their bikes. A few of the leaders rented houses in town, however. Those individuals, Duncan learned, were their targets.

"What're our orders?" Duncan asked, trying to keep the worry out of his voice.

"To roust the people who've rented that two-story green house at the end of the block," Lieutenant Magnum said, sipping from a flask.

"What then?"

Lieutenant Magnum smiled malevolently. "Send half your squad around to the back of the house, Sergeant. You and the rest follow me. At my signal, we'll break down the front and back doors."

Duncan relayed the orders, then turned back to the lieutenant. "How many are inside? Are they likely to be armed?"

Duncan watched as the lieutenant jutted out his chin. "Scum like this always are. There could be a dozen or more."

Duncan felt he had little choice. To refuse to obey would result in his being relieved of duty. Investigated. Perhaps found out, in which case he might just "disappear." On the other hand, if he went along, he might save someone's life, and live to do damage to New America another day.

Duncan's men smashed their way into the house, M-16s at the ready. Three people slept in the living room on a pull-out sofa bed. Others lay on the floor inside sleeping bags. All were now awake, confused, and afraid.

Chaos broke out. Duncan's men screamed at the top of their lungs at the bikers, gesturing ominously with their gun barrels. Others ran up the stairs, following Lieutenant Magnum.

Duncan raced after the lieutenant. When he got to the

top of the stairs, his men already had kicked open doors to two bedrooms. Inside one bedroom, a long-haired, heavily-tattoed man wearing only briefs sat on the side of the bed. His female companion lay quietly, wide-eyed and clutching a sheet to her neck.

The biker coolly lit a cigarette. "What do you boys want?"

"Shut your filthy mouth!" Lieutenant Magnum commanded, as he consulted a piece of paper. "What's your name?"

"Dooley."

"You one of the organizers of this rally?" Lieutenant Magnum demanded.

"No, man, I'm just one of the attendees."

Duncan intervened. "You want me to get 'em outside, Lieutenant?" Outside, they were less likely to get hurt. Duncan was especially afraid for the woman, who looked terrified.

"Not just yet, Sergeant," Lieutenant Magnum replied, walking slowly to the end of the bed, where he pivoted, so all present could behold his splendor, including knee-high, black leather boots shined to a high gloss and a perfectly creased uniform. He tugged on the black, leather brim of his campaign hat.

"Look, man, we got a right to be here," Dooley said, looking sideways at the lieutenant. "We ain't breaking no laws."

"That's where you're wrong," the lieutenant said, drawing his side arm.

Duncan again said, forcefully, "Lieutenant, shall I escort the prisoners outside!"

"You're breaking God's laws!" Lieutenant Magnum shouted, and shot Dooley in the side of the head.

The gunshot caused Duncan to jump back, nearly knocking over one of his men who was standing too close behind. The woman in bed began to scream hysterically, as she frantically scooted away from her dead biker friend, who lay twitching on the bed, blood and brains oozing out of a red-black hole in the side of his head.

Lieutenant Magnum walked around the side of the bed

and brought the barrel of his nine millimeter down on the woman's head. She collapsed onto the bed beside the dead man.

"Now you can haul their sorry asses outside, Sergeant!"

Downstairs, several bikers lay unconscious on the floor. Duncan looked daggers at members of his squad who'd obviously used their rifle butts to crack heads.

They prodded those bikers who could walk out of the house onto the lawn. Other state police squads similarly emptied out adjoining houses. Officers yelled at them to load the bikers into the M-35s.

Lieutenant Magnum finished speaking into a walkie-talkie and pointed at an approaching armored personnel carrier. "Get most of your squad in that APC, Duncan, except for a couple of men up by the driver. Put your best man on the machine gun. You follow these trucks around to the rest of their stops until they're all full. If any of these bastards tries to escape, shoot 'em! Is that clear, Sergeant?"

Duncan felt sick to his stomach. "Yes, sir."

"I'll meet up with you later. We'll form up a convoy and head toward the camp."

"Camp, sir?"

"Just get going, Duncan."

As they went about their rounds, Duncan got a better perspective of what was happening throughout Sturgis. The state police obviously had been assigned to drive the bikers out into the streets and take prisoners, while the National Guard responded to any serious counterattack by the bikers. Two M-1 Abrams tanks rolled down city streets, crushing as many parked motorcycles as possible. In a panicked rush, bikers mounted up and rode away.

The machine guns on the tanks and accompanying APCs had been altered to fire rubber bullets, which inflicted serious, although nonlethal, damage to the fleeing bikers. Exploding tear gas canisters added to the noise and chaos. Like the others in the APC, Duncan wore a gas mask.

As near as he could tell, the bikers put up little resistance. The guardsmen were content to inflict maximum physical damage and then let most of the bikers through their lines. It wasn't kindness, Duncan understood. They just didn't have vehicles and jails to hold all fifty thousand bikers.

As the convoy headed out of town, Duncan was amazed to see that General Simpson had been true to his word. Several television camera crews were filming the rout.

Duncan and Lieutenant Magnum rode in a jeep leading the convoy of trucks filled with manacled bikers. About twenty miles south of Deadwood, they turned onto a black-topped road that led to a security checkpoint, where guards furiously waved on the military trucks streaming into the camp.

"See those emplacements," Lieutenant Magnum shouted above the wind, pointing toward the hills above the camp. "Ground-to-air missiles in case any aircraft try to fly over."

Duncan knew he could pinpoint the location of the camp later so it could be photographed from space by a Defense Department satellite. He was nagged by the thought that the Pentagon should already know about this place. Or did they? He'd been around long enough to be aware of the Byzantine motivations of the military brass and politicians in Washington. Maybe they wanted this outrage to occur as justification for military action against New America. At any rate, he'd do his job and find a way to use the miniature camera hidden in a pocket of his uniform. The news media certainly wouldn't be following them here.

"What is this place?" Duncan asked, as the convoy came to a stop.

"It's a temporary prison for felons who will not observe the law," Lieutenant Magnum replied tersely, getting out of the jeep. "They are rehabilitated, if possible, and returned to society, or they are expelled from New America, according to provisions of the Social Contract."

Duncan doubted the lieutenant. Allowing large numbers of New Americans to leave would be an admission that God's plan for his chosen people had gone awry.

An imposing fence topped with razor wire surrounded a camp the size of three or four football fields. Inside the wire, prisoners lived in tents. Walkways connecting the four corner towers gave guards an open field of fire into a crowded inmate population, which Duncan estimated to number as many as five thousand. He knew this wasn't the only detention camp in New America.

A mountain stream flowed through one corner of the prison, serving as an open latrine. The stench of human waste was nearly intolerable. Duncan concluded that when winter came, it would be a death camp.

"This place is almost full," Duncan observed, as he and the lieutenant watched the camp guards use truncheons to prod, beat, and herd the bikers through the main gate into the milling crowd of prisoners. Even the tough bikers looked afraid.

Duncan felt the hair on the back of his neck stand up as someone in the far recesses of the camp screamed in fear and pain.

Looking around, he noticed that one truck had pulled out of the convoy and parked in front of a large metal building that served as the camp motor pool. Beyond it a dozen or so cabins had been built into the side of a heavily forested hill.

Dazed biker women jumped from the truck's tailgate and were herded into the motor pool building. Duncan's heartbeat accelerated. God, he hoped the "flag" wasn't among them.

"What's with the women?" he asked the lieutenant, who was taking a pull from his flask.

"They're for the amusement of the guards."

Duncan whirled away, suppressing an urge to pull out his nine millimeter and blow the lieutenant to hell. Instead, he yelled at several men in his squad who were ogling the women and shouting obscenities. "Get over by the fence! You're here to make certain none of the prisoners escape, not for fun and games!"

Duncan slipped out of his pocket a slim, rectangular camera about the size of his hand. He walked between two trucks to make certain no one could see him, including the tower guards. He focused the camera by hand and held it chest-high, pointing and clicking away. He moved around to several other safe locations, so he could get as many views of the camp as possible.

Duncan didn't want to be gone long, however, and soon returned to where the lieutenant stood, conversing with several fellow officers. Duncan stood apart respectfully, as if awaiting orders. It gave him time to think, but the only questions that came to mind were: *Why in the hell are they letting this go on? Why aren't U.S. paratroopers dropping from the sky at this very moment?*

Lieutenant Magnum sauntered over to where Duncan stood. "I guess we can leave now. The guards have everything under control."

"Where're we going?"

"Back to Sturgis, first. We'll get our orders there. You and your men probably will return to the bivouac, at least for tonight."

As they walked toward the jeep, Duncan asked, "What will eventually happen to the bikers we rounded up today?"

The lieutenant shrugged. "I figure they'll interrogate the lot of them and sort out the leaders. Let most of the followers go, so they can spread the word. I don't think there'll be a Bike Week next year, do you, Sergeant?"

Duncan laughed on cue and shook his head. "What about the leaders?"

Lieutenant Magnum shrugged. "They periodically empty out this cesspool."

"Where do the prisoners go?"

The lieutenant snickered. "You obviously don't know much about the geology of this part of the state, do you, Sergeant?"

9

Jeremiah watched one of his followers create a new page on the New America Internet web site. On this page he planned to progressively post *The Epistle of Jeremiah the Prophet to the New Americans*. It was the Prophet's duty to soothe the concerns of New Americans, bolster their spirits, interpret the word of God, and be their beacon into the future.

When completed, the collected epistles would be called *I New Americans*, and comprise a second new book of the revised Christian Bible, following right after *The Book of Second Jeremiah*.

THE EPISTLE OF JEREMIAH
THE PROPHET
TO THE NEW AMERICANS

CHAPTER ONE

1 To all the Brethren who strive to implement His Word in the land called New America, as well as those who support our efforts from afar;

2 The Grace of God the Father is with you, and He watches and guides your effort to achieve His plan for

the Chosen Few. Blessed are those who observe the Social Contract set forth in The Book of Second Jeremiah. Amen.

3 As Paul the Apostle spoke to the community of Christian converts following the crucifixion of Christ, providing them guidance and correction in their efforts, so I, Jeremiah the Second, called to serve God as His emissary on earth during these momentous times, will also minister to the faithful.

4 Those of a cynical, blasphemous nature who oppose New America and work evilly to thwart God's Will have said I was dead or disinterested; nay, for God has protected me and instructed me as to His Will during a long period of isolation and meditation. I am sent to guide you again. If ye are weak, I have the strength of the LORD.

5 As the Twelve Apostles were persecuted and scattered by Herod Agrippa, as Peter was jailed and Paul stoned, so the authorities of this wicked time seek to silence me, believing falsely that to kill the Leader is to kill the Idea.

6 My actions are ordained by God and I can no more be arrested, tried, and judged than Jesus could be judged by Herod or Pilate, who had the good sense to wash his hands of the demands of the Mob, and those Jews in high places who manipulated it. Were the government of the united states so wise.

7 In New America we see God's hand everywhere. Think ye are here by accident! That this beginning is not part of God's plan! If so, ye are of little Faith and Faith, as Christ said, can move mountains.

8 The work ahead of us is as a mountain, and will

test your Faith and Allegiance; yea, even your willingness to give up your life for the LORD. Ye of little Faith best be gone! New America is not for the faint of heart, and the uncommitted. Ye who have waited patiently, come now and join the Army of the Lord. The Battle looms ahead, as does the Glory promised by God.

9   New America is the Way, and it will encounter the same resistance faced by the early Christians battling against the ominous military might of Rome. Your battle is comparable and the result will be the same in the end; for the plan of the Eternal God of Goodness always will triumph over Evil and the petty concerns of Philistines.

10 Ask ye the way! Read the Book of Prophecy. Evil or good is man's personal choice but "no man is an island"; he is by necessity part of a social organization, which cannot take away his freedom by institutionalizing Evil and Inequality. In New America there is no room for Injustice, Greed, and the Lust for Power; nor for a Morality flexible enough to indulge and forgive all Evil intention and acts.

11 Know ye the results! Read the Book of Prophecy. New Americans are the Chosen of God, destined to take control of their Evolution, to escape the confines of earth, know the Universe, and be absorbed into the Mind of God. So it is written, so it is ordained.

10

Steve flew into the Denver airport. As instructed by Attorney General Thompson, he waited near the baggage claim carousel, trying not to look conspicuous.

He regretted not being able to see his ex-wife, Jennifer, and the kids, who lived in a nearby suburb. Even though he'd taken many precautions, Jeremiah's men could still be trailing him. Steve didn't want to give the terrorist any ideas, such as kidnapping his family and offering to exchange them for Laura.

Steve had mentioned his fears to Thompson, who'd promised to dispatch FBI agents to guard and protect Jennifer and the kids. Steve knew the agents would operate in the background, hoping to bag Jeremiah if he came calling.

About 6:00 P.M., two muscular young men wearing Levi's, tight-fitting black T-shirts, and aviator sunglasses approached Steve and uttered the correct password: *false prophet.* Steve thought cynically they might as well have worn signs on their backs: *"Assassins for Hire."* On the other hand, they obviously were smart enough to have memorized his photograph.

The driver of a black Seville wordlessly chauffeured them north on Interstate 25, while Steve chatted idly with his companions about sports, until he grew bored with the topic and pretended to sleep. They bypassed Cheyenne, Wyoming, and continued to drive north, roughly parallel to the Laramie Mountains. Four hours after they'd left Denver, the driver exited at an isolated interchange, and said, "This is where you get out."

No sooner had the Cadillac turned back onto the interstate than headlights popped on a hundred yards down a narrow access road. Steve tensed, hoping it was a signal from fellow CAT members, not Jeremiah's supporters who had learned of their mission. They took the last available seats in a fifteen-passenger Ford van and were driven on back roads another hour northeast into the grasslands of east-central Wyoming. Eventually they turned down a dirt lane toward a farmhouse, set well back from the road.

Although it was after 11:00 P.M., a buffet had been set out in the kitchen and the weary travelers filled their plates and eagerly took advantage of soft drinks, beer, and wine on ice. Their tensions began to ease and the team members introduced themselves, using only first names.

Steve scrutinized the thirty or so CAT soldiers crowded into the three first-floor rooms joined by arched doorways. Most were younger and appeared physically fit, determined, and confident. Steve didn't recognize anyone.

With the sound of metal on glass, the conversations ended and everyone turned their attention to a middle-aged man dressed in combat fatigues, who held a spoon in one hand and a glass of beer in the other. He had positioned himself in the dining room, so he could see into the kitchen and living room.

"Welcome to Wyoming," the man said. His appearance and voice of authority suggested he was or had been a military officer.

"You know why we're here, so I won't go into that," he said, crisply. "We're about platoon size as you can see and each squad leader will provide you with more detailed instructions about your particular role.

"Our first objective tomorrow morning will be to move into the Black Hills area of South Dakota, about fifty miles east of here. Those of you familiar with the area might ask why we didn't just fly into Ellsworth Air Force Base near Rapid City and drive south. The reason is that Rapid City is a bastion of New America, and too many of the new people who live there also work at the air base. Its security has been compromised in my opinion, although not everyone in Washington agrees with me."

A restless stir rippled across the room, punctuated by the sound of someone crumpling a beer can.

"You'll travel in three cars and two vans. Wear civilian clothes. Your uniforms, weapons, and equipment will be transported separately. Each squad will go to a different staging area, generally a motel or hotel, to await instructions as to the location of the target. Hopefully, the mission will kick off after dark tomorrow. You'll be lightly armed. This is a quick in-and-out operation."

Steve knew that meant assault and sniper rifles, side arms, grenades, a light machine gun, perhaps even an 81- or 82-mm mortar, all items that would fit nicely into vans and car trunks.

The briefing officer rocked back and forth from his heels to his toes. "This mission is very important to our nation, I believe. Don't treat it as a lark or a run-of-the-mill exercise. We're here to kill Jeremiah the Terrorist. If you're captured, you can expect the same treatment you'd get within any enemy nation. Or worse. Most of you saw on television what happened recently in Sturgis. The U.S. government will rightfully deny any association with our effort. If any of our own are killed, we will *not* leave their bodies behind." He paused, then taped a piece of paper to the doorway frame. "Find your name on this list and get together briefly with your squad leader. Finish eating and get a good night's sleep. Good hunting tomorrow."

After everyone had checked the list, the squad leaders introduced themselves as Alpha, Beta, Charley, and Frank. Alpha walked over to where Steve sat.

Approximately Steve's age and nearly as tall, Alpha wore wire-rimmed glasses and chewed gum vigorously. "I feel I know you well, Steve, even though we've never met. You don't mind if I call you Steve?"

Steve shook his head and followed Alpha to a corner of the living room, where they had more privacy.

"I read the book you wrote with your wife," Alpha explained. "I even feel like I know Laura, having watched her on television so many times." Alpha paused and looked around, working the gum. "In your book, you wrote about American agents working undercover in Europe, who discovered Jeremiah's relationship with Walter Dorfler, and Dorfler's dealings with the Ukrainian gangsters."

Steve understood. "You were one of the faceless, nameless agents." CIA, probably.

"Yes, my mother can take no pride in my work, which indeed is a cross for her to bear." The blond-haired squad leader, whose English was too perfect, leaned closer to Steve to impart a confidence. "I'm working undercover in New America as Hans Dietrich Hoffman, captain of artillery."

Flattered that the undercover agent trusted him enough to impart such life-threatening information, Steve nevertheless wasn't certain he wanted to know these details.

"Maybe they paired us together for another reason," Hoffman said.

"What's that?"

"I also know Katrina Dorfler up close and personal."

"Really?"

"Yes, in fact, there's another operative here who knows her." Hoffman motioned to someone across the room and they were soon joined by a balding, husky man, who Steve concluded was the only CAT member besides the platoon leader who might be over forty.

"I'm Doc," the man said, offering Steve his hand.

"The only other member of our squad you need to know is the driver, over there," Hoffman said, pointing. Steve looked across the room at a thin man, who gave a feeble, two-fingered salute in acknowledgment.

"He's called Wheelie," Hoffman said. "Not very original, but apropos."

"What do I do?" Steve asked.

"We'll be going to Hot Springs tomorrow to question a man we've lured there," Hoffman explained. "He's the key to the operation. You've studied him."

"Who?"

"The governor of South Dakota," Doc replied, affably, "Davey Schropa."

In the morning, the vehicles left the farmhouse one at a time, every twenty minutes, beginning at 7:00 A.M. Wheelie piloted a four-door Oldsmobile, with Doc in the front beside him, and Steve and Hoffman sitting in the backseat. Within a half hour they were in South Dakota, near Edgemont, in an area where row crops grew in the flat lands between the dome-shaped hills covered with prairie grasses and grazing cattle. A large billboard sign informed them that prehistoric woolly mammoths once had roamed the area. Some had fallen in sinkholes, where their remains were perfectly preserved and viewed now millions of years later by curious tourists. Steve hoped New America eventually would be only a relic, a curiosity.

"How did you persuade Schropa to come to Hot Springs?" Steve asked Hoffman.

"He's been followed for a long time now," Hoffman replied, "to establish his patterns. He comes here a lot to relax and relieve the tensions of his job, although of course he's only a figurehead. He accepted an invitation to visit the local VA hospital and listen to a proposal from the director."

"What's the plan?" Steve asked. "Capture Schropa and force him to tell Jeremiah's whereabouts?"

Doc turned sideways in the front seat, so he could look at his companions. "Torture? That's medieval! We use more sedate methods." He laughed heartily at his private joke, although Steve thought Hoffman's smile didn't quite hide an element of distaste.

"What methods?" Steve asked. "Hypnosis?"

Doc shook his head. "Nobody in our business believes in this anymore. All that business about trance states, that's for Las Vegas magic shows. It's illusion, not reality, although the CIA experimented for years with hypnosis, searching for a technique to program themselves a Manchurian candidate. They wanted to send him to Cuba, where he'd assassinate Fidel Castro after getting a telephone call from someone who read him poetry by Robert Frost."

Doc snickered, causing Steve to smile.

"So you're not going to torture him or hypnotize him," Steve said, playing along. "Whaddaya gonna do, say 'pretty, pretty, please, tell us where Jeremiah is'?"

Doc winked at Hoffman. "Sounds okay to me."

"Doc believes in chemically altered states of consciousness," Hoffman explained.

"You've seen it before, Steve," Doc suggested, a twinkle in his eye.

Steve frowned. "I don't think so."

"You've never been in a bar?"

Steve shook his head. He was on a life-and-death mission with a comedian. At least it broke the tension.

"You got a whole bunch of guys drinking a chemical potion from a bottle, which causes them to say and do things they ordinarily wouldn't," Doc explained, "and the next day, they can't remember anything!"

"Come to think of it, I've done that experiment a few times," Steve admitted, trying to be a good sport.

"Yeah, well, I got a mixture of chemicals we inject intravenously that's much more effective than alcohol," Doc said, suddenly serious. "We don't know exactly how it works, but it seems to tap into subconscious conflicts. It promotes confession as a way of unburdening the soul. Chemicals by Freud. The people who planned this operation think Schropa is an excellent candidate for such intervention."

Steve looked out the window, thinking of what he knew about the one-time insurance agent from Sioux Falls. Schropa seemed a likable young man caught up in this maelstrom. Wasn't that the way it happened? When Jeremiah asked his high school buddy to be a front man, what could Schropa do except agree?

The VA Medical Center sat high on a hill overlooking Hot Springs, a small town on the southern edge of the Black Hills National Forest. A few remaining bathhouses were evidence of the town's original claim that its

warm, mineral-rich waters had therapeutic powers.

Wheelie drove up a hill to the medical center administration building, a sandstone structure with a distinctive domed, red-tile roof that could be seen for miles. Doc, Steve, and Hoffman entered the building through a side door and went into a room equipped with an examination table and medical cabinet.

Schropa arrived shortly thereafter for his luncheon date with the hospital administrator. In a nearby private dining room, the administrator outlined a proposal for turning the medical complex over to New America, to be used for the treatment of sick and wounded members of the state police and National Guard.

While they discussed this proposal, Schropa drank a white wine laced with one of Doc's chemical concoctions, which soon caused the governor to lapse into a stupor. Several attendants carried him to the treatment room and placed him on a gurney. Elsewhere in the building, a comely nurse entertained Schropa's bodyguard and driver, a corporal in the state police.

Steve leaned against a far wall, watching as Doc inserted an IV line into the governor's arm.

As the chemicals flowed into his vein, Schropa revived. To Steve's amazement, the governor suddenly sat up and swung his legs over the edge of the gurney. He looked around at those in the room as if nothing were wrong. On the other hand, Steve detected a film across the subject's eyes.

"Do you know Trent Dillman?" Doc asked, picking up on a line of questioning he'd pursued years ago with Katrina Dorfler on an American army post located near Nuremberg, Germany.

"Yes," Schropa answered.

"Is Trent Dillman alive?"

"Yes."

"Is he now known as Jeremiah the Terrorist Prophet?"

Steve fiddled with his tie, making certain the small camera lens was pointed at the "patient."

"Yes."

Laura had arranged for the miniaturized movie camera,

compliments of the technical staff of the United Broadcasting Corporation. The "guts" of the camera were inside a case about six-by-one-by-four inches, which fit nicely in Steve's inside suit-coat pocket. A small cable led to the camera lens, which appeared as a tie tack. It had infrared capabilities, which he thought might come in handy later.

Steve wanted this assignment documented, although his fellow CAT members might not be happy to know about the camera's existence. Steve knew Laura would fuzz over faces when she edited the tape.

"Is Jeremiah in New America?"

"Yes."

"Is he alone?"

"No."

Doc looked at Hoffman. "Who's with Jeremiah?"

"His men and . . . Katrina Dorfler."

Doc gave the thumbs-up sign to Hoffman.

"Where is Jeremiah, exactly?"

"In the Black Hills."

"Tell me how to get to Jeremiah's hideout, Davey."

And the governor did.

By midafternoon the other squads had been informed of the location about fifteen miles directly west of the Mount Rushmore monument, in the heart of the Black Hills—a three-thousand-square-mile area of minimountains rising as high as seven thousand feet above the surrounding prairie.

Wheelie drove Doc, Steve, and Hoffman north to Custer, where they checked into a motel and waited for darkness. Near midnight, they left and drove west and north on gravel roads until they reached the rendezvous point, where the four squads were given their assignments by the man who'd briefed them at the farmhouse. Hoffman's squad, including Steve, would guard the rear and provide reinforcements, if necessary.

The team hiked a hundred yards up the side of a steep hill, through dense stands of ponderosa pine and black spruce. The men stepped carefully to avoid twisting an ankle on the many protruding and loose rocks. They were aided by a bright moon, although the CATs wore black and had smeared black grease paint on their faces to prevent moonlight reflection. At the crest of the hill, the men hunkered down while the squad leaders located the cabin with their night-vision binoculars and agreed upon the best approach.

Steve carried only his 9-mm Sig-Sauer. There were enough expert marksmen in the group that he didn't need to be toting a rifle. The snipers had memorized Jeremiah's face and their orders were to wound him, if possible, but use deadly force against everyone else, except Katrina Dorfler or any other women present. Steve hoped the terrorist could be taken alive and that he would be allowed a few minutes alone with Jeremiah, before Doc took over.

The hideout provided several advantages to Jeremiah and his entourage. The weathered pine cabin sat at the bottom of a canyon, between the base of an overhanging granite cliff and a meandering mountain stream. It was largely invisible from the air. A winding gravel road leading to the cabin provided several natural checkpoints and sniper perches, which was one reason why the CATs had come over the opposite mountain.

By 2:00 A.M. the three lead squads had formed a semicircle around the cabin and were in place for the final assault.

Everything seemed perfect and that bothered Steve. He remembered other times when Jeremiah had been cornered—in Laura's hotel room in Kansas City, in a beachfront house at Ocean City, New Jersey. Near the pond at the farm. Each time Steve had been within a few feet of the terrorist, yet each time he'd escaped. Why? Because Jeremiah always had a contingency plan. Why would tonight be any different?

Steve looked again through the night-vision binoculars. Jeremiah couldn't escape across the stream, where the CATs would pounce on him. The cliff behind the cabin looked too steep to climb. South of the cabin the stream entered a minigorge. To the north was the road, running through a meadow. *That would be the best escape route,*

Steve thought, *if Jeremiah could somehow get by the squad in that area.*

"I'm going to move off to the right," Steve whispered to Hoffman, who frowned but shrugged.

Halfway to the meadow, Steve saw a flash off to his left, followed by an explosion, and the chatter of automatic rifle fire. Steve turned his binoculars on the scene and saw one of his comrades fall in the small stream, which was no more than fifteen-feet wide and knee-deep. Two guards on the porch of the cabin crumpled to the ground as the windows of the cabin exploded in a shower of glass. After dumping several flash/bang grenades through the broken windows, three CATs burst through the cabin's front door and Steve heard more automatic weapons fire.

Steve waded across the stream and stood behind a tree at the edge of the meadow. He heard his companions shouting. Someone yelled, "All clear!"

Suddenly, about seventy-five yards to his left, a figure materialized out of nowhere. Steve pointed the Sig-Sauer at the running man, waiting for the right moment, the clean shot.

Was it Jeremiah? Should he kill him, as Peter suggested? *Drive a stake through the fucker's heart and bury him in an unmarked grave.* No, Steve wanted him alive! He disagreed with his former boss. Jeremiah *should* be put on trial, so the myths could be stripped away, revealing him to the public as nothing more than a monster.

This internal debate ended as Steve felt a sharp blow to his head, which caused an explosion of bright pinpoints in his brain. Followed by a panicky descent into darkness.

He woke up a half-hour later, disoriented and nauseous. It took several minutes for Steve to orient himself and decide he was lying on a bed in the cabin.

"I should have gone with you," Hoffman said. Steve looked at the German, trying to focus his eyes and thoughts. The realization came gradually. There had been at least two others: a scout out front and a trailer. The precaution had worked. One of them had spotted Steve and knocked him out. Steve cursed his stupidity. For the first time since he'd begun hunting the terrorist, Steve doubted his own abilities. Peter had been wrong again.

Steve rose unsteadily and looked around the bedroom. Two dead men lay on the floor. Carrying a Heckler and Koch MP-5 submachine gun, the platoon leader wedged his boot toe under each of the dead men and flipped them onto their backs.

"Recognize them?" he asked Steve.

"No."

"There are three more dead guys in the back bedroom."

But Steve didn't know them either. A bed had been turned over to reveal a trap door. Steve knew the exit was in the meadow.

"There's someone you should meet," Hoffman said, directing Steve toward the cabin's main room. The German pulled a stocking cap over his face to prevent Katrina Dorfler from recognizing him as the one who'd helped snatch her off the streets of Nuremberg.

She sat on a sofa, shaking with fear. *It's like Jeremiah to leave her to her fate as he escaped,* Steve thought. *Why can't she see this?*

Steve sat beside her, not bothering to mask himself. He wanted the terrorist to know who was hunting him.

"We need to talk," Steve said, gingerly feeling around the cut in his scalp, which somehow reminded him to position himself so the camera lens poking through a buttonhole of his black jacket pointed at Katrina.

"I won't tell you anything," she said, shrilly.

Steve looked at a robust woman in her mid-thirties, with dark, purple-streaked hair, and an interesting face.

"I don't know anything important," she persisted.

"We have much in common," Steve replied, introducing himself.

"I know you. You killed my father!" Katrina screamed, raising her fists as if to hit Steve, although clearly afraid to do so.

"No, I was with your father when he took cyanide," Steve said. "If Jeremiah told you differently, he's lying.

You father wasn't even talking to me when he took the pill. It's on film. I can get you a copy."

Katrina's eyes narrowed to slits, but Steve detected a sliver of doubt.

"That's not the only lie that sonofabitch has told you," Steve said, through clenched teeth. He moved closer on the sofa, so he could whisper his secret into Katrina's ear. "About six weeks ago, he raped my wife at her parents' home in Austin, Texas. Did you know that?"

Katrina stole a look at him, and Steve saw a series of emotions ripple over her face, ranging from disbelief to horror.

"How can you live with an animal like him?" he asked.

Katrina shook her head, as she sobbed. "I've always loved him. I can't help it. Now there's another reason." Implausibly, she told him, "I'm pregnant with his child."

11

Laura thought compulsively about *him* as she maneuvered the Land Rover through early morning rush-hour traffic. A car horn jarred her to reality, causing Laura to fear that *they* were trying to run her off the road.

She hated traffic jams inside the Washington D.C., beltway and remembered that *he* had restricted the use of automobiles in New America. Laura shook her head wearily. Jeremiah had come to occupy the whole of her mind, in ways both logical and deranged.

She'd insisted on driving herself to the Rosslyn headquarters of the United Broadcasting Corporation. Maria had objected strenuously until Laura reminded her bodyguard that she was an "employee" and would do as she was told. Nevertheless, Laura had slipped a snub-nosed .38-cal. Colt inside her purse.

She drove into the high-rise parking lot adjacent to the UBC building and maneuvered upward by executing tight U-turns onto ascending ramps.

"Damn!" she said, coming to her designated parking space on the fourth floor near the elevators, only to find another car in her spot. She wasn't surprised someone had taken her little-used space. This perk had been conferred upon her as a retirement present by Arthur Kingsley, the founder and guiding light of UBC until his death a year ago.

Laura infrequently visited the network, where she'd been

anchorwoman of the newsmagazine show *American Chronicle,* and then only to use the secretarial services or lunch with friends and colleagues. To escape the confines of the farm.

Laura continued her upward spiral until she spotted an empty spot near the back of the eighth level, nearly two hundred feet from the elevators. After pulling into the space, Laura applied lipstick. When she readjusted the mirror, she saw a man standing near the rear of a car parked behind her. A thin man with a thin face. Where had he come from? Had he been following her?

She pushed the door lock button and waited nervously, occasionally sneaking glances at him. Although many commuters parked here and transferred to the subway at the nearby Rosslyn metro station, this guy was loitering. Why?

She shouldn't be afraid. Should she be afraid? Yes! To this guy lurking in the garage, she could be nothing more than a piece of meat.

Again Laura's thoughts wandered to Jeremiah and his draconian legal code, as set forth in *Second Jeremiah* and demonstrated several times by the terrorist. What would he have his police do to this malingerer? Beat him? Throw him into a detention camp? Brutalize him? Did Jeremiah— a rapist and murderer himself—get his support from frightened people such as herself? Was it nothing more than irrational fear that kept people from communicating with each other, turning them into clansmen, who hated everyone else they didn't know or who were in any way different from them?

Knuckles rapping on the window of the truck caused Laura's head to snap forward from its position against the headrest. It was him!

"You Laura Delaney?"

Laura felt around in her purse for the gun. "What do you want?" she asked, cracking the window.

"My name's Wheelie," he said, holding out a manila envelope for her to see. "Steve Wallace told me to give this to you. That you would know what it is."

Laura immediately forgot her fears, opened the door of

the Land Rover, and stepped out into the garage. "What else did he say?"

"To tell you he was staying in New America." Wheelie's eyes darted around the garage. A toothpick bounced nervously from one side of his mouth to the other. "I don't think his plans have the approval of the bigwigs, but who can tell him what to do."

"Is he safe? Was the mission successful?"

Wheelie shifted his weight from one foot to the other, obviously anxious to be off. "The false Prophet escaped. I wasn't at the point of action, but I drove one of the cars. Getting away wasn't easy once the alarm was out and the state police arrived."

"You didn't answer me," Laura insisted. "Is Steve safe?"

"He's okay. He's with a guy who can take care of him." Wheelie looked at his watch. "Look, that's all I know, lady. I only did this as a favor because Steve said you'd give me a thousand bucks." He held out his hand, a bored look on his face.

Although shocked, Laura took a checkbook from her purse and wrote out the check.

Wheelie frowned, examined the piece of paper, folded it, and pocketed it. "I guess you're good for it."

Laura viewed the miniaturized videotape alone in her office, often rewinding and playing certain sections. Steve had taped a brief summary at the end, although he didn't appear on camera. But she knew everything that had happened, and she knew her husband wasn't about to give up his mission because of this setback. His last words were, "Use this film and information any way you see fit, Laura. I love you."

How much we've both changed, she thought, sitting alone in the oppressive silence of her office. There was a time when Steve was suspicious of the news media and guarded in his conversation with reporters. He believed law-enforcement agencies such as the FBI should conduct their business out of the limelight. Jeremiah's terrorist campaign had convinced him otherwise, and Laura understood.

A consummate master at manipulating the news media, Jeremiah could only be neutralized by a more effective public relations counteroffensive. Otherwise, he'd continue to win public support.

She'd changed, too. Once, the CAT raid would only have been a "story" she'd have reported "objectively" without considering the consequences to any private person. The public's "right to know" superseded individual rights. Her attitude had been tempered, however, now that those rights belonged to her and Steve.

When Steve had told her about the CAT, Laura had implored him not to go. She'd tried logic, threats, and tears, until she realized he couldn't be dissuaded. He wouldn't be going, she was certain, if he didn't feel obligated to avenge her dishonor.

Laura edited the tape in her office, copying various segments to a full format tape, always careful to block out the faces of CAT members. When recording the interrogation of Davey Schropa, Laura carefully picked frames of that event that didn't show his interrogators or the intravenous line jabbed into his arm. The sanitized version clearly indicted the governor of South Dakota in a conspiracy to aid and abet a fugitive wanted on numerous violations of federal law.

Laura replayed the new tape from the beginning. One question remained. Why had Steve cut short his interview with Katrina Dorfler?

Laura dialed the intercom number for Mel Crawford, telling him she'd be up to see him shortly. It was the same office where she'd first met Steve in 1995. Mel hadn't moved to a more spacious suite, even when Kingsley appointed him president of the news division two years ago. It was a corporate reward for Mel's stellar performance as producer of *American Chronicle*. The show that had chronicled Jeremiah's rise and fall had brought in so much advertising revenue over a two-year period that UBC's stock had doubled in price and then split.

*   *   *

When Laura walked into Mel's office, he

came from behind his desk and embraced her. She held on a bit too long to the best male friend she had, and Laura saw the concerned look in his eyes when she drew back.

"You okay?" Mel asked, steering her to one of the chairs in front of the desk.

"Yeah. How 'bout you?"

"Couldn't be better." He sat on the edge of his desk, cocked his head, and looked appraising at Laura. "You look great. I really like your hair longer."

Laura fluffed her tresses à la Mae West. "It's almost as long as yours, Mel."

"When I was a producer, nobody gave a shit if I had long hair and wore jeans. Now that I'm allegedly a member of management, even my secretary tells me to get a haircut. I feel like a teenager."

His gunmetal gray hair ended in ringlets. "I like your hair longer, too, Mel."

"Married life and retirement seem to agree with you, Laura. You've got color in your cheeks. You're more beautiful than ever."

Usually unflappable, Laura blushed. She wore a simple mocha-colored tunic with ivory highlights and matching pants. The thigh-length tunic hid the fact she'd added nearly two inches to her waist.

"It's been too long, Laura. You should come around more often. I miss you. Hell, I wish you'd come back to work."

Laura chuckled, partly in remembrance of the many exciting times they'd had on the firing line, with Mel functioning as a ring master, coordinating all the diverse elements that went into the production of an hour-long newsmagazine show. At the last minute, he'd turn it over to "the talent," meaning Laura, whose job it was to convey all the information to the audience in a smooth, practiced manner.

"I have something you might be interested in," she answered, standing and walking to a VCR and inserting her tape.

When it had played through, Mel exhaled nosily, as if

he'd been holding his breath. "Jesus, Laura, this is dynamite! Where'd you get this tape? No, forget that. Are you giving it to me?"

"Yeah." Although not as spectacular as the recent television coverage of the Bike Week massacre in Sturgis, it was compelling evidence that Jeremiah was alive and directing events in New America. His "coming out" epistle had been met with much skepticism regarding its authenticity. Not so confessions by his best friend, cousin and lover.

"It'll be a real coup for us, Laura."

"Let's hope it finally compels the government to take action," she responded.

The Carpenter administration had been reluctant up to this point to take strong action against New America and was supported by public opinion polls. At least until Bike Week, two-thirds of Americans told pollsters they didn't feel "New America" constituted a clear and present danger to the United States. Even in the wake of Bike Week, people were ambivalent. While 75 percent deplored the violence against the bikers, nearly half thought a state had the "right" to regulate large demonstrations within its borders, especially those whose purpose could be considered "reckless and immoral."

"He's a master tactician," Mel said, begrudgingly. "Jeremiah commits acts that appeal to people's best and basest instincts at the same time."

Laura reluctantly agreed. "Like when he kicked off his campaign four years ago by assassinating a pedophile."

"Exactly. You know vigilantism is wrong and you have to say so, but inside you're glad that that monster is dead."

"Everyone needs to understand that freedom and democracy are at stake," Laura said.

"Who approved this raid, Laura? Who are these guys?"

Laura lied. "I'm not sure, Mel. We'll have to decide how to handle that."

Laura planned to warn Peter Thompson about the upcoming broadcast, so he could protect himself, his office, and his reputation. The attorney general was one of a handful of people who eventually would bring down Jeremiah, and therefore he had her unwavering support, regardless of his tactics. Maybe that made her and Peter and Steve just like Jeremiah. Maybe the end result did justify the means in some cases.

"There's another problem," Mel said. "I'd like to use the hour-long format of *American Chronicle*. But as you know, we're still trying to replace you after three years. Several who've tried out for the job haven't exactly made a hit with the viewing public. The mark you set is too high, Laura."

"I liked the good-looking guy who used to be a football quarterback," she teased.

Mel chuckled, indicating he didn't believe her for a minute. "That guy was nothing more than a trained dog. You know how you used to ignore the TelePrompTer material and wing it. He was struck dumb if someone else's words weren't flashing before his eyes."

"You gotta make a choice, Mel. Beauty and brains, or the beast."

"I might have stumbled across someone with potential," Mel announced, walking behind his desk. "I want you to meet her and help me decide." He picked up the phone and dialed his secretary.

Ten minutes later, Laura was introduced to
Julie Burton, formerly a reporter with the Midwest News Service, headquartered in Kansas City.

"I can't tell you how pleased I am to meet you, Ms. Delaney," Burton gushed as she burst into the room. "You're a legend in this business!"

As they stood face-to-face in front of Mel's desk, Laura felt she was looking in a mirror—fifteen years ago. Burton had a fuller, more youthful face, brown instead of blue eyes, and was maybe an inch shorter than Laura. Even so, the resemblance was uncanny. Burton projected a perky, yet sensuous image, although the navy jumpsuit the younger woman wore made her look almost like a teenager. She needed polishing.

"Julie came to our attention when she fed us an exclusive report that public stocks were being used for punishment in Anathoth, one of the new settlements in New America," Mel explained.

"South Dakota," Laura corrected.

"I was lucky," Burton confessed, breathlessly, conveying unlimited youthful energy. "We got a tip and I was already on assignment in Omaha, so the production guys said, 'Hey, let's truck on up there and see what we can see!'"

Laura bobbed her head as she sat down. "That's how it's done."

"Julie also was at the Bike Week massacre," Mel said.

Burton scooted a chair close to Laura. "The state police commander called to invite me."

"We're gonna give Julie a shot at anchoring *American Chronicle*," Mel announced from his perch on the edge of his desk. His and Laura's eyes locked momentarily. "Laura, I'd like you to be Julie's mentor. Give her some tips. A leg up."

"That would be great!" Burton exclaimed.

Surely the network wasn't so hard up for an anchor that they needed to bring in untested talent from Kansas City, she thought. Then Laura remembered that that's how she had been discovered, with not much more experience than Burton.

"You'd be a paid consultant." Mel laughed, adding, "as if the money matters."

Do it for me, for old times' sake, he seemed to be saying. She didn't necessarily feel any obligation to Mel or the network, but it would be something to do for a few weeks, while she made other decisions. It would keep her mind off her internal turmoil; *serve as an excuse to stay away from the farm.* She could mold her replacement's attitude about the terrorist.

"What do you think about him?" Laura asked Burton.

"You mean Jeremiah," Burton said, a smoky film descending over her eyes, giving her a seductive look Laura knew the camera would love. "He's news."

"There you go," Mel chimed in.

Laura remembered his oft-stated view that UBC simply reported news about the terrorist. It didn't mean those who put the show together agreed with Jeremiah's views. Conversely, they would be abrogating their professional responsibilities if they censored news about him, simply because they didn't like him. Ordinarily, Laura would have agreed with Mel, had she not then, and now, been so deeply involved personally.

"If you were standing on the *American Chronicle* set right now, giving an intro to a show about Jeremiah's reappearance, how would you describe him?" Laura persisted.

The perky smile faded a bit. "I'd say he started a terrorist campaign nearly four years ago, in which he attacked what he called symbols of American decadence: crime, the judicial system, immorality, Wall Street, Congress. What would you say about him, Laura?"

"That he's a terrorist, fascist, racist, and sexist." Rapist. "That he wants to establish a bogus theocracy in the middle of the country to use as a base to destroy the United States. That he's trying to justify all his activities with the preposterous claim that God speaks to him. He's a psychopath and cult leader, like Hitler and David Koresh."

Burton frowned. "David Koresh?"

"You remember Waco?" Mel prompted.

"Oh, yeah."

Laura stood, having made her decision. "I'd be glad to help out, if Julie is agreeable."

Burton stood also and said, "I've heard about the various attacks on you lately, Laura. I'm sorry."

"You mean the incident at my farm?" The story about the gun-toting intruder had made the national news.

"That and the break-in at your parents' ranch in Texas. Weren't you visiting them at the time?"

Laura stepped backward, stunned. "Where did you hear that?"

"Another reporter from Midwest News Service. He said he'd heard it from a local newspaper reporter in Texas, who was trying to put together the story."

It seemed to Laura that Burton's smile now had a cruel twist to it. "It was nothing. Vandals. Local high school kids, I think." She'd never been on this side of a reporter's inquiry. She'd always wondered what prompted people to lie. Now she knew.

"Thanks, Julie," Mel said, dismissing the young reporter. As the door closed, he turned to Laura. "What did you think?"

"I think you've got your work cut out for you, Mel. It'll be like teaching Broadcast News one-oh-one."

"I know, but her charisma rating before a test audience is through the ceiling."

"Well, careers in this business have been woven out of lesser material."

"You can make her better, Laura."

For the moment, Laura could only nod dumbly.

Over the next few days, Laura and Mel agreed upon a rough cut for the next *American Chronicle* show, which would begin with a shadowy figure running in a meadow, followed by the CAT assault on the mountain cabin, the terrorist's dead bodyguards, a glassy-eyed Governor Schropa telling everything he knew, and Katrina Dorfler refusing to tell what she knew—or at least not telling it on camera.

After a commercial break, film of the Bike Week massacre would be replayed, along with still photographs of a large, outdoor prison camp. The photos had come in an envelope mailed from the District of Columbia to Laura's UBC office. On the back of each a label read: NEW AMERICA CONCENTRATION CAMP. An enclosed note warned against a news helicopter flyover, saying the camps were protected by SAMs.

The night of the broadcast Laura stood nervously at the back of the production booth suspended above the studio floor, along with Mel, the show's producer, director, and other network executives gathered to watch this important show.

Looking down at the floor toward the anchor desk, where Julie Burton awaited her debut, Laura suspected her replacement's stomach was fluttering with butterflies.

"Some people think she looks a little like you," Mel said.

"Really?"

Mel smiled. "Personally, I think God broke the mold after he made you."

Laura squeezed her old friend's hand, noting he'd exchanged his usual uniform of jeans and denim shirt for a suit. And he'd gotten his hair cut.

The set had changed since Laura's time, although it still featured a series of panels showing picturesque scenery from ocean-to-ocean. Four panelists sitting to the right of the anchor desk represented various areas of expertise regarding each show's subject matter.

Mel planned for Burton to move out from behind her desk during certain segments and approach the audience to solicit individual opinion. Laura had never mingled regularly with the audience on the theory that a peripatetic host invited comparisons with various daytime talk shows specializing in outrageous topics, such as the difficulties concerning relationships between transvestite husbands and their mothers-in-law.

On the other side of the anchor desk sat the computer operator, who would relay to Burton comments by the "online" audience.

Resplendent in a powder blue suit, Burton opened the show by reporting a UBC exclusive: taped footage of a raid on a secluded cabin located in the Black Hills of South Dakota and "interviews" with two of Jeremiah's confidants.

Afterward, the panel members discussed Jeremiah's recent epistle, concluding that in the wake of all these developments it could be assumed the Prophet was alive and well, directing events in New America.

Following her script, Burton "threw" the show to a senior correspondent at the White House, who had at his side Col. Samuel Douglas, military aide to the president's national security advisor. The White House wasn't wheeling out any big guns for this interview, indicating to Laura that they were unprepared to comment or preferred to say nothing substantial. Colonel Douglas denied any government involvement in the failed effort to capture or kill Jeremiah.

"Then who authorized and conducted this raid?" UBC reporter Roy Webster asked belligerently. Laura smiled. While she had attempted to project warmth during her career in television, Webster carefully cultivated an "attack dog" approach.

"I couldn't speculate on that," Colonel Douglas replied evenly.

Webster was unrelenting. "There's speculation that the raid was conducted by the American Patriots. Can you comment on that, Colonel."

"No, Roy, all I can say now is that the disturbing news that Jeremiah is directing efforts in South Dakota through a puppet government will cause the administration to reassess domestic security implications and take appropriate action."

"Hasn't the government known for years that Jeremiah was planning another terrorist campaign designed to destabilize the government and the economy? Haven't some of your colleagues at the Pentagon so advised the president?"

"There's been speculation to that effect, Roy, but no concrete proof," Colonel Douglas replied. "The recent letter or epistle, if you will, could have been a fake. In fact, we still haven't seen him."

"You don't believe Governor Schropa or Jeremiah's girlfriend, Katrina Dorfler, when they say he's alive?"

Douglas shrugged good-naturedly, indicating to Laura that the White House had been caught unawares and offered up a sacrificial lamb to the media "wolves."

"What about speculation that New America has developed a military capability?" Webster persisted. "Does the administration have any evidence of foreign military advisors in New America?"

"No," the colonel replied, cryptically.

"Jeremiah once gained possession of a nuclear weapon, which he threatened to detonate near the nation's capital," Webster said. "And he used a biological agent to kill inmates in a federal prison. Is there any evidence he now possesses such weapons of mass destruction?"

"Not that we know of," Douglas replied.

Webster sneeringly bounced the interview sequence to his UBC colleague at the Justice Department, Curtis Griswold, who read a statement issued by Atty. Gen. Peter Thompson, saying the department still had outstanding arrest warrants for Jeremiah; that the FBI had never closed the case and would continue its effort to capture the terrorist and bring him to justice.

Based on the photographic evidence broadcast by UBC, the Justice Department said it would open a new investigation into the existence of concentration camps in New America, as well as numerous complaints of civil rights violations occurring during the Bike Week debacle.

Thompson's statement explicitly denied that FBI agents had participated in the recent raid. Forewarned by Laura, Thompson didn't make available any spokesman who could be grilled about the attorney general's relationship with the American Patriots or the assassination team.

When the show resumed, Burton questioned the various "talking heads," beginning with Alexander Bennett, a former FBI assistant director and regular UBC consultant, who reviewed the various criminal charges against Jeremiah and speculated about the Justice Department's next move.

A retired general pooh-poohed the idea of New America's military capability, although Laura thought he was less convincing in his denial that Jeremiah might possess weapons of mass destruction.

"Have you ever heard of a former Lt. Gen. Benjamin Arnot?" Burton asked.

"It doesn't make any difference if Arnot is in New America," the general snapped, "because there's no way the South Dakota National Guard can challenge the military might of the United States."

A woman civil libertarian cautioned the audience about indicting everyone in New America because of Jeremiah's actions. Laura silently mouthed Governor Schropa's oft-repeated remark that "New America is just a place where people live." She wondered about Schropa's fate, now that he'd led the dogs to the predator's den.

A widely-recognized expert on international terrorism said Jeremiah could have doomsday weapons at his disposal; that such weapons now were no more complicated than the use of dynamite, which Jeremiah had used devastatingly at the New York Stock Exchange and again at a trade association conference in Florida.

As the hour neared an end, Julie Burton walked among the audience, asking their opinions, which ranged from one extreme to the other.

"The army should invade South Dakota and arrest that whole lot of traitors," an elderly, white-haired gentleman suggested.

A soft-spoken women demurred. "Let's not tar them all with the same brush. Some of the leaders may be breaking the law, but many people in New America are just exercising their constitutional and God-given rights."

A UBC scientific poll of five hundred individuals conducted halfway through the show indicated nearly two-thirds of the respondents thought the federal government should take aggressive action to arrest Jeremiah.

Burton was about to break for the show's final commercial when Ken, the UBC computer expert, interrupted. "This is weird, but someone, somehow, has taken over the UBC web site. There's an image coming up on my screen."

Burton rushed to Ken's side. "Can we go live with this?"

"I think so," Ken said, looking up at the production booth.

Laura and Mel stared at the monitors in the booth as the technicians frantically tried to adjust their equipment. As the computer pixels took shape, Jeremiah's image appeared.

"I'll be damned!" Mel said.

"Good evening, America," Jeremiah said. At first, his computerized voice sounded spooky, causing a chill to pass over Laura.

"He's broken in with some kind of video-conferencing software," Mel said. "Put him on the air."

Laura understood. Jeremiah was being filmed from a remote site and his image and voice scrambled through a computer mainframe. They couldn't trace the call and locate him even if they'd been prepared, which they weren't.

"UBC continues to top the ratings with provocative shows," the terrorist said, "but these allegations about New America are false or concocted. We are a society of righteous individuals attempting to live a life prescribed by God, who has chosen to speak through me. Who among you can deny this possibility?

"As for the charges that I conducted a terrorist campaign in the United States, or ever possessed a nuclear weapon, those are simplistic, misleading charges, the evil inventions of the federal government, which simply wants to silence my voice for fear that people everywhere will be attracted to our cause."

"So, you're charging a government conspiracy," Julie Burton said.

"Julie, you're trying very hard and in time you will do well," Jeremiah replied. "However, I see Laura Delaney's hand in all this. I can't understand why she hates me so much and published that pack of lies about me and my devoted followers. In fact, as usual, Laura's not telling all. Laura, have you decided what color to paint those nursery walls yet? Blue or pink? A father has a right to know."

Everyone in the production booth turned to look at Laura, who backed away, paralyzed with shock. She grabbed her purse and ran from the booth, down the stairs, and burst out a side door, setting off a fire alarm.

Laura sped through the streets of Rosslyn, nearly blinded by her tears. She careened onto the highway and headed toward the mountains and home. The farm she'd come to hate now seemed a sanctuary; somewhere she could hide, protected by a fence and armed guards.

The show had been a disaster. He'd turned the tables on her once again. As her pregnancy became obvious, there would be rumors that *he* was the father of her child, which, of course, was entirely possible. If she remained silent, some would interpret that as an admission of an affair with him. If she publicly charged rape, she'd inject herself into a media circus she couldn't control. And she could never actually prove her charge.

Jeremiah would eventually reveal Steve's role in the failed CAT raid and make him out to be nothing more than a jealous husband. The terrorist would surely plant stories in the media about the close relationship between Steve and Peter Thompson, possibly even causing a political crisis for

Peter, especially if it could be implied that Peter knew of, or had initiated, the CAT raid.

A sudden summer rain began and Laura turned on the windshield wipers, comforted by the rhythmic sound. She listened closely and heard the words: a-bor-shun, a-bor-shun, a-bor-shun. She smiled and regained some confidence. She still could control her destiny.

12

Since the failed CAT raid, Steve had stayed with Hoffman and Duncan. The apartment of a military officer and a state police sergeant seemed a safe place to hide. In fact, single members of the military and police apparently were often assigned to live together so they could spy on each other. Given the steady stream of visitors to the apartment and the nature of their business, Steve had become aware of the extent to which Duncan and Hoffman had turned this state policy upside down.

On Saturday evening in the middle of the long Labor Day weekend, both Hoffman and Duncan received telephone calls ordering them to report to their respective duty stations. This unusual command at an unusual time prompted them to telephone colleagues and pump them for information. After several conversations, both men concluded that something big was about to happen.

"What do you think it is?" Steve asked.

"A lieutenant I know who's also from Germany said it looks like our entire regiment will be moving out," Hoffman said.

"My barracks is to move directly south and stop all westbound traffic on Interstate 90," Duncan added.

"Maybe it's an internal crackdown." Steve said.

"Or maybe D day has arrived," Hoffman replied, grimly.

"What'll I do?" Steve asked.

"You can hide out here or come with me," Hoffman said.

"That's dangerous," Duncan said. "There're wanted posters of Steve everywhere."

"Hiding out isn't my style," Steve said. "And it doesn't get me close to Jeremiah."

"In uniform, wearing grease paint, it's unlikely he'd be recognized," Hoffman said. "In fact, I can make him my driver. I rate a jeep."

Duncan shrugged, pulling on his uniform. "He's one more guy to throw a monkey wrench into the machinery."

Before they left, Duncan turned on his laptop and quickly created a file containing information about the developing situation and their analysis. He then transferred the file to a disk and popped that into a pocket of his uniform.

"Let's go," Hoffman said, already changed into a battlefield uniform. He'd exchanged his glasses for contact lenses.

They piled into Hoffman's BMW and drove through downtown Pierre, stopping in front of a Best Western hotel near the bridge leading west across the Missouri River. Duncan got out.

"Where's he going?" Steve asked.

"He'll use a data port in one of the hotel conference rooms, transmit the information to a phone number in Washington, and then destroy the disk."

"Won't someone be suspicious?"

"No one in New America would interfere with a state police sergeant on official duty. The guys at the other end of the phone line will make certain the call can't be traced back to the hotel."

They dropped Duncan at the new state police barracks across the river in Fort Pierre, and then sped west on state highway 14.

"We're headed to the military post where I first met Jeremiah," Hoffman told Steve. "He was observing an exercise in which the troops attacked a facility with three large buildings, perhaps on the edge of a river or lake. I wish I knew the real target."

*   *   *

Hoffman parked the BMW behind the motor

pool and told Steve, "Wait here. I'll be back as soon as possible."

Steve locked the doors and scrunched down in the seat to avoid being seen. Powerful lights lit up the army post like a football stadium. Steve heard men shouting above the roar of motors; lots of diesel engines were being started, as well as helicopters.

After what seemed an eternity, Hoffman returned, knocked on the car door, and shoved a duffel bag into the backseat. "Here's a uniform, boots, helmet, and some grease paint. Hurry up! I volunteered us to be in the lead unit."

Steve stripped down and struggled into the uniform. He flipped on a light beside a mirror on the back of a sun visor and smeared black paint on his face. Steve jumped out of the car, slapped the helmet on his head, and took out after Hoffman, who already was on a dead run.

They ran around to the other side of the motor pool, where chaos reigned. Steve watched Hoffman size up the situation and then move with a purpose toward an armored vehicle. He climbed on top and motioned for Steve to follow.

There were two openings: one high and in back, the other lower and toward the front. Hoffman directed Steve into the front slot, so that only his shoulders and head stuck out. Steve squatted down into the cavity and found himself looking at gauges and a steering wheel. He obviously was the driver!

"This is a Commando Scout," Hoffman yelled above the din. "Reconnaissance vehicle." Steve looked over his shoulder at what appeared to be a 7.62-mm machine gun mounted near the back opening. Hoffman lowered himself into the hole and came up with a headset, which he held up for Steve to see. Steve looked around below until he found similar communications gear.

With Hoffman's instructions in his ear, Steve mastered the seven-ton vehicle in about ten minutes, while they continued to move forward. Steve listened in on Hoffman's conversation with his battalion commander, Lt. Col. Roger

Miles. Miles ordered Hoffman to the head of the column, and Steve felt exhilarated as he complied with the command, gunning the armored car out front, where at least they wouldn't be breathing dust.

As they dipped and bumped across the undulating prairie, Steve kept a sharp lookout for rocks and other objects that could immobilize them or even flip them over. Wherever they were going, he wanted to get there first, and alive.

The armored column consisted of other reconnaissance vehicles, self-propelled artillery and antiaircraft guns, towed artillery, and several dozen armored personnel carriers (APCs) filled with infantry troops.

Hoffman switched the communications equipment to the intercom mode, so they could talk privately. "Miles says we're headed toward Rapid City. We should be there in less than an hour."

"What's there?"

"Ellsworth Air Force Base."

"Oh, my God! You've got to be kiddin'."

"There's nothing funny about this nightmare, my friend."

Eventually, Colonel Miles ordered the artillery battalion to halt on a high plateau north of the air base. Both the base and Rapid City in the background were well lit in the early morning hour.

"Where's the rest of the regiment?" Steve asked.

"Good question. But the artillery is here."

"What do you know about Ellsworth?"

"Home of the U.S. Air Force Twenty-eighth Bomb Wing, including two squadrons of B-1B Lancers."

"The stealth bomber?"

"The most deadly death delivery machine in the world," Hoffman answered. "It's virtually undetectable by radar. It can fly seventy-five hundred miles without refueling, and carries both cruise missiles and nuclear bombs."

"You don't think we're here to capture them!"

Hoffman didn't have time to answer, as he responded to a rapid-fire series of orders from Colonel Miles directing the battalion into action. Mortar and artillery fire rained down on the eight concrete bunkers placed strategically around the base.

Looking through night-vision binoculars, Steve saw that "his comrades" also had targeted a mine field extending a hundred yards in front of the perimeter. He felt helpless. What could he and Hoffman do?

The massed artillery barrage quickly took out the bunkers north of the base, and cleared a path through the mine fields, allowing the APCs to dart inside the wire and unload infantry squads. Steve's spirits rose as he watched U.S. airmen put up a stiff resistance. Perhaps the attack would be repulsed.

A thundering noise came from behind their position. Steve turned and watched in horror as military helicopters popped up from the cover of the many domed hills and buttes surrounding the base. The second-hand Russian "Hinds" hovered over the base, using their formidable armament to chop up the defenders. Transport helicopters followed and dropped more troops inside the five-hundred-acre base.

Steve saw Hoffman jump to the ground and confer with Colonel Miles and a lieutenant, who held a map with both hands.

Steve focused his binoculars on the unfolding battle. New American troops concentrated their attack on the hangars and runways on the west side of the base, where a half-dozen sleek black bombers sat silently. Through the glasses he watched a heavy firefight break out near one of the hangers. U.S. airmen in an APC equipped with a 30-mm automatic cannon briefly mowed down the attacking troops until their vehicle was destroyed by a New American soldier firing a handheld antitank rocket. Steve grimaced and lowered the glasses.

Suddenly, a red fireball lifted one of the B-1s off the ground. Steve initially thought it was an errant hit by one of their artillery guns. Then he saw U.S. airmen running on the tarmac, throwing satchel charges under other bombers—blowing up their own aircraft to prevent them from falling into enemy hands!

Hoffman crawled on top of the armored car and said, "This is about over."

"You sure? Maybe they can turn it around."

The German shook his head. "Miles says there're only about thirty-five hundred airmen here, and most of them are support personnel. There're less than four hundred armed men guarding the base. They only have one small armory. We've got four infantry companies inside the fence now, besides all this firepower. Believe me, it's nearly over."

"They blew up some of the bombers," Steve noted, hopefully.

Hoffman pointed upward and Steve saw several of the B-1s taking off, blending into the night sky.

"New American pilots," Hoffman said. "Guys who know how to fly those planes."

"Who are they?"

"Russians, Chinese, Iraqis. Who knows. We can be thankful for several things. According to Miles, none of the B-1s are loaded with nuclear bombs. And there aren't any intercontinental ballistic missiles here any more."

"What happened to them?"

"Dismantled by treaty requirements and moved."

Suddenly, the distinctive sound of jet aircraft caused them to look up. Even in the night sky, Steve recognized the fighter planes: mostly F-15s and F-16s. "The air force to the rescue!" he said.

"Don't be sure," Hoffman cautioned. "Miles is a great source of information. At the same time we attacked here, other New American units overran Air National Guard bases throughout the Midwest: Sioux Falls and Fargo in the Dakotas, Sioux City and Des Moines, Iowa, Great Falls, Montana. New America now has its own air force. However, you can be certain the U.S. Air Force will arrive shortly in force, which is why we need to get the hell out of here."

"What are your orders?"

"I'm supposed to lead two companies into Rapid City, where sympathizers will help us hide and camouflage our equipment. Then we're to fade into the civilian population. In fact, many of the attacking troops apparently came from inside the city. You remember what the CAT briefing officer said? Rapid City is a Trojan horse."

"What're we gonna do?"

"We're not hiding out."

Hoffman ordered Steve to drive the armored car onto the base and head for the runways. Bullets bounced off the car as pockets of defenders targeted them. They abandoned the Scout at the edge of the taxiway and ran toward a Lockheed 130 that was revving up its engines. Before the stairs could be pulled up, Hoffman bluffed his way on board, followed by Steve.

The transport plane immediately lifted into the air, but stayed close to the ground. Steve looked out a window at an aerial dogfight in progress above them. Something zipped across the sky, creating a narrow trail of smoke. One of the F-16s had exploded in a ball of fire. As the pilots fired missiles at each other, Steve could only guess who the good guys were.

The airplane transported artillery, other equipment, and a platoon of infantrymen, whose first lieutenant eyed Steve and Hoffman suspiciously.

"Don't mean to crash your party, Lieutenant," Hoffman shouted over the engine noise. He lapsed expertly into an Alabama accent, causing Steve to suppress a smile. "Our Commando Scout blew a piston, and I figured if we didn't get the hell off the base quickly, I was gonna wind up the loose asshole in a Yankee jail. You know what I mean?"

Steve watched a smile crease the young lieutenant's face, which was a signal for his men to also begin chuckling.

"So where the hell we going, Lieutenant?"

"Fort Riley."

"Kansas?"

"Yeah."

"Well, don't that beat all."

As Hoffman went to sit beside the lieutenant, Steve decided on a quick catnap, since he'd been up now going on twenty hours. But his mind whirled with thoughts of their destination—Fort Riley, home of the fabled Big Red One, the First Infantry Division.

* * *

An hour and a half later, they landed at Marshall Field on the south edge of Fort Riley. They disembarked and immediately raced for cover, since it was obvious the airfield had been the scene of a battle. Parachutes and bodies littered the ground. The charred remains of several helicopters sat on a runway to the south.

They made it to a hangar where mechanics wearing the uniforms of the New American Army worked feverishly on several Apache gunships and Blackhawk transport helicopters.

Hoffman approached a captain who was smoking a cigarette and barking orders. "Captain, we just came in on that 130 out there, from Ellsworth."

"How'd it go up there?" the captain asked.

"Good. They got a lot of bombers off the ground. Hell of an air battle going on when we flew out."

"I'll bet." The captain scrutinized Hoffman's uniform patches. "Artillery, huh?"

"Yeah. I need to get with my own kind."

"That'd be over at Camp Funston. That's the post railhead."

"Can you get some transport for me and my driver?"

"Sure," the captain said, whistling shrilly while motioning to someone on the other side of the hangar.

"What're you gonna do with these helicopters?" Hoffman asked.

The captain shrugged. "I'm waiting for orders. You know how that is."

A short ride across the airfield and a bridge over the Kansas River brought them to Camp Funston. The dawn's rosy glow in the east illuminated the terrain, allowing Steve to see that this river valley surrounded by high hills was nearly identical to the one in which the New America Army trained.

Their jeep driver cut across a field and raced down Twelfth Street, dropping them at the west end of Camp Funston, where furious activity surrounded three rail spurs.

Again, Hoffman wielded his captain bars with authority,

questioning several soldiers until he ran across an angry, exhausted major. After Hoffman explained once again how they'd gotten here, the major shook his head in disgust. "I don't know why the fuck you came here, Captain, since we're busting our hump to get outta here. You see all this equipment? We seized it from the training area, and I got orders to get it moving by rail before dawn." He shook his head. "Fat chance."

"Where to, sir?" Hoffman asked. "Where's it all going?"

"Kansas City. Don't ask me why, Captain. I don't know. I'm just a motherfuckin' logistics officer."

Steve and Hoffman walked north along the spur lines, watching as switch engines positioned a string of flatcars near loading docks. Steel ramps bridged the gap between the docks and the flatcars, allowing various tracked vehicles to inch their way onto the train.

Hoffman catalogued the various weapons for Steve: "M-1 Abrams tanks, Bradley fighting vehicles, multiple-launch rocket systems, big-caliber artillery pieces, hun'red-and-fifty-five to two-oh-three millimeter. They can fire conventional, nuclear, chemical, or biological shells. Up to six rounds a minute for as far out as twenty miles. Jesus, they made a helluva haul here tonight."

Steve was amazed. "How'd they do it? *This is a U.S. Army post.*"

"Superior numbers, superior firepower, superior planning, the element of surprise. It wins every time. Remember, Steve, it's peacetime, in the middle of the nation, in the middle of the last big holiday of the summer. They hit this place with a whole division, outnumbering the defenders three-to-one."

"What are we going to do now?"

Hoffman turned to face Steve. "Looks like we jumped from the frying pan into the fire. You ever been to Kansas City?"

Jeremiah thought it prudent not to be in New America as his army attacked military installations in the Midwest. If those efforts failed, the United States undoubtedly would occupy New America and launch an all-out search for him. So Jeremiah went to Virginia, where the final, critical phase of his plan would be implemented. If successful, it would prevent retaliation by the U.S. military, which otherwise could easily retake Ellsworth and Fort Riley, and leisurely recapture its lost equipment while destroying his army.

About midnight, he rode in a powerboat across Lake Anna toward the nuclear power–generating plant located on the opposite shore. The seventeen-mile-long, man-made lake provided cooling water for the nuclear reactors. Unlike his soldiers, Jeremiah came from the northeast shore because he calculated it to be a better avenue of escape, being only twenty miles from Interstate 95, running the length of the East Coast.

The nuclear power station was well lit even in the middle of the night, and Jeremiah noted that General Arnot and his staff had done a good job of reproducing the various buildings at a military training area in New America. Even so, the two fourteen-story dome-shaped nuclear reactors and the adjacent 600 feet long turbine-generator building dwarfed the models.

Jeremiah knew the attacking battalion had approached the Lake Anna plant using the same technique employed by the division of New America troops that had infiltrated and attacked Fort Riley. They'd arrived in small groups over a period of several days, staying in hotels and the homes of sympathizers, until the hour of the attack. Here at Lake Anna, the seven hundred troops had moved into position in large, modified Ryder and U-Haul trucks. The officer corps had arrived days ago in motor homes, which also served as mobile headquarters.

He'd chosen this power plant carefully. It was less than seventy-five miles southwest of the nation's capital. Northeasterly winds were the general rule in this part of the country; therefore, the resulting fallout of a "nuclear incident" at Lake Anna could reach all the way to Boston—encompassing an area containing about a fifth of the nation's entire population, and many of the symbols of the federal union: the Capitol and White House, Independence

Square in Philadelphia, the Revolutionary War icons located in Boston. And New York, the nation's financial and communications center.

Those not killed by a nuclear explosion would become ill, and radiation contamination would render a sizable area uninhabitable for centuries.

"Stay here," Jeremiah told the boat driver, as he stepped ashore with his three bodyguards. "We may need to make a quick getaway."

A major waited for him.

"Any trouble?" Jeremiah asked.

"None," the major replied. "As planned, we approached up the fire road and the rail spur, and used shaped explosives to blow in the doors of the three buildings."

"Any resistance?"

"We had to kill a few security guards, but there was only a skeleton crew on duty after midnight. Less than twenty."

A hissing, crackling sound caused Jeremiah to turn to his right. Several of the transmission towers that carried electricity away from the reactors had been dynamited. Broken, blazing electrical lines whipped about in the air like giant Fourth-of-July sparklers.

"Several hundred thousand customers of the Virginia Power Company are now without electricity," the major noted.

Jeremiah nodded with satisfaction. Part of the message had been sent. He looked up the road at New American soldiers milling about the information center—a sleek, long, gray building emblazoned with the red-and-white logo of the Virginia Power Company.

"We've got three companies setting up a perimeter, digging in, and establishing machine-gun and mortar positions," the major explained. "When the state and local police show up, we'll be ready for them."

"What about antiaircraft missiles?" Jeremiah asked.

"That, too."

Inside one of the reactor buildings, the major escorted him down a series of hallways. Jeremiah knew how they'd taken over the power station so easily and quickly. Not only did they have overwhelming numbers and firepower, New

American hackers had stolen diagrams of the plant from the computer files of the Nuclear Regulatory Commission.

Jeremiah arrived at control central and swept into the room imperially. As usual, he wore black. "Colonel Morten," he said, acknowledging his battalion commander. "How's it going?"

"As planned, sir. Our computer people are doing their job now."

Jeremiah looked about the room, a semicircular mezzanine overlooking the reactor floor below. The outside wall contained computer terminals, gauges, and machinery that controlled the reactor, which was successively encased in a steel reactor vessel, a steel containment liner, and the exterior, dome-shaped concrete containment building. Inside the reactors, uranium-enriched fuel rods were manipulated to generate a controlled nuclear fission process. The boiling water produced steam to drive the Westinghouse turbines, which produced electricity for nearly four million customers in Virginia.

"It really wasn't necessary for you to be here, sir," Colonel Morten said, taking off his helmet. "It's dangerous."

"I know," Jeremiah replied, taking the colonel's arm, and moving him away from the others. "Colonel, I had to make certain you and your men are willing to make this sacrifice, if necessary. In a few hours, I'm going to address the American people, and begin negotiations with the president of the United States regarding the independence of New America. My balls are going to be out there on the chopping block, if you know what I mean."

A twisted smile took over Morten's face. "Jeremiah, you don't know me. Oh, I'm sure there's a dossier somewhere, but I'm talking about feelings you can't put on paper." The colonel tapped his chest. "I hate what this country has become. Hate it all. Hate the greed, the crime, cynicism, immorality, political corruption, injustice. Someone's gotta change it. I figure that's you."

"I'm only the Lord's instrument."

The colonel chuckled softly. His cheeks were concave, and the circles under his eyes as dark as death.

"The U.S. Army asked me to put my life on the line

several times, Jeremiah. And I did, without question. Then I'd come home on leave, look around, and ask myself why. I don't have any of those doubts today."

Exactly what Jeremiah wanted to hear. Even God hadn't revealed the outcome of the air battle taking place in the upper Midwest. If U.S. forces were lucky enough to destroy his new B-1 bomber fleet, Lake Anna would serve as his new lever.

"You're a good man, Morten, and I'll need you in the future. If things get dicey here and you have to do what you have to do, I think you can figure out a way to get out ahead of the firestorm. You've got my blessing, okay?"

"Yes, sir."

"Now, where's the plant manager?"

Morten motioned to a group of men standing across the room, and a sergeant shoved a man toward them.

"You the plant manager?" Jeremiah asked, bending to read his name plate. "Mr. Kincaid."

"Yes, I am," the frightened, bespectacled man responded.

"You know who I am?"

"I can guess."

"Let me tell you what my men are in the process of doing," Jeremiah said, clasping his hands behind his back. "Demolition experts are on top of this building right now, planting charges to blow a big hole in the concrete containment building. Am I right, Colonel?"

"Yes, sir."

"Over here are some of our best computer wizards and nuclear scientists," Jeremiah said, pointing to a half-dozen men sitting at the control panel. "They're reprogramming your computers."

Kincaid managed a tight smile. "You can't do that! There are too many safeguards."

Jeremiah laughed. "Oh, yes, we can and will. Believe me, my people are the best. Let's walk over and take a look."

Jeremiah moved confidently across the room and tapped the shoulder of a man sitting in front of a computer screen. "How's it going, soldier?"

"We're there already, sir," the soldier said. "If I change

this line of code, I can reduce the boron content of the reactor coolant."

"Take a look, Mr. Kincaid," Jeremiah said.

The plant manager leaned in and studied the computer screen. When he drew back, his face was ashen and his hands shook.

Jeremiah faked a look of uncertainty. "Let me see if I understand this, Mr. Kincaid. We reduce the boron content, fiddle with the placement and number of reactor rods, and what we get is a nuclear . . . BOOM!"

The plant manager staggered backward. "My God, you can't do that!"

"Can and will, Mr. Kincaid. Do you know Sheila Rodenberry?"

"Head of the Nuclear Regulatory Commission? Not personally."

"Well, you should meet her, and tell her what's happening here." Jeremiah put his face close to Kincaid's, to whisper a confidence. "I know where she lives."

13

Alerted by his staff, Pres. Robert Alan Carpenter turned on the television at 9:00 A.M. Eastern time, Sunday morning, when most Americans were just waking up or preparing to go to church. UBC and the other major television networks had interrupted their regularly scheduled programs to broadcast a television address by Jeremiah, Terrorist Prophet. Aides told Carpenter the networks had received an advisory an hour earlier, giving them the coordinates for a private consortium satellite, which would make the broadcast available.

The president had been up since the middle of the night, receiving reports from the Pentagon about the series of attacks launched against U.S. military facilities in the Midwest. Occasionally, he had compared this information to that being broadcast by the networks.

Jeremiah sat on a straight-back chair placed in front of a blue backdrop. Nothing in the picture gave away his location. By design, Carpenter assumed, the terrorist had dressed conservatively, wearing a navy, pin-striped suit, a light blue shirt, and a red-white-and-blue patterned tie. His curly, sandy-colored hair was flecked with more gray than four years go, when he'd gone on national television to broadcast similar demands. Although Jeremiah smiled pleasantly, Carpenter thought the terrorist's faded blue eyes lacked expression, as if he'd looked too long into the sun.

The president watched in fascination and disbelief as the performance began.

"Citizens of the United States, I have the unfortunate duty to report to you today that the armed forces of New America undertook several defensive actions last night and early this morning in response to serious provocations by your government," Jeremiah said, sounding somber and aggrieved.

"Recently, in violation of long-standing Geneva accords and international standards of conduct, a U.S.-sponsored terrorist squad attempted to kill me at my home in the Black Hills. This assassination team included Steve Wallace, a former FBI agent with close ties to Atty Gen. Peter Thompson, who reports to the president of the United States."

Carpenter frowned. Military intelligence had arrived at the same conclusion about Thompson. He couldn't allow his attorney general to freelance within the government as if he were head of state.

"The people of New America have demanded a forceful response," Jeremiah continued, "so our armed forces briefly occupied several military bases and posts in the Midwest, to prevent the government of the United States from using these facilities and weapons to attack our people."

Carpenter detected a harder edge to the terrorist's voice, as Jeremiah said, "We now have in our possession fighters and bombers equipped with nuclear weapons that are capable of striking anywhere in the United States—with impunity.

"Don't fear for a moment that this force will be used against you, our neighbors. We can and must learn to live in peace, side-by-side. We know that's what you want. New Americans desire only the opportunity to peacefully construct our society and live our lives as ordained by God in *The Book of Second Jeremiah*."

The mention of the hated blueprint disgusted Carpenter.

"So that people in both nations can achieve their goals, we need to establish several principles," Jeremiah said.

"First, the United States must refrain from attempting to retake the military facilities we've occupied. .

"Second, New America's expanded borders must be rec-

ognized and respected. New America includes that territory
within a line extending roughly from San Francisco to Saint
Louis and Pittsburgh, and then north to the Canadian border. All U.S. military facilities and equipment within our
borders must be abandoned in place.

"Third, a treaty must be negotiated detailing this agreement and establishing a demilitarized zone between the two
Americas."

"For those of you already living within the new borders
of New America, you are automatically accorded citizen-
ship in our great, vibrant nation. For those of you who want
to join us and observe the Social Contract of *Second Jeremiah*, please come as soon as possible."

Jeremiah concluded by smiling warmly into the camera.
"Thanks for tuning in, and be assured that New Americans
want nothing but peace and goodwill between our two
nations throughout the new millennium."

An hour later, Carpenter walked into the ornate
cabinet room located in the west wing of the White House.
Members of his cabinet, VP Richard Trainor, congressional
leaders, and the Joint Chiefs of Staff sat around the oval-
shaped conference table. Lesser staff aides sat in chairs arranged around the perimeter of the room, except in front
of the French doors leading to the Rose Garden.

Carpenter took off a navy blazer and draped it over the
back of his chair. Should he have worn a dark suit, instead
of khaki slacks and a yellow golfing shirt? A patriotic tie,
like Jeremiah?

The president couldn't escape his image and physical
appearance. God knew, he had enough people advising him
about them. His hair had gone gray, but it was a dull gray,
which now was tinted silver, although he had to deny that
vanity.

His wife, Milly, and other staffers had him on a diet that
didn't include burgers, fries, and ice cream, which he considered staples. At six foot two, his chart weight should
have been two-oh-five, thereabouts, but they tried to just
keep him under two thirty. More pragmatic advisors urged

him to use his bulk in an intimidating fashion when necessary.

It didn't always work. Carpenter liked to dress down, laugh—even giggle, sometimes—hug people, and gossip with them. It's why he enjoyed campaigning more than governing. Nothing beat a company picnic with tables heaped high with fried chicken and potato salad.

But, today, Carpenter felt and looked grim.

"I assume you all saw Jeremiah's broadcast this morning," he said. "I consider it significant he made no mention of his forces occupying the Lake Anna nuclear power plant. He's more sophisticated now than four years ago when he openly threatened on national television to explode an atomic bomb unless we recognized New America."

Carpenter had rejected the entreaties of several advisors that he and the first family leave Washington, D.C., either to seek refuge at Camp David in the nearby Maryland mountains or a military command center located deep inside the mountains west of Denver. The American people would interpret such acts as a sign of panic or, worse, cowardice. Instead, he'd ordered all U.S. military forces, domestic and worldwide, placed on a state of high alert.

The president's eyes came to rest on Sheila Rodenberry, chairman of the Nuclear Regulatory Commission, a short, homely woman whose physical shortcomings belied an inner hardness and extraordinary intelligence. "Sheila, tell us about your visitor early this morning."

"Dennis Kincaid, manager of the Lake Anna plant, knocked on the front door of my house at about 3:00 A.M. Said he'd been dropped off by Jeremiah and had a message from him."

Expressions of shock escaped from many around the table, who undoubtedly wondered if Jeremiah knew where they lived.

"Kincaid told me that over five hundred well-armed troops had occupied the power plant grounds and buildings," Rodenberry continued. "That they'd blown a hole in the concrete container building and were prepared to initiate a runaway nuclear reaction. Kincaid convinced me the raiders indeed have such capabilities."

"Since they haven't done it, I assume this is Jeremiah's big stick to force our acceptance of his demands," said Atty. Gen. Peter Thompson.

"That would be a reasonable assumption, Peter," the president said. Turning back to Rodenberry, he asked, "Sheila, how could this happen?"

She shrugged. "It just happened, sir. We weren't prepared for an assault of this nature. They knew what they were doing and they did it. Efficiently, remorselessly."

"What would the damage be if they carried out this threat?" Carpenter asked, looking ruefully at his reflection in a mirror on the far wall. When he'd become president seven years ago, his hair had been mostly brown, and there'd been far fewer wrinkles in his face.

"A meltdown of the nuclear core would cause a fireball explosion, sending radioactive material high into the air. The contamination around the plant for a radius of a hundred miles would be immediate and long-term. Decades."

"Including Washington?"

"Yes."

"Beyond that?"

"The whole North American continent could be contaminated to some degree or another," the NRC chairman said. "After the Chernobyl explosion in 1986, radiation levels increased even in this country. Mortality rates would depend on wind patterns, exposure levels, and duration of exposure."

"What's your best estimate of casualties?"

Rodenberry squinted and shook her head. "Everyone within ten miles of the plant would die within a few days. Luckily, it's primarily a rural area. Scientific studies of the aftereffects at Nagasaki, Hiroshima, and Chernobyl would indicate thirty-to-forty thousand long-term deaths within, say, a fifty-mile radius of the plant, mostly from radiation-caused cancers. Farther out, mortality is hard to predict."

"Goddammit it, Mr. President, let's retake that power plant," growled four-star Army Gen. Milton Haase, chairman of the Joint Chiefs of Staff. The burly soldier turned toward Rodenberry. "Isn't there some way we can be immediately prepared to cap that containment building, Sheila? To minimize the damage."

Rodenberry looked from the general to the president, shaking her head. "I doubt that's possible."

General Haase looked boldly at Carpenter. "I'll say it if no one else will, Mr. President. The casualties Sheila projected are acceptable."

"To whom!" Carpenter said. "The six million people living here in the nation's capital who'd be exposed to high levels of radiation? Where do you suggest we move the capital of the United States to, General Haase?"

"Jeremiah's bluff is already working," said Thompson.

His attorney general wore a business suit and starched shirt, Carpenter noted, distastefully, as if this were any other day at the office.

Haase glared at the president. "You can't let this madman blackmail the greatest nation on earth!"

"Then our internal security should have been much better," Vice President Trainor suggested, almost casually. "How in the hell could Jeremiah overrun all these military installations in the Midwest, including a major air base and army post?"

"You can have my resignation, Mr. President!" General Haase said through clenched teeth.

The president looked at the general. "I'll consider that offer later, General Haase, as well as the possible resignations of many others in this room." Carpenter stared daggers at the uniformed personnel around the table. "Right now, let's stick to the issues at hand. General Avery, tell us what happened at Ellsworth."

Avery, chief of staff of the air force, coughed delicately. "They hit us with about 2,500 men, outnumbering armed base personnel by five-to-one. They even had infiltrators inside the wire, who presumably came in with the civilian workforce or *were* the civilian workforce."

"And the bombers?"

"Of the twenty-eight B-1s they got into the air, our interceptors shot down twelve with air-to-air missiles, and we located and destroyed six on the ground. We've retaken Ellsworth, so they can't use that air base."

"But they managed to get away with ten of the best low-level penetration bombers ever made," the president said.

"Yes, sir," General Avery replied, his cheek muscles twitching visibly. "We'd have got all of them if they hadn't put our own aircraft in the air against us."

"You mean the F-15s and -16s they hijacked from National Guard bases in the Midwest?"

"We destroyed most of them in dogfights extending all the way to the Canadian border."

"Most of them?"

"We don't have a complete inventory yet," Avery said, "but they may have managed to hide a dozen or more F-16s."

"Do you know where?"

"We're currently reorienting our surveillance satellites and we should know the location of most of them by the end of the day tomorrow," General Avery said.

"But not necessarily all of them," the vice president noted.

"What kind of weapons were seized?" Carpenter persisted.

"General purpose bombs, air-to-air missiles such as the Sidewinder, air-to-ground missiles like the Shrike," Avery replied.

"Nuclear weapons?"

"None were stockpiled at Ellsworth or at any of the Air National Guard facilities."

"Jeremiah has nuclear weapons," Thompson said. "He said so in his television address, and we know where he got them."

"All of the aircraft captured are acceptable platforms for nuclear weapons," Avery remarked, grimly.

"Jesus!" Carpenter stared at Avery, thinking that an air force general who wore glasses probably couldn't see beyond the end of his nose.

"Let's be thankful he didn't overrun our missile bases in North Dakota, Wyoming, or Montana," said three-star Gen. Buster Franklin, chief of staff of the U.S. Marine Corps. "There are more than five hundred Minutemen and Peacekeepers at those locations."

Carpenter knew he looked puzzled, prompting Franklin's explanation. "The underground missile silos at Minot and Grand Forks are individually sealed and guarded and hidden in an area the size of Massachusetts."

"Jeremiah's forces would have gotten bogged down there," Haase interrupted, irritably. "Ellsworth was a quick in-and-out. Besides, the bombers are more flexible. We could have subverted the computerized missile launch codes."

Col. Samuel Douglas, military aide to the president's national security advisor, who was traveling abroad, spoke up. "There's intelligence information suggesting weapons of foreign manufacture may have been smuggled into New America, including nuclear weapons, as well as artillery shells and bombs containing chemical and biological agents."

"Can we defend against the B-1s?" Carpenter asked, swallowing with difficulty, "if they were fitted with such weapons?"

"We have air superiority," Avery answered, "and we can deploy many air defense missile systems, such as the Hawk and Patriot, which were effective in Desert Storm against Iraqi SCUDs. But with that many B-1s attacking at one time, especially now before we can deploy our defenses, I'd expect one or more to . . ." The general's voice trailed off, as he looked around the table and shook his head sadly.

"There is no effective ABM system, as you know, Mr. President," Haase interjected. "For decades now, we've relied on the fact of mutually assured destruction as the primary deterrent to all-out nuclear war."

The president sat back, as if all the wind had escaped from his body. *MAD. An appropriate phrase,* he thought. It was insanity. With the end of the Cold War, he'd considered the possibility of nuclear war remote, at best. Now a madman had nuclear weapons and threatened the very existence of the United States. With only sixteen months left in his term of office. He'd be remembered for all time according to how he handled this situation.

Carpenter could imagine the developing firestorm of criticism: Why hadn't he taken action earlier against New

America? Why had he waited? Why had he ignored the advice of his cabinet and military advisers? Perhaps it sounded like an excuse, but he believed in constitutional remedies. Conflicts between states and the federal government were to be resolved in the legislatures and the courts.

Truthfully, he hadn't imagined this military development, even in his wildest nightmare, although several of the men sitting around the table, especially General Franklin, had warned him about New America's military capabilities. Capabilities, that's all he'd thought they were. New America! *Christ, it's South Dakota,* he thought.

What should he have done? Ordered a preemptive military strike against a sovereign state? Should Roosevelt have done the same against Japan before Pearl Harbor? Truman against China and North Korea? Kennedy against the Soviet Union? The historians would argue about that, and maybe he'd be found negligent.

"Let's take a break," Carpenter said.

The White House staff brought in coffee, fruit juices, soft drinks, pastries, and sandwiches and placed them on a sideboard. Although it was nearly noon, Carpenter noted that few in the room exhibited a hearty appetite, with notable exceptions. Attorney General Thompson, Colonel Douglas, and General Franklin ate heartily while carrying on a quiet but animated conversation.

The president walked through a secretarial suite to the Oval Office, where he washed up in an adjacent bathroom before stepping out into the Rose Garden and waving confidently at reporters standing outside the far fence.

Fifteen minutes later, Carpenter returned to

the Cabinet Room and held up his hands to quiet the chatter. "Let's talk briefly about Fort Riley. What happened there, General Haase?"

"They managed to infiltrate a division of men into the area," General Haase said. "We had about three thousand combat-ready soldiers on post. They attacked the training area first, causing a great deal of confusion because they wore U.S. Army battle dress. They were individually well-armed to begin with and now they have all the weapons an army needs."

"Such as?"

"They seized at least 200 tanks, 135 Bradley fighting vehicles, 75 rocket launch systems, and 100 big artillery pieces. They fought a running battle with the post defenders and moved most of this equipment out by rail."

"Where to?" the president asked.

Haase looked to Colonel Douglas, who said, "Kansas City. Intelligence indicates they've moved some of the vehicles and guns into a main rail yard near the downtown area."

"They abandoned Fort Riley?"

"Yes," Haase answered. "They also got away with about thirty helicopters from the airfield."

"Gentlemen and ladies, if I may summarize," Carpenter said, standing. "It appears Jeremiah has temporarily outmaneuvered us. He did the unthinkable and overran two of our largest mainland military facilities, which were undermanned and extremely lax in their security."

"It was the Labor Day weekend," Haase protested.

"Yes, it was, General. And the Japanese attacked Pearl Harbor on Sunday. That doesn't mean we shouldn't have been ready, in either case.

"He's blackmailing us by threatening to blow up the Lake Anna power plant if we counterattack," Carpenter said. "If we call his bluff, we can't guarantee the American public he won't retaliate with the B-1s. One of them—perhaps loaded with nuclear, chemical, or biological weapons— could get through our air defenses and annihilate half the East Coast."

Carpenter looked around the room, inviting dissent, but there was none. "I don't see any option but to negotiate with him. Buy some time."

Wounded voices erupted throughout the room.

"That's just what he wants," Thompson protested.

"It's tantamount to military surrender!" General Haase thundered.

"It's totally unacceptable!" said Secy. of State John Tremain. "It would immediately undermine our credibility around the world, and we'd be facing flare-ups all over the globe, starting with the Korean peninsula."

"Any treaty you might negotiate with this madman would require Senate approval," said Sen. Donald Gilmore, the majority leader in the Senate, and, in Carpenter's opinion, the likely Republican Party candidate for president in next year's elections. "I doubt that approval would be forthcoming, Mr. President, especially given the two-thirds' majority requirement."

"The American people can be made to understand the necessary sacrifices," Thompson said, looking icily at President Carpenter. "All they are waiting for is unwavering leadership. Every hour you delay in attacking him will make Jeremiah stronger, if for no other reason than the fact that his supporters abroad will sense our weakness and reinforce him with men and weapons."

"The attorney general is absolutely right!" General Franklin said. "Attack now and destroy his army and their weapons. We'll take our chances with the B-1s and sacrifice several northeastern cities, if necessary."

"I agree," Haase chimed in, casting his vote.

"And if Jeremiah decides he wants to go down fighting?" Carpenter asked, rhetorically. "If he successfully devastates part of the nation with nuclear weapons, how will that make us stronger against external threats? Which one of you brave men will stand before the American public and take the blame?"

"Defeating the New America Army in the Midwest might not be as easy as everyone thinks," Colonel Douglas said. Carpenter watched the generals glare at the colonel, as if he were a child speaking in the company of adults.

Undeterred, Colonel Douglas continued to play the devil's advocate. "The rest of Jeremiah's army, about five divisions, is reported to be moving south to Kansas City. Within forty-eight hours, an army of over one hundred thousand experienced, motivated, and well-equipped mercenaries will be dug into a major American city. We'll have to destroy it to destroy them. What if they won't let the citizens out of the box? What if they defend themselves with those big guns, lobbing nuclear, chemical, or biological shells at our attacking forces? What might those casualties be? What would be the public reaction?"

Carpenter signaled for silence, deciding it was time to be presidential. "I was elected president to make these decisions, not any of you in this room. I'm still commander-in-chief. That's how it is, unless some of you agree with Jeremiah's opinion of the Constitution. I'll explain my decision to the American public in a television address tonight." Carpenter looked around the room belligerently. "I don't intend to preside over the capitulation of our nation to terrorism. Neither do I intend to see its cities and people needlessly destroyed and killed. If we negotiate, we buy time, so all you military geniuses and backbenchers can come up with a better plan than slugging it out on a nuclear battlefield located in our backyard. Or can someone around this table convince me—guarantee the nation—that we can counterattack now and prevail without suffering disastrous consequences?"

The president dared anyone to lock eyes with him. Instead, he watched them all look away.

14

THE EPISTLE OF JEREMIAH
THE PROPHET
TO THE NEW AMERICANS

CHAPTER TWO

¹ Having been sanctified by God to guide the Chosen People, I, Jeremiah, convey to those in New America, and its many Supporters around the world, the LORD's approval of your actions and your Victories in attempting to implement the Prophecy of *The Book of Second Jeremiah;*

² The Grace of God the Father is with you as He watches and guides your Effort to achieve His Plan for Mankind on Earth. Blessed are those who observe the Law. Amen.

³ The Egyptians of our time have tried to enslave the Chosen People; and the Pharaoh of our time has hardened his heart against God's Will that the Chosen People be allowed to live in Peace in the Promised Land.

4 Some say Egypt is first in prosperity among the nations of the world. Why would anyone, slave and citizen alike, want to leave and start anew in a desolate land! God's answer, provided through His servant, Jeremiah, is this: Egypt is eternally corrupted because it has erected Mammon as its principal God. Man can only progress to the knowledge of Ultimate Truths when all are truly Equal, not only in opportunity, but in sharing the bounty of society's Wealth, which can only be produced cooperatively.

5 The Devil's representatives on Earth have long lied about the Divine Right of Kings, the natural order of Aristocracy, the privileges of the Priesthood, the righteousness of Representative Government, the necessity of actual slavery, and Wage-Slavery. In New America, the ageless conflict between Individual Rights and Property Rights will be resolved to reflect the LORD's Will that all law-abiding citizens are Equal in all respects. This is the LORD's ultimate gift of Love to Mankind.

6 Those who would stop the Exodus of the Chosen People would well remember the Devastation wrought upon Egypt by the LORD and remember the victory song of Moses and his people: "In the greatness of thy majesty thou overthrowest thy adversaries; thou sendest forth thy fury, it consumes them like stubble." Only the strong, sanctified New Nation can achieve God's Will for Man.

7 The means we use to fulfill God's plan are God's means, and not subject to the criticism of Man. In *The Book of Second Jeremiah*, God promised a great Victory

for His Chosen People in the New Year Three, dating from the beginning of the migration to New America. That Prophecy has now come true.

8 The God of Moses again speaks to the Chosen People, reminding them that the struggle to establish the Promised Land will continue to be difficult, and the path strewn with many obstacles. Final Victory will come to the People only if they do not stray from their Purpose, through a Weakness of Will, and fall into the worship of False Idols, for which they, too, can suffer the Plague ordained by God.

9 Those in our midst who are Traitors, not True Believers, who are faint of heart, who will not observe the Law, will be found and cast out. Best ye leave first of your own accord, while ye are able.

10 Beware the Assassin who attempts to kill to create Chaos and further Evil; confuse him not with the One who is the Righteous Sword of the LORD.

11 Those New Americans who are Faithful, but troubled, should Pray. As Christ said, the Hypocrites love to pray in public, so they may be seen as pious. "But when you pray, go into your room and shut the door and pray to your Father who is in secret; and your Father who sees in secret will reward you." Remember that our Cause is our Church, and the LORD's Representative thy conduit. Convey thy thoughts on the Internet to Jeremiah, who can put your heart at ease.

12 In the Promised Land, we will be Good Neighbors, as the LORD decreed to Moses and his people. We will Negotiate in good faith, even with those whose hearts are dark and given over to our

destruction. Then, if words fail, we will Fight for that which is rightfully ours, using all Means at our disposal, so sayeth the LORD to His Prophet, Jeremiah.

15

Steve and Hoffman didn't stay in Kansas City, instead returning to Hoffman's apartment in Pierre at the direction of his CIA handlers. They'd hopped another air transport and were among the few passengers "going home." Most other New American troops headed to Kansas City. Military convoys carrying equipment and supplies clogged highways south for hundreds of miles.

Early Tuesday morning, they sat at the kitchen table with Duncan, drinking coffee.

"How'd you sleep?" Hoffman asked his friends, indicating by his tone of voice that he had tossed and turned most of the night.

"I didn't," Steve admitted, rubbing the black stubble on his face. "Every time I dozed off, I'd see that bastard's face."

"The ultimate nightmare," Duncan said.

"I don't like this waiting game," Steve said.

"Neither do I, but we can't kill Jeremiah if we don't know where he's at," Hoffman replied. "Washington said he was back East, but they think he'll return here. We've got lines out. As soon as someone sees him, we move."

"It's amazing," Duncan said. "The president and Jeremiah both go on TV and talk about peacefully settling this conflict, while behind the scenes Carpenter orders a hit on Jeremiah, and Jeremiah is turning Kansas City into a fort. It's enough to make you cynical about politics."

"I heard rumors last night that Jeremiah's troops have occupied a nuclear power plant south of Washington," Hoffman said.

Steve bolted out of his chair. "Get me on a secure telephone line. I've got to warn Laura."

They spent the next two days running the traps, as Hoffman put it, but none of the undercover operatives in New America had seen Jeremiah or heard of his whereabouts.

Duncan told them about a notice on the Internet community bulletin board concerning public executions to be held Friday at noon in Pierre.

Hoffman paced about the living room, digesting this information. "Think about the language in Jeremiah's recent epistle. He talked about a weakness of will, the faint of heart, traitors."

"I thought he was talking about us," Duncan joked.

"As New America faces off with the United States, they need to be strong within," Hoffman continued.

"He has to rekindle that fanaticism that caused them all to pull up stakes elsewhere and come here," Steve said. "He first won converts with his campaign against criminals, lawlessness, immorality."

"So Jeremiah stages a pep rally," Duncan said.

"Exactly," Hoffman agreed, excitedly. "Complete with entertainment, speeches, and scapegoats to divert attention from all their problems. It's a guiding principle of dictators."

"Bread and circuses."

The look on his two friends' faces convinced Steve they all were thinking the same thing: *Jeremiah quite possibly will be at the executions tomorrow.* In that case, so would they.

Hoffman, Duncan, and Steve left their apartment building on Harrison Avenue early Friday morning and walked down the hill toward the Capitol.

Hoffman wore his military uniform, while Duncan had on a white uniform. A plastic-enclosed permit pinned to the FBI agent's breast pocket identified him as one of the many food vendors sanctioned for the event. Steve played a wounded veteran of the military strike against Fort Riley. Bandages covered his head and the left side of his face, except for an eyehole. His left arm rested in a sling. A military tunic bearing lieutenant's bars was draped over his shoulders. As a final touch, Steve walked with a cane.

Despite an overcast sky on this breezy, cool September day, it didn't feel like rain. The growing horde of spectators shuffling across the landscape sent dust devils swirling into the air. From television reports they'd watched this morning, Steve knew that buses had rolled out of Bismarck, North Dakota, before dawn, picking up New Americans at frequent stops on the way south along the "83-corridor" to Pierre. Community leaders actively encouraged "citizen participation" in the executions by all nonessential workers.

The rally goers disembarked in assembly areas established around the perimeter of Pierre. Although *Second Jeremiah* expressly forbid possession of firearms, everyone entering the capital city this day passed through a metal detector at a state police checkpoint. Distinctive in their taupe uniforms, campaign hats, and big, black boots, state policemen seemed to be everywhere.

They breezed through the checkpoint without trouble and walked west on Broadway Avenue toward the state government complex, a two-hundred-acre site, including the Capitol Building and, to its east, Capitol Lake. An atmosphere both festive and grim prevailed, Steve thought.

The celebration centerpiece—the gallows—had been constructed on a tear-shaped peninsula jutting approximately a hundred-and-fifty-feet into the ten-acre, artesian lake.

"In the past, that peninsula usually was lined with the flags of the other forty-nine states," Duncan said.

"All I see today is the ROSE flag," Hoffman said.

"How many people do you think are here?" Steve asked.

"According to television, the goal is four hundred thousand *observers*," Hoffman answered. "Which would be about 10 percent of the New Americans living up here."

Not much vacant ground remained, Steve saw. Spectators even occupied the lawn of the executive mansion. They'd staked out precarious footholds on the steep hill near the State Library and Cultural Heritage Center, leading up to a plateau where other eyewitnesses stood in ranks, like dark sentinels.

"Hilger's Park in the valley around the corner is reserved for families with kids," Duncan said. "So they can picnic and play games." He looked disgusted. "Some family event. Since they won't be able to see the gallows, giant television screens have been placed strategically throughout the park for their viewing pleasure."

"There are giant TV screens all over," Hoffman noted, reading from a flyer handed him by a state worker. "Including the football field up at Riggs High School and the American Legion baseball stadium on Capitol Avenue."

The spookiest scene in this grotesque, developing tragedy, Steve thought, was the large number of people standing on top of the treeless hills rising sharply above the south shore of the Missouri River, more than a mile away. How could they hear or see what was happening? Or did that concern them or the organizers? Perhaps their presence alone was required.

Duncan bid his companions farewell. "My ice cream cart is being held for me on Broadway Avenue, right behind the gallows." He grinned. "Very convenient, huh?"

His gallows humor is admirable, Steve thought. Explosives had been placed in a false bottom of the ice cream cart by another undercover agent masquerading as a groundskeeper. If and when Duncan set off the charge, there was a good possibility he'd be killed.

As the three men shook hands, Steve hoped it wasn't the last time they'd be together.

"Good luck, Ralph," Hoffman said. "I hope sales are sky-high."

Hoffman and Steve continued along Governor's Drive, walking by the executive mansion into Memorial Park, located on a wedge of land between Capitol Avenue and the southeast corner of the lake. They could hardly push through the crowd at this prime viewing area.

As they crossed the street, Steve looked up at state police sharpshooters on top of the Capitol and other state office buildings. *Yes, yes! It's clear evidence that Jeremiah will be here!* He wished the U.S. military would launch a massive airborne assault on Pierre this afternoon, but he understood why that wouldn't happen, so long as Jeremiah's troops occupied the nuclear power plant and the New America armed forces had several B-1s loaded with nuclear bombs.

A three-story office building on the south side of Capitol Avenue was a perfect sniper's nest. *Surely we won't be so lucky as to get inside,* Steve thought, noting that several policemen stood guard outside the entrance.

Hoffman told them he needed to go inside and get some antibiotics for the lieutenant, a brave and wounded soldier. Still, they might have been stopped except for the intervention of a state police lieutenant. Perhaps it was his imagination, but Steve thought a look of recognition passed between Hoffman and the policeman.

Indeed, they went to a doctor's office on the second floor, although it was deserted, since all the building occupants had been evacuated hours ago. From the north window of the office to the gallows was about four hundred feet, Steve noted—an easy shot for a marksman, and Hoffman claimed to be very good.

Hoffman opened a clothes closet, then a concealed door in the back. He took out a German-made Heckler and Koch PSG-1 sniper rifle. Hoffman handed two grenades and a 9-mm Beretta to Steve, who could only guess how this cache of weapons had been smuggled into the building.

"Go outside and walk one block west to Ree Street, just across from the Capitol. That street runs south all the way to the river. Station yourself there."

"Why?"

Hoffman shrugged. "A hunch. The governor's motor launch is moored on the river. It's a natural escape route for them if trouble starts." Hoffman winked at Steve. "And there's damn sure going to be trouble."

"Won't they come looking for you soon? What if the police ask me about you?"

"Tell them I have orders from General Arnot to stay in the building." The German shrugged, indicating he planned to play it by ear. "I'll think of other excuses if they come around. If something goes wrong . . . well, that's why there're three of us and more."

Steve put the grenades and the pistol in his arm sling and bid Hoffman good hunting. Outside on the street, Steve made his way slowly to his post, using the cane to good advantage in securing a pathway. At the corner of Ree and Capitol, he backed up against a fence in front of the base-ball stadium, where someone with a microphone warmed up the crowd by reading passages from *The Book of Second Jeremiah*. Steve held the cane protectively in front of him, so no one could accidentally bump into his sling and dump out its contents.

At six-three, Steve could see over the top of the crowd. On the wooden gallows, four ropes swayed ominously in the breeze. Workmen repeatedly tested the trapdoors be-neath them. Every time one of the doors banged open, the sound was magnified by microphones, and the crowd oohed and aahed. More ominous for their cause, workers placed on the platform a Plexiglas shield, which Steve assumed to be bulletproof.

Suddenly, he was there! Jeremiah bounded up the stairs of the gallows and stood momentarily with his legs spread, his arms held high above his head. His usual black garb contrasted with the curly blond hair Steve could see even at a distance. The crowd roared its greeting. Steve silently mouthed the words: *Shoot the sonofabitch now!*

But Jeremiah quickly moved into the bulletproof Plexi-glas cage that shielded him on all sides, excepting narrow entry and exit slots. Steve knew Hoffman had just missed a golden opportunity.

"Citizens of New America! Welcome to the first of many public displays of justice!"

Hooded executioners marched four condemned men up the stairs and positioned them beneath the ropes. *All were naked, presumably to add to their humiliation,* Steve thought. The crowd applauded and many whistled, causing Steve to wonder about these people, since not all their actions appeared rehearsed. Many laughed, gestured animatedly, and generally acted as if they were at a celebration.

"I had a dream!" Jeremiah continued, his loudspeaker-enhanced voice seemingly omnipresent, as if he were shouting from the heavens. "I dreamed of living in a country where there was no crime! I dreamed of my wife being able to walk on the streets without fear of being raped and murdered! I dreamed of my kids being able to go to school to learn, without fear of violence! I dreamed of a country where I could leave the doors to my house unlocked, without fear of anyone stealing from me and my family. *I dreamed of living without fear.*"

Steve noticed the crowd around him had become strangely quiet, although many nodded their heads affirmatively.

"But that wasn't possible in the old America," Jeremiah said. "Because that America has cancer—the cancers of crime, injustice, economic inequality, decadence, political corruption, and, worst of all, a lack of enduring, God-given rules and values!"

An orchestrated demonstration broke out, as a woman with a beautiful voice began to sing "God Bless New America. . . ." Off to his left, Steve saw Jeremiah's image on a huge television screen located in front of the Capitol. The Prophet sang, too.

When the revised song ended, Jeremiah resumed his tirade: "There are many critics of our efforts in New America to deal with lawbreakers. We put them in public stocks, we cane them, we send them to reeducation camps, we put the mark of Satan on the evil ones. We're accused of violating their rights. But who invited these rule breakers to New America? Didn't they come of their own free will?"

The crowd shouted out its agreement, which became a mighty roar that ebbed and flowed for miles.

"You know what the real problem is? These people grew up in the culture of old America, where breaking the law is winked at. Even God's law. Ministers preach every Sunday to congregations that get up and leave the church and pay no attention to the sermon. They call themselves Christians and break the Lord's commandments every day! The only reason they read the Bible is to find excuses to lie, hate, and steal."

The crowd around Steve buzzed with excitement, punctuating Jeremiah's remarks with such endorsements as, "That's right," "Yes, sir," and "Tell it like it is." *It's similar to a revival meeting,* he thought.

"Some people who came to New America apparently didn't think we'd actually enforce the rules of *Second Jeremiah.*" The Prophet paused and looked around, as a big smile spread slowly across his face. "Surprise! Surprise!"

Laughter swept through the crowd, which began to stamp its feet, generating a rumble that sounded like drums.

Jeremiah cupped a hand behind one ear and asked the crowd, "What is our motto?"

A thunderous response came back, "Obey, or die! Obey, or die! Obey, or die!" The bogus motto echoed for miles over the hills. Steve knew crime resulted mainly from psychological dysfunction brought about by a host of situations. Hanging criminals wouldn't reduce the root causes of crime.

"Today we're here to cut out the cancers of crime and injustice!" Jeremiah shrieked, pointing at one of the condemned men.

"This man invaded a home and abducted a fourteen-year-old girl!" the Prophet on the TV screen thundered. "This abduction was witnessed by four other young girls. Their fathers actually found this beast raping the innocent young virgin in a nearby field!"

The camera focused on the accused rapist's genitalia, shrunken with fear. One hooded executioner put a rope around his neck. A primal roar erupted from the crowd, and Steve wondered if they would feel the same indignation *if they knew about the rape of his wife by the man screaming for a rapist's blood!*

"There's not going to be any trial for this evil man!" Jeremiah continued. "No prosecutors to cut him a deal. No jury to let him go. He's guilty! He confessed! We don't care if his mommy and daddy didn't love him!" Laughter exploded from the observers. "We don't care if he secretes too much testosterone! We don't care if Santa didn't bring him enough toys when he was a little boy."

Jeremiah's television image suddenly took on a different persona. No longer the madman cheerleader, he now appeared thoughtful and spoke barely above a whisper. "All we care about is the violated virgin. All we care about is justice. The death penalty isn't a deterrent; it's the solution! This man broke God's law. Thou shalt not rape! Here is his reward." Jeremiah pointed at the hooded man, who pulled a lever, causing the alleged rapist to drop to his death.

A storm of approval rumbled through the crowd, and Steve steeled himself to shout out his endorsement also, so as not to arouse suspicion among those pressed against him.

Jeremiah's emergence several years ago had caused Steve to reread his Bible. Much of it was comforting; other parts disturbing. He'd been particularly struck by the story of the Old Testament David—the greatest king of ancient Israel, author of much of the Psalms, chosen of God. Because of his lust for Bathsheba, David had her husband, Uriah, murdered. Yet in the first verse of the first book of the New Testament, Christ is called "the son of David."

And the confusion regarding sin and punishment and rehabilitation, and who should sit in judgment, continued to the present. Steve only knew for certain that today's circus in Pierre was legally and morally wrong. Although no longer a sworn peace officer, he'd taken it upon himself to bring Jeremiah to justice. Capturing him wasn't likely, so he'd have to kill him. Steve would be judge, jury, executioner. He didn't want to think long about the possibility that, at least for today, he and Jeremiah were alike.

Jeremiah's ranting shook Steve from his philosophical musings and he listened to the terrorist describe the crime of the next condemned man, who the führer of New America said was guilty of murder—the murder of his neighbor during a dispute over the burning of waste and garbage. The camera switched back and forth from Jeremiah to the alleged murderer.

"Oh!" Jeremiah said, cupping his ear, to indicate the condemned man had spoken. "He has an excuse! He wants to tell us about it! Cain wants us to sympathize with him for killing his brother! His fellow New American! Do we want to hear his excuse?" Jeremiah cupped a hand to his ear, and the mob collectively yelled, "No!"

"You mean no excuses are allowed when a man breaks the law?"

"No!"

"You mean 'Thou shalt not kill' is an absolute rule?"

"Yes!" The crowd sounded like angry bees.

"Don't you think we should appoint this man a liar?" Jeremiah stepped back, shook his head, and pretended to be embarrassed by his *faux pas*. "Excuse me, I meant a *lawyer*!"

"No liars!" they yelled.

"A liar would twist all the facts and find some excuse for mercy. To a liar, the courts are but a means of getting rich and achieving notoriety. After the lawyers lie and confuse the issues, a judge might let this man go, or put him in a nice prison where he could watch HBO, take a homosexual lover, and enroll in college courses!"

"No!" said the crowd, its collective anger obvious.

"U.S. courts have constructed so many safeguards for the accused and placed so many handicaps on the police, it's impossible to convict criminals even when there's a mountain of evidence pointing to their guilt. I say that's wrong. Unjust!"

The throng sincerely voiced its agreement.

"In New America, we're going to dispense justice day and night, if necessary," Jeremiah continued, "including capital punishment for the crimes of treason, murder, assault, rape, kidnapping, and major theft. It won't take us long to get rid of the criminal 10 percent so the rest of you can live without fear."

Off to his left, Steve saw a section of the crowd waving placards, some of which displayed drawings of a noose.

"But don't we have to tolerate these rule breakers, these murderers, to have a democratic society?" Jeremiah asked, acting confused and troubled.

"No!"

Jeremiah looked pleased. "All right. You exercise your democratic rights. Vote to set this man free or hang him." Jeremiah demonstrated a thumbs-up and thumbs-down response, as if he were a Roman emperor. The crowd turned thumbs-down as the chant went up and grew in intensity, "Hang him! Hang him! Hang him!"

Jeremiah pointed to the executioner and the second condemned man dropped to his death, amid an approving roar from the multitude.

The same fate befell a man accused of stealing twenty computers, which he'd attempted to smuggle out of New America in a moving van, saying he was going home to Texas.

"We've dealt with the major crime categories today!" Jeremiah yelled. "A rapist, a murderer, a thief! But we have saved the best for last." Jeremiah shouted out the crime, "A drug dealer! Someone who poisons people's minds so they don't know right from wrong, or don't care. This drug dealer was caught red-handed by the state police trying to sell crack cocaine on our streets! In his house were found many cases of whiskey, as well as marijuana. Read from your book. What is the commandment of God?"

Steve listened as those around him opened their copy of *The Book of Second Jeremiah* and, in unison, read: " 'Thou shalt not imbibe intoxicating alcohol or drugs, except those revealed to cure serious mental or physical afflictions, for these foreign substances are a direct cause of Evil.' " Steve thought of Peter Thompson's statement that narco dollars provided significant revenues for New America. What hypocrisy!

"Let me read a verse for you," Jeremiah said calmly. "*Second Jeremiah* 2:25. 'There is no right of life for Evil Men; Good Men shall pluck Evil Men from society as weeds are plucked from a beautiful garden. The Social Contract knows no exception, nor qualification. No need exists for judges and juries, prisons and parole, rehabilitation and pardon. Obey, or die!' "

*   *   *

Jeremiah moved out from behind the bulletproof shield, apparently prepared to pull the handle himself and drop the trapdoor out from under the drug dealer's feet.

Steve saw Jeremiah suddenly stumble backward, tumble off the scaffold, and disappear from the television screen! Steve resisted an impulse to cheer and jump. Hoffman was a marksman! Due process wasn't served, but justice damn sure had been.

The crowd sucked in its breath. Then a murmur of uncertainty and fear swept through it. People began moving, pushing, trying to run.

A loud explosion sent a cloud of white smoke into the air behind the gallows. Steve nodded grimly. Duncan had just served dessert. The crowd stampeded, trampling its weaker and less fortunate members. Many people were forced to jump into the lake. Steve stayed against the fence, preparing himself for action. He took the Beretta from the sling and stuck it behind his belt. He put the grenades in his pants pocket. He dropped the cane and sling to the ground, and put on the tunic.

Across the street near the bronze statue of "Dueling Stallions," Steve saw the crowd part as an open-topped, military jeep drove through. A state policeman stood in the passenger's seat, pointing an automatic rifle. The jeep knocked people down and ran over one prostrate woman, as it accelerated toward the river. *Had the bastard somehow survived?*

Steve pulled the pin on one grenade, flipped it underhanded into the jeep, and dropped to the ground just before the explosion. When he got up, a sharp pain in his shoulder and blood on his shirt indicated he'd been hit by shrapnel. He had no time to think about that, however, as a Chevy van with darkened windows drove around the blazing, gutted jeep and the two charred bodies.

Fearing the worst, Steve ran after the speeding van, which rocketed through the intersection with Sioux Avenue, hitting a half-dozen people whose bodies exploded high into the air. The river was two blocks away.

"State police!" Steve shouted, running hard. That and the

Beretta cleared a path for him. The van had screeched to a stop near the river. Several men waded toward a large boat bobbing close by.

Steve didn't recognize Jeremiah from the back, although two men in the water wore black. Whoever they were, they were bad guys. Steve knelt and fired at the boarding group. The two men in black flung up their arms as if in surprise and then fell forward into the water.

Steve was tackled by two men and the Beretta went flying. He jumped up and ran toward the river, looking over his shoulder at his pursuers, who had multiplied in number.

The boat executed a sharp U-turn in the river, its motor emitting a high-torque whine. Although Steve had the remaining grenade in hand, the boat was already out of his throwing range.

Standing at the water's edge, he momentarily held the crowd at bay with the grenade while considering his options. Observors from Griffin Park to his right advanced slowly toward him. To his left, a narrow street also was filled with people. There was only one avenue of escape. He put the grenade in his pocket, dove into the Missouri River, and swam toward La Framboise Island, about two hundred feet away in the middle of the channel.

Once there, he climbed up a steep, muddy bank and stepped onto an asphalt hiking trail. A dense growth of brush and trees covered the island. Steve ran on the path to the opposite side, where his pursuers could no longer see him.

He took off the tunic and tore the bandages off his head and face. If he followed the trail to the west end of the island, he could slip back into Pierre over a dam. But what good would that do? He'd be back in the devil's den, and a noose might be waiting for him.

A hundred yards across the river in Fort Pierre, he saw people milling about a park. They wouldn't know what he'd done. They'd think he was just trying to escape the mayhem on this side of the river. He dove again into the water and swam toward the far shore. Halfway across, a huge floating tree nearly rammed him. In defense, he grabbed a short stubby branch and hung on. He was tired and needed a breather. He ducked under the water to get on the other side of the log.

As the strong current rapidly moved the tree downriver, Steve looked back at La Framboise Island and saw men on the hiking trail. Two powerboats patrolled both sides of the island. If he'd kept swimming toward the opposite shore, they'd probably have run him down. In fact, they'd notice the log soon and put two-and-two together.

When he saw a small, marshy island off to his left, Steve let go of the log, ducked under water, and swam in that direction. He popped above water twice for quick breaths before finally feeling mud with his feet.

He crawled military style to a stand of tall grass, where he lay on his back in the shallow water and muck. He blackened his face with mud and broke off several reeds, until he found one that was dry and mostly hollow.

At first, the boat roared by, staying in the main channel of the river, but then it executed a tight U-turn, skidding on the water. Turning his head sideways, so one eye looked along the top of the water, Steve saw the wedge-shaped bow of the boat bearing down on him. He put the reed in his mouth and submerged, pressing himself as far down into the mud and cold water as possible.

16

Laura's early morning routine was to sit in the kitchen nook formed by the ground-to-roof turret, sip coffee, and stare out the windows into the yard and the woods across the far road. As autumn approached, the flowers had disappeared, the grass had withered, and the tree leaves had faded to brown. Soon they'd die and drop to the ground. Laura shuddered at the symbolism. Where was Steve?

She hadn't left the farm since that Thursday-night edition of *American Chronicle,* when Jeremiah had humiliated her before the world by mentioning her pregnancy and insinuating he was the father of the baby.

Laura relished not being a player in the current media circus, which had been ongoing since Jeremiah's troops had launched their offensive a week ago. The public now knew about the occupation of Lake Anna. The news media and politicians used each other to discover the facts, report the news, shade the truth, manipulate public opinion. It was another world, alien in its concept.

Maria walked into the kitchen and headed for the coffeemaker. "How'd you sleep?"

"Okay." Actually, Laura hadn't slept well since the rape. She alternately hated the embryo in her stomach and wondered about "it." In the genetic mixing of him and her, who would it be like? Was evilness an inherited or acquired trait?

Her face puffy from sleep, and her long, curly, jet black hair in disarray, Maria sipped coffee. Saturday mornings she slept in until eight. "So what're your plans for the weekend?"

"I forgot what day it is." Preoccupied as she was with ageless questions, Laura had lost track of time. "I guess I'll get drunk tonight, hop some bars, get laid, that kinda thing." Laura sighed. Being clever and cool lately was nearly impossible.

"Sounds good to me," Maria replied. "I could tag along. Of course, all that booze and smoke and sex wouldn't be good for the baby."

Laura rose to refresh her coffee, fighting back another urge to slap Maria, at least give her an acid tongue-lashing. She couldn't forget or forgive Maria's remarks after the pregnancy test, when they'd left the doctor's house to drive home. Maria wasn't worried about HIV infection because Jeremiah was too strong, too virile. Too big.

"Have you heard from Steve?" Maria asked.

"No, but I know he'll be home soon."

For Maria's benefit, Steve was on an FBI consulting job in Los Angeles. Laura remembered Steve's admonition not to confide in Maria, whom he distrusted after the events at her parents' house.

Twenty minutes later, Laura heard a rumbling noise that sounded like an approaching tornado. She looked out the front window and saw a helicopter hover into view and set down on a level portion of the front lawn. Steve got out, ducked down, and ran toward the house, as the mechanical bird went airborne again.

Laura ran out onto the front porch to meet Steve, who wore ill-fitting clothes and looked haggard. Nevertheless, Laura leapt at her knight in shining armor, knowing Steve would catch her with his strong arms and that she'd finally feel safe again. They kissed and hugged for a long time.

"Where've you been, Steve?" Maria asked, standing in the entryway.

"Working." Steve took Laura's hand, walked into the

house, and headed toward the kitchen. "I need something to eat. Maria, why don't you give us some privacy." He looked at the bodyguard until she flinched under his gaze, smiled feebly, and walked outside.

"What can I fix you?" Laura asked eagerly.

"Toast, eggs." Steve went into a coughing fit.

"Where'd you get the terrible cold?"

"Swimming in the river."

"What?"

"Fix the eggs and I'll tell you about it."

Laura became so absorbed in Steve's account of how he and "his friends" had tried to kill Jeremiah that she forgot her breakfast preparations, which Steve took over.

"I lay in the mud near the end of a small island until dark," Steve said. "They nearly ran over me twice with a boat. Then I floated downriver probably another half hour. There was a bright moon and I saw two guys in a fishing boat, so I dog-paddled over to get a better look."

"Did they see you?"

"Not at first. When I stuck my head above the side of the boat, they almost jumped out."

Laura whooped with laughter, thinking how much more alive she felt having Steve around.

"So I said, 'Whacha fishin' for?' and one guy squinted at me and said, 'Walleye.' "

"Who were they?"

"Two Indians from the Lower Brule Reservation," Steve replied. "They asked who I was, and I said, 'Just someone trying to get out of New America.' The one guy nodded and said, 'Can't blame you for that.' So I crawled into the boat and they took me to the reservation, where I called Peter. He sent the helicopter."

While Steve ate ravenously, Laura asked the big question, "You don't know if he's dead?"

Steve shook his head.

"Or what happened to your friends?" Laura knew enough not to ask their names, in case someone was listening.

"They're pretty resourceful guys," Steve said. "If anybody could get out of that hell, they could. Has there been anything on the news about all this?"

"No."

"That could be a good sign," Steve said. "He might be dead or badly wounded. Otherwise, he'd use the assassination attempt to whip up support or as an excuse to launch another terrorist attack."

"Maybe he doesn't want to admit New America is so easily infiltrated that he can't even appear in public without fear of being killed," Laura said.

"Maybe he can add that to his 'I dreamed of living without fear' speech."

Laura beamed, enjoying immensely their effort to belittle "the Prophet."

"In Jeremiah's case, I'd need to see a dead body to be certain he's dead. Time will tell, I guess."

"What happened to Katrina Dorfler?" Laura asked.

"We left her at the cabin. They decided to use her as a 'marker.' Any time she's spotted, Jeremiah is probably nearby."

Laura saw Steve hesitate, as if prepared to say something else about Katrina. But he remained silent, sipping from his coffee mug.

"The news is all about Lake Anna," Laura said, "and President Carpenter's decision to negotiate with Jeremiah."

"What's happened at the power plant over the last week?"

"Nothing. Everyone's freaked out. A lot of people are moving out of this area. There're all kinds of bizarre ideas floating around. One member of Congress insists that the air force has this gluelike stuff made from secret space materials, and that they could drop it from the air on the Lake Anna reactors, where it would solidify and prevent them from blowing up."

"And I thought all the crazies were in Pierre."

"President Carpenter is taking it on the chin from everyone. Some of his opponents in Congress are talking about impeaching him. I don't think the president should negotiate with Jeremiah, but they should give Carpenter a chance."

"And Peter?"

"There are rumors he'll resign as attorney general or that

Carpenter will fire him. In the meantime, he's staying quiet. The media's trying to hang the CAT raid on him, and if that happens, he could be indicted."

Steve showered and slept, while Laura kept watch from a chair, holding his gun. Near dusk, after he awoke, they went for a walk in the northeast pasture, as they'd done before when she'd told him about the pregnancy. Now she had even more bitter news.

"You're not the father of the baby," Laura said. That's all Dr. Helen Cureton could tell her for certain. To identify the father with scientific precision, they'd have to do blood tests on other likely candidates. But Laura knew there was only one.

"What are you going to do?"

Laura spoke decisively. "We're going away, tomorrow. I'll have an abortion and we'll take a vacation."

"Go where?"

The glorious sunset in the west uplifted her spirits. "How about Europe? Scandinavia. I've always wanted to go back there. I can easily get the *procedure* done in Copenhagen, for example. Then we can relax. Sit in Trivoli Gardens, drink schnapps, and watch the jugglers." Maybe never come home to the insanity that had taken root in America. Live abroad, with the liberal-minded, easy-going Danes.

Laura looked at Steve. "Well, what to you think?"

He smiled forlornly and Laura understood. It would be sad to leave the country in the midst of this crisis, but it was egomania of the highest order to think they could make a difference now. Steve had taken his best shots and someone else could take a turn at the plate. Europe would be a nice diversion. Except.

"You can bail out of this relationship, you know," Laura said, swallowing a lump in her throat. "I'd understand. No one would blame you."

Steve looked amazed. "You can't get rid of me that easily, Laura. Europe's fine, but instead of leaving tomorrow, how about the day after tomorrow? Give me a day to fly to Denver and visit the kids."

Laura squeezed Steve's hand and smiled in relief. "It's a deal! I'll make all the arrangements while you're gone."

Later, when they were having dessert in the kitchen, and Maria sat in the living room, Steve called an airline and made his travel arrangements.

"My flight is at nine in the morning," he announced. "Can you take me to the airport, Maria?"

"Why can't I come?" Laura protested.

"I thought you had plenty to do here," Steve argued.

Laura reluctantly nodded her agreement. Most transatlantic flights left Dulles International Airport in the late afternoon or early evening. That gave her only two days to accomplish a hundred things.

While Maria took Steve to Dulles airport, Laura drove into Middleburg and used a pay phone to call a travel agent and made arrangements for her and Steve to fly to Copenhagen. She asked the agent to book them into a Palace Hotel suite for a month. That would give her and Steve time to decide what to do with their lives.

Laura also spoke to Dr. Cureton, who said she'd make an appointment with a competent Danish doctor who could perform the abortion.

Laura segregated clothes in her closet, selecting those she'd take and those she'd leave behind. There were so many things she should do, such as talk with her parents, her brother and sister, the property manager and his wife, her lawyer. Mel and her friends at UBC. A dozen other people. But she couldn't do that, at least not now. Their departure and destination had to be a secret.

Laura flopped on her bed, overwhelmed by everything. After several deep breaths, she decided to do it one step at a time. First, the abortion. Then she'd call everyone from overseas, although she wouldn't be able to tell them of their whereabouts or give them a telephone number. Maybe Steve's FBI friends could figure out a safe method of communication.

Later that evening, Laura found herself in the nursery-to-be, for no particular reason other than to think of what might yet be with her and Steve.

Her skin tingled as she felt someone behind her and turned to see Maria standing in the doorway.

"You startled me!" Laura said.

"Thinking about changing your mind?" Maria asked, stepping into the room. She wore black Levis, a black, turtleneck sweater, and a shoulder holster and gun.

"About what?"

"About the abortion." The voice came from behind Maria and Laura recognized it. As Jeremiah walked around Maria into the room, fear caused the hair on the back of Laura's neck to rise and her heart to pound. His left arm was in a plaster cast, supported by a shoulder sling. Scratches and bruises covered his face. None of the injuries had diminished his sardonic smile.

"You bitch!" Laura said, realizing Maria's perfidy. She swung her fist at Maria, who easily deflected the blow.

"You let him rape me!"

Maria put her hands defiantly on her hips, a sneer smeared across her face. "Only after he got into the good stuff."

Laura recoiled, looking in disgust at both of them. "How could you? He killed José!"

Maria shrugged. "José did not believe in the cause."

"What cause? Terrorizing and killing people."

Maria snarled. "No! Bringing about a revolution, so the have-nots are on top for a change! It's in the Bible. 'But many that are first will be last, and the last first.' "

Laura recalled her conversations with Maria about the discrimination she'd suffered growing up Hispanic and poor in south Texas. Still, Laura was angry. "You're a Judas goat!"

Maria shook her head. "Personally I don't know what you see in this skinny bitch, Jeremiah! I bet she ain't got no fire, like a Latino woman."

Jeremiah laughed at the quarreling women. "No one has your enthusiasm, Maria. For the cause, or in bed. But, nevertheless, I am bewitched by Laura. We're going to be parents of a fine bouncing..." He stopped talking and frowned. "Just what sex *is* the baby, Laura?"

Laura knew it was a boy, but she remained defiantly silent, turning to watch Jeremiah walk about the room, inspecting its contents, including the crib.

"I think it's a boy," Jeremiah concluded. "That's the prophecy, Laura. God's will. When he's twenty-four, or thereabouts, he takes over for me as Prophet of New America."

"You really are one sick sonofabitch, aren't you?" Laura spat. "In addition to being a madman, you're obsessive. You raped me just so you could impregnate me!"

Jeremiah shrugged. "It's not my fault Steve is impotent."

Laura rushed at him, beating him with her fists, causing him to protectively cover his arm. Before she could follow up, Maria slammed her against the wall.

"Take it easy! Take it easy!" Jeremiah cautioned. "Let's not cause a miscarriage here."

"You're right, Laura. You're just a brood mare," Maria spat, venomously. "That's all you're gonna use her for, isn't it, Jeremiah?" She turned to look at him.

He shrugged and winked at Laura. "You'll be my wife officially, Laura, although, like the Bible's patriarchs, I'm not really a one-woman man."

"Well I'm a one-man woman," Laura retorted. "You'll never really possess me." Then her spirits sagged. "Why are you doing this?"

"I'm in love, Laura. Love makes us crazy; that's what the songwriters and poets say, isn't it? When you're in love, you can't think straight. You can't sleep or eat. You can only think about the object of your affection. Love is obsession, Laura. At least in the beginning."

"I'll never belong to you. Steve will come after me again." Laura pointed at the cast. "Next time you won't be so lucky."

Jeremiah responded affably. "Indeed, he and his friends almost killed me in my own country. He's got balls, even if they don't make sperm."

Laura made a break for the door but Maria tripped her, sending Laura sprawling on the floor.

"Okay, enough fun, you two," Jeremiah declared, helping

Laura up. "While Steve's in Denver, let's get packing. You're going on a trip, Laura, but not to Denmark. You'll love New America in the fall. I've got a wonderful new hideaway where we'll be comfy and safe."

"I hate your guts!" Laura yelled. "I'll kill this baby somehow, believe me."

Jeremiah pondered Laura's remarks, and his face turned red with anger. "No, you won't, Laura, even if Maria has to watch you day and night. We'll have long heart-to-heart talks during your pregnancy and you'll come to know me and love me, and embrace our cause."

Maria threw Laura's clothes into a suitcase, while Jeremiah paced nervously nearby. On the way out, Laura attempted to throw herself down the stairs, but Maria held her arm tightly. Laura continued to struggle as they stepped onto the front porch. She wondered about the other security guards, but she knew Jeremiah had somehow disposed of them; perhaps they, too, had secretly been on his payroll all along. Just like the outside guards at her parents' ranch.

They made it only as far as the porch, however, because Steve stepped from the shadows of the house, pointing the Sig-Sauer at them. "Don't move!"

"Steve!" Laura said, breaking away from Maria and running down the steps to his side. He pushed her behind him with his left hand, while keeping the gun pointed steadily at Jeremiah and Maria.

"I took you to the airport!" Maria protested, in amazement.

"Exactly."

Jeremiah laughed. "How long have you known about Maria?"

"I've suspected it for months," Steve replied.

Laura gasped as Maria reached for her gun, dropped down and rolled off the porch. Steve's gun hand calmly followed her movements until she came up on one knee, the gun out of her shoulder holster. Steve shot her, the bullet entering the middle of Maria's forehead. She fell backward, spread-eagled on the ground, as Steve swung the gun back toward Jeremiah. Laura smiled and sighed in relief.

"Very good shot!" the terrorist declared. He had one foot on the steps and one on the porch, and was turned slightly sideways. Suddenly, fire exploded from the cast on his left arm, and Steve staggered backward against Laura who tried to break his fall as he collapsed to the ground. She screamed at the sight of blood pouring from the side of his head.

Jeremiah grabbed her by the arm and roughly jerked her upright. He'd taken his arm out of the sling, and she could see the gun. Before she could react, he fired again, the impact causing Steve's body to bounce off the ground.

"No!" she cried, attacking Jeremiah, pummeling him with her fists, pushing him backward so that he lost his balance and nearly tripped. She fought with him as he shoved her toward the Land Rover, opened the backseat door and pushed her inside. He put a knee on her chest, and handcuffed one of her wrists to a door handle.

Laura watched Jeremiah walk back toward Steve, presumably to deliver the coup de grâce. She stretched one leg into the front seat, putting her heel on the horn.

The blaring sound caused Jeremiah to jerk around, a worried look on his face. The incessant horn might attract the attention of the property manager and his wife in the apartment above the barn. She watched Jeremiah stare at Steve's body, turn, and walk back toward the truck. Laura heaved a sigh of relief. Jeremiah got behind the wheel, glared at her, and began driving down the hill. She looked through the rear window at Steve lying motionless on the ground and a piercing shriek escaped her.

17

In the Oval Office at the White House, Pres. Bob Carpenter sat behind a walnut desk that had belonged to his grandfather, who'd been governor of Oklahoma and a federal judge. The tall, stocky president with the silver mane leaned back in the swivel chair, a stunned look on his face. "That's an extraordinary proposal, Colonel."

"These are extraordinary times, Mr. President."

Indeed, Carpenter thought, *although my experience, after nearly seven years in office, is that most people who sit in front of this desk are usually motivated by a lust for power or money, or both. But this . . . this suggestion by Colonel Douglas is totally selfless, the single greatest patriotic gesture I've heard. Ever. Or is it just insanity?*

"At least appoint me to the negotiating team," Colonel Douglas suggested. "That way you can decide at the last minute. I know you think I'm crazy, but maybe it'll be the only alternative left."

Douglas might have a point, Carpenter thought, as he stood and looked out over the Rose Garden. He'd already violated several laws by authorizing the FBI director to use his "assets" in South Dakota to attempt to kill Jeremiah. That effort failed. Douglas's plan might have a greater chance of success.

"All right, Sam. You're on the team. Make whatever

preparations are necessary, but do *nothing* without my approval."

The army colonel stood and saluted. "Yes, sir."

Alone again, Carpenter considered the pressure that had been exerted upon him by those lobbying for themselves or their friends to be on the negotiating team. Several politicians thought the limelight of the negotiations with Jeremiah would enhance their careers, although Carpenter considered that view shortsighted. Organizations representing women, gays, African Americans, Hispanic Americans, and Asian Americans were unhappy over their lack of representation, especially given Jeremiah's many racist, sexist, and homophobic pronouncements.

Carpenter chose three men initially: Attorney General Thompson, General Haase, and Secy. of State John Tremain. The nation's top legal officer, military officer, and diplomat. Obvious choices. Now Douglas, a second-level White House aide, had been added to the team. Four was enough.

Carpenter busied himself with necessary paperwork until his secretary opened the door and poked her head into the room. "The vice president asks to see you."

Carpenter hesitated. "Send him in."

Vice President Trainor burst into the room, as if reacting to a starter gun.

"How are you, Richard?"

"Fine, Mr. President. And you?"

"Very busy today." Carpenter liked Trainor, who had been a good vice president, meaning he had stayed discreetly in the background, like a piece of furniture. In private, however, Trainor often lapsed into philosophical meanderings about the nature of man and the challenges of the next millennium, as if he couldn't stop campaigning. His wooden movements, fake smile and dyed hair hardly inspired confidence, however.

"I passed Colonel Douglas in the outer office," Trainor said. "Anything new on the military front?"

"I decided to appoint Colonel Douglas to the negotiating committee."

"Really? I'm surprised."

Most people will be, Carpenter thought. "As you know from the recent meeting in the cabinet room, he's not afraid to speak his mind."

"I'll say. I thought General Haase might break him to buck private."

"Douglas is an insightful intelligence officer, and he's gained a lot of experience in national security matters during his tenure here at the White House. I value his opinion."

Trainor shrugged, and Carpenter wondered again why his vice president hadn't pressed to be a negotiator. It was a high-visibility assignment, and Trainor obviously would seek the party's presidential nomination next year. On the other hand, if the negotiations failed, or if any agreement was perceived as a sell-out, then the negotiators would be held responsible.

"What about the military situation?" Trainor asked.

"The Pentagon has a plan for retaking Lake Anna. I think I'll okay it."

"What's involved?"

Carpenter hesitated. Trainor was vice president. He should know, in case. "They plan to explode a laser-guided missile above the containment buildings. It's a high-tech device that will create an electromagnetic field that temporarily disables the plant's computers, so Jeremiah's men can't control the nuclear reactors. An overwhelming military force will then retake the power plant. That's the way it's supposed to work, anyway."

"You're going to do this before the negotiations?"

"Yes."

"And if Jeremiah breaks off the talks and sends one of the B-1s against us?"

"The whole country is bristling with antiaircraft guns and missiles. Fighters are flying thousands of sorties a day. Last night a rocket blasted off from Cape Canaveral to put up a new spy satellite. My generals tell me the B-1s aren't likely to get through."

"Very gutsy, Mr. President. Very gutsy. So you really don't plan to sit down and talk with him."

"I didn't say that, Richard. We could retake Lake Anna, he could refrain from launching the B-1s against us, and we could still talk. There's still the situation in Kansas City to be resolved."

"He's continuing to pour troops and equipment into the area?"

Carpenter nodded. And he appeared powerless to stop the invasion of an American city. Jesus! If only the military could retake Lake Anna and recapture or destroy the B-1s, then they could crush the sonofabitch at Kansas City and end this nightmare.

Otherwise, he might actually have to negotiate with the terrorist. Offer some kind of commonwealth status for New America. The thought of such a capitulation sickened Carpenter. He had a choice of being the president who presided over the breakup of the United States, or the one who started another civil war. This time with the possibility that nuclear, chemical, and biological weapons could be used. For many of his critics, it was a simple choice between cowardice or patriotism. Carpenter still hoped for a third way. Maybe that would be the Douglas option. Even then, what could ever be done about those six million New Americans? Wouldn't they always be a thorn in the nation's side?

"It's a heavy burden you carry, Mr. President."

Yeah, and you might want to reconsider shouldering it, Carpenter thought. Suddenly, he wanted out of the White House.

"Richard, excuse me, but I need to get some work done, and then I think I'll have the Secret Service sneak me out of here."

"Where are you off to?" Trainor asked.

Carpenter voiced his thoughts. "To Washington Cathedral, then maybe to Camp David. Yeah, that would be nice." He and Milly could bowl, watch a movie, take a late afternoon walk on a mountain path. The prospect of such an escape heightened the president's spirits.

Trainor stood and held out his hand. "Everything will work out for the best, Bob, believe me."

"I hope so." Carpenter thought it unusual for Trainor to use his first name.

"I know so," Trainor said, as he continued to grasp the president's hand. "Godspeed, sir."

Sitting in the backseat of the presidential limousine, Carpenter thought about the reasons he'd selected Trainor in 1991 as his running mate. Mainly, the senator from Kentucky demonstrated significant fund-raising abilities, with seemingly no end to his contacts among the rich. Directly and indirectly, Trainor helped raise nearly $30 million from private contributors during the 1992 campaign; in 1996, the figure was closer to $50 million.

Nevertheless, Carpenter thought about taking the unprecedented action of abandoning support of his own vice president and endorsing Peter Thompson in next year's presidential primaries. Although he and his attorney general had been butting heads for nearly all of the second administration, largely over the threat posed by New America, Peter had been right. Carpenter knew that now, and he reminded himself to never let personalities influence politics, which was about shifting alliances at best. Yesterday's enemy could be tonight's bedfellow—especially if it was best for the nation.

He'd forgive Peter for launching the CAT raid against Jeremiah's hideout without telling him, especially now that both of them were guilty of the attempted murder of an accused felon who hadn't had his day in court. Any number of partisans would relentlessly search for evidence to impeach him or indict Thompson. To them, a political victory counted for more than the national interest.

It troubled Carpenter that Trainor never missed an opportunity to downplay the New America threat, characterizing the secessionists as harmless religious fanatics, protected by the Constitution in the exercise of their beliefs. Trainor had argued that the Chinese had Jeremiah on a short leash, and that "the Prophet" no longer posed a threat. Not that any of these assessments by the vice president excused his own poor judgment, Carpenter noted. But what about all of Trainor's moneyed friends who felt the same way? Especially the Chinese-American businessmen who'd donated millions in campaign funds. Were there underlying interests he'd failed to detect because of his own ambition and greed? Carpenter now wondered.

The presidential motorcade—consisting of a bulletproof limousine surrounded by Secret Service cars—moved at a fast pace up Massachusetts Avenue toward Washington National Cathedral, located on the heights above the city. Carpenter wasn't a religious man—a lifetime in politics had seen to that—but in the past he'd found peace of mind in the solitude of the old cathedral. Sometimes solutions to problems had even come to him there.

The huge Gothic structure planned by George Washington had been constructed in the shape of a cross. Another president, Woodrow Wilson, was buried in the cathedral. President Carpenter had toyed with the idea of being interred there himself when the time came.

He entered through the central portal, noting that the carved tympanum was unfinished, due in part to a dearth of craftsmen. *My problem, too*, Carpenter thought. *I am surrounded by men who lack vision and skill.*

Followed discreetly by his Secret Service detail, the president walked halfway down the main aisle and slipped into one of the padded pews. At the far east end of the cathedral was the high altar and the central figure of Christ, carved from stone taken from quarries near Jerusalem.

He fingered the gold embossing of *The Common Book of Prayer,* provided for penitents such as himself. What prayer would he say today? Was it forgiveness or guidance he sought? Would a prayer launched from below attain such speed as to burst through the Indiana limestone a hundred feet above his head? The president prayed for . . . good luck.

Shafts of light from the outside passed through stained glass windows depicting Bible stories. Which story was being played out today in America? Carpenter wondered. On whose side was God? Did God intervene in human affairs, or did he let men decide their own fate? Did God talk to men, or were the voices Jeremiah heard the product of a diseased mind? Was Jeremiah a prophet, or merely the opportunistic leader of mercenaries now pouring out of the Trojan horse that was New America? Were the noncombatants in New America dangerous fanatics or just frightened, disillusioned individuals in search of something solid in a society seemingly built on quicksand. Carpenter waited for an answer, but all he heard was the coughing of a Secret Service agent behind him.

Outside, a small crowd had gathered on Wisconsin Avenue, possibly attracted by the limo or the readily identifiable Secret Service Agents. Standing on the steps of the cathedral, President Carpenter waved to the crowd. Impulsively, he began walking toward the fence, invigorated by the brisk autumn air.

"This isn't wise, sir," the head of his Secret Service detail said. "I suggest we forgo this."

Carpenter looked at the man in the dark suit and dark glasses, thinking his choice of words was funny. *"I suggest we forgo this?"* "Why? No one knew we were coming here. I want to talk to them."

Carpenter reached out to the crowd with both hands, and their hands quickly filled his. His face lit up and there was a new bounce in his step. Two excited young women squealed in delight and hopped in place. He could have watched the bosomy one jump up and down all day. Part of their fascination with him had to do with the office, which made him a celebrity, even a superstar. He'd grown accustomed to the adoration, without letting it unnecessarily swell his ego. Still, he loved the perks, and he loved campaigning in the fall. Some of his best days in life had occurred on the first Tuesday in November.

"How'm I doin'?" he asked, repeating a phrase that had become his campaign trademark.

"Great!"

"You praying up here or what, man?"

"Mr. President, can I please have your autograph?"

"Sir, can't you do something about taxes. They're too high."

The president laughed at the last remark and had begun to explain his budget program when a voice demanded his attention.

"You sold our country down the river!"

Carpenter turned toward the thundering voice and saw a face dark with anger, eyes gleaming with the fanaticism of purpose.

"You sold our country down the river!"

When the man raised his arm as if to point, Carpenter saw the gun. Everything happened in slow motion, just as it did in his recurring nightmare. He couldn't get away. The Secret Service agents couldn't shield him in time. It was going to happen. He saw the gun barrel spit fire and felt the blow to his chest.

As he lay on the ground, everything became deathly quiet. Carpenter saw the panic in the eyes of those bending to help him, comfort him. It didn't hurt as much as it had in his nightmare, and for that he was thankful. Off to his left, agents struggled to subdue the gunman, but the sky held Carpenter's attention. It was amazingly bright and calming. Beckoning.

He thought about the negotiations. What would happen now? Would Vice President Trainor give Colonel Douglas the go-ahead? What would be the result? It didn't matter anymore to Carpenter. Maybe none of the so-called big issues had ever really mattered. Maybe he'd be judged on the every-day way he'd led his life. Maybe he'd be judged solely on the basis of how he'd treated his fellowman. *I'm about to find out.*

18

Laura stood on the deck of the house, smoking a cigarette and contemplating her surroundings, which were unique, to say the least. Elevated on pilings, the cedar cabin resembled a beach house anchored into solid ground far below the shifting sands.

Except this "beach house" was underground, positioned against one wall of a huge, oval-shaped chamber that was dark and dank, with water dripping and running from many crevices. Stalactites hung from the ceiling and stalagmites appeared to sprout from the cave floor. Quartz crystals resembling clumps of diamonds had formed in cracks in the limestone walls and floor. Other crystalline formations looked like popcorn, needles covered with frost and slightly inflated balloons. Under other circumstances, she would have been fascinated.

Covered wood stairs led downward steeply from the deck to the cave floor, approximately twenty feet below, ending in front of an imposing chain-link gate that was locked. Despite some lighting at ground level, Laura couldn't see an exit. On the other side of the cave, an underground stream fed into a small pool. A possible escape route, she noted.

Laura recalled bits and pieces of her journey that had ended in this underground Hades. After Jeremiah had abducted her from the farm in Virginia, they'd driven only a few miles on back roads to a clearing in the trees where a helicopter waited. With their arrival, the speed of its rotors increased, blasting dirt and grass into the air. It was so noisy and conspicuous that Laura couldn't understand why people in the area hadn't complained to the sheriff's department.

They abandoned the Land Rover and the helicopter rushed them across the dark countryside, flying low, hugging the ground. The noise inside had been deafening, although Jeremiah quickly donned a headset to converse with the pilot. Laura decided they were headed northwest toward the area where only a few miles separated Virginia, West Virginia, and Maryland.

Within a half hour the helicopter landed near a silver metal hangar located beside a concrete runway. In the distance, a light illuminated a one-story building with a flat roof. Laura made mental notes of all the landmarks, certain she could retrace their route. Shortly before midnight, they boarded an executive Learjet, which turned onto the runway and was quickly airborne.

As the hours ticked by, she knew their destination: *New America/South Dakota.* They landed just after 3:00 A.M. by her watch. Before getting into a Mercedes, one of the men who'd met their plane bound Laura's hands and blindfolded her. She cried out when a needle pierced the skin on her upper arm. After that, the world became fuzzy and out-of-kilter. Still, Laura calculated the car ride to have been nearly an hour.

They put her in a contraption similar to a sedan chair, and two men carried her several hundred yards, first downhill and then uphill. She heard their labored breathing, their boots scattering rocks, and she smelled pine needles.

A strong man hoisted her over his shoulder like a sack of potatoes and carried her into a cold and damp place. At the time, Laura thought it was a walk-in freezer, similar to those at meat-packing plants, and she feared being butchered.

Then the floor seemed to drop from under them, causing Laura to be sick to her stomach. Only when they stopped and she heard doors whoosh open, did Laura realize it was an elevator. The strong man carried her up what she now knew to be the stairs leading to the deck. Once inside the cabin, they'd forced her to take a pill and she'd slept until an hour ago, although she had no idea of the time of day, and wasn't entirely certain of the day of the week. They'd taken her watch with its calendar function.

Laura looked at her shift and tights, suddenly realizing they'd changed her clothes. Why? She pulled up the dress and reached a hand inside the tights, making sure she had on panties. She reached between her legs, but couldn't feel evidence of a discharge.

As Jeremiah walked out of the house to join her on the deck, Laura flicked the cigarette over the railing. She'd never been a steady smoker, but in recent weeks it had become a nervous habit.

"Not much of an environmentalist, are you?" The terrorist uncharacteristically wore jeans and a baby blue windbreaker over a checkered flannel shirt.

Laura's eyes narrowed in abject hatred. "Every time I get stalked, raped, and kidnapped, I forget all about my social responsibilities."

Jeremiah chuckled. "Just remember that 'a prudent wife is from the Lord.'"

"What?"

"Proverbs nineteen, verse fourteen. You are given to me by the Lord and ye best be prudent."

"Fuck you."

Jeremiah shrugged. "It's the Lord's word, Laura."

"I'm not your goddamned, fuckin' wife!"

"Oh, you are, in God's eyes and mine. Furthermore, you need to be more dutiful, Laura. As the Good Book says, 'Wives, submit yourselves unto your own husbands, as unto the Lord.' Ephesians five, verse twenty-two."

"Fuck you and fuck the Lord, too."

"That's blasphemy," Jeremiah said, without rancor.

"You're just another hypocrite who's given religion a bad name," Laura said. "Using God's word to further your own interests or as a justification for killing someone."

"I'm the real Prophet, Laura."

"In that case, I'll choose not to believe in God."

"Your soul is in danger."

"My soul's fine. You believe in the Golden Rule?"

"Of course."

"In that case, when they put you in prison, figure on someone fucking you, pretty boy."

Laura smirked as she lit up another Salem, fully intending to eventually throw the butt onto the cave floor.

Jeremiah reached over and snatched the cigarette from her mouth. "You're pregnant. The child doesn't need to breathe nicotine and carbon monoxide."

"Fuck the little bastard!" It wasn't that she didn't have a wider vocabulary; it just seemed the most appropriate response, given the circumstances.

"How can you talk about our son that way, Laura?"

She stared daggers at him but then looked away, her anger melting into despair. Tears formed in her eyes. Steve was dead, and she was at the mercy of his killer, her rapist and captor.

Jeremiah leaned on the railing of the deck, and Laura calculated her chances of rushing him and pushing him to his death. In her mind's eye, she envisioned him falling to the cave floor where his head split open like a ripe melon, his spongy red brains full of black seeds. While she contemplated this fantasy, Jeremiah turned to face her and she concluded her plan was not feasible. Despite the cast on his left arm, he was sinewy and quick, like a cat. And strong, she knew, from past experiences.

"Forget about trying to escape," he said, as if reading her mind. "This underground cave system is hundreds of feet below the surface. There are no stairs leading above ground, only elevators, and they're locked and guarded. There are hundreds of miles of passageways and dozens of rooms down here, many of them unexplored. It would be easy to get lost, and your body might never be found."

Laura froze, remembering the packet of photos someone had mailed anonymously to her, showing New America's internment camps. Evidence existed that people regularly disappeared from New America. Now Laura had an idea about where to find their bodies.

"You've got to start taking better care of yourself, Laura, and we need to work on our communications. How are we going to get to know each other if you can only respond in two-word sentences."

"Fuck you!"

"You're going to have our child."

"Don't bet on it. I'll find a coat hanger lying around some day and be rid of this cancerous growth inside me."

She smiled, seeing the impact her words had on him; her many more words than two. He seemed shocked and she rushed to maintain her advantage.

"And when you get rid of the coat hangers, I'll search for another tool. A knife, spoon, fork. A splinter off the floor. I'll let my fingernails grow until they're long enough!" She searched desperately for the words necessary to form other images that threatened his seed. "I'll jump off this deck! Yes, that's what I'll do." Laura put her foot on one of the lower boards, as if preparing to leap over the railing to her death on the stone floor below—or, at least, make the gesture. She really didn't want to die.

Jeremiah restrained her. He had a sour, disappointed look on his face. "Then someone will watch you day and night. I won't let you murder our son." Suddenly, he pleaded: "I chose you! *Years ago when I first saw you whirling on a dance floor.* A vision of beauty. Why won't you accept me? Steve is dead!"

She slapped his face, although he didn't wince. "I don't believe you!"

"You saw me shoot him! You held him in your arms as blood poured from the hole in his head!"

Her hands balled into fists she shrieked, "I don't believe you! I don't believe you!"

"All right. Maybe you'll believe news reports by your own network. The United Broadcasting Corporation, Julie Burton reporting." He looked nostalgic. "She's really not as good as you were, Laura."

Her mouth hung open, as she stepped closer to him. "What do you mean?"

"Come inside, Laura. I have something to show you."

While she sat compliantly on a sofa, Jeremiah walked to

an entertainment center and placed a tape inside a VCR atop a Sony television set. He pressed several buttons and stepped aside, looking first at her and then at the TV screen.

"This is Julie Burton reporting the midday news on UBC," Laura's replacement said. "There are unconfirmed reports of the death of Steve Wallace, a former FBI agent well-known across the country for his efforts several years ago to apprehend the Prophet, Jeremiah. For further details, we go now to Roy Webster, reporting live from Wallace's farm near Middleburg, Virginia."

Webster, an old friend of hers, stood near their front gate. The cameraman framed Webster and then zoomed over his shoulder to bring the farmhouse on the hill into view.

"Julie, we're told there was a deadly assault here last night," Webster announced. "As you can see, law-enforcement officials are scouring the grounds of this estate, where Wallace lived with his wife, former UBC newscaster, Laura Delaney. Here with us now is a spokesman for the FBI, Matt Henley. Mr. Henley, can you tell us what happened?"

The FBI agent, who Laura remembered vaguely as a member of Steve's counterterrorism squad, said, "We're not certain. Ordinarily, we might speculate it was a robbery gone bad, except, as you know, Roy, many people viewed this ranch as a shrine of sorts, and it was constantly being invaded."

"Has anyone been killed?"

"Yes, we've found five bodies. Four males and a female."

"Were they found inside the house?"

"No, sir. Three bodies, those of security guards, were discovered at various locations on the property. The bodies of a male and a female were found near the front porch of the house."

Roy clenched his jaws and Laura teared up, knowing how much her friend hated to ask the next question. "Are those the bodies of Steve Wallace and Laura Delaney?"

"The dead woman definitely is not Laura Delaney," Henley replied.

"And the man?"

Henley hesitated. "I knew Steve Wallace very well, but I can't confirm his death at this time, until the investigation is completed and the dead man's next-of-kin are notified."

Webster looked into the camera for his wrap-up. "Julie, confidential sources tell us that the dead man is Steve Wallace, and that Laura Delaney is missing. That's all we know right now."

Jeremiah turned off the VCR. "That was taped a few hours ago while you were sleeping, Laura." He looked solemn, but then broke out in laughter. "The husband is dead; the husband is dead. Long live the husband!"

"You sick sonofabitch!" Laura snarled, before being overcome by grief. She slumped on the sofa, thinking of Steve lying dead in a morgue, in an ice-cold vault like this cave. She struggled instead to remember him as he was: tall, handsome, athletic, strong, confident.

It wasn't his physical features or courage that had endeared him to Laura, however. She'd loved his humor and sensitivity best. They had easily interchanged the role of straight man and comic. He'd arrived at the farm for a date several years ago with an expensive bottle of wine, and she had commented on his ability to make such extravagant purchases on a G-man's salary. He'd cracked her up with his deadpan remark that his liquor store had financing for steady customers.

Several times, he'd worried about what to do with his life after the FBI years, even though she'd explained to him how much money she had in the bank. He feared being bored. That had opened the way for her to chide him affectionately. "Oh, I see! All the money and sex one man could possibly handle, and it's not enough for you!"

He'd responded by jumping her bones on the living room sofa, where they had made love, oblivious to the world around them. At that time they hadn't worried about who might be listening, or watching.

Steve was tolerant, understanding. When he'd learned about the rape, he could have walked away. She knew many men couldn't handle that, let alone a pregnancy resulting from a rape. Especially when the two of them had tried so long and unsuccessfully to conceive a child.

The fond memories caused her to smile and laugh softly. Her change of demeanor startled Jeremiah, who smiled and said, "That's it, Laura. Steve's gone! Laugh it off. Better days are ahead, I promise you."

Laura laughed at Jeremiah, who didn't understand at all. Then the despair returned as she thought about how they'd almost made it to Europe, putting an ocean between them and the madness developing in America—their America, not Jeremiah's *New America.*

She and Steve would have been happy there, Laura knew. Who wouldn't have been happy with him. He was the sun, the moon, and the stars—her universe. At least she'd known true love in her life, which would always be a comfort. Jeremiah could never take that away.

"Exciting days, in fact," Jeremiah babbled. "Now that Steve's out of the picture, I can focus on the important things." Jeremiah's voice held a begrudging admiration. "I actually was more afraid of Steve than the U.S. Army." Jeremiah looked at the cast on his arm. "Only the direct intervention of God could have allowed me to escape that murderous assault in Pierre."

"God, my ass! You were just lucky! That kind of luck won't last forever."

Jeremiah smirked. "Well, God's luck continues to hold. President Trainor wants to negotiate with me in Minneapolis."

"President Trainor?"

"Oh, more news, Laura. President Carpenter was shot to death. Poor fellow. He was at the right place at the wrong time."

"Did you have him killed?"

Jeremiah feigned indignation. "I'm not an assassin like Steve was. I'm a prophet king. Wise and magnanimous. Let me give you an example, Laura. I'm going to order my men out of the Lake Anna nuclear plant."

"What's the real reason?" Even in her grief, Laura was curious.

Jeremiah's eyes narrowed. "They've developed an excellent plan to retake the plant."

"How did you find out?"

"God told me."

"Bullshit."

"No shit. I'll appear conciliatory and peace loving, and the American people will demand that the negotiations go forward—that I be given a fair hearing."

"Anyone would be crazy to negotiate with you."

"There're always my bombers to compel them to sit across the table from me."

Laura couldn't resist the urge to argue with him, even under the present circumstances, when her life's dreams had been dashed and she was a prisoner in a cave. "And what would be left for you to rule, if you initiate a nuclear holocaust?"

Jeremiah staggered backward several steps and put his good hand over his heart, as he pretended to be shocked. "My God, Laura, I hadn't thought of that!" He doubled over in laughter.

"You are fuckin' crazy!"

"There's not going to be a nuclear holocaust, Laura," Jeremiah said, wiping tears from his eyes. "Probably not, anyway." He frowned, calculating. "Well, maybe there's a chance, but I plan to stop short of a holocaust, if possible. I'll negotiate in good faith in Minneapolis, sorta, if I get what I want. If not, I'll make a few moves that'll send them scurrying back to the bargaining table." He held out both arms and smiled broadly. "In the end, we'll win, Laura. You and I together, forever, in New America!"

"Fuck you!" *It can't happen,* Laura thought. *Surely President Trainor and his military advisors had a plan to outsmart Jeremiah. To kill him. At least capture him and put him on trial, so the nation could recognize him as a demented egomaniac. Someone with a death wish, who didn't mind killing millions of Americans in the process.*

Jeremiah turned and walked toward the door to the deck, speaking over his shoulder to her, "Well, gotta go. It's a busy time of year in my business. You take care of yourself, Laura. Get a lot of rest. The guards will look after you. Don't waste your time planning to escape. It's hopeless."

*   *   *

After he'd left, Laura considered his warning. Was it hopeless? The cave system undoubtedly was beneath the Black Hills. But what good was that knowledge? Laura couldn't imagine getting out of this hellhole without help.

As Jeremiah had promised, a guard appeared to shadow her every movement as Laura wandered about the cabin, seeking an escape route. On the second level were three bedrooms. Downstairs was a kitchen, den, and great room. All the windows and doors on both levels were locked and barred, and the log walls were at least a foot thick. She looked under the many rugs covering the wood floors, but couldn't find a trapdoor.

The lower-level great room, with its cathedral ceiling and stone fireplace taking up an entire wall, was the cabin's focal point. Laura wondered if she might crawl up the chimney, out onto the roof.

"You plan on following me into the bathroom?" she asked the guard, a muscular giant who showed off his physique by wearing a black T-shirt two sizes too small. He probably had carried her into the cave and up the stairs to the house.

"Those are my orders," he replied.

"What's your name?"

"Chuck."

Laura sat on the sofa in front of the fireplace, trying to think of a way to get out of the house and the cave. But her mind drifted back to thoughts of Steve.

Would she ever see him again? Was there an afterlife? A God? Laura didn't know. She hoped so, but she couldn't conceive of a God of the universe, or even the universe. All this arguing and killing over the *correct religion* was insane. It shouldn't be necessary to profess a "faith" or go to a particular church. It should be enough just to live by the Golden Rule. Her version, not Jeremiah's. Would God really punish her for lacking a fanatic's faith? Wouldn't the real God understand and welcome her and Steve home?

Later, as Laura sat on the sofa near the fireplace, picking at a pasta dish prepared by Chuck, she heard the front door open and high heels clicking across the floor. A woman of medium height and build, with dark hair cut short and streaked purple, entered the room. She wore a baggy, off-white sweater, tight, black leather pants, and high-heeled, black boots.

"Hi, I'm Katrina Dorfler," she said, with a noticeable foreign accent.

Laura stood, stunned. "Walter Dorfler's daughter?"

"Yes," she answered. While appraising Laura, she said to the guard, "Chuck, serve us some coffee, will you?"

Laura also evaluated Katrina, who sat on an easy chair. The German woman was pretty, in a rough way, although she wore too much makeup. She had an interesting face, characterized by a quizzical expression.

"You knew my father?" Katrina asked.

"Yes, I was talking to him in his hotel room in Quebec when he took . . ." Laura let her voice trail off.

"The cyanide pill," Katrina said, completing the statement.

"I had no idea he'd do that," Laura said, helplessly, sitting down.

Katrina shrugged, sadly, took out a pack of Marlboros and offered one to Laura. "You smoke?"

"Sometimes," Laura admitted, "but I've got my own."

Katrina lit up. "I'm gonna quit pretty soon."

"Me, too, whenever it looks like I might live a long life."

Katrina snorted smoke into the air. "Nothing will happen to you. Jeremiah wouldn't allow it. You are his goddess."

"Where'd you come from?" Laura asked, intrigued. Maybe Katrina would provide the information or means necessary for her to escape.

"From the outside. Don't ask any more questions about that. I couldn't help you get out of here even if I wanted you gone, which I do."

From her research for the book she and Steve had written about Jeremiah, Laura had learned much about Katrina. She and Trent Dillman had been teenage lovers in Germany, before Katrina's father took over the instruction of Jeremiah, programming him to become America's most famous terrorist. Jeremiah had rejected Katrina in favor of their younger first cousin, Emma Dietze, who eventually became an international tennis star and later was killed in Florida by a street mugger. Katrina had become active in right-wing politics in Bavaria, and there were rumors that the CIA had interrogated her there with an intravenous truth serum.

Laura first learned Katrina was in New America after viewing the tape Steve had made of the unsuccessful effort to assassinate Jeremiah. Had Steve told Katrina about the rape? The pregnancy? Should she fear that a jealous Katrina would have her killed? Was that the reason for her visit?

"I don't want to be here," Laura declared, in an attempt to set Katrina's mind at ease.

"And I don't want you here!" Katrina angrily swung her arm, accidentally knocking a vase off an end table. Chuck heard the crash, rushed into the room and asked what had happened. They both remained silent as the guard picked up pieces of broken vase and took them to the kitchen.

"Help me escape," Laura whispered, just before Chuck returned with a coffee service.

Katrina poured for both of them as she spoke to the guard. "Chuck, why don't you go out on the deck, so us girls can talk in private. I promise not to break anything else."

They both watched Chuck go out onto the deck, although he kept watch on them through a glass porthole in the door.

"I'd help you escape if I could," Katrina said, "but Jeremiah's already thought of that. He thinks of everything. He'd catch you or come after you again. As for me?" She shrugged, indicating Laura could imagine the punishment.

"If I get away, he'll never find me again. I can promise you that!"

Katrina shook her head. "No, you can't promise me that. Jeremiah has eyes and ears everywhere, believe me. Even your government hasn't figured that out yet. Remember Maria? That's how close he can get to you."

Maria. The name incensed Laura. At least Steve had paid her back. In spades.

"Did you know about him and Maria?" Laura asked.

Katrina sipped her coffee and returned the cup to the saucer. "I know about all of them. He has many women, no matter what he tells you. Some of them would surprise you. He can be faithful for only a short time. Maybe you're the exception, maybe not."

"Why do you stay with him?"

Katrina shrugged. "He was my first love long before this. Long before he and my father made their plans."

Laura understood first love. It often developed into a myth that little resembled reality, especially with the passage of time. But Katrina had been a sidelines observer for many years. She, of all people, knew what Jeremiah had become. Was her love that blind?

"Besides, my father always encouraged our relationship," Katrina continued.

"Was he unhappy when Jeremiah began his affair with Emma Dietze?" Laura asked, which indeed is what Walter had implied shortly before he killed himself. In fact, Walter said he'd had to "do something" about that relationship. Laura had never understood exactly what the old man had meant.

"My father did not approve of their romance," Katrina said, "and he always told me that eventually Jeremiah and I would be together. That it was fated. Maybe I believed him. Maybe that's why I could never let go. Now, I can't go."

Laura shook her head incomprehensibly. A father promoting romance between his daughter and nephew. Was it just another control measure?

"Jeremiah liked being in Emma's limelight. She became world famous, like he wanted to be. She was rich and independent, like he wanted to be."

Laura remembered Emma, the wonderfully athletic Teutonic beauty who had ruled the professional tennis world for a decade, and probably would have continued to do so for several more years, had she not been killed.

"Jeremiah is attracted to fame and wealth, you see," Katrina continued. "It's a fire and he's a moth. That's why he chose you, I think. That and the fact that you don't want him, which is something he can't comprehend or tolerate."

Laura was stunned. Walter also had spoken of Jeremiah's obsession with certain women, implying it was his Achilles' heel. She knew Jeremiah had selected her originally to get his twisted message across to the public. But she'd never really understood the obsession beyond that. Until now.

"Was Emma in love with Jeremiah?"

Katrina took her coffee cup and walked near the fireplace, where several logs had been reduced to charcoal. She lit up another cigarette. "I knew Emma all my life, since we were little girls. We were very close. In the beginning, it was just an infatuation, I think, on both their parts; but Emma also had problems with her fame. Too many people wanting to use her. I don't know if she loved Jeremiah, but she saw him as, how would you say, a buffer against the world. Just before she was killed, Emma told me she was thinking of marrying Jeremiah. Wanted to know if she and I could still be friends." Katrina shrugged. "What could I say? Her mistake was telling my father."

Laura couldn't fathom the reason for this conversation although she instinctively knew it was important. "Is there something else I should know about Emma's death?"

Katrina waved her cigarette through the air, its lighted end inscribing a jagged figure that lingered on Laura's retinas for several seconds. "We can't get into that now."

But they might later? Laura sensed that Katrina had an agenda, but wouldn't be rushed into revealing it, either out of wariness or because the timing wasn't right.

"Make certain you understand, Katrina, that I don't want Jeremiah," Laura said, feeling suddenly sick to her stomach. "He raped me and now I'm pregnant. I don't want the baby either."

Laura began to weep. Katrina snubbed out her cigarette in an ashtray, sat on the sofa and put her arm around Laura. "Your husband told me about the rape."

"Did you believe him?" Laura asked.

"Yes, I just didn't know about the baby."

Laura's head sank into Katrina's shoulder and she began to sob uncontrollably. "Steve's dead, you know."

Katrina squeezed Laura's arm. "Maybe."

Laura jerked back, so she could look Katrina in the eyes.

"What? You think Steve might be alive!" Laura could barely breathe. "What do you know?"

"I don't know anything for certain, but think about the tape recording you saw. Did you see his body?" Katrina looked at the door leading to the deck. "This is just between you and me. I don't want to give you false hope, but the FBI might just have *said* your husband is dead."

Suddenly Laura had hope! She so wanted to believe that Steve was alive.

"I will try to find out for you," Katrina promised.

Laura's fears reemerged. "What does Jeremiah believe?"

Katrina shrugged.

Was Jeremiah trying to deceive her, knowing all along that Steve wasn't dead? Was he now on his way to kill Steve, who could be lying wounded in a hospital bed? Could he have just been wounded? Laura despaired as the memory came back: the bleeding head wound, the shot fired into his chest that had caused Steve's body to literally bounce on the ground. She fought against an awful pessimism that threatened her hope.

"Will you come again?" Laura asked, thinking that would give her another chance to work on Katrina.

Katrina looked at Laura analytically, as if making up her mind. "Yes, I think so. I didn't know when I first came here." She smoothed Laura's hair. "You are so beautiful, I was threatened, but now I see that you are a warm and caring person. This is not your fault, what has happened."

Laura begged, "Please help me get out of here. I don't want to be here when he comes back. You know what he's going to do to me, don't you?"

Katrina nodded, slowly and sadly.

19

Steve listened to the footsteps in the hallway and could tell who it was by the way he walked.

The sailor stationed outside came to attention and saluted as the attorney general entered the private room at Bethesda Naval Medical Center.

"How are you today, Steve?" Thompson asked, placing his hands on the bed's guardrail.

Steve, his head bandaged, lay in bed, watching television. "Peachy. I've had great success on *The Price Is Right.* If I'd been there, I'd've won a Honda Accord."

"That's not bad."

Compared to being dead, Steve thought. The first bullet Jeremiah had fired from his hidden gun had cut a groove through his hairline, fractured his skull, and knocked him unconscious. The second bullet, fired into his Kevlar bulletproof vest, broke two ribs and collapsed his right lung.

He would have died without the quick action of Seth Schuyler, the farm manager who lived with his wife above the barn. The old man heard the shots and a car horn. He ran to the front of the house and gave Steve mouth-to-mouth resuscitation and CPR until the ambulance arrived.

Steve knew Jeremiah and/or Maria had quietly killed the other three security guards. Ordinarily, he didn't celebrate the death of a human being, even the many vicious criminals he'd encountered in his career as an FBI agent, but he'd kill Maria Inglesias a dozen times more, if possible.

Schuyler's wife had called an FBI number Steve had given them in case of such an emergency. As a result, Thompson got involved and Steve was taken to Bethesda and admitted five days ago as a John Doe. Fortunately for him, military personnel were accustomed to keeping secrets.

"Have you located Laura yet?" Steve repeated the question he'd asked every day when Peter came to visit. Like the rest of the nation, he should be mourning the death of Pres. Bob Carpenter, but Steve could only grieve for Laura.

"No. We assume he took her back to New America, although we're not hearing much from our sources there. The state police have cracked down, arresting thousands of suspected spies and restricting travel into and out of the area. All telephone calls are being monitored."

"But you're getting some information?"

Thompson smiled tightly. "We've heard from Hoffman."

"He's alive?"

"Yes."

"And Ralph Duncan?"

Thompson shook his head. "He apparently didn't make it. I don't know the details."

Steve pushed a button and the top half of the bed moved him to a sitting position. He swung his legs over the side and stood, his bare feet chilled by the cold tile. He'd done this exercise several times over the past two days, and each time it generated a blinding headache and a searing pain in his side.

"I don't think you're supposed to be up."

"No, and what happened to Laura wasn't supposed to happen," Steve said. "Not in a sane world."

He begrudged his wounds; even felt ashamed that he was lying in a bed, being cared for and served his meals, while that madman held Laura captive.

"I'll find her," he said, "and this time he won't get away."

"You could rest a few more days."

"Arrange for me to meet Hoffman," Steve said, in a tone that didn't allow argument. "Tomorrow."

Thompson examined his manicured nails for several seconds and then nodded, giving Steve a strange, fatherly look. "All right. I'll take care of everything."

"I'll need some clean clothes. And a hat." To cover his partially shaved head and the bandage covering the ugly scalp wound, which had bled profusely and probably scared Laura half to death.

"Okay."

"I hear from the television news you'll be going to Minneapolis soon."

"We shouldn't be negotiating with Jeremiah," Thompson said, "but if it's going to happen anyway, I should be there."

From his hospital bed, Steve had seen Peter on television, criticizing the new president, Richard Trainor, for deciding to go ahead with the negotiations and allowing Jeremiah to pick the site. The death of President Carpenter had strengthened the nation's resolve not to negotiate or compromise with Jeremiah, who the people initially thought might be behind the assassination. Then Julie Burton at UBC revealed that Carpenter's assassin was a member of the American Patriots—the ultraconservative organization that supported Thompson. Public opinion swung again, this time in favor of the talks.

"He'll use the nuclear weapons if the government doesn't find a way to satisfy his demands," Steve said.

"Perhaps," Thompson replied, "but at some point, we'll have to call that bluff or completely surrender. Better to bite the bullet now than allow him to strengthen his position."

Steve appreciated all points of view—Peter's, the administration's, the public's. Democracy's strength and weakness was the obligation to consider all points of view, none of which might be absolutely right or wrong. That's why compromises occurred so often in politics and government. But people like Peter would have to deal with that dilemma.

"Will the government try to kill him in Minneapolis?" Steve asked.

Thompson stared at him—that icy, cool stare Steve had seen before, which gave no indication of the attorney general's true thoughts. "There are no such plans that I know of."

Steve understood. The U.S. government had met officially or unofficially many times with other dictators and terrorists, from Hitler to Saddam Hussein. Certain rules applied, the foremost being that neither party would attempt to kill the other. Otherwise adversaries would never talk, and all problems would be solved on the battlefield, which was unacceptable in the nuclear age.

Steve had decided against another attempt on Jeremiah's life at the negotiations. "Don't worry about me doing something to upset the apple cart," he assured Peter. "I know there's much more at stake here than my personal situation."

"Keep in touch," Thompson proposed. "We might be of use to each other."

Steve flew via military jet into Ellsworth Air Force Base, arriving in time to witness the installation of a new commander, a ceremony that included an air force band playing a spirited rendition of "Stars and Stripes Forever." This island of federalism within the heart of New America had been extensively reinforced after Jeremiah's troops had briefly occupied it.

MPs escorted Steve to a room in billeting. After they left, the door to an adjoining room opened and Hans Dietrich Hoffman walked in. They embraced awkwardly and sat on opposite sides of a small circular table located at the foot of the bed.

"What happened in Pierre?" Steve asked.

"I had a clear shot at him," the German explained, "but at the last minute he moved slightly. At the time, I didn't even know I'd wounded him."

"And Duncan?"

"One of our spies on the hillside saw the whole thing through binoculars. The cart explosion killed several of Jeremiah's bodyguards, but a police sniper shot Duncan as he attempted to flee."

Steve gritted his teeth. They'd all missed. Despite their

best efforts, Jeremiah had suffered only a superficial gun-shot wound to the arm, and a good man was dead. The best, in fact.

"Maybe we'll get another chance," Steve said.

Hoffman shook his head. "My superiors were very clear about that. I'm on ice for the duration. They're going to fly me back to Germany in a few days. After that, I'm supposed to play the role of a freelance journalist investigating Islamic terrorism in northern Africa." He gave Steve a sad smile. "There's a good chance you'll never see me again."

Steve popped two ibuprofen tablets into his mouth and washed them down with orange juice he'd purchased from a vending machine. "If I wanted to find Laura, where would I look first?"

Hoffman thought for only a few seconds. "The Black Hills. The same area where we hunted him before. It's still the best hiding spot in South Dakota."

"How would we find her?" Steve asked.

"She's pregnant. She'd eventually have to see a doctor or go to a hospital. Of course, Jeremiah could bring the doctor to her."

"There's only one hospital in Rapid City, I think. It makes sense to get a list of gynecologists and obstetricians. Try to figure out some way to narrow that list to a likely prospect. It'd have to be someone Jeremiah trusted. I wish you could help."

Hoffman shrugged. "They didn't say I couldn't visit the tourist sites in Rapid City."

Until the current national crisis was resolved, no tourists would be visiting the Badlands, Black Hills, Wind Cave, and Mount Rushmore. Strangers checking into a local hotel would stick out like a sore thumb.

Hoffman made several telephone calls and found them a bedroom in a mobile home on the city's east side. They slipped off the air base in the back of a bread truck. The fifth-column supporters living in the trailer park were a man-and-wife team working as janitors. The woman helped them with disguises, although with the onset of cold weather in the Great Plains the most effective means of hiding their features were bulky winter coats with high col-lars or hoods. Ski masks wouldn't even arouse suspicions. Just to be safe, Steve let his beard grow and knew a dark stubble would soon cover his face. Hoffman ditched his glasses and gum, and let the woman dye his hair a dark brown.

"Photographs of both of you are posted in many locations," the woman reminded them.

Steve knew he and Hoffman were public enemies number one and two, after having been identified as the ones who had twice tried to kill the Prophet.

The next day they rode a mass transit bus into the downtown area and began putting their plan into motion.

As they traveled through town, Steve looked out the window at the people on the streets, concluding that life seemed relatively normal in Rapid City, save the presence of many policemen. What had he expected? That the residents calling themselves New Americans would suddenly renounce their allegiance in this time of crisis and return home? That wasn't going to happen. When people made such an important lifestyle decision, it was difficult to reverse, for economic reasons and matters of pride. Frankly, his experiences—especially at the public executions—had convinced him that most of them were true believers; only a few were trapped by the rumblings of war.

Rapid City was wrapped around a large hill extending from Rapid Creek on the north to the southern heights, which led to Mount Rushmore. The hill also had become a cultural divide, Steve had been told by their trailer park colleagues. On the east side were the majority of businesses and the downtown area, as well as the modest homes and trailer parks housing many who worked in the tourist industry.

On the west side of the hill were the upscale homes of those who'd done better economically—the owners of hotels, restaurants, and businesses, including the many gift and trinket shops that predominated in the area. Many of these shops sold Black Hills gold, a malleable material combined with copper and silver, and shaped into rings, bracelets, and charms.

Downtown near the city administration building, Steve and Hoffman switched buses and traveled south on Mount Rushmore Road, getting off at the southern edge of the city, where they walked six blocks east to a regional hospital complex.

As Steve approached the desk in the Emergency Room, Hoffman took a seat in the waiting room. While many of the promises Jeremiah had made to his followers about New America hadn't been implemented, they were entitled to free health care, if they presented an identity card—such as the forgery Steve possessed—indicating they observed the Social Contract, as set forth in chapter 2:6–26 of *The Book of Second Jeremiah,* and worked a "socially necessary" job.

"What's the problem?" a doctor asked, coming into the examination room. Steve read her identification badge: May Liang. She looked to be in her early thirties.

Steve gingerly removed a knit cap, revealing his head bandage. "I'd like you to take a look at this and some other wounds to make certain they aren't becoming infected."

"How'd this happen?" she asked, removing the bandage. Dr. Liang was delicately pretty, he thought, and very businesslike.

"Gunshot and shrapnel wounds," Steve replied honestly, before telling the necessary lie. "I'm a member of the National Guard, and I was wounded in a recent battle." Maybe she wouldn't even think of him as a potential assassin and remember the wanted posters.

"What are your other wounds?"

"Broken ribs."

"Who treated you?"

"A corpsman."

The doctor looked surprised. "He or she did a good job. Did they administer antibiotics?"

"Yes, but I used them up."

"And the ribs, they still hurt? I doubt X rays were taken. We should do that."

Steve was about to object, but he didn't want to arouse

her suspicions; not before he got to the real reason for his visit. Besides, a checkup might not be a bad idea. He needed to stay healthy, for Laura's sake.

"Someone will be along shortly to take you to the lab."

The whole process took an hour-and-a-half before Dr. Liang returned.

"The broken ribs seem to be healing nicely," Dr. Liang said, looking at the X rays. "Same for the head and shrapnel wounds, but to be safe I'll write you a prescription for an antibiotic." He could tell she was about to leave. "Anything else?"

"Yes, my wife is pregnant. Can you recommend an obstetrician?"

"There are several in the area. I'll have the nurse give you a list."

Somehow, he had to narrow down that list. "How can we find out something about their reputations? How they handle these things. There are differences in their approaches to childbirth, aren't there?" He was fishing desperately.

"They're all competent physicians," Dr. Liang replied, somewhat testily. "Your wife should visit several doctors and select the one she's most comfortable with."

At least he'd get the list. But he decided on a more risky gambit, using Katrina Dorfler's secret about her pregnancy. "Once, on state television, I saw Katrina Dorfler, Walter's daughter, with a doctor I think is an obstetrician. Do you know him?"

"No," Dr. Liang replied, and then hesitated. "Well, there is a Dr. Connolly, who's active in political affairs. You probably saw him with Jeremiah. Maybe Katrina was with them. I don't know."

Steve remained silent, thinking enough had been said.

"Come back if you need to," Dr. Liang concluded. "And don't worry. You'll recover and your wife will have her baby, and you can make a new life here. The truth is, we don't really need an army. We don't need to fight them. We have an idea about a better way to live. The force of the idea will eventually prevail. Otherwise, it's not worth anything."

Having dispensed that wisdom along with the medication, Dr. Liang disappeared, leaving Steve to wonder how many other New Americans thought like her, especially about the army.

They located Connolly's office downtown on Saint Joseph's Street. Hoffman waited outside while Steve entered the office and approached the receptionist's desk.

"I'd like to make an appointment next week for my wife," he said, handing over his identity card in the name of Larry Stevens.

While the receptionist checked her appointment book, Steve took a card from a plastic holder. Dr. Connolly's business card included a small photograph of him. Connolly might or might not be Katrina's doctor, but he was another link to Jeremiah.

"Hanging around out here makes me nervous," Hoffman said, as Steve came out onto the street. Two state policemen sat in a jeep parked at a nearby intersection, although the streets were nearly deserted.

Steve spotted a restaurant on the next block. "If we can get a seat there by the window, we can see this office."

"What if he goes out the alley door?"

Steve disparaged the alternative. "You want to stand in the alley? Think we'd be less conspicuous there?"

The old-fashioned restaurant advertised "home cooking," and Steve was hungry, having skipped breakfast. At 1:15 P.M., several booths near the large picture window were vacant. The maroon vinyl covering on the bench seats was cracked and ripped in several places, revealing an off-white ticking.

A bored waitress handed them a menu, obviously typed by a poor speller. Steve decided on the "meet loaf."

The food arrived at the same time Steve saw a man in a suit leave the clinic. From this distance, he couldn't tell if it was Dr. Connolly. On the other hand, he hadn't seen any other men in the office.

"Enjoy our food," Steve said to Hoffman. "I'll try not to be gone long."

Outside, Steve put up his coat's hood, crossed the street, and fell in behind the man wearing a bulky gray overcoat and fedora. He followed him around a corner and into an old hotel.

The plain brick exterior didn't do justice to the lobby, a large room with plush carpeting, comfortable furniture, and rich woodwork. A large, cut glass chandelier hung level with an open mezzanine located above the registration desk.

As the man he'd been following waited to be seated in the restaurant, Steve pretended to read brochures about local attractions. The man turned and Steve saw the face of the man on the business card, Dr. Connolly.

Steve waited a few minutes and then walked through the sparsely populated dining room to a secluded booth in the back, where the man sat spooning his soup.

"Dr. Connolly?"

"Yes?" the physician answered, quizzically. He had a round face, bushy eyebrows, and was bald except for a closely cut semicircle of hair just above his ears. Probably in his sixties, Steve calculated. "I was in the lobby when you came in, and I thought I recognized you." Steve held out the business card. "I just stopped by your office to make an appointment for my wife. She'll be coming out next week from Sioux Falls. I was recently with the army at the battle of Fort Riley." He hoped the doctor would bite on something, otherwise he'd have to leave.

"Really, Mr . . . ?"

"Stevens. Larry. Do you mind if I join you for a few minutes?"

"No, go right ahead," Connolly said, pointing his spoon at the empty seat across from him. "I don't have much time, however. Got a full house back at the clinic. If my practice is any indication, the population hereabouts may double soon. Is this your wife's first child?"

"Yes," Steve replied, thinking of Laura.

"Well, that's always the worst, of course, but she'll do fine. I tell all my patients that women have been doing this successfully since long before there were doctors. I look forward to meeting her. What's her name?"

"Lynn." It was Laura's middle name; the name he'd used to make the appointment.

"Well, you were lucky to survive the battle, weren't you, son?"

"Certainly was," Steve replied. He could only hope Connolly wasn't in the habit of memorizing the faces on wanted posters.

The doctor shook his head. "Terrible business, this civil war. But as Jeremiah asks, why won't they just let us go our own way?" He pointed his salad fork at Steve. "We have to have independence, not some commonwealth status. If we're subject to their laws, how could we ever really change things? Create a new economy, draft a new constitution, establish our own form of government, mete out our own form of justice."

Steve ached to ask how it was a physician could condone the violence and torture that went on in New America. But did Connolly and other private citizens know the full extent of that?

"The politicians in Washington and the news media are hysterical about Jeremiah threatening to use nuclear weapons." Dr. Connolly smiled and shook his head again. "Would they let us go if we threatened them with anything less?" He then answered his own question. "Absolutely not!"

"I agree with you, sir," Steve replied, privately amazed that a well-educated man could so blithely justify New America using any means to achieve its goals.

"Larry, I've learned a thing or two in my life," Connolly continued. "You can only get some people's attention by whacking them between the eyes with a two-by-four. You remember several years back, when Jeremiah killed those people who were symbols of what's wrong with America? The pedophile, the teenage rapists, the criminals, stockbrokers, lobbyists, and politicians. Hell, they needed killing. Some people do, you know. Like it says in *Second Jeremiah*, evil people don't have a right to life. By killing those evil folks, Jeremiah compelled people to start thinking about a New America. That's right. That's how he got people's attention. That's when I started listening to him."

There were many innocent victims among the thousands Jeremiah had killed during the first phase of his so-called crusade, Steve thought. *And thousands more now had been forced from their homes, as war looms on the horizon. What about their rights? Where would it stop? Apparently the good doctor wouldn't lose any sleep over millions of his fellow humans dying in a nuclear holocaust. God forbid he'd bring Laura's child into the world.*

"I bet you carry around this book," Connolly said, taking a compact copy of *Second Jeremiah* from his coat pocket. Steve, as prepared as a Boy Scout, did the same.

"Turn right here to the last chapter. Verse three: 'Ye who oppose my people should read the Old Testament, for I will send afflictions on you as I did on Pharaoh, except yours will be greater by far, causing much death and destruction and a pox on future generations.' Guess the politicians in Washington didn't read this, huh?"

Actually, some had, Steve thought, remembering a meeting nearly four years ago in the lead-lined "submarine" room in the FBI Building. Those gathered there at the time, including himself and Peter Thompson, had taken Jeremiah's writings seriously, although no one could have imagined his prophecies would actually come true. *How had that happened?*

"Well, enough of this talk," Connolly concluded, twirling his fork through a plate of pasta a waiter had set in front of him. "You just send that wife of yours around—Lynn, right?—and I'll take good care of her."

"Thanks, Dr. Connolly. Oh, by the way, one more thing and I'll leave you to your lunch. I suppose there are Lamaze classes offered somewhere in town, where Lynn and I could go." *Where there'd be other pregnant women. Where Katrina might show up if she was still in this area.*

Connolly spoke with his mouth full. "I'll tell her all about it when I see her next week."

Steve offered his hand. "It was a pleasure to meet you, sir. Let's pray that the Lord continues to protect Jeremiah."

Connolly dabbed his lips with a napkin. "They haven't been able to kill him so far."

"I saw Jeremiah up close a couple of times," Steve said. "Once he was with a woman, I think her name was Katrina something-or-other."

"Katrina Dorfler. Walter's daughter. Everyone knows her."

"Oh, yes. I hope she's bearing up well under all this strain."

"She's fine. I see her now and then." Connolly frowned and looked intently at Steve, who wondered what he'd said to occasion the additional scrutiny. In any event, it was time to leave.

"Thanks a lot, Dr. Connolly, and have a good meal."

"Take care of yourself, son."

Bingo! Steve said to himself, as he walked back to the café, where Hoffman was on his second dessert and fourth cup of coffee. As they walked toward the bus stop to return to the mobile home park, Steve told Hoffman what he'd learned from Dr. Connolly.

"If he sees Katrina, it's likely he'd also see Laura," Hoffman agreed. "We'll set up surveillance on the good doctor, and maybe we'll get lucky."

20

Later that evening, Jeremiah returned to the cave house and Katrina disappeared quietly into the world aboveground. As Jeremiah "made love" to Laura, she pummeled his back with her fists and battered his legs with her heels, just as she'd done during the first rape at her parents' house.

"Do you have it in, motherfucker!" she howled, her voice a rumbling bass, as if she was possessed by the devil. "What a pitiful little prick you are. Cocksucker. Bitch."

She continued to spit out cuss words, and they had their effect, as Jeremiah eventually gave up, pulled back, and looked at her. She feared he might kill her.

The look on his face faded to resignation, however, giving Laura a sense of exhilaration.

Jeremiah rose from the bed and began putting on his clothes. "I wanted to give you everything," he said. "I wanted us to be perfect together, Laura. I wanted you to be part of this great movement."

Laura laughed, the near hysteria in her voice frightening even to herself. "This is nothing but a great bowel movement! New America is a pile of shit, and you're nothing more than the head fly!"

"Laura, if you'd just give it a chance, we could learn to love each other."

"Are you fuckin' crazy! Yes, you are! You lost touch with reality a long time ago, buddy-boy. You've developed some psychotic fixation on me, but to me you'll never be anything except a terrorist, murderer, rapist, and madman."

In his eyes, Laura saw the hurt and she silently celebrated her victory. *Maybe it would be the last time he'd enter her bedroom. Maybe he'd send her home!*

Laura was ecstatic the next morning when Chuck knocked on her door and yelled for her to get dressed. They were leaving shortly, he said. When she emerged from her room and looked over the balcony railing, she saw Jeremiah standing near the fireplace—dark, silent, brooding.

Chuck blindfolded her and led her out of the cabin onto the deck and down the stairs, which Laura counted. Twenty-three. Another fifty-eight steps on the cave floor and they came to an elevator. Laura estimated it took twenty seconds until the elevator came to a stop. Someone opened a door with squeaky hinges and they stepped outside. Laura felt the sun's warmth on her face, although there was a fall chill in the air.

She remained blindfolded for a thirty-minute car ride and was helped into another vehicle, which she recognized as a helicopter once its blades began to whirl. After they were airborne, Chuck took off the blindfold and Laura could see out the right side of the aircraft.

She saw forest-covered mountains, then grasslands and the dome-shaped hills so characteristic of many parts of South Dakota. They flew east into the sun. Within twenty minutes, the scenery below changed to a desolate moonscape of jagged, multicolored spires of limestone, clay, and sandstone. It could only be the Badlands, she thought. They had definitely come from the Black Hills, probably south and west of Rapid City. Jeremiah didn't seem to care if she knew the general location, and why should he? Laura could only pinpoint the cave home as being located within a several-thousand-square-mile area. The underground Hades where she'd been held could be attached to either Wind Cave or Jewel Cave, popular tourist attractions that were forty miles apart.

"Where are we going?" she asked, speaking into her headset.

"You'll see," Jeremiah replied. Within an hour, they landed on a pad near the sprawling Science Center located northeast of Pierre. Laura recognized the complex from photographs and television reports. From the air it resembled a giant wagon wheel lying on its side, complete with "spokes" in the form of tube-shaped buildings connecting the rim to the thirty-five-story hospital at the center of the complex.

A large crowd waited at the entrance to greet and cheer Jeremiah, as if he were a returning hero. A television film crew also was present. Laura stared in amazement at the camera, cameraman, and technicians, as if the people and tools of her former profession had become alien to her.

"I've been kidnapped!" Laura shouted. "Kidnapped and raped. He's keeping me in a cave."

The camera crew ignored her outburst. Chuck clamped a hand over her mouth and said, "Shut up or I'll gag you!"

But when Chuck removed his hand, Laura resumed her tirade. She was promptly gagged and moved to the rear of the entourage. She couldn't understand why no one would help her. Were they afraid? Could the New America Dictator for Life—God's Prophet—indulge any whim and commit any crime without fear of criticism? Did they know about her situation and simply not care? Or had they been told some other story? That she was demented, perhaps! Why, when it was a question of "he said, she said," did most people always believe the man?

The crowd followed Jeremiah as he walked briskly down a series of hallways that seemed a labyrinth to Laura, who struggled to keep pace. As they walked, Jeremiah talked into the camera. Laura could hear only some of his words, enough to understand he was conducting a "public tour" of the Science Center. Laura assumed this broadcast could be picked up across the United States. It was her chance to be seen; to let her loved ones and law-enforcement officials know she was alive, but not compliant.

Jeremiah dropped back to Laura's side. For the first time, she noticed he was dressed like a college professor, wearing black slacks, a brilliant white shirt, gray-and-white herringbone sports coat, and matching patterned tie. "So you think I'm crazy and New America is an aberration? Maybe today will change your mind, Laura, and a lot of other minds."

They entered a small auditorium, where students sat listening to a lecture given by a man wearing a white lab coat. In the semidark room, the lecturer used an overhead projector to show slides illustrating his thesis.

While Jeremiah and the camera crew stayed up front, Chuck steered Laura to a seat near the back of the room. She protested by yelling into the gag, prompting Chuck to squeeze her carotid artery until she felt faint. After that, she remained quiet, aware that having her air supply cut off could cause brain damage to the baby. She had mixed feelings about having a dead fetus inside her.

Following this brief disturbance at the back of the room, Jeremiah nodded at the lecturer, who continued, "When deprived of water, many organisms, including microscopic tardigrades and rotifers, as well as brine shrimp and nematodes, simply cease the metabolic processes that constitute normal cell life. Reinvest them with water, and they resume life. This process is called cryptobiosis."

"Is this a form of hibernation?" Jeremiah asked.

"No," the lecturer responded, politely. "It's more than hibernation, during which metabolic activities simply slow down. These cryptobiotic animals actually cease all cellular activity. Significantly, however, none of their cellular integrity is compromised during this suspension of metabolic activities."

"It's almost as if they had been frozen," Jeremiah observed.

"Yes, but without the cellular damage that results from freezing."

"So what is our research here in New America attempting to discover?" Jeremiah asked.

"Scientists have known for some time that these animals

produce a glucose sugar called trehalose," the lecturer said, "which forms a noncrystalline casing that preserves the structural integrity of the cells and tissue. When the animal is rehydrated, the trehalose goes back into solution and can be consumed as a sugar for energy. The animal resumes life."

"It has theological implications, doesn't it?" Jeremiah asked. "What is life and what is death? And is there a bridge between them?" Jeremiah looked directly into the camera. "The answer to the last question, incidentally, is God."

The balding, diminutive lecturer said, "If we could manufacture a human gene to replicate this process and inject it into humans, we might achieve the same effect."

"In which case, we could certainly extend life," Jeremiah guessed. "It would also have beneficial applications on interstellar space flights, isn't that right, doctor?" Jeremiah looked to the professor for confirmation and was rewarded with a smile. The students applauded their insightful leader.

Jeremiah addressed the camera. "Don't go away. Our tour is just beginning. We have many more interesting topics to talk about."

As Jeremiah left the auditorium, Chuck pulled Laura to a standing position. "Nod if you want me to take out the gag. It's not going to do you any good to act up because no one's going to pay any attention to you. The cameras are not going to focus on you, but I will hurt you again."

Laura nodded sullenly. What choice did she have? At least she looked bad today, and that would come across on television if she behaved and could get in front of the camera. Her appearance alone would convey to those who knew her that all was not well. She wore no makeup and had done nothing with her hair except run a brush through it. She'd put on loose-fitting slacks and a faded, gray "Longhorns" sweatshirt over a T-shirt. Or was Jeremiah happy for her to look like a frumpy, suburban housewife?

Jeremiah and his followers moved on to a science laboratory, equipped with many workstations. The scientist supervising the class explained to Jeremiah and the camera that they were helping to construct the human genome map and determine the functions of the nearly one hundred thousand genes contained in each human body cell. She stressed that much of the actual work was performed in a nearly isolated, sterile environment, while those in this laboratory used computers to construct a three-dimensional model of human DNA.

"Aren't genetic laboratories throughout the world involved in similar efforts?" Jeremiah asked.

"Yes," the scientist in charge said, adding smugly, "but we intend to be the first to finish the task."

"And the rewards of this knowledge?"

The scientist spread her arms and hands expansively. "A knowledge of all life processes, including whether or not there is a so-called 'death gene' that naturally limits our life span, or whether humans, with appropriate genetic intervention, might live hundreds of years."

"I suppose obvious benefits of this research would be the development of cures for various forms of cancer and the elimination of diseases caused by defective genes or mutations," Jeremiah said.

"Definitely. It might even reveal a means by which we could induce diseased human organs to regenerate themselves," the scientist answered.

"Wow!" the Prophet exclaimed to the camera. "This, too, is New America."

Laura snorted her disgust at this obviously sanitized version of a totalitarian colony. Also, this tour was too elaborately planned—and Jeremiah too well rehearsed—for this to be a spur-of-the-moment response to her characterization of New America as "a pile of shit."

"Ma'am, could you tell us your background," Jeremiah asked the scientist.

"I'm a cellular biologist, Jeremiah. I came to New America from a large university where I was doing similar work until my research grant was canceled."

Jeremiah faced the camera. "There's no higher priority in New America than scientific research, which is a central part of our religious philosophy. We don't do such research to gain power or make a profit. We do it to discover the handiwork of God. Ultimately, it is the means by which we will understand him. It is his plan for us, and his gift to us.

"Furthermore, as these students will attest, we don't charge tuition to attend New America University. Intellectual ability, desire, and an individual work ethic are the only admission criteria. What kind of society charges money for education? Isn't that a social birthright?"

The camera panned the students at their workstations and Laura watched all of them enthusiastically nod their agreement.

Next they went into a huge, cold room, where a quiet, whirling computer mainframe occupied space equivalent to half a football field. Jeremiah interviewed a technician, who spoke in phrases generally incomprehensible to Laura, although she understood the subject to be current computer processing speed and storage capacity vis-à-vis the human brain, implying that artificial intelligence research in New America was narrowing the gap.

"Let's try and put this into English, if we can," Jeremiah said, hamming it up for the cameras. Those in his retinue laughed as if on cue, but Laura caught his attention and placed a finger in her mouth, simulating a gagging response.

"We already have computers that can store as much information as the brain," Jeremiah continued, ignoring Laura, "but the human brain processes information about five times faster. Is that correct?"

The computer guru smiled indulgently. "That's true of the best human brains, not the ordinary ones."

"Oh." Jeremiah laughed, effecting an excuse-me tone. "How long before we build a computer here in New America that has processing skills equivalent to the smartest of humans?"

"Five years at the most," the researcher answered.

Jeremiah focused on the camera, his playful expression replaced by one of contemplation. "What then would distinguish a computer from a human?"

"There would be no difference, especially if the computer had the capacity to learn."

Jeremiah appeared skeptical. "You mean, if there was a computer behind one door and a human behind another, I could talk to both and never know which was a machine and which flesh-and-blood?"

"That's what we call a Turing test in our field, Jeremiah. If you can't tell the difference between a computer and a human, whether on an intellectual or emotional level, then artificial life has been created."

Jeremiah frowned. "But it's only a machine."

The computer scientist responded without hesitation. "A silicon-based intelligence, rather than a carbon-based human model. Who's to say which is the preferable form?"

Jeremiah arched his eyebrows and nodded thoughtfully before resuming his peripatetic tour.

They entered a classroom where a physicist lectured his students about antimatter. "Most known matter comes in two forms," he told them, "particles and antiparticles. One with a negative electrical charge, the other with a positive electrical charge. Bring them into contact with each other and mass is converted to energy. All of the mass, not just 1 percent, as is the case with nuclear fission. Therefore, the resulting energy conversion is ninety-nine times more efficient."

"Let's see if I understand this, Professor. An antimatter explosion is the most efficient form of energy production in the universe?"

"That's correct, Jeremiah."

"Why doesn't it occur naturally?"

"Under ordinary circumstances, oppositely charged particles naturally repel each other."

"So if it proved possible to somehow bring them together in a controlled environment, the result would be the greatest energy source in the world?"

"Exactly. A hydrogen-antihydrogen rocket system could travel at the speed of light."

"And what would that make possible, Professor?"

The lecturer, a bear of a man with a full, salt-and-pepper beard, said, "A new propulsion system of this sort, coupled with nanotechnology—which is technology on the scale of atoms—would allow us to explore the far reaches of the universe." Laura watched a glow akin to rapture spread across his ruddy face. "Such stellar probes could be built to be self-reproducing, especially as our knowledge of physics and genetics increases, in which case they could land on far stars and build colonies, while yet launching other probes traveling toward the outer reaches of the universe."

"Where we'd find what, Professor?"

The physicist returned to earth, shrugging. "I don't know."

Jeremiah looked into the camera. "I know. We'd discover our destiny." He stared pensively into the camera for several seconds before abruptly moving on.

The next auditorium Laura entered had seating for several thousand people. It was filled to capacity, including the various scientists and students they'd met previously in other locations within the Science Center.

As Chuck steered Laura to a seat in the front row, Jeremiah took his place in front of the audience, near an odd-looking structure consisting of three stairs covered with a luxurious dark blue carpeting. He took off his sports coat and dropped it casually on the floor beside him. He sat on the top step, his feet on the first step, his elbows resting casually on his knees.

Experienced as she was in appearing before studio and television audiences, Laura admitted to herself that Jeremiah looked extremely relaxed and confident, even distinguished. Rapist bastard!

"In the United States, they tell jokes about New America," began the Prophet. "About us. Have you seen the TV show with the comedian who's made up to look like me? He goes to the top of the mountain to talk to God, who gives him twenty commandments on two stone tablets. Carrying one tablet under each arm, the prophet walks down the mountain until he encounters his people, at which point he begins to tell them, 'God has given us twenty . . .' " Jeremiah paused for effect. "Before he can complete his statement, the prophet drops one of the tablets, which breaks into a thousand pieces." Jeremiah looked about the audience, most of whom also were smiling, some already tittering. "So the prophet amends his remarks, 'And God has given us ten commandments. . . .' "

Jeremiah chuckled as laughter swept the audience.

"Let's face it, it's funny," Jeremiah admitted. "But there're jokes about you, too." He pointed at the audience. "Yes, you! We have few cars up here, no booze and drugs. We don't believe in pornography and promiscuous sex, nor do we use foul language or view violent, sadistic movies. We strictly observe the values of *Second Jeremiah* and the Social Contract. Therefore, we can't go out to a topless bar on Saturday night, get wasted, and drive around later on the highways, drunk and shooting at our fellow citizens."

Boisterous whooping erupted from one section of young students, as Laura turned to look at them with amazement and despair.

"So the joke is, 'What do New Americans do on Saturday night? They sit home and pray—pray they can get the hell outta there!' "

There was less laughter this time, and Jeremiah looked soberly at his attentive audience. "Today, those watching this broadcast—watching throughout the United States, we hope, if our satellite broadcast signal isn't being jammed by the government there—have seen a small part of what New America is *really* about."

Spontaneous applause followed this statement, again causing Laura to look more closely at those seated around her. What was wrong with them? Had they been totally brainwashed by this lunatic? Were they, too, afraid to say anything for fear of being physically harmed? She hoped so, but feared that wasn't the case. Their enthusiasm didn't appear to be forced.

"Let me try and bring it all together for you," Jeremiah continued. "Yes, we've given up some creature comforts to come live here in New America. Our economy is new and it exists in large part to accomplish social goals, so it's truthfully not as efficient as we'd hoped. It doesn't help that the U.S. government forces many suppliers to deny us raw materials and supplies. They also regularly attempt to sabotage our power stations and conduct other armed intrusions into our country. We're constantly fighting legal battles with them in court."

Jeremiah shook his head, looking both sad and disgusted. "But they can't deter us from our purpose. You've seen it today. Our society is dedicated in large part to the task of discovering the meaning of life, of finding ways to fulfill our highest potential and know the mind of God. No, we're not partying up here! We're not worried about earning enough money to buy that new sports car or the home at the beach or expensive clothes and jewelry. We're not trying to get ahead at the expense of our brother or sister. Let's admit it, audience: *We are anti-American!* We're not into the petty concerns of the marketplace, buying and selling this and that, as if consumer consumption were the sole purpose of life. We don't measure the value of our life by the value of our material possessions. We celebrate Christ's birthday with joy by honoring the messenger and living the message. We don't suffer depression because we don't have enough money to buy all the Christmas gifts the advertisers persuade us we absolutely need to be happy."

The crowd voiced its discontent with Old America, and its encouragement of the Prophet.

"Let's tell a few Old America jokes," Jeremiah suggested, slyly. "What do they have that we don't? Well, they have their much vaunted democracy, although a majority of disillusioned voters don't participate in the electoral process. Politicians in old, worn-out America are forever arguing about something petty, while they line their pockets with bribe money and talk endlessly about how they're going to create jobs, lower taxes, and eliminate crime. None of which they ever accomplish. Washington, D.C., is the hot-air capital of the world!"

The Prophet's partisans rocked with laughter and encouragement.

"Politicians are like American schoolchildren, always fighting, lying, accusing each other of various crimes. Aren't you glad we don't have partisan politics and social disorder in New America?"

The audience hissed.

"Aren't you glad our leaders in New America don't act

like spoiled children? Aren't you glad our children don't act like adults in the United States?"

That got Jeremiah the laugh he'd worked for. Now, Laura thought, it was obvious to the television watchers that citizens of both "nations" considered each other to be a joke.

"We have different priorities here," Jeremiah continued. "We have absolute values we live every day. We fight evil tooth and nail. We believe in economic equality, and we plan to implement this goal eventually. There is no other type of equality worth having." He paused. "When you have order, values, and justice, you can move to a higher plane, which is to discover the secrets of life, the laws of the universe, and achieve a union with God at the highest level. We're living a life of meaning, not a meaningless life."

The Prophet took a drink of water from a glass sitting nearby on the floor. "Let's talk about God for a few minutes. The God worshipped in the United States is different from New America's God. Their God is incomprehensible, unpredictable. They pray to their God for material things, or to deliver them from a tight spot. The beliefs of their God are periodically readjusted to reinforce their own prejudices and selfish desires, and provide an excuse for attacking their neighbor. The hypocritical Old Americans always have their hand on the Bible, but never incorporate its contents into their hearts.

"The God we worship in New America is different. He expects us to observe his word and commandments, without excuse or qualification. The reward for this obedience is His love. Our God is not an enemy of science. The so-called creationists have perverted God's word. Science is a tool that man can use to unlock God's secrets. Evolution is part of God's plan."

Jeremiah nodded for several seconds. "Yes, we are evolving, the universe is evolving, the laws governing the universe are evolving. It's obvious. Just look around you. Read history. Review in your mind the lessons we've learned today. Progress is everywhere. Purpose is everywhere for those who want to see it."

The audience again interrupted with applause and several members stood, clapping wildly, whistling, and cheering.

Jeremiah silenced them with a motion of his hand. "All that distinguishes man from the other animals is that we think. We have intelligence. We can discover and comprehend. That is God's plan; his plan for us, the Chosen People."

Laura looked around at the nodding heads. So they were fanatical believers in Jeremiah's peculiar philosophy. The problem always had been that some of the things Jeremiah said made theoretical sense. That was how he trapped them in his web. The gulf between his words and actions had always horrified Laura. New America's emphasis on science and technology had nothing to do with theology. It was the means by which even a small nation could have disproportionate power in the world.

Nevertheless, Laura found herself listening to Jeremiah with the same rapt attention as those seated around her.

"What is life about? What is our individual purpose? Why is the world the way it is? Why does evil exist? I don't know." Jeremiah shrugged. "Some things God doesn't reveal, even to me. Some things we must accept on faith. Some things we must learn ourselves. God rewards diligence and hard work. God has a plan, some of which he revealed to me in *The Book of Second Jeremiah*. I'm not a god. I'm not as smart as any of the scientists we've met today or many of the students in this room. I was just called to speak for God."

The chant went up softly, "Jeremiah! Jeremiah! Jeremiah!"

Laura remembered the TV footage shown in the rest of the United States several days after the public executions in Pierre, where Steve and his colleagues had tried to kill Jeremiah; videotape shot secretly by dissidents and smuggled out of the colony later. It showed Jeremiah ranting and raving, a madman in stark contrast to his cool demeanor today. Couldn't they see he was little more than a talented chameleon? An actor. An opportunist of the highest order.

"Isn't it odd that in a religious nation like the United States, so many people sneer at the idea that God would talk to an individual," Jeremiah scoffed, as if he were one of the doubters. "If God talks to you, you're obviously insane. If God dictates his word to you, that's blasphemy. Yet the Christian Bible my enemies hold in their hand like a weapon was put together by a committee, and revised and interpreted so many times that most people really don't understand what it means." He looked lovingly into the lens, a tear forming in one eye. "God speaks to all of us, if we listen.

"Let me tell you several scientific truths that God has revealed to me, which I willingly share with the world. First, the idea that the universe was born in a big bang singularity is correct, but our existing laws of physics are seriously flawed. There are other worlds and dimensions. Time and space are human inventions. Our universe is finite, but it will not reach a state of entropy and collapse upon itself. Nor will it explode. Our universe will expand into infinity and eventually transform itself. Scientists of New America will one day scientifically validate what God has told me."

Jeremiah looked unblinkingly at the glass lens of the camera, as if to project to the viewers his utter sincerity. Laura understood the technique, and its intended effect. Jeremiah looked so at ease, and so confident, Laura feared he would hypnotize those watching.

"God has reaffirmed to me the promise of the New Testament that there will be a resurrection of the dead and life eternal for good people—those who strive to live his word. This resurrection will be much different than expected." Jeremiah wagged a cautionary finger at the audience. "Remember, knowledge and thought evolve also. It is the rule of God's universe. Our work here in New America will shed additional light on the resurrection God promises, but I will give you a glimpse today."

Many in the audience were actually on the edge of their seats, Laura observed. Including herself, despite her feelings about *him*.

"To survive in a changing and evolving universe, humans must evolve to survive," Jeremiah continued. "Earth could be destroyed tomorrow by an asteroid or a black-hole quasar. What would save the human race then? Consumer economics or science? Remember First Corinthians fifteen, fifty: '. . . flesh and blood cannot inherit the kingdom of God.' That means something fundamentally different than what is commonly taught. Remember what we learned today about intelligence, both carbon-based and silicon-based. Remember that life is energy. Energy cannot be diminished or created; it can only change shape. It can therefore be resurrected in ways we can only dream of now, but which are directly related to the work we do here in New America, especially with computer-processing speed, artificial intelligence, genetics, and quantum physics. I can assure you that eternal life is possible because God has told me so."

Laura spotted a monitor on the wall and watched as the camera panned the audience, which was applauding politely but fervently. She saw herself, sitting there calmly, raptly watching Jeremiah. Her lips were parted in an expression of . . . awe. Suddenly, she understood. It was a delayed transmission, with a minute or two allowed for editing. They'd filmed her when she was engrossed in Jeremiah's performance. *The look on her face could be interpreted as . . . love!* Laura buried her face in her hands and cried. Now the people watching—her family and friends—would assume she was one of them!

Jeremiah stood on the carpeted steps. "All we ask of the United States is: Let us go! Let us travel our own path!"

The chant went up in the room, "Let us go! Let us go! Let us go!"

Jeremiah motioned for silence. "Those who choose the values of the United States can pursue their pettiness; we'll pursue our goals!"

As if on cue, he was interrupted by cheering and applause.

"If the forces of the United States hadn't attempted to assassinate me, not once, but twice, we would not have been forced to respond as we have," Jeremiah said, unbuttoning his shirt cuff so he could roll up the sleeve and reveal his bandaged arm.

"On a conciliatory note, in preparation for our bargaining

session to be held in Minneapolis, I have asked the armed forces of New America to abandon the nuclear power plant they seized in Virginia. We will not endanger the lives and homes of Americans if they will not harm New America."

More cheering and applause.

"What are you afraid of? Let us go! Let us go!"

The rally continued as Jeremiah and Laura and the bodyguards left the auditorium and walked toward an exit and the helicopter pad. Jeremiah slowed to walk beside her. "I have a concession for you, too, Laura. You do not wish to have me in your bed. So be it. You have your wish."

"Let me go! Let me go!" she chanted cynically, mimicking the crowd response.

"Not until you've given birth to our son. That, too, has been ordained by God."

"Those voices you hear in your head don't come from God." Laura seethed, as Jeremiah walked away from her. She was too tired to keep up the pace; too tired to worry anymore about how she looked on camera, if they were still filming. She was emotionally and physically exhausted and nearly four months pregnant. Jeremiah already possessed a part of her, and there didn't seem to be anything she could do about it.

21

Peter Thompson looked out a window
of the jetliner as it began its landing approach to the
Minneapolis–Saint Paul International airport. On this clear,
unseasonably mild October day, the landscape below appeared as a checkerboard. Some of the dark brown squares
had been recently plowed, while others were straw-colored
with nearly ripe corn; a few were green with winter wheat.
Summer's promise of endless growth and renewal had
given way to the bleak reality of the approaching winter.
Nearer to the airport, houses, trees, lakes, and golf courses
combined into patterns that resembled Rorschach ink-blot
patterns. What did it portend for the future of the nation?
Thompson wondered.

As the plane taxied toward its arrival gate at the northwest wing of the airport, Thompson saw off to his right
buildings of the U.S. Air Force Reserve and the Minneapolis Air National Guard, both airlift wings. Several C-130
Hercules transport planes usually were parked on the tarmac, but weeks ago Jeremiah's marauders had hijacked
them. They were used to drop airborne troops on Fort Riley, and then presumably diverted to various hiding places
on the ground.

As prearranged, a stewardess showed Thompson from
his first-class seat to the exit door. He walked down stairs
to the tarmac, where an army lieutenant and sergeant stood
beside a jeep. They drove across the taxi runways toward

one of the large hangars at the Air National Guard facility, where the historic meeting with Jeremiah would take place at 10:00 A.M.

The ANG facilities bristled with troops from both sides, as well as tanks and APCs. Three military policemen, one with a handheld metal detector, frisked Thompson for weapons and searched his briefcase.

He was taken inside a building to the negotiating room, ordinarily used for meetings of the local military brass. Inside the room was a conference table, ten chairs, and a credenza containing coffeepots and platters of pastry and muffins.

Secy. of State John Tremain was holed up in a nearby private office, talking on the telephone. Col. Samuel Douglas sat on a chair along the wall of the main corridor, reading a Bible.

"Hi, Sam, how's it goin'?" Thompson asked.

"Good, Peter. I'm finding some comfort here." Douglas tapped the Bible page and resumed reading.

Thompson walked outside and discovered Gen. Milton Haase off to the side of the hangar, puffing pleasurably on an obscenely long cigar. Two U.S. MPs stood guard a discreet distance away.

"Do you have any idea when or how he will arrive?" Thompson asked.

"Nope," replied the general, who wore a Class A military uniform heavy with decorations and insignia, including four Silver Stars.

Thompson looked up as four jet fighters blasted across the sky. "I'd think he'd be afraid to fly in."

"We won't shoot down his plane, Peter. He has the president's guarantee of safety. However he comes, I'm certain it'll be a dramatic entrance. On television this morning, I saw people south of the city standing on a steep hill overlooking Interstate 35. Apparently they think he might arrive by auto caravan, like Christ coming to his fate in Jerusalem."

Thompson chuckled at Haase's cynical humor. Certainly, thousands of reporters and technicians had come from all over the world to record this historic event. The majority of onlookers were simply curious, waiting to see what would happen. Officials of the U.S. government and rebel representatives would talk about the possibility that the federal union could be modified: a state, or several states, might be allowed to secede, or be given commonwealth status in a *new* America. If the talks failed, civil war on American soil—perhaps even nuclear war—could result.

"Our new president inherited his predecessor's willingness to accommodate Jeremiah's never-ending demands," Thompson said. "I fear this so-called conference could go down in history, along with Yalta, as the worst example of negotiators selling out the lives of millions of people."

The general flicked ashes from his cigar. "I'm certain you'll have a chance to make your case in next year's elections, Peter."

"If I run, I hope you'll support my candidacy, Milton. Perhaps even consider advising me on military matters after your retirement. I think we have similar beliefs about what is best for the country."

The general seemed more interested in the cigar, Thompson thought. Haase took a tool from a pocket of his uniform, snipped off the burning end, and brushed away the remaining embers with stubby fingers. He carefully placed the cigar in a breast pocket of his dark green uniform. "Well, I'm not certain about that, Peter. I think I'll just do what old generals do, and fade away."

As Haase walked away, Thompson stared at the Minneapolis skyline. He thought about the terrorist's televised tour of the Science Center. It had been three days since the telecast, and the polls showed that nearly 65 percent of Americans wished their government had such a high priority on scientific research, especially that impacting health and longevity. Pinpoint polling showed Jeremiah's "favorables" were high among the well-educated, among those who labeled themselves as "very religious," and, inexplicably, among women. Pollsters noted that a majority of women always react well to a message directed at "excessive materialism."

Thompson, who like many politicians lived by poll numbers, was startled that nearly 20 percent of Americans—

one-in-five—thought "New America" should be granted some type of independent status within the United States, especially if such a concession was the only way to avoid a nuclear civil war.

On the other hand, Thompson was buoyed by the fact that 78 percent of those polled "strongly condemned" Jeremiah's military actions against the United States, although nearly a third thought he had been driven to his actions by a "secret" government plot to assassinate him. As he'd surely planned, Jeremiah's "favorables" rose as a result of voluntarily surrendering the Lake Anna nuclear station. Inexplicably, immigration *into* New America had increased.

Overall, the numbers weren't that bad. Thompson was confident he could convert a majority of Americans to his viewpoint, given enough time and the right forum.

As a Learjet approached the airport, Thompson sensed it was "him" and wished fervently that someone would seize this golden opportunity and direct a missile at the jet. But he knew that wouldn't happen because the people wanted the two parties to talk before fighting.

The airplane taxied close to the hangar before shutting down its engines. It sat ominously for several minutes until a limousine and three military vehicles arrived, braking sharply near the jet. Soldiers of the New American Army spilled out of the jeeps and took up defensive positions around the airplane, glaring at their U.S. counterparts.

Finally the door to the jet opened downward, forming steps. Jeremiah appeared in the doorway, where he paused, waving like a politician, presumably for the benefit of the one television pool camera present, Thompson concluded.

Surrounded by tall, praetorian guards, Jeremiah walked down the steps and got into the limo. Within moments, he emerged and started toward the hangar, surrounded protectively by his gunmen. As he came close, their eyes met. Jeremiah smiled, pointed a finger-and-thumb handgun at Thompson, and shouted something the attorney general couldn't hear above the hubbub. Thompson thought it might have something to do with their standoff at the pond behind Laura's farmhouse. Four years ago he had commanded men who had Jeremiah in their gun sights, and today the attorney general bemoaned the fact that the terrorist was still alive.

Another limo arrived shortly, disgorging South Dakota senator Rupert Carlson and Lt. Gen. Benjamin Arnot, military commander of the New American Army. Their negotiating team was present. Thompson wondered why the news media hadn't made an issue about the absence of Gov. Davey Schropa, who had disappeared from public view after he had revealed Jeremiah's hiding place to the CAT interrogators.

Thompson followed at a discreet distance, until Jeremiah and his entourage encountered General Haase and several MPs. An acrimonious discussion followed until Jeremiah waved his hands in exasperation, allowing the MPs to search them.

In the conference room, Secretary of State Tremain, always the diplomat, made the introductions as the negotiators took their seats around the table.

Thompson saw that Haase could barely conceal his contempt for the turncoat Arnot, who wore the uniform of the forces he commanded, although the decorations displayed on it were mostly for achievements in another army. The burly, graying warriors, once West Point classmates, glared at each other. The other military man present, Colonel Douglas, remained inscrutable, as always.

Considerably ill at ease, Thompson made small talk with Senator Carlson, sitting to his right. The ruddy-faced senator, long-rumored to be the financial genius behind the formation of New America, prattled on about this "historic event."

Arnot, his chin thrust out belligerently, said, "We want our bomb-detection dog to go over this hangar!" The renegade soldier struck his fist repeatedly on the table, punctuating his every word.

"This hangar has been under guard by forces from both sides since it was agreed upon as the site for negotiations," Haase said. "The negotiating room has been searched thoroughly by a team that included your people."

Arnot's belligerence increased. "I haven't personally conducted an inspection!"

Jeremiah put a restraining hand on his general's arm. "That won't be necessary, General Arnot."

Thompson had been this close to Jeremiah only once before and carefully observed him. The terrorist looked relaxed, confident, and physically fit. Six feet tall, one-eighty, fair complexioned, with a smattering of freckles here and there. Thick blood veins were visible on the back of his hands, and neck. His thin, slender nose divided piercing, light blue eyes. His hair was light brown and wavy, although Thompson knew its natural color and texture varied. The FBI had photographs and videotape of Jeremiah with many different hair disguises—blond, black, gray, straight, and tightly curled.

Jeremiah wore a diplomat's navy blue, pin-striped suit, and Thompson could see the edge of a bandage beneath the left sleeve of his shirt.

As decided by President Trainor, Tremain was the principal spokesman for the United States. "I've been asked by Pres. Richard Trainor to extend to you, Mr. Dillman, his greetings and warm wishes, as well as the appreciation of the American people for turning over to us the nuclear power plant your forces seized in Virginia."

"You should," General Arnot boomed. "If a runaway reaction had *accidentally* occurred at that plant, all the eastern seaboard cities would have been rendered inhabitable!"

"Bullshit!" General Haase interjected, taking the cigar out of his pocket and lighting it, without asking anyone's permission. "That wasn't a humanitarian gesture and you know it, Arnot. It was a public relations ploy."

"I think it would best be characterized as a good-will gesture, General Haase," Jeremiah said, "but let's back up a moment and clear up a major confusion." He looked directly at Secretary Tremain. "Despite the endless speculation in the news media, Secretary Tremain, I am not Trent Dillman of Sioux Falls, South Dakota. Never was. My name is Jeremiah, Chosen of God. Please address me as such; otherwise I will immediately leave these negotiations."

Thompson looked at Tremain, who was reed thin and short. Almost fragile. The secretary of state nodded once, the equivalent of a blink. Jeremiah had won this round.

"The B-1s won't be so easy to stop," General Arnot said.

"We're here to make certain there are no nuclear incidents, gentlemen," Tremain said.

"That's correct," Senator Carlson replied. "Peace is what the people want, not just the millions of New Americans I represent, but the majority in the country at large."

"Excellent point," Jeremiah agreed, and Thompson suddenly had the feeling "the Prophet" was toying with them. He could see it in the terrorist's face. This was a game, a "show" event. Jeremiah had no intention of negotiating.

"What do you want?" Thompson asked, cutting to the chase.

Jeremiah shifted in his seat so he could look directly at Thompson. "I want New America to be recognized as an independent nation, with recognizable boundaries, and I want the United States to pledge publicly that it will refrain from attacking us militarily. I've said this many times before, as you all know."

"Those demands are unacceptable," Thompson replied. "What do you really want?"

"To whom are my demands unacceptable?" Jeremiah asked, smiling broadly. "Are you speaking for yourself, Peter? The American people? Congress? President Trainor? Or maybe just the American Patriots."

"New America is a fascist dictatorship, and dictatorships always fall."

"The United States isn't a democracy, Peter. It's an economic oligarchy controlled by the heads of the seven hundred largest multinational corporations. In the history of humankind, representative government will be but a passing moment."

"That's your hope, I'm certain."

"No, it's a historical inevitability. People naturally don't like government, and if a collective decision is necessary, they prefer a direct democracy."

"You call what exists in New America a direct democracy!"

"Peter, Peter, give us time. In the computer age, direct democracy is imminently possible, and inevitable."

"Maybe you should allow your people a referendum on your actions."

"Peter, they've voted by staying. You know why? They're willing to freely trade some of your so-called individual freedoms for safety, security, and a high moral purpose."

"In time, they'll regret that trade-off," Thompson said.

"No, Peter, they won't, especially when we have economic equality in New America. When people realize that everyone's work and contribution is valued equally, they'll greatly prefer collective goals over selfish, individual goals."

"Everywhere in the world that a socialist-communist government and economy has been tried, the people have suffered," Thompson replied.

"Then they didn't do it right, because it's inevitable. History will trample in the dust kings, aristocrats, oligarchs, and all others who attempt to rule the masses from a position of privilege and wealth. People will be equal, whether you in this room like it or not."

Thompson sneered at the terrorist. "Very good, Jeremiah. You've found a propaganda message that resonates with some people. But that's all it is, propaganda."

Jeremiah looked amused by Thompson's attempt to insult him. "I wonder what would happen if your government's decisions were put to a referendum, Peter." He smacked his forehead. "Oh, I forgot! That will be next year's presidential elections in the United States. Tell me, Peter, do you think people will vote for nuclear war or a principle that allows everyone to live as peacefully as they please?"

"I believe the people of the United States will do the right thing, as they've always done throughout history," Thompson said. "They will do whatever is necessary to preserve this union, knowing that if they allow it to disintegrate, their freedoms and prosperity will soon evaporate."

"Good luck, Peter," Jeremiah said, shaking his head at the immensity of his adversary's task. "But I must tell you,

I think it's already too late. The seed of New America has been planted, and it will hereafter be as perennial as the grass, no matter what happens in this room."

General Haase sighed audibly and interjected, "Enough of the college debate. Do you really believe this army of yours will fight for all these ideals?"

"They'll be up to the task, Milton," General Arnot answered. "Believe me."

"But they're little more than mercenaries," Haase insisted.

Jeremiah shook his head wearily. "And what do you think your largely black and Hispanic army is, General? Your soldiers are in your army because your racist, sexist society doesn't make any place for them in the mainstream economy. Do you really think they'll fight and die to preserve your system?"

"Absolutely!" Haase replied, confidently.

"Please, gentlemen," Secretary Tremain said, "you're making speeches and hurling insults, instead of attempting to find a common ground." Looking at Jeremiah, Tremain asked, "Sir, would you consider any situation in which New America, as you call it, would remain a part of the United States?"

"No."

"Under what circumstances would you retire the six armed divisions you have in the field?" General Haase asked. "As well as turn over to us the military aircraft you have illegally seized."

"Do you think we're fools, Milton!" Arnot yelled.

"In your case, Benjamin, yes!"

Arnot stood, quivering with anger. "I outmaneuvered you, Milton! Just as I always could! At the Point and on the battlefield! You're nothing but a worn-out, armchair general. I've had the best of you and, by God, I'll do it again, given the chance!"

Jeremiah motioned for Arnot to sit and said, "If you recognize New America, we will redeploy our troops to their training areas."

"Well, then we've made some progress." Tremain smiled, displaying the perennial optimism of an experienced negotiator. "Now if you were to promptly return the B-1s, I am authorized to promise you that President Trainor will submit a constitutional amendment to the Congress proposing a form of commonwealth status for New America—the details to be worked out at a future conference."

"This is not acceptable," Senator Carlson whined. "The Congress—the Senate where I sit—would take months or years to debate such an amendment, and they might not approve it. Meanwhile, New America would be defenseless."

Jeremiah spoke forcefully, "Give us independence now or give us death. Roughly equivalent to Patrick Henry's words, I believe."

A gloomy silence prevailed around the negotiating table. Thompson looked briefly at everyone. Jeremiah smirked. General Arnot fidgeted. Senator Carlson seemed put-upon. Haase aggressively smoked his cigar. Tremain—well, Tremain always had the same noncommittal look on his face. Colonel Douglas stared into the distance, apparently absorbed in his own thoughts. He held tightly onto the Bible. Thompson watched the colonel's head bob up and down, as if affirming some private judgment.

"I suggest we take a brief break for coffee," Tremain said, standing, as if that point was nonnegotiable.

"You know goddamned good and well that if we give you back those bombers, you'll attack us, Milton!" General Arnot yelled, pointing belligerently at his adversary and demonstrating why their careers had diverged so sharply.

Tremain led the way to the side table, but Jeremiah abruptly left the room, walking rapidly down the hallway toward the main exit. Alarmed, Thompson followed, wondering if he dare shout a command to the U.S. troops to detain the terrorist if he tried to leave.

Outside, Jeremiah slipped into the backseat of the black limo, but reemerged within a few minutes. He walked briskly back toward the negotiating room, failing even to acknowledge Thompson, who was forced to conclude the terrorist had simply retrieved something from the car. Or made a secure phone call to someone.

Tremain reconvened the meeting and launched into a

long-winded dissertation about the benefits and ground-breaking nature of his government's proposal. Thompson looked at Jeremiah, who seemed suddenly on edge, his eyes darting nervously about the room. Something was wrong, but before Thompson could decide what it was, an MP entered the room and whispered in his ear, "You have an urgent call from the White House. There's a lieutenant outside with a secure telephone."

Thompson rose immediately and excused himself, walking rapidly from the room. What could President Trainor possibly want? The lieutenant with the portable phone stood outside the hangar in the bright sunlight.

The explosion ripped apart the middle portion of the building, the shock waves knocking Thompson to the ground. He instinctively covered his head with his arms and curled into a ball. He felt a sharp pain in his back. Gunfire erupted as the opposing soldiers recovered from their initial shock and began shooting at each other. Thompson crawled toward two metal barrels of the type usually filled with oil or grease and wedged himself between them for protection.

The skirmish ended quickly, and a soldier helped Thompson to his feet. He limped to the area that had been the negotiating room. Little remained. Pieces of wood, tin, and glass were scattered over a wide area. An unusual, acrid smell hung in the air. Thompson saw bodies and parts of bodies scattered about, although he couldn't identify them individually. It was only certain that none of the negotiators had survived the blast, except himself. And he didn't know why. At the moment, it seemed sheer luck that the White House had called.

Thompson wondered who had planted the bomb? Surely it had been someone on his team, because Jeremiah was obviously dead. Or was it a missile? Or did "they" bring the bomb, which exploded prematurely? In that case, wouldn't it have been Jeremiah who'd have excused himself from the room?

Thompson couldn't think straight at the moment, as a

22

Thompson flew from Washington, D.C., to Whiteman Air Force Base near Sedalia, Missouri, where Gen. Buster Franklin had reserved a seat for him on an airborne command post.

"How are your wounds?" General Franklin asked, as they boarded an EC-130E Hercules, just as the sun peeked above the eastern horizon.

"Almost healed." Two of the shrapnel wounds he'd suffered in the Minneapolis blast two weeks ago had required over twenty stitches each. "Where are we going?"

"Kansas City. Above Kansas City, to be precise."

They walked through an electronic suite crammed with the latest camera and computer equipment and entered a deluxe cabin filled with other high-ranking military officers. General Franklin introduced Thompson around and then steered the attorney general to two adjacent seats in the back.

"Why did you want me on this flight?" Thompson asked, looking around, thinking the cabin was as luxurious as Air Force One.

"It's good for your image," the general answered. "I told the PR flacks back at the Pentagon to make certain the news media knows. You gotta start running for president some time."

He was the only civilian in the cabin, Thompson noted, and the only one wearing a business suit. At the risk of being compared to Richard Nixon, who walked on the beach in a suit, Thompson wasn't about to wear an undistinguished camouflage uniform, presidential ambitions be damned.

"I'm certainly going to need a new job, Buster. President Trainor told me yesterday my days at the Justice Department are numbered."

The Marine Corps chief-of-staff snorted contemptuously. "Don't worry about *him*. He doesn't exactly have a lot of support right now."

True, Thompson thought. Trainor's support had melted away following the bombing two weeks ago in Minneapolis, especially when the president urged caution in the face of demands within Congress and at the Pentagon that action be taken against the rebel army dug in at Kansas City. Polls showed that most people wanted to settle the mess now, when the opportunity presented itself.

"It makes sense to strike now," General Franklin said, talking around a cigar stuffed in the side of his mouth. "With Jeremiah and General Arnold dead, the rebel army is leaderless."

"During a television interview with UBC, Trainor voiced the opinion that the New American Army would disband shortly and bloodshed could be avoided," Thompson said. "When they asked me to comment, I disagreed. Trainor called and said if I couldn't be a member of the administration team, I should resign."

"Do that and run for his job."

"Still, Trainor made one valid point. No matter what happens, there are millions of dissident citizens in the Dakotas, and we have to find a way to accommodate their beliefs."

"The best way to make certain they behave in the future is to corner their army and kill it."

Thompson reluctantly agreed with that logic, although he now was convinced that the "New America phenomenon" wouldn't go away, even with a military victory. In his heart of hearts, he agreed with Jeremiah's statement at the negotiations that a seed had been planted.

Thompson also knew the current political environment demanded that he lead or get out of the way. No one would tolerate a namby-pamby who wanted to "talk about the issues." He wasn't the only politician in Washington who entertained the idea that he might be the next commander-in-chief. The powerful chairman of the House Judiciary Committee, who harbored hopes of becoming the presidential nominee on the Republican ticket, warned Trainor that a bill of impeachment could yet be drawn against him for allowing a mercenary army to occupy the farm belt with impunity.

"I'm still surprised that President Trainor seems to have folded his political hand and retreated to the sidelines," Thompson said. "I know his cabinet and staff advised him to out-hawk the hawks and ensure his own election next year."

"Trainor's a pussy."

The cabin of the huge, modified transport plane had no windows. On the other hand, several strategically placed television screens broadcast live images of the action taking place on the ground below. Some scenes were filmed by the plane's external cameras; others by ground cameras that bounced their images off satellites. Computer screens displayed constantly changing drawings and graphics showing the location of troops, tanks, and artillery.

"Are we in danger?" Thompson asked.

"We can expect some antiaircraft fire in the beginning," General Franklin replied, "but we're armed and equipped with countermeasures. We got fighter support." The general had a mischievous look on his face. "In a worst-case scenario, there's an escape pod in the hold, but there's no room for civilians."

"Thanks, Buster."

Thompson watched as General Franklin pointed at TV screens showing high-altitude shots of the New American Army's defensive line, between the Kansas and Missouri Rivers, including downtown Kansas City, Missouri.

"You can see they also got strength on the high ground south and west of the downtown area," General Franklin said. "Right now both armies are probing each other. Depending on how we come at them, they'll reposition themselves north or south of the Missouri. If they have time."

"Is this going to be a bloody battle?" Thompson asked.

"By necessity, yes."

"What do you mean?"

"Look around this cabin, Peter. You got a lot of aging warriors with stars on their uniforms. Most don't get to participate in more than one or two real battles during their careers, not counting the daily infighting at the Pentagon. They want this one badly, to avenge what the rebel army did to Ellsworth and Fort Riley, and to get even for the fact someone assassinated the army's senior officer at a peace conference."

"I understand."

"We probably could destroy most of the New American Army with air strikes and carpet bombing, but that wouldn't allow us to regain our honor on the field of battle."

"Do they have any kind of chance at all?"

"Not really. They got maybe a hundred thousand troops in the area. We have three times that many. They're outmanned and outgunned. They have no airpower. As a result of air surveillance, satellite photos, and tips from ordinary citizens, we've destroyed all but four of the eighty F-16s they hijacked, as well as five more of the B-1 bombers. They wouldn't dare bring those few planes over the battlefield, where we could easily shoot them down."

"If they have no chance, why would they fight?"

"Same as us. Pride. That army down there is commanded by a professional, competent officer corps. The troops are either mercenaries or fanatics, who've already accepted the likely fact of being killed in combat. It goes with the profession. These soldiers aren't about to cut and run. They don't have any place to go anyway, except jail."

Thompson knew another important reason to dislodge the rebel army was that it sat astride one of the nation's main food supply lines—key highways, railways, and water routes bringing grains and beef out of the nation's heartland to the major East and West Coast cities, which already were suffering some food shortages.

"Here's the scary part," General Franklin said, leaning close to Thompson. "Their army is widely dispersed throughout the city. Squads of soldiers have taken over private homes. Larger units are hunkered down in civic buildings, retail shops, malls, hotels, even hospitals and nursing homes. They got their artillery hidden in warehouses and parking garages. If we go after all these assets aggressively from the air, it would mean destroying a good part of Kansas City and killing tens of thousands of civilians."

"I understand the rebels have been hard on the local population, anyway, especially women," Thompson said.

"That's another reason to give these bastards no quarter," General Franklin said, his face twisted in anger.

Thompson's heart jumped into his throat as the huge transport rolled sharply to the right. Even in the soundproofed cabin, he could hear the four engines straining. "What's going on, Buster?" he asked, his voice squeaking.

General Franklin pointed at one of the television screens, showing the sky filled with paratroopers, and the smoke from antiaircraft shells exploding in the air. "It's begun," the general replied.

Thompson looked at his watch. It was nearly 7:00 A.M., November 12, 1999.

By midday, Thompson learned from Franklin and the other generals in the flying command post that the battle below was going their way. The federal forces were divided into two armies: one approaching from the west and drawn from soldiers mobilized at Fort Riley and Fort Sill, Oklahoma, the other coming from the east, having been assembled at Fort Leonard Wood, Missouri. The two armies had secured the east, west, and south suburbs, and formed a pincher around the main rebel army located along the Kansas and Missouri Rivers.

Thompson watched televised images of warplanes firing "smart bombs" at antiaircraft and artillery batteries, and tanks. *War is depersonalized for the observers and commanders*, he thought. It was as if they were sitting in a theater, watching a movie; a fictional account of a real war. Except Thompson knew that men were dying on the ground below in large numbers. Even the laser-guided missiles weren't that surgically precise.

"Jesus!" someone yelled above the constant buzz of voices in the cabin. "They're using chemicals."

The big plane rolled and dipped to get over the area in question. Thompson followed General Franklin's pointing finger and watched a television screen that had zoomed in on a sector on the city's east side, where federal forces were concentrated. A white cloud engulfed these troops and oozed through their lines.

General Franklin went into the communications center, while Thompson remained strapped into his seat. He didn't want to be standing if the huge aircraft took evasive measures again. This possibility didn't seem to concern the military personnel, who stood, talked, cursed, and gestured. Thompson detected a hint of urgency in several voices.

General Franklin returned shortly.

"What's going on?"

"They've fired chemical shells at our troops advancing from the east," Franklin said. "First reports are that it's sarin, a nerve gas."

"Don't the troops have gas masks and other protective gear?"

"Certainly, but it takes awhile for them to put protective clothing on. This was unexpected. God, in our own country!"

"How toxic is sarin?"

"In high dosages, it can kill up to 90 percent of the troops exposed. We'll lose thousands in this attack."

A calm soon returned to the observer cabin, as the generals and colonels discovered the source of the chemical attack. One TV screen provided a crystal-clear view of a rebel MLRS-12 rocket tubes on a tracked vehicle that rocked violently as it pumped shells at U.S. troops. Then it was obliterated, presumably by an air-to-ground missile.

"There's another one," General Franklin said. "Third screen from the right."

Thompson saw a single artillery piece mounted on a railroad flatcar. It fired and a switch engine moved it to another location.

"There are deep limestone caves northwest of the city, used as a foreign trade zone," General Franklin said. "The enemy hid hundreds of large artillery pieces there and we couldn't get at them. Now they're rolling them out. But it's only a matter of time before the pilots and our own artillery nail them."

The battle continued on into the night, and Thompson was bone weary by the time the flying command center touched down a second time at Whiteman to refuel. General Franklin directed an aide, a lieutenant, to find a bed in billeting for the attorney general.

Joe Lambert stood in the hangar, looking at the apocalyptic bomber. Designed for low-level bombing runs, the adjustable-winged B-1 had a penetration speed of six hundred miles per hour at a height of two hundred feet. The bomber skin was radar-absorbent and its fuselage designed to resist nuclear blast rebound pressures.

Nothing can stop it, he thought, *especially in this weather*. A storm system blanketed the East Coast of the United States, from the Carolinas to their location in Nova Scotia. The rain and high winds would provide natural cover for the B-1, and the bad weather would keep interceptor aircraft on the ground. No one expected a raid on a night like this, which was exactly why they were flying, he concluded.

Lambert's job required him to check the three bomb bays. The center bay contained a rotary launcher loaded with three SRAMs. Each of these air-to-ground missiles carried a 170-kiloton nuclear warhead. Four B-61, 500-kiloton nuclear gravity bombs hung in the other bays. They were designed to be delivered either by free-fall, parachute-retarded airburst, or low-level "lay down," with immediate contact burst or delayed surface burst. Lambert knew strategic nuclear weapons of this size would cause massive damage and kill millions of civilians.

Lambert acknowledged the other three crew members as

they arrived and climbed inside the bomber. The Russian pilot had logged thousands of hours flying the Blackjack, the "black" bomber of the former Soviet Union. The North Korean copilot handled the mechanical flight controls. The defensive systems operator from Japan analyzed data from onboard AN/ALQ-161 detection systems, which provided scary, computer-voice warnings about ground fire, incoming missiles, or hostile aircraft. Lambert, the offensive systems operator, would arm and release the atomic weapons at the appropriate time.

The pilot taxied, and they were soon airborne. The high winds made it a bumpy ride as the B-1 rocketed over the predawn landscape at a dizzying speed. Lambert calculated that in approximately a half hour they'd be over Boston, where he'd lay down one of the B-61s. His orders were to repeat the same procedure at fifteen-minute intervals, as they flew over New York, Philadelphia, and Washington, D.C. Drop one of the monster bombs on each city and speed on ahead of the hurricane-force winds resulting from the explosion.

After destroying Washington, their orders gave them free rein to use the SRAMs on the U.S. Navy's Atlantic Fleet parked at Norfolk, Virginia. If the fleet was crippled, it couldn't be used against New America's friends abroad, especially in the Middle East.

As they flew across the Atlantic Ocean, Lambert considered how he'd come to this critical juncture in his life. A former air force pilot, he'd flown fighters in Desert Storm and over the Balkans after that, in support of NATO troops trying to restore peace in the former Yugoslavia. Even so, he wasn't on the promotion list to lieutenant colonel, and he'd left the service to become an airline pilot.

He'd progressively lost faith in America for any number of reasons: while he performed his patriotic duty overseas, his wife had been mugged in the parking lot near the building where she worked, and permanently injured; his father had died of cancer while an insurance company dragged its feet on a potentially life-saving but expensive medical procedure; and, finally, the airline company for which he worked merged with another carrier and he'd lost his job.

He'd volunteered his piloting skills once he'd moved himself and his family to Fargo, thinking the new nation surely would start up an airline. He even agreed to be on call in case his fighter-pilot skills were needed. Lambert envisioned such a situation involving a federal air attack on South Dakota, during which time he'd be piloting a fighter engaged in defensive actions.

But this . . . this situation he hadn't imagined in his worst nightmare. As they approached Boston without any sign of detection, he thought about simple, hardworking people like himself asleep in their homes below. Men, women, and children awaiting the day, when they would rise to cook breakfast, walk the dog, go to school, drive to work. They couldn't imagine the death machine streaking toward them in the predawn sky.

Luckily, he was the key to their salvation, today, and for that Lambert was as happy as a person can be, knowing his own death was likely.

"We'll be over the target in two minutes," the pilot said, breezily, in unaccented English, as if he were announcing the next station on the underground metro. "Navigator, arm bombs and release at your discretion."

At his discretion. Lambert looked at the digital and analog instruments and typed in a series of commands on a keyboard. He thought he heard the bomb bay doors whirl open. He punched in another command and pushed "Y" twice, to confirm his intentions.

"Bombs away."

They flew on and Lambert imagined his fellow aviators tensing their shoulders for the shock—which didn't come.

"What's the problem?" the Russian asked.

"I don't know," Lambert said. But he had his orders, and he'd already decided to follow them. He believed God had a plan for the "Chosen People," and that he had a critical role to play. He would be a martyr for the movement, remembered forever. That's what the *Prophet* had told him in person, several weeks ago when they'd talked for hours. Lambert had looked deeply into the Prophet's eyes and saw his destiny. This mission *would not be successful.*

Lambert looked over at the Japanese DSO, unable to see

his eyes inside the helmet, behind the dark shield designed to prevent radiation-flash blindness. Still, Lambert knew his seatmate knew, and he listened as the DSO said, "I think the problem is that the OSO failed to perform his mission."

Lambert felt the g-force increase as the pilot banked sharply to his right and upward, rotating the wings to a maximum sweep of sixty-seven degrees. They were going ballistic! The DSO swung at Lambert with his left arm. Amazingly, inside this deadly instrument of destruction, that was his only weapon. The four crew members weren't even carrying side arms. Lambert warded off the blows, as he flipped a switch activating an SOS beacon. The copilot turned in his seat, reached back, and grabbed at him. Lambert struggled desperately to pull the yellow ejection handles on either armrest, but the copilot and DSO had pinned both his arms.

"Oh, shit!" the pilot said.

Lambert looked at the control panel and saw a yellow circle around the bomber's screen image, indicating a missile lock on the B-1. He began to pray.

Thompson stayed on the air base the next

morning, compelled by the television news. An F-16 Falcon had brought down a B-1 with a Sidewinder missile, and the bomber had crashed north of Boston, near Ipswich. According to CNN, reports from the crash scene indicated the B-1 had carried at least four nuclear bombs.

In Washington, a delegation of congressmen from eastern seaboard states held a press conference, suggesting that President Trainor offer a cease-fire in the current conflict with New America and attempt to resume negotiations with whomever was in charge of the secessionist colony.

Some of these same congressmen had been braying for blood only a few days ago, Thompson thought, with disgust.

Those demanding a ceasefire pointed to the carnage in Kansas City. U.S. casualties on the first day of the battle approached ten thousand, according to news reports. Before going aloft again, General Franklin told Thompson at an early morning breakfast that actual federal casualties, both dead and wounded, probably would go even higher. Enemy casualties were twice as high. Another week and the rebel army would be entirely destroyed, the general told Thompson.

But the battle wouldn't last that long. At noon, eastern standard time, all television networks carried live President Trainor's address to the nation. Thompson was one of many crowded around a television set in a lounge at base headquarters in Sedalia.

"As of this moment, I have ordered the military forces of the United States to observe a cease-fire in the conflict at Kansas City," Trainor said. "And I ask the New American armed forces to do likewise. This madness has gone far enough, and I think I speak for the majority of Americans when I say that a continuation of fighting will benefit no one other than our enemies abroad.

"In the last twenty-four hours, chemical warfare has been initiated within the United States. And we have narrowly averted a nuclear incident that could have destroyed the very foundation of our nation. Can anyone deny that it is now time to talk, rather than fight?"

Thompson feared that most Americans would agree. Trainor looked and sounded presidential, Thompson thought, ruefully.

"Obviously, we have a constitutional crisis of unprecedented proportions on our hands," President Trainor continued, "which I am prepared to address directly, without prejudice and without any hidden agenda. We can peacefully resolve our philosophical and political differences.

"As president of the United States, an office conferred on me by circumstances I wish had not occurred, I had absolutely no prior knowledge of the treacherous bombing in Minneapolis that claimed the lives of conscientious and peaceful negotiators both from the United States and New America.

"This was a dastardly attack," Trainor told a watching nation, "which we can only speculate was the work of those who desire to stoke the fires of discord within the United States for their own purpose. Let us not destroy ourselves, while our enemies around the world applaud our self-destruction.

"I have taken an oath to protect and defend the Constitution of the United States, and that Constitution has many clauses protecting the rights of individuals to dissent from the wishes of the majority. It guarantees a host of states' rights. The Constitution can be amended by a majority of the peoples' elected representatives in Congress. In the days ahead, I will be talking more about this process, as well as specific proposals.

"I believe beyond a shadow of a doubt that all Americans, regardless of their religion, creed, or race, or their social or political beliefs, want to resolve our differences peacefully. I promise those individuals who comprise New America that we their brothers will be sensitive to their concerns, needs, hopes, and dreams."

The president was emphatic: "Please take me at my word. Give peace a chance. Thank you and God bless everyone who lives within the borders of these two great nations."

It was Trainor's last words that left a bitter taste in Thompson's mouth. *Two great nations.* No, it was one great nation, and a rebel colony. On the other hand, Thompson wondered what he would have done had he been in Trainor's shoes. New America had four of the B-1s left. What if the next one got through? Was it worth the risk?

Maybe he was just tired, Thompson thought. Unable to think straight. One thing he knew for certain: U.S. military forces would be denied a victory in Kansas City, and their reputation would be even more tarnished, given the thousands of casualties they had suffered in a stalemate. The rebel forces could even claim a victory, in that they survived.

By the time Thompson had returned to Washington, the first poll results were in. President Trainor's call for a cease-fire and a resumption of negotiations had the support of 60 percent of the people. The president, who only a week ago had been ignored and threatened with impeachment, now appeared to have the support of a solid majority of American citizens.

23

THE EPISTLE OF JEREMIAH
THE PROPHET
TO THE NEW AMERICANS

CHAPTER THREE

1 Jeremiah, being a Prophet who spake the words of the One True God to His people;

2 And on behalf of all the Brethren who strive to implement His Word in the land called New America, as well as those Martyrs who in support of our Cause and Way of Life have made the Supreme Sacrifice in the Great Battle of Kansas City:

3 The Grace of God the Father is with you and guides your efforts, and makes a place for you in Heaven; and protects and preserves the One who is His Righteous Instrument. Amen.

4 In light of the recent Treachery in Minneapolis, and the Carnage inflicted on our troops in Kansas City, I direct your attention to the Revised and True Words

of the first Jeremiah, wherein much can be learned, about Yesterday and Tomorrow:

5 "Righteous art Thou, O LORD, when I complain to Thee; yet I would again plead my case before Thee. Why does the way of the Wicked prosper? Why do all who are Treacherous thrive?

6 "Thou plantest them, and they take root; they grow and bring forth bitter fruit; Thou art near in their Mouth and far from their Heart.

7 "But Thou, O LORD, knowest me; Thou seest me, and triest my mind toward Thee. Pull them out like Sheep for the Slaughter and set them apart for the day of Slaughter, I beg you. Show them not mercy a second time.

8 "How long will the land mourn, and the grass of every field wither? For the Wickedness of those who destroyed it the beasts and the birds are swept away, because a Godless nation said, 'I will not bend my knee to the LORD!'

9 "I have forsaken my House; I have given the Beloved of my Soul into the hands of her Enemies, whom She recognizes not.

10 "Yet my Heritage surely cannot be like a speckled bird of prey, about which assemble all the Wild Beasts, come to devour that which they did not sow, nor can harvest.

11 "Many masquerading as shepherds seek to destroy my Vineyard; trample it down and make it a desolate wilderness. The land and the people in it cry to me for Deliverance and Revenge.

12 "Oh, LORD, have they not sown wheat, and will they not reap thorns, profiting nothing! Shall they be

ashamed of their harvest and Fear the Anger of the LORD?

13 "Thus sayeth the LORD concerning my Evil Neighbors who touch the Heritage which He has given my People to inherit: 'Behold, I will pluck them up from their land, and after I have plucked them up, I will again have compassion on them, and I will bring them again each to his heritage and each to his land. And it shall come to pass, if they will diligently learn the ways of My People, to swear by My Name, 'As the LORD lives,' even as they taught My People to swear by Mammon, then they shall live beside My People. But if Any Nation will not listen, then I will utterly pluck it up and Destroy it, sayeth the LORD.' "

24

For the last month, Laura had been alone in the cabin within a cave, except for her bodyguards. She hadn't seen Jeremiah since the day after the Science Center tour, when he'd left, saying he was going to the peace negotiations in Minneapolis. More disturbing to Laura, Katrina Dorfler had quit coming around. She was Laura's only companion and only real hope of escape.

One day in mid-November, Katrina appeared out of nowhere, striding briskly into the cabin. She seemed confident, happy, excited, in contrast to her usual depression over her imperfect relationship with Jeremiah. Katrina wore a beautiful, ankle-length turquoise winter dress coat and a gray knit beret. She took off the cap to reveal newly-dyed blonde hair. Keeping her coat on, Katrina sat on the sofa near the fireplace and patted a place beside her. "Come sit with me, Laura."

"Where have you been?" Laura asked, hurrying to Katrina's side.

"Keeping busy," Katrina said. She shouted into the kitchen, "Hey, Chuck, bring us girls some coffee."

"I've been going nuts here," Laura complained. "There's nothing to do." She looked down at her bulging stomach and felt disgusted. "I should exercise more or even dress up now and then, so I'd look nice like you."

After the bodyguard sat the coffee service on the table in front of the sofa, Katrina asked, as she always did when she came to visit, "How about some privacy, Chuck?"

He ignored Katrina and returned to the kitchen, but shortly Laura heard him go outside. She didn't go onto the deck anymore, since she'd quit smoking. She hated the cold and dampness in the cave, where the temperature was a constant forty-nine degrees, with humidity near 90 percent.

"So how are you?" Katrina asked, gaily.

"I've been raped, kidnapped. I'm a prisoner. My husband may be dead."

Katrina couldn't be deterred from her new optimism. "You look okay to me."

"I need to see a doctor," Laura said, getting right into her revised spiel for help.

"Why? Are you having trouble, Laura?"

"Morning sickness, mainly, but the baby hasn't been checked. You know, his heartbeat and such. I should have a sonagram." Soon, she'd be beyond the point at which she could safely abort the child. That thought gave birth to a sense of despair and panic.

"I know how you feel," Katrina said, nodding sympathetically.

"No, you don't," Laura declared, thinking that someone had to be pregnant to fully appreciate the feeling and accompanying emotions.

Katrina persisted. "Oh yes, I do."

Laura became more attentive. "You mean you've been pregnant before, Katrina?"

Katrina stood and walked toward the door to the deck, where she could see Chuck. Laura heard the bodyguard talking loudly with the guard who patrolled the cave floor.

Katrina turned back toward Laura and opened her coat to reveal a stylish maternity outfit. "I'm pregnant now. I thought you knew and were keeping my secret. I told Steve. Didn't he tell you?"

Dumbfounded, Laura stared at Katrina's protruding belly. "No, he didn't say anything to me." Why? Steve obviously had had his reasons.

"Well, it's true," Katrina said, beaming. She rebuttoned her coat and sat back on the sofa, where she fished a Marlboro out of her purse.

"You shouldn't be smoking," Laura said.

"I know, I know. Did you quit?"

"Yes." Laura regretted doing anything to ensure the viability of Jeremiah's seed, but she had a conscience.

Katrina looked determined. "This is my last pack."

"The baby," Laura said, pointing at Katrina's stomach, "is it Jeremiah's?"

"Of course!" Katrina snapped.

"Does he know?"

Katrina shook her head.

"How far along are you?"

"Same as you, Laura. About four-and-a-half months. That's why I've had to stay away lately. Not just from you, but Jeremiah, too. So he doesn't find out."

"Where do you live?"

"With friends who protect me, and my secret."

Laura was flabbergasted. Jeremiah had fathered two children by two different women at approximately the same time, but he didn't know it! *Or did he?*

"Where is he, anyway?"

Katrina smiled kindly. "You don't know much about what's going on in the outside world, do you?"

Laura shook her head in frustration. No newspapers or magazines were allowed in the cabin and she could watch only those television programs preapproved by Jeremiah and supervised by Chuck. "What's going on?"

"At the negotiations with the government in Minneapolis, a bomb went off and killed most of the negotiators, but Jeremiah escaped somehow. There was a big battle at Kansas City, and now a truce. Jeremiah's in China, I think."

Laura couldn't picture these momentous events.

"You can't keep your pregnancy a secret much longer," Laura said, still trying to think of a way to turn this information to her advantage. Then it came to her. "Is the baby a boy or a girl?"

"A boy."

Laura's hope soared. "If Jeremiah wants a son to fulfill his prophecy and eventually take his place, he has one. Yours and his. He can let me go!"

Katrina bit her lip and fumbled for another cigarette. "I

can't predict his reaction and that makes me afraid."

Laura reached across the table and patted Katrina's hand. "Why would Jeremiah be mad that you're pregnant?"

"Because it is unplanned. He always told me, 'Katrina, birth control is your responsibility. Don't forget it.' If he wanted me pregnant, he'd say so."

"Did you get pregnant on purpose?" Laura asked.

Katrina smiled slyly. "Yes and it was only an accident that it happened at the same time, you know . . . that you became pregnant. He planned that, but I didn't know, of course."

Planned by him! The rapist!

"Jeremiah doesn't allow anything to change his plans," Katrina said. "In that way, he is just like my father."

Instinct told Laura they were again skirting the edges of the secret that involved Jeremiah and Emma Dietze, Katrina's other cousin, whom Jeremiah once planned to wed. Laura remembered Walter Dorfler's words on his death-bed in a Quebec hotel. He had told Laura that Jeremiah ". . . was so obsessed with my niece Emma, I had to do something so he would complete God's work."

Now Laura understood. *Walter had had his niece killed and used her death to stoke Jeremiah's fanaticism about the decadence of America.*

Katrina stared at Laura for several moments and repeated, slowly, with great precision, "My child is not part of the plan. Do you understand?"

Laura's stomach flip-flopped, as the horrible implications of Katrina's remarks became clear. "What will you do? The first time he sees you again, he'll know."

"Yes, I must leave today, before he comes back. I'm going home to Germany to be with my mother until the child is born. I'm telling you this, Laura, so you will understand why I cannot help you right now. If I should fail, nothing would happen to you, but I might be killed." She added for emphasis, "And my baby."

"You don't have to do anything yourself," Laura pleaded. "Just call Peter Thompson, the attorney general, and tell him exactly where I am. Don't use your name. That's all you need to do, Katrina, and then they'll rescue ne. I'll get a late-term abortion. You can tell Jeremiah about your pregnancy. You and he will be together. Then he'll want you to have the baby." Laura nodded her head, attempting to entice Katrina to agree to her plan.

"He'd know. He'd see right through my denials. It's not that I don't want to lie to him to help you, Laura, *it's that I can't.*"

Laura saw the fear, the real fear. "Does he beat you?"

Katrina winced, as if a blow had been struck.

Laura exhaled, her breath coming out in a long, slow sound of defeat. "I understand and I won't involve you, Katrina. Your secret is safe with me. But some day he'll have to know. He'll find out."

"Maybe, maybe not. I have a plan."

"What kind of plan?"

"I can't talk about that now."

Exasperated, Laura no longer believed Katrina would or could help her. "Have you heard anything more about Steve?" she asked.

A smile played at the corners of Katrina's mouth. "I told you before that Steve might be alive. I didn't have any reason at the time to believe that, only my hunch. But a few days ago, I overheard something."

"What? What did you hear?"

"Someone saw Steve recently in Rapid City."

Laura's spirits soared as she experienced a renewed sense of hope; hope that had been dashed by what seemed the certainty of Steve's death. How had he survived the gunshot wounds?

"You mustn't repeat what I've just told you," Katrina warned. "I don't want Steve to kill Jeremiah, but I don't want you to give up hope either. Do you understand?"

Laura did, sort of. Katrina could be lying, fearful she'd settle for Jeremiah if she thought Steve was dead. Or was Katrina telling the truth but hesitant to contact Steve for fear he'd kill Jeremiah while rescuing her?

Katrina stood. "I've got to go now. Take care of yourself, Laura. If you need to see a doctor, tell Jeremiah to take you to a Dr. Michael Connolly in Rapid City."

"Do you see him?"

"No. But Jeremiah knows and trusts Connolly."

Sensing she wouldn't see her for a long time, perhaps never, Laura embraced Katrina.

"Don't worry, Laura. Somehow, it will work out for both of us. I feel certain."

Jeremiah returned two days later. Buoyed by his many successes, he told Laura the details of how he'd outsmarted the federal authorities time after time.

Because he seemed in an magnaminous mood, Laura made her pitch. "I should go see a doctor. Katrina recommended Dr. Connolly."

Jeremiah wrinkled his forehead and nodded. Elated, Laura immediately began plotting. If she got out of the cave and into Rapid City, she at least had a chance of escaping. A slim chance, she knew, but maybe some unanticipated opportunity would present itself. She could try to break free, drop a note, appeal to a nurse, or the doctor. If all failed, she should see a doctor anyway. She didn't want to die in childbirth due to some unforeseen complication.

Just before Thanksgiving, Chuck told Laura they were going to see Dr. Connolly—she and him and another guard. Jeremiah was away again "on business." They went through the usual blindfold routine to exit the cave and get into the backseat of a car.

Although she couldn't see, Laura nevertheless paid careful attention, creating landmarks with her other senses. She calculated the speed of the car, so she could establish a time frame for this trip to Rapid City. Approximately seven miles into the trip by her calculations, they turned right onto a paved road. Two minutes later, they passed a farm. Laura smelled the silage. Eight minutes later she heard a train whistle, and felt the car bump over railroad tracks. A mental image complete with pictures, sounds, and smells began to form.

Chuck removed her blindfold as they neared the outskirts of Rapid City. Laura longed to look outside at the world—the land, trees, houses, people, the sky. What she saw horrified her.

On the heights south of the city, bodies hung from lampposts, trees, and hastily improvised gallows. Crudely lettered signs were attached to each body: TRAITOR, COLLABORATOR, BLACK MARKETEER, U.S. WHORE, THIEF, QUEER, DRUG DEALER. Laura hid her eyes with her hands, seeking the serenity of blindness and ignorance.

Steve had almost lost hope. After nearly two

months, there had been no sign of Jeremiah, Katrina, or Laura. He and Hoffman had set up an observation post in an empty second-floor office located across the street from Dr. Connolly's clinic. They jimmied the lock to get in originally and then changed it, so only they had a key and couldn't be surprised by a janitor or, worse, the state police.

"Maybe we should give up," Steve said to Hoffman.

"Maybe." The CIA agent had renewed his obsession with chewing gum. "I'm getting a bad feeling about this."

Steve hoped the news reports were right, and Jeremiah had been killed in Minneapolis. *Blasted to pieces.* At first, he thought the terrorist's death would mean Laura's imminent release. What reason did Jeremiah's lieutenants have to hold her now? Several horrible scenarios came to mind and made him sick to his stomach.

"It's even more dangerous here now," Hoffman said. "The state police are everywhere, arresting suspected spies and saboteurs, and exacting vengeance against anyone thought to be a collaborator."

President Trainor's actions had dashed everyone's hopes, Steve thought. New Americans considered the cease-fire a victory. Not only had the rebel army survived in Kansas City, but federal troops that had occupied South Dakota at the start of the battle had been withdrawn after the cease-fire.

"Let's give it a few more days," Steve said. "Then we'll try something else."

That evening at dusk, Steve climbed up to the roof of the building and looked out over Rapid City. With the exception of the big hotel where he'd first talked to Dr. Connolly, most of the buildings were three- and four-story structures. He could see for miles in every direction of the downtown area, but he never saw Laura.

It reminded him of times in the FBI when they'd searched for a body. They'd walk right by it, time after time, never seeing it, until one day they stumbled upon it by accident and wondered how they'd missed it before.

"Come look at this!" Hoffman said, standing to the side of the uncovered window so as not to be seen. "Isn't that Laura?"

Steve grabbed his binoculars. It was Laura! She wore a long, gray coat, but he could see her face. She stood beside a black Mercedes, conspicuous on the otherwise deserted street. A large bodyguard took Laura's arm and led her into Dr. Connolly's office. Steve watched, but no one else got out of the car, although he couldn't see through the tinted windows.

"Let's go!" Steve said, heading for the door and the stairs leading to the first floor.

In the first-floor hallway, Steve said to Hoffman, "I'll go to Connolly's office. The receptionist might remember me from the time I was there to make the appointment for Laura." Actually, Lynn, his fictional wife. "I'll tell them my wife is in the back and I need to talk to her. That it's an emergency."

"I'll walk casually over to the limo."

Yes. Steve thought, desperately. This one time in his life he had to be smart, and lucky. He prayed for divine guidance. *Please, God!* "If the bodyguard with Laura gets suspicious, I'll kill him right away." Steve felt reflexively for the gun and commando knife attached to his belt and hidden from view by his thigh-length coat.

"I'll knock on the window of the limo," Hoffman said, "and if no one is inside, I'll get in and jump-start it. If there's a driver, I'll take care of him." Hoffman opened his coat to reveal an Uzi equipped with a silencer.

"Drive around back to the alley entrance. We'll be there."

"If everything goes well, we could have as much as a half-hour head start," Hoffman said.

Exactly the time we'll need to drive to Ellsworth Air Force Base, Steve thought. Even if they were prevented from getting to the air base, they could hide in several safe houses and summon massive reinforcements.

Hoffman took a cell phone from his pocket and said, "Go! I'll call our friends and tell them what's happening."

With Hoffman following, Steve put up the parka hood, stepped out onto the sidewalk, and walked across the street past the Mercedes.

Inside the doctor's office, Steve glanced briefly at Laura's bodyguard, who was reading an old issue of *Sports Illustrated.* Steve kept his face averted, walked to the receptionist's window, and tapped on the glass. The hairs on his neck tingled at the thought of the bodyguard behind him and Steve kept one hand inside the coat, near the Sig-Sauer.

"Can I help you?" the receptionist asked, opening the window after what seemed an eternity.

"My wife just went into the back," Steve whispered. "I have some medical records she needs before talking to the doctor. I need to give them to her."

"What's her name?"

Steve eyeballed the registry and tried to read the names upside down. "She sometimes uses her married name, sometimes her maiden name." He picked out a name. "Nancy. Nancy Ogilvy. What room is she in? I'll just go back."

"I'll give the doctor the records." The receptionist held out her hand.

Steve leaned forward to impart a confidence. "Part of this concerns a virus I have. The doctor said I should be present when they talk about it. You understand?"

The receptionist drew back. "All right. Go through the door over there, then down the hallway to room three."

There were only four examination rooms. Steve checked the patient records placed in plastic holders attached to each door. On the second door, the name at the top of the folder was: LAURA DELANEY. Steve's spirits soared. He opened the door slowly and saw Laura sitting in a chair, looking forlorn. Steve quickly stepped into the room, holding a finger to his mouth.

Laura rose and fiercely embraced him. "How . . . ?" she started to ask.

"Later!" Steve said, taking her hand. He stuck his head into the hallway before pulling Laura after him. They walked quickly toward an exit door less than fifteen feet away. A sign warned of an alarm that would sound upon opening the door.

Steve pushed open the door, dragged Laura into the alley, and silently rejoiced at the sight of the limo waiting for them. With the alarm wailing mercilessly in the background, he opened the back door and pushed Laura in before entering himself. As he shut the door, a gun pressed against his temple.

There were three men in the backseat of the limo. One had a hand clamped over Laura's mouth.

Steve instinctively drove his elbow into the face beside him. The gun dropped to the floor, but before Steve could lash out again, he felt a numbing blow to his head.

Someone shoved him out of the car onto the ground, where Steve tried unsuccessfully to stand up. He sat with his arms on his knees and his head on his arms as he tried to clear the cobwebs from his brain.

Steve looked up to see Jeremiah and two of his bodyguards appear at the entrance to the alley, prodding Hoffman ahead of them. The German's face dripped blood and he could barely walk.

"Laura, I thought you were going to see Dr. Connolly," Jeremiah said, a mocking smile playing at the corners of his mouth.

"You bastard!" Laura shrieked, breaking loose from the guard. She attacked Jeremiah, pounding at him with her fists. While Steve watched helplessly, Jeremiah backhanded Laura, knocking her back against the car. Her knees buckled as blood gushed from her nose. She would have collapsed to the ground, except for the strong arm of the blond bodyguard.

Jeremiah squatted in front of Steve. "This is getting rough on both of us, Steve. Your head's taken quite a beating lately, what with the gunshot wound and now this. Your brains will soon be mush. I think you're in line for a long rest in one of our special institutions."

Steve remained silent, although he had regained his senses for the most part and was calculating his next move. Steve rolled backward as his right leg shot powerfully outward and upward, aimed at Jeremiah's face. If his shoe heel hit the terrorist's nose just right, it would drive the bone into Jeremiah's brain.

Steve felt his shoe land solidly, but as he scrambled to his feet the blackjack fell again and everything turned black.

25

Thompson stared at the television set broadcasting a UBC news bulletin. *Jeremiah was in Beijing shaking hands with the Chinese premier!*

The former attorney general listened as the announcer explained to the audience that the Terrorist Prophet and Chinese officials had signed a treaty of friendship in which the world's most populous nation recognized the existence of one of the least populated.

"The treaty establishes a special trade status between China and New America, and provides for a mutual nonaggression pact," the newscaster said. "It says that each signatory will come to the aid of the other if either nation is attacked by external enemies."

The crisis facing the United States just got more complicated, Thompson thought, *given the stalemate on the Kansas City battlefield and the political paralysis in Washington.*

He was surprised Jeremiah was in Beijing, surprised by the terms of the treaty, but not surprised that the terrorist was alive. FBI medical examiners had determined several weeks ago that Jeremiah wasn't among the dead at the Minneapolis bombing site. Thompson had sat on that information, trying to think of a way to take advantage of it. Now everyone knew.

"I'll bet Russia is next," predicted Matty Terwilliger, Thompson's former chief aide. She'd been standing beside her boss's desk when the news flash was broadcast.

"I'm sure," Thompson sighed. He respected Matty's political acumen, and understood her thinking. China and Russia aspired to world leadership. They wanted to impress their culture and political ideas on the peoples of the world and shape the global economy to their benefit. If they could aid Jeremiah's cause, it was one more means of crippling their chief competitor.

The United States had played this game in reverse many places around the globe, Thompson knew. They'd stirred the pot in China and Russia's backyards by aiding insurgents in such places as Afghanistan, Tibet, and the Baltic states. Many of these rebels were little better than Jeremiah.

How did he do it? Thompson wondered, as he watched the tape of Jeremiah signing the documents. A terrorist who had started his campaign four years ago in Los Angeles with a sniper rifle was now treated as a head of state. How much of it was planning and how much luck? Divine intervention?

"We've had a dozen press calls this morning asking you to speculate about how Jeremiah survived the bombing in Minneapolis," Matty said.

Reporters who'd already found out about Jeremiah's presence in China. "That's not my business now."

"What are you going to do?" Matty asked her boss.

Thompson continued cleaning out his desk, knowing that the press conference at which he'd announced his resignation an hour ago now would be a footnote on the evening news.

"I'm having a guest for dinner tonight," he answered.

Thompson lived in an unpretentious townhouse he'd purchased years ago for half a million dollars because it was located in a fashionable neighborhood near Georgetown University, where other capital movers-and-shakers lived. Its most attractive feature, Thompson thought, was a spacious, private dining room perfect for frequent dinner parties.

Tonight, only a few weeks before Christmas, he and

General Franklin sat around one corner of the long dining table. Nevertheless, Thompson wore a burgundy dinner jacket and gray cravat, and General Franklin a navy blue suit. The perfection of the table settings, the efficiency of the service, and the anticipated excellence of the food and drink conveyed to Thompson a sense of order and predictability, even in these troubled times. *All yet could be put right.*

After an entree consisting of marinated lamb kabobs, with fresh mint and assorted vegetables, was served, Thompson dismissed the waiter and cook for the evening.

"This is quite exquisite," General Franklin said.

"I had to repay you somehow for the thrilling ride and meal over Kansas City, Buster."

General Franklin chuckled at Thompson's facetious remark. "You don't like meals ready to serve?"

"I don't like being shot at while I'm dining."

"The news today was interesting," General Franklin said, a mischievous look on his face. "Some cabinet officer resigned." Then he became serious. "Were you surprised to see him in Beijing?"

"No. The FBI had Jeremiah's fingerprints on file from the time he left his gun in a Kansas City airport hotel four years ago, when he was surprised there by Steve Wallace." Thompson paused and added, sadly, "That was the first time he attempted to assault and kidnap Laura Delaney. Anyway, the body of the man posing as Jeremiah at the negotiations was *not* Jeremiah."

General Franklin's eyes narrowed. "So he knew what was coming down the pike."

"He had a double present," Thompson said. "Actually, Jeremiah was there, in the beginning, I believe. The switch occurred during a break. Later I recalled that the double didn't have a bandage showing beneath his left shirt sleeve, as Jeremiah did in the beginning."

"How'd he get away?"

"Hid in a secret compartment inside the limo that brought General Arnot and Senator Carlson to the meeting. The man who arrived on the Learjet probably was the double, just in case someone shot down the plane. After the bombing, the MPs drove the limo to a hangar. FBI investigators think Jeremiah may have walked away disguised as a U.S. Army major."

"Probably commandeered a jeep and drove off."

"Entirely possible."

"So who planted the bomb?"

"Colonel Douglas. The FBI found pieces of his briefcase embedded in the bodies."

"How'd he get it by security? I understand it was tight as a drum."

"The bomb wasn't in his briefcase, Buster. His briefcase was a bomb. Undetectable Semtex. Very sophisticated construction."

"Obviously he had help. Someone among the security detail."

"Maybe."

"Any possibility he was an unwitting mule?"

"Everything's possible. We'll never know all the answers." Thompson rose and walked to a sideboard. "Dessert, Buster?"

"No, thank you, Peter."

Thompson sat two snifters on the table and poured a generous measure of brandy in each one. He offered General Franklin a choice of cigars nestled in an elegant wood box. The tough-looking marine with the close-cropped red hair smelled several before selecting a Montecristo.

Thompson stood behind his chair. "I think Colonel Douglas hatched this plot himself. I've learned that President Carpenter appointed the colonel to the negotiating team, although Carpenter was killed before he could make an official announcement. What did Douglas have to offer? Why did Trainor keep him on? I think Douglas proposed to sacrifice himself if Jeremiah proved intransigent at the negotiations, which of course he did." Thompson paused. "I certainly underestimated Carpenter."

"I can't believe Douglas would blow up himself and the others on our team," General Franklin said, the unlit cigar shoved into one side of his mouth.

Thompson inhaled deeply. "I knew Sam for many years. He was not only a soldier and patriot, he was a *very* religious man. He viewed Jeremiah as a false prophet, and was deeply disturbed by the heresy."

"I wonder how Douglas squared his high moral standards with his willingness to blow up Haase and Tremain?" General Franklin asked. "And you, Peter, assuming Douglas wasn't behind the telephone call that got you out of the meeting."

"I'm certain Douglas struggled mightily with that," Thompson answered, "but it's obvious the assassination wouldn't have succeeded if Douglas had suddenly advised his fellow negotiators to leave the room. It was a hard, even callous decision, but the only one he could make."

Thompson sat down. "The key is the telephone call, Buster. That's why I invited you here this evening. To discuss its implications. Do you know that the MP who told me about the call was killed in the firefight after the explosion?"

General Franklin lit the cigar. "That's too much of a coincidence."

"Exactly. Now I have no corroborating evidence that I received a call from the White House. Trainor denies making the call."

"Immediately casting suspicion on you as the person who planted the bomb."

"Reporters already are speculating that I did it. Several members of Congress want a special prosecutor appointed to investigate my role in the Minneapolis bombing and the CAT raid that targeted Jeremiah."

"Meanwhile, Trainor can force you to resign without any fear of criticism, and your presidential ambitions are in the shitter. As we say in the Marine Corps, Peter, you've been screwed, blued, and tattooed."

Thompson laughed at his friend's graphic description. "Back to the telephone call. I tried desperately to get telephone company records, but they've conveniently disappeared."

"Naturally."

"Someone made the call."

"Not necessarily, Peter. If someone at the site knew about the bomb, which seems likely, they could have just aid there was a call to get you out of the room, so you'd immediately become the scapegoat. Another possibility is hat Douglas had the call made. I know he liked you, Peter. He wanted you to be president."

Thompson put down his brandy snifter. "But he didn't ell Jeremiah about the bomb, and neither did I. So that eaves only two possibilities. Jeremiah found out about it ome other way, or Trainor knew and told him."

General Franklin blew smoke at the ceiling. "I'd already arrived at the latter conclusion, Peter, knowing you were nnocent. Just to play devil's advocate, what if Trainor didn't know? What if Carpenter didn't tell him, and Douglas kept quiet?"

"Then Trainor is innocent, and Jeremiah found out some other way, as I said."

"But you think Trainor and Jeremiah are in league, don't you, Peter? Why? For God's sake, what would Trainor have to gain?"

"The presidency. He might not have gotten there the legitimate way. He's not exactly a charismatic personality. He's been successful in politics largely because he's always been able to raise large amounts of campaign funds."

"Do you think Trainor was involved in Carpenter's assassination?"

"I think it very suspicious that the accused assassin, Harvey Wilkinson, managed to hang himself in jail."

"Another major breach of security. Another convenient coincidence. Go on, Peter."

"Harvey Wilkinson was twenty-five years old, unemployed," Thompson said. "Married, one child. Left his wife about six months ago after quitting his job as the manager of a car rental agency in Cincinnati. Not active politically, although he joined the American Patriots. Had a real hard-on for the federal government."

"That doesn't make him unique," General Franklin wisecracked.

"Wilkinson's dad, Boothe, was a Vietnam War vet who claimed disability as a result of exposure to Agent Orange. Fought for two decades with the Veterans Administration and joined several law suits against the government, seeking disclosure and compensation. Eventually committed suicide about two years go, when he was about to die of cancer. His son wasn't seen sober after that. Guess where the Wilkinsons are from?"

"Where?"

"Louisville, Kentucky. Trainor was a senator from Kentucky and he was an army intelligence officer in Vietnam. He and the elder Wilkinson are about the same age."

General Franklin put both hands on the table, looking down in disturbed thought. "I've got a lot of friends in the military intelligence community. If Trainor and Wilkinson knew each other, I'll find out."

"You're also going to have to shoulder the responsibility of finding the remaining B-1 bombers, Buster. Only you can do that. Without them, Jeremiah's nothing more than a cowboy."

"I'm already on that in a big way, Peter. I've got a team going over satellite photos day and night."

"Where do you think they are?"

"Despite the one that flew out of Nova Scotia, I think the other four are right in our backyard. We're on high alert now, but our whole electronic interception system faces outward. A long flight into the United States greatly increases the possibility of detection. But if they were hidden in Wyoming, for instance, they could pop up and hit their targets before we knew what was going on."

"How could they not be seen?" Thompson asked. "They're pretty distinctive."

"They're the same size as a big jetliner," General Franklin answered. "With its wings retracted, a B-I is eighty-by-a-hundred-and-fifty feet and forty feet high. One of them would fit in any hangar at most airports in the country."

"If you need help on the ground, I still have friends in the FBI," Thompson said.

"I'll take all the help I can get, Peter, but what you really need to do is make that run for president. Someone has to carry the banner for the union, especially if we're right about Trainor."

"I'm severely compromised, Buster, as you know. Trainor will get the nod from the Democrats. I'm not a Repub-

ican. That only leaves a third-party bid. No one's done that
successfully in nearly a century."

"Then you'll have to be the first, Peter. Otherwise, we'll
lose everything."

"I know. Trainor's supporters in Congress are preparing
to introduce a constitutional amendment that would allow
states to secede from the federal union, with approval by
two-thirds of the registered voters."

"It's impossible to believe any congressman with a conscience would vote for it," General Franklin said.

"People are frightened, Buster, and want this whole thing
behind them. There's no great love of the federal government anyway. All politics is essentially local. This constitutional amendment might just fly."

General Franklin stood, as if anxious to get going. "Then
we got to get humpin'."

Thompson showed his guest to the front door and said,
"Watch your back, Buster. You've got to be number one
on his hit list." He saw that his comment had a sobering
effect on the general.

26

Their food flew through the slot at the bottom of the cell door. Steve picked up the tin plates and examined their contents. Vegetable stew, he guessed, unless the wiggly things counted as meat.

He walked to the back of the cell and put one plate in the sink and dumped onto it the contents of the other. He used the edge of the empty plate to retrace the grooves of the words he'd previously etched on the cinder block wall: FUCK JEREMIAH. FUCK NEW AMERICA. Perhaps it was juvenile, but he derived genuine pleasure from his only method of protest.

Each day the guards filled in and painted over the grooves, and criticized his artwork in the form of a beating. Every day, he redid it. *God forbid they ever think of paper plates.*

The cell was approximately eight-by-ten feet, with two beds suspended from each wall. A narrow pathway ran from the cell door between the beds to a lidless toilet and a sink, both anchored to the back wall. A barred window high on the back wall was much too small for a man to squeeze through. Every evening about dark a low-wattage bulb located inside a barred ceiling cavity came on and burned until dawn.

They'd been here about ten days, Steve calculated. Once again he contemplated the chains holding the iron bed frame to the walls, calculating what use he could make of hem, if he could get them off. Given the pristine condition of the beds and the paint on the floor and walls, the jail appeared newly constructed. *Jail construction probably is a growth industry in New America,* Steve thought.

He replayed in his mind the scene in the alley, where Jeremiah and his thugs had foiled their escape. He had Laura in his arms when the whole escape plan blew up in their faces. Why hadn't he seen it coming? Taken precautions. Obviously he and Hoffman had been under surveillance for some time. He'd been so anxious to rescue Laura, he'd ignored Hoffman's misgivings. He'd been careless and now Laura was once again paying for his inadequacies and failures.

Jeremiah has outmaneuvered me in every confrontation over the past four years, Steve thought, even though he'd wounded Jeremiah in Kansas City, and nearly killed the terrorist recently in Pierre. Being close, however, only counted in horseshoes. He'd let Laura down, and this time he'd pay for it with his life.

A scream echoing down the cell-block corridor caused a knot of fear to form in Steve's stomach. The horrible sound wasn't distinguishable as human or animal, only someone or something experiencing terrible pain. It probably was Hoffman. Steve knew they'd come for him soon.

Twenty minutes later, two of the jailhouse

goons unlocked and entered his cell. They carried truncheons and eyed Steve warily, with good reason. He'd broken another guard's arm several days ago.

"Put your hands on the wall and spread 'em!" one of the goons shouted. "Now, or I'll bust your head again!"

Steve complied, not wanting to suffer another severe beating just to get in several good licks before goon reinforcements arrived.

They cuffed Steve's hands behind him and walked him down a hallway, past other cells occupied by frightened and beaten men, who looked at him with eyes filled with terror and sadness and curiosity.

"Leave him alone!" someone yelled.

"What did you do?" another asked.

"I just wanted to go home," someone else answered.

The protests went on all night, until the guards used their billy clubs as a sleep aide.

At the end of the hallway, the two lunkheads shoved him through a door into a large room, approximately twenty-by-thirty feet and painted an institutional white, like his cell and the color of his jailhouse uniform. In the middle of the room were a desk and chair.

Along one wall, a gurney sat beside a metal cabinet. Through the glass doors, Steve saw various gleaming steel instruments lying on the shelves and shuddered to think how they were used.

On the other side of the room, arm, neck, and leg restraints were anchored into the wall. A block-and-tackle was rigged from the ceiling. In a far corner, a hose dripped water into a floor drain.

So far the thugs hadn't used the equipment and were satisfied to punch and kick Steve every day, while trying unsuccessfully to make a videotape of him confessing to "crimes against the state." Steve responded by reciting Jeremiah's crimes against humanity. They ended each session by hosing him down with ice-cold water before taking him back to his cell. It sufficed as his daily shower.

Today his jailers broke with tradition and made Steve stand in front of the desk for nearly ten minutes. He heard a door open and someone walk toward him. Steve flinched in anticipation of the blows. He looked out of the corner of his eyes and saw—Jeremiah!

"So, Steve, how do you like New America's equivalent of the confessional booth?" Jeremiah inquired, as the two guards snickered. "Here, the confessor tells all!"

Enraged and energized by the bastard's presence, Steve pivoted, dipped his shoulder, and charged, hoping to knock Jeremiah down. But the terrorist stepped back and shoved Steve, who lost his balance and sprawled onto the floor. The guards jerked him to his feet and brought him face-to-face with Jeremiah. One of the goons grasped a handful of Steve's hair to control him

"How about you take these handcuffs off and we go at

it man-to-man!" Steve yelled. "Hand-to-hand combat until one of us beats the other one to death."

"You'd take that chance? In your shape?"

"Damn right! What are you afraid of? You're God's boy, aren't you? You don't have to worry about losing a fight with a mere mortal like me." Spit flew out of Steve's mouth. "You already have a handicap. I've got broken ribs and a cracked skull!"

"I'm sorry about that," Jeremiah said, insincerely. "If Laura had just let me kill you that night at your farm, you wouldn't be in all this pain."

"You're afraid of me, aren't you, shithead! Afraid I'd kick your ass in front of these mental midgets! C'mon, let's get it on!"

"My, my, you are feisty today, Steve. I attribute that to sexual frustration. Lack of pussy. Now me, I'm contented as an old tomcat. Gettin' it everywhere! And now that you're here, I've persuaded your old lady to get back into my bed."

Steve struggled to move toward Jeremiah, but one of the jailers pulled his hair and the other simultaneously lifted his handcuffed arms, igniting a fire in his rib cage.

"No, Steve, we're not going to fight like a couple of school-yard gang leaders. You wouldn't be a match for me, although you did get in one good lick in the alley." Jeremiah frowned, gently rubbing a yellow bruise on his jaw. "Besides, God has already demonstrated he's on my side; otherwise you would have escaped with Laura. Ever think of it that way?"

Yes, I have. Steve silently cursed God, wondering once again why He—if He existed—always appeared so uncaring when bad people were doing bad things to good people.

"Take a look around this room," Jeremiah said, "because you'll be spending a lot of time here over the next few months." The Terrorist Prophet walked behind Steve. "I doubt you have anything useful to tell us, Steve. I know your motivations, your friends, and supporters. The two trailer rats who hid you and Hoffman are hanging from lampposts on the edge of town." He completed the circle and stood in front of Steve.

"I've just returned from Beijing, where I signed a treaty with the Chinese. That and the B-1s I've got hidden away convinced President Trainor to cave in to me. The leader of the free world pulled down his pants and bent over right on national television! You are now in the internationally recognized nation of New America, Steve!"

Jeremiah began to chant the name, as did his minions, as if they were urging on their favorite sports team. "New America! New America! New America!"

"Didn't you know, Steve? Haven't you been watching television in your cell?"

The goons laughed on cue.

Jeremiah put his face close to Steve's. "You know, on the way back from China I could have stopped to visit your ex-wife and kiddies in Denver." He raised his eyebrows knowingly, as Steve recoiled in shock and fear. For the first time in their various confrontations, he felt willing to give in, to do anything Jeremiah wanted, if the madman would just promise to leave his loved ones alone.

"Steve, you've read *The Book of Second Jeremiah*. We don't tolerate lawbreakers in New America. People who steal cars, attempt to kidnap people, and plot against the state. You can get in real trouble doing that here." He paused and looked calculatingly at Steve. "You'll be here until about the end of March. That's when Laura will give birth to our son."

Steve strained against the hands that held him, trying again to get at Jeremiah. If he could just get on top of him he could sink his teeth into the side of the monster's neck, biting down until his teeth punctured the carotid artery, until he felt that black blood gushing out of that evil body.

"In fact, here's my promise to you, Steve. I'll bring by some videotapes now and then so you can watch Laura and I make love. I think you'll agree I'm a stud when you see me in action. You will definitely view a video of the birth and the happy family." Again, they were nose-to-nose. "Then I'm going to personally spend an entire afternoon killing you as slowly and painfully as possible. Afterward we're going to grind up your body and sell it to the local Indians as hamburger."

The jailhouse dolts could hardly contain themselves as they howled appreciably at their leader's grotesque sense of humor.

Jeremiah pretended to lightly knock the dust off Steve's dirty white shirt. "In the meantime, boys, have your daily fun with Mr. Wallace, but don't do any permanent damage. That's my job."

They shoved Steve into his cell and he saw

Hoffman lying on his bed, curled into a ball. After rolling him over, Steve recoiled as if snakebit. The German CIA agent had been beaten severely, his right eye gouged out and suspended by its optical nerve.

"Oh, my God!" Steve cried, rushing to run water on their one, dirty towel. He dabbed at the blood that covered Hoffman's face and head, fearful that the eyeball might suddenly focus on him.

"He was here today!" Hoffman wheezed, hardly able to breathe.

"I know," Steve replied, sitting on the bunk and gently lifting Hoffman's head onto his lap.

"He did this. He said they'd been too soft on me!" Hoffman started to hyperventilate. Steve rubbed the cold towel over his friend's face, arms, and chest, trying to soothe him.

"I told him I worked for the CIA," Hoffman admitted, his breath coming more evenly as a result of Steve's efforts. "I told him all about my service in Europe, even the interrogation of Katrina Dorfler." Hoffman grabbed the front of Steve's soiled shirt. "I even gave him names of Russian and Chinese double agents!" Hoffman smiled conspiratorially, looking with his one good eye at Steve, who understood. A textbook response to torture was to give the enemy names of its own spies and accuse them of being double agents. If you died, you'd at least have planted the seeds of suspicion and confusion among your adversaries.

"But I didn't fool him," Hoffman allowed, his head slumping back onto Steve's lap. "Tomorrow . . . tomorrow, the guards are going to rape me! Then they're going to castrate me! Jeremiah said he'd be here to watch!"

Steve couldn't divert his attention from the eyeball lolling on Hoffman's cheek. He wondered how much it hurt, or if it was numb. *Could it see?* Could he somehow put it back in! He felt sick at his stomach, but was determined to try. He used the towel's edge as a grader, trying to gently push the eyeball toward its socket, but Hoffman moaned in pain and turned his head away. Steve placed the wet towel over the eye and that half of Hoffman's face. Astonishingly, that seemed to soothe him.

"I can't tell 'em what they want to know," he said to Steve, as if it were a solemn pledge. "But I can't go through that either."

Steve knew what Jeremiah wanted—the names of U.S. spies within New America, as well as sympathizers who hid infiltrators and saboteurs. Hoffman had endured ten days of savage beatings to protect these people; protect them from his fate, and also keep them in place. They were critical to the effort to undermine New America. Hoffman pointedly had never revealed their identities to Steve.

"They're stupid," Hoffman gasped, seeming to regain some strength and a measure of his dry sense of humor. "If the major was here, he'd show them how to get the information in ten minutes!"

Hoffman meant "Doc," the interrogation expert who'd accompanied them on the CAT raid. Did they lack this expertise in New America, or did they just prefer sadistic methods?

"You know what you've got to do?" Hoffman asked, focusing his good eye on his cell mate.

Steve nodded.

"You see, they've discovered my greatest fear," Hoffman whispered, as if this information was confidential. Steve didn't want to know the details of Hoffman's innermost fears, although he could guess, given Jeremiah's plans for tomorrow.

Hoffman slept fitfully for several hours. When he awakened, Steve offered him the tin plate of food, but Hoffman shook his head. Always thin, the German now

looked like a scarecrow. Steve considered ways to smash
the light bulb above, but that would only attract attention.
He had to do what he had to do right under their noses, in
one of the intervals between the times the hall guard
checked their cell.

Hoffman sat up, holding the towel in place over his damaged eye. He and Steve looked at each other briefly, communicating without speaking. They scooted back on the
bunk so that their backs rested against the wall. Sitting between Hoffman and the cell door, Steve put his arm around
Hoffman's shoulders and pulled his friend closer.

"Tell me about Germany," Steve said. "You were raised
near the Black Forest, weren't you?"

"Ja. In Stuttgart."

Steve smiled at the way the German pronounced the
name of his city, drawing out the double-consonant sound.
"Tell me everything about it and your family. Your life
there."

"I wish I had some gum," Hoffman said, using the towel
to support his gouged-out eyeball. He brought the German
state of Baden-Württemberg alive for Steve, who could en-
vision the Hoffmans' Alpine-style home on a hill above the
city, smell its unique odors, picture each member of Hans
Dietrich's family, and hear their guttural speech and booming laughter.

Hoffman enthusiastically told stories from different eras,
when he was a son, a student, a soldier, a spy. Steve found
them amazingly similar to the "growing-up" legends of
young American boys and men.

Together, they roamed mentally throughout the majestic
countryside of southwest Germany, up steep mountains to
breathtaking meadows and back down to cool, babbling
streams. Hoffman recalled a memorable motorcycle ride
down a mountain road at night, with a beautiful female
friend hanging on for dear life, her arms and long legs
grasping his body as they whipped through hairpin curves,
propelled on this death-defying trip by youthful exuberance
and too much good German beer.

"Life is always good, Steve, but during moments like
that, it's heavenly. It tells you there's something more."

Hoffman talked about the women he'd loved, and the women he wished he'd loved. The kids he'd never had. That was his only real regret.

"Thank you for this early Christmas present, my friend. It was the best funeral I could have had."

They sat some more in silence.

"Maybe you will go to Stuttgart some day and see my family, Steve. Tell them you were with me when I died and that my last thoughts were of them." He looked kindly at Steve. "You don't have to tell them how I died."

Steve struggled mightily to blink back tears and hold in the silently building scream.

"I'll tell you a secret, Steve. If you're very lucky, like me, and you have time to prepare for your death, one thing becomes clear. It isn't the symbols of your achievement or wealth that you reach out your hand for, it's to touch someone you love and who loved you."

Hoffman squeezed Steve's hand and held it tight. Steve knew he was a surrogate for many who couldn't be here this evening to say good-bye to their loved one, Hans Dietrich Hoffman.

When Hoffman finally relaxed his grip, Steve turned slightly so that Hoffman's neck rested in the crook of his left arm. Steve grasped the wrist of his left arm with his right hand and brought the pinchers together forcefully against each side of his friend's neck. He rested his cheek on Hoffman's head, happy not to be able to see his face. From the hallway, it would look like he was comforting his injured cellmate.

Hoffman struggled only a little, his instincts not wanting to let go of life. But he never said a word. Steve applied more pressure and kissed Hoffman's head.

Minutes passed, or was it hours? Steve felt for Hoffman's pulse, but there wasn't any. He covered the body with a blanket, and walked to the small window at the back of the cell. He hoisted himself up to try once again to look through the opaque glass and see outside. Was it raining? Were nonexistent trees bending to the will of the wind? Or was that just a memory? He felt disoriented. In shock.

Hoffman's recital had caused Steve to think of his dead

father. He whispered out the window into the night, "Dad. Dad, where are you? Help me. Help me!" There was no answer. Only a question.

Who would do this for him when his time came?

27

On March 7, 2000, Peter Thompson, candidate of the newly-formed American Patriots political party, won the Kansas presidential primary election, tallying 38 percent of the votes cast.

As he relaxed in a Wichita hotel suite, Thompson relished winning this "mini-presidential primary" over his opponents, Pres. Paul Trainor, the Democrat, and Ohio senator Donald Gilmore, the Republican. Despite what happened today, Thompson knew all three likely would be nominated during summer conventions as the standard bearers of their respective parties.

"Open primaries like Kansas are difficult to read," said Daniel Perez, Thompson's campaign manager, who sat at a desk going over tally sheets. "Voters who cross party lines to vote for a candidate may actually be sending a message to their party's candidate, trying to change his mind on a particular issue. Many will return to the party fold in the general election."

"I understand," Thompson said. "I still think it's significant we've won more open primaries so far than either Trainor or Gilmore. And I like the coalition we put together here."

"It cuts wide and deep," Perez agreed. "Political moderates. Catholics, Jews, Muslims, and every other religious group that doesn't buy into Jeremiah's theology."

"We've been getting the solid support of workers at multinational corporations, such as Boeing in Wichita," Thompson added. "And minorities. African-Americans, Hispanics, and Asians. They know a fractured nation could put them at the mercy of governments in states where racial/ethnic hatreds still run deep."

"Don't forget the Kansas farmers. They saw what happened to landowners in the Dakotas."

"Let's hope this coalition and momentum carries through the rest of the primary season," Thompson said.

"Only ten more elections, boss."

Thompson shook his head wearily. "The next hundred days will seem like a lifetime."

"You've got to do better than to keep coming out on top by a hair, Peter."

"Why, for God's sake?"

"You got 38 percent here, Trainor 34, and Gilmore, 28. If those splits hold up through the general election, none of you will win a majority of electoral votes. Then the House of Representatives will elect a president. Gilmore has more supporters in Congress than either you or Trainor."

Thompson took a clean shirt out of an open suitcase lying on the bed. "It's amazing I'm even in the race, let alone doing well."

"You gotta give it to the American Patriots," Perez said. "They've been tireless in their efforts to build an organization, raise money, and get your name on all the primary ballots. Too bad they couldn't field candidates in every congressional race, so we'd have some muscle in the House of Representatives."

"We'll have to concentrate our efforts this fall in states with significant numbers of electoral votes," Thompson said, putting on the clean shirt and pulling up his suspenders. "New York, Pennsylvania, New Jersey, the old industrial Midwest, Florida, Texas, and California. It's a long-shot, but doable."

"We need to more aggressively court Gilmore," Perez said. "He can be the kingmaker. He could throw his support to you in the general election if he decides he can't win. Or maybe you two can make a deal."

"His people think I'll eventually throw in the towel. That's why Gilmore's straddling the fence. He doesn't want to offend anyone, so it'll be easier to convert them to supporters later."

"It's a smart strategy," Perez said. "The people are looking for a middle ground between war and capitulation. Congress knows that, which is why they put off a vote on the secessionist amendment. They want to wait and see what happens in the primary and general elections."

"Jeremiah and Trainor are analyzing the numbers, too," Thompson said, already having filled Perez in on his conspiracy theory involving the president and the terrorist. "If they see they can't win legitimately, we can expect some actions designed to swing voters their way."

Perez nodded his agreement. "Here come the B-1s again."

Thompson inserted American flag cufflinks through the French cuffs. "However you look at it, this was a great win. Jeremiah couldn't win a battle here, nor an election. That says something. I think it's similar to the fight waged in Kansas before the Civil War by the pro- and antislavery forces. Kansans once again came down on the right side."

"At least Jeremiah's army is crippled," Perez noted.

Thompson didn't argue with this common perception about an army that had lost one-third of its troop strength, with nearly thirty thousand dead and wounded at Kansas City. But General Franklin had told him the New American Army, now repositioned along the South Dakota/Nebraska border, was reinvigorating itself with new recruits. The carnage at Kansas City amazingly had become a positive recruitment device abroad. Mercenaries couldn't resist the opportunity to pit themselves against the best, with a two-third's chance of survival, Franklin had explained.

"You need to address your supporters, sir," Perez interrupted, handing over a sheaf of papers. "These are suggested remarks."

Thompson glanced briefly at the printed mush, folded the papers in half, and shoved them into an inside coat pocket. He had time to think as he left the hotel suite with Perez and walked toward the service elevator, surrounded by other aides and his private security detail. He'd spurned Secret Service protection, even when offered by President Trainor, not quite trusting those who ultimately reported to the White House. That thought troubled him and suggested one theme he could speak about downstairs.

The service elevator opened into a hallway. They walked by the kitchen toward a back entrance to a first-floor ballroom, where Thompson's supporters waited. He knew only a few of them. The majority were spectators. His "show" was currently the most lively in town. Next week, it probably would be a rodeo or NASCAR event.

Thompson stopped short of entering the ballroom and collected himself, ignoring the prattle of those about him, all of whom offered some type of advice.

Finally he entered the room and walked down an aisle toward a lectern at the front. His supporters stood and clapped. A festive atmosphere prevailed in the room, fueled in part by the open bar.

When Thompson turned to face his supporters, lights suspended from the ceiling effectively blinded him to certain areas of the room. That made little difference, since he generally spoke into a void in front of him. The political pros suggested he pick out one person in the audience and speak to him, or her. But that technique was forever spoiled when his selected audience of one flashed him the middle finger several weeks ago.

"I want to thank the people of Kansas for this victory," Thompson began, and then halted for the cheers and victory whoops that followed.

"But I must temper my enthusiasm—our delight with this victory—by noting that we only won 38 percent of the vote today." Silence. He'd thrown cold water on his own victory celebration. He could almost hear the groans of Perez and other campaign aides. "About 60 percent of the voters voted for candidates who either want to give into blackmail and split this great nation into pieces, or who want to find a way to live side-by-side with a terrorist neighbor."

Perez walked over and whispered in Thompson's ear "Remember the speech in your coat pocket, Peter."

Thompson understood the chagrin of his staff. Questioning the judgment of voters violated a basic campaign tenet It would solidify the opposition, while making those who'd voted for him feel unappreciated. But Thompson wanted to speak to the broader television audience also. Hopefully, he could mollify his supporters and convert some doubters.

"I won't spend time this evening talking about the obvious, which is that Jeremiah is a madman and a terrorist," Thompson continued. "But we must also acknowledge his talents as a strategist and astute social psychologist.

"He's holding our nation hostage to nuclear blackmail, but more importantly he's tapped into our worst prejudices. He's fanned our hatreds to a fever pitch."

Thompson's voice rose passionately. "In this immigrant nation, which once welcomed everyone, regardless of religion, race, or national origin, so long as they loved liberty and democracy, worked hard, and observed the law, Jeremiah has set us one against the other."

Thompson nodded for emphasis and was encouraged to see some in the front row mimicking his body language. "He's managed to set black against white, Christians against all other religions, and citizens against their government. He's tried to ignite economic class warfare. These are simply tactics to Jeremiah, nothing more." Thompson elevated his voice again. "Do you really believe the God of the universe condones fratricide to settle theological, social, economic, and political differences?"

"Hell, no!" The cry from the back of the audience caused Thompson to grin, encouraging others to chant the same response.

"Who in the hell would want to live in New America?" Thompson asked, his mild profanity—unusual and out-of-character for him—eliciting a titter from the audience. "Up there with the intolerant Aryan elite, with their amended Bibles and their mercenary army that pillaged and raped an American city, and used chemical weapons on the battlefield. Four terrorists flying a hijacked B-1 came within a hairsbreadth of killing tens of millions of Americans in a nuclear holocaust.

"Inside that armed compound called New America, the state police summarily execute dissidents by the hundreds, perhaps thousands."

A chorus of boos erupted from the audience.

"In New America, they've chosen to ignore the fundamental message of Christ in the New Testament, which is to treat your fellowman and woman as you would want to be treated. That is a message of tolerance, people. It's the message we've tried desperately to enshrine in the United States. It's the primary reason for our greatness. The reason we were able to achieve in two hundred years a level of democracy and economic prosperity that has eluded most nations on earth."

Thompson took a breath. "We took in those poor, huddled masses yearning to be free; those people from Europe, Africa, Asia, anywhere in the world, and they gave us their best—the best of the sweat of their brows and the best of the creativity of their minds. We are what we are today because of our diversity and our tolerance, not our intolerance. Yet Jeremiah says diversity is a handicap that won't be tolerated in his *new* America."

The audience was silent. Thompson had no idea what they really thought, those in this room and those in the vast television audience, but he'd gone too far now to turn back.

"Tolerance. We seem to have run out of it. The population is splintered into a thousand special interest groups, all of which have some litmus test. Disagree with them on that, whatever it may be, and they want you out of their midst, or they want to isolate themselves from society. In a democracy, citizens don't always agree. Do you always agree with your neighbor? Your coworkers? Your spouse? Your children? Your parents? No, you don't!"

He swallowed the word before it escaped his mouth. *Compromise. This is why political candidates read from TelePrompTers,* he thought, struggling to recover. "In a democracy, people arbitrate their disagreements through peaceful, constitutional means, but there are some principles that can never be compromised. We can't give in to terrorism, murder, and blackmail, especially when the price is the future existence of the United States."

The audience cheered loudly and Thompson saw that even his staff was applauding the fact that he was "back on message." But he wasn't done.

"We can't continue to unfairly demonize our federal government, our federal union," Thompson said. "In our nation, there's always been a healthy suspicion of government because it has the power to suppress the inherent rights of people, about which our Declaration of Independence speaks so eloquently.

"Nevertheless, only the federal government can do certain things if we are to be one nation. Only it can provide a national defense, a foreign policy, an effective worldwide economic strategy, a stable currency, an intercontinental transportation system. Exploration of space. In a large nation such as ours, we need a federal effort to explore space, protect the environment, ensure educational standards, and guarantee justice.

"Yet we've heard an increasing drumbeat of propaganda from those who insist only states or local governments can really reflect the will of the people. That they shouldn't be constrained by a federal government isolated in Washington, D.C. You know what I say to this argument—baloney! It doesn't hold water."

His audience applauded tepidly and Thompson knew he probably should quit now. Defending "big government" was a political liability.

"The World War II generation is about gone from our midst, but for those of you who remain and remember, let me ask you a question: if the United States had been fifty separate nations, or five or six sectional groups in the nineteen-thirties and forties, do you think we'd have been able to resist the combined military forces of the Axis powers? Or would the swastika be flying today in this country? Do we want to see the ROSE flag displayed throughout the land?"

He'd broken another inviolate rule of politics: *don't appear overly emotional about the issues.* Stick with the facts and carefully chosen neutral words and phrases.

"We have many problems in this country to solve. We've ignored them because the issues are complicated and the choices are difficult. But we can't continue to do that! We have to be tough and resolute. We have to revive that patriotism and dedication our parents and grandparents had. Our immigrant ancestors. We've got to rebuild this nation. Chart a course into the future. It won't be easy; it wasn't in the beginning. Democracy isn't easy, either. It takes a great commitment by the people. Oftentimes, it's not efficient. Sometimes, the people in government are inadequate or corrupt. But it's better than a dictatorship, people! We don't need to create a new nation, a new economy, a new religion. We just need to recommit to the principles and institutions that have seen us through nearly two-and-a-half centuries."

He had run out of breath and words. His rhetorical inadequacies briefly depressed Thompson. He was suddenly bone tired. "If you elect me president, our federal union will not be dissolved. I will arrest Trent Dillman, who is masquerading as Jeremiah the Terrorist, and any and all other New Americans who have committed treason against this nation. And I will not surrender to New America if it threatens us again with nuclear weapons, any more than I or my patriotic predecessors would have surrendered to any foreign power that threatened our national existence."

Thunderous applause rewarded this reiteration of his campaign theme, and both his staff and supporters were rejuvenated.

"Thank you for your support," Thompson said, waving good-bye, "and remember the words of the song, 'America the Beautiful,' which asks God to bestow his grace upon us, 'to crown thy good with brotherhood, *from sea to shining sea.*'"

As he walked back toward the hallway leading to the kitchen, Perez whispered into his ear, "Jesus, Peter, talk about a loose cannon rolling about on deck! What got into you?"

Thompson stopped and turned toward the man said to have been personally responsible for electing governors in five states during the last election. "Loose cannon? Because

I spoke my gut? Said what I believe in? What do you people want, Daniel, a robot you can manage?"

"Okay, so this one time I'll let you speak your gut," Perez quipped. "You didn't do that bad. Just don't do it on UBC! I've got you lined up for a remote interview with Julie Burton, host of the *American Chronicle* show."

A UBC technician led Thompson to an improvised pressroom and wired him for sound. A television monitor to the right of the camera allowed him to see his inquisitor in the UBC studio in Rosslyn, Virginia.

"Mr. Thompson, this is Julie Burton in Washington. Congratulations on your primary victory today in Kansas."

"Thank you, Julie." Thompson forced himself to smile at the image that filled the television monitor. Unlike her predecessor, Laura Delaney, whose physical beauty was enhanced by warmth, compassion, and intelligence, Burton was cold and calculating, and Thompson didn't trust her.

"Your speech just now to your supporters was extraordinary, Mr. Thompson. You implied that all those opposed to your policies regarding New America are bigots, traitors, or stupid and shortsighted. Was that your intent?"

"No. I was merely attempting to put the national debate into perspective." *No wonder all politicians hate the news media,* he thought. *No wonder politicians are afraid to speak their mind and, instead, deliver up philosophical drivel.*

"Mr. Thompson, wasn't the American Patriots Party, which you now represent, founded primarily by conservatives suspicious of the powers of the federal government?"

"The American Patriots Party is comprised of people who believe, as the name implies, in democratic institutions and a federal union to be preserved at all costs."

"Even if that cost includes nuclear war?"

"Absolutely, Ms. Burton."

"Mr. Thompson, one of the issues we've been discussing on tonight's *American Chronicle* show concerns the continuing mystery of the bombing of the negotiations in Minneapolis, an event that many believe precipitated the current constitutional crisis."

Who are the many, he wondered, *except Julie Burton and other rabble-rousers in the news media who wouldn't let this issue rest? They're snooping down the wrong path, anyway. Perhaps soon, I'll have a real story for them.*

"You survived the bombing, Mr. Thompson, yet you deny any prior knowledge of that horrendous event."

"That's correct."

"The evidence apparently indicates a briefcase carried into the negotiations by Col. Samuel Douglas contained the explosives. Wasn't Colonel Douglas a friend of yours, Mr. Thompson? Indeed, wasn't he a member of a task force you assembled years ago to capture and arrest Jeremiah, when you were deputy director of the FBI?"

"The answer to all those questions is yes, Ms. Burton."

"Then, sir, you might understand how it's difficult for many observers to believe your denial of any involvement in the bombing. You say you left the room to take a telephone message from the White House, but President Trainor denies calling you. Is he a liar?"

"I can't say for certain, Miss Burton, but as I've said before on your show, Jeremiah also survived the bombing, indicating he clearly knew about it. Who told him? Certainly not me. Perhaps you're not asking the right questions of the right people."

"During a recent interview with the New America media, Jeremiah insisted he had a double at the negotiations because of his fear of assassination," Burton countered, "not because he planted the bomb or knew about it."

"First, Miss Burton, there is no independent news media in New America," Thompson sparred, "only state-run newspapers and television. You of all people should understand that. Second, Jeremiah, as you refer to him, is a demonstrated terrorist, murderer, and liar. I'm surprised UBC gives credence to anything he says."

Burton flashed a dazzling smile. "On another issue, Mr. Thompson, a special prosecutor is investigating whether or not you ordered an assassination team into New America to kill Jeremiah while you were attorney general. Are thes[e] charges true?"

"No," Thompson lied. "And all Americans should b[e] skeptical about an investigation that appears to be politi[-] cally motivated and which leaks more than a sieve."

As Thompson headed to his hotel room, following tw[o] more press interviews, he felt dejected. He'd "won" a[n] election, but perhaps botched that victory in his imprompt[u] remarks and his disastrous interview with Julie Burton, wh[o] he suspected was a supporter of President Trainor. Mayb[e] she was angling for a job in Trainor's second administra[-] tion, or trying to maintain her show's high ratings by bein[g] controversial. At any rate, by keeping alive various rumors[,] she undermined his political appeal.

Thompson took a long, hot shower. When h[e] emerged from the bathroom wearing dark blue pajamas[,] General Franklin, dressed in civilian clothes, sat in a chai[r] beside his bed.

"How'd you get in here, Buster?"

"I'm a general. By the way, congratulations on your vic[-] tory and your speech. I liked it."

Thompson chuckled, thinking that if Buster liked hi[s] speech, it undoubtedly was over the edge. "The press wil[l] eat my lunch over it."

"Fuck 'em. Look at these." The general spread severa[l] photos on the bed for Thompson's examination. "Thre[e] more B-1s have been located."

Thompson could barely contain his excitement. Three down, one to go. If all the bombers were neutralized, the nation would be saved.

"Don't worry, we'll find the other one soon."

"What if Jeremiah detects the surveillance and moves the bombers or launches a preemptive strike?"

The general snorted. "The United States Marine Corps i[s] the best fighting force in the world, and we have our own little air force, in case you've forgotten. They try to move those planes and I'll destroy them. They'll never get air-borne again under the control of New American pilots."

"This is wonderful news, Buster!"

"One baffling tidbit, Peter. The crew of the B-1 shot down over Boston apparently fought among themselves. That might explain why they pulled out of the bomb run and presented themselves as a fat target."

"What does it mean?"

"I don't know. Maybe nothing more than a great break for us." General Franklin stood. "I know you're tired, Peter, but I thought you'd want to hear all this directly."

"You're taking a lot of risks, Buster."

"I'd rather be an American hero than a traitor. You just keep givin' 'em hell, Peter, and leave the rest to me. You're doing the right thing."

Before Thompson collapsed into bed, he had one more question. "What do you hear about Steve and Laura?"

"No one's seen them, or Hoffman, for about three months, not since that day folks in the underground in Rapid City got a call from Hoffman, saying they'd soon have Laura and would head toward the air base."

"What do you think happened?"

"Jeremiah turned the tables on them. Steve and Hoffman could be dead."

And Laura would soon give birth.

"Any way we could mount a private raid to try and find her?"

"It wouldn't be smart right now, Peter. We don't have any sightings. Besides, you can't be taking a political risk like that right now. It'd just be more ammunition for your enemies. We've got bigger fish to fry. You've got to win this election."

Thompson sighed and sat on his bed.

General Franklin walked to a bar in a corner of the presidential suite. "You get some sleep, Peter. I'll help myself to some of your bourbon before I take off."

28

THE EPISTLE OF JEREMIAH
THE PROPHET
TO THE NEW AMERICANS

CHAPTER FOUR

1 Jeremiah, being a Prophet who spake the words of the One True God to His people;

2 And on behalf of all the Brethren who strive to implement His Word in the land called New America, especially those who believe in the true Equality of Mankind:

3 The Grace of God the Father is with you and guides your efforts, and protects and preserves the One who is His Righteous Instrument. Amen.

4 We are a Peace-Loving people and respond eagerly to our Brethren's enlightened call for Compromise; our prayers to the Almighty are answered and New America will soon be granted its Independence.

5 Yet Nebuchadnezzar continues to threaten New America in his Campaign, banging frantically on the

Drums of War, inciting to Violence those blinded to the Evil and Corruption about them. Babylon cannot further illuminate the Beacon on the Hill which is New America. If our Cause were not Right, would the LORD grace us with Success?

6 We have attacked Evil relentlessly and vigorously and we are Safe in our Homes and on our Streets, unlike those who live in Babylon. The critics of New America bemoan the lost rights of Criminals, but I tell you this on behalf of the LORD: better that ten percent of those charged with Evil be mistakenly punished or killed, rather than ninety percent of the Guilty be set free time and again to plague one hundred percent of the Innocent and Law-Abiding.

7 We are in the process of eliminating Representative Government and most individual Taxes, the bane of the Working Man; no longer do the Prideful strut and crow at the Center of Evil, manipulating all for their Private gain and glory.

8 New Americans observe the Social Contract and the LORD's Word. We respect and live the motto of our banner: Reverence, Order, Service, Equality. We probe the secrets of the universe, to discover God's intent for Mankind; and the treasures of knowledge found will be freely shared with all, even our Enemies. Does Old America think it can match these achievements by electing once again a Lustful, Prideful one who speaks only Evil?

9 As for the benefits of Diversity about which Nebuchadnezzar speaks, why does he not extol diversity of purpose and belief? Why are we not free to choose a different way of life? Why must everyone conform to

the philosophy of Babylon? And have its values and economic system forced upon them. Is this not Repression, designed to achieve Uniformity?

10 Is it because New Americans are primarily white that Nebuchadnezzar denies us the right to think differently? To chart a New Way into a glorious future.

11 Nebuchadnezzar says only the United States can ward off foreign aggression. This is contrary to God's Word to the Chosen People of old and the Chosen People of the future. Observe the Word of God, and ye shall not be conquered by Babylon, or any warlike nation that worships False Idols.

12 While Babylon seeks to subject people, New America works to free people, and achieve True Equality.

13 Hence, the LORD has told me a parable of the Physician and the Garbage Man: he who gathers our waste products is hard-working and strong; he who ministers to the needs of the sick and infirm truly is an Instrument of God. Both are beloved of God; yet in Old America, the Garbage Man is held in low esteem and often paid a subsistence wage, while the Physician is usually honored and rewarded with riches.

14 If a Man and Woman are clean and hard working, if they eat nutritious food and avoid Alcohol and Drugs, they will be healthy and may never need the services of the Physician. But if the Garbage Man doesn't perform his work, wastes will accumulate and become a breeding ground for Diseases spread through the air and water, or by insects and animals. Plagues could occur, striking equally the Good and Evil person.

15 In a Righteous Society anointed by God, each In-

dividual holds hands with his Neighbor, creating a Human Chain originating in the misty past and stretching into a glorious and bright Future. In this cooperative effort, the Garbage Man is as important as the Physician; each makes the other's religious, social, and private life possible and fulfilling. When all Necessary Work is valued and Rewarded Equally, the Root of Evil will no longer have nourishment, and true Equality of Opportunity will exist for all. So sayeth the LORD to his Prophet, Jeremiah the Second.

16 When there is True Equality, and when New America's scientific achievements eliminate humankind's Genetic Defects and biological hindrances, then we will have a true Master Race dedicated exclusively to the Achievement of Knowledge, and the eventual attainment of the Omega Point.

17 The LORD has instructed the Leaders of New America to begin gradual implementation of the Wealth Exchange for all Workers, including managers. This less-than-perfect process is unfortunately necessary in this time of shortages of food and goods resulting from the efforts of our Enemies. We who are Chained together for all time will suffer Equally, as we will eventually share Equally the fruits of ultimate Victory and Prosperity.

18 The only temporary exemption to the Wealth Exchange will be for those Investors who have helped make New America possible; and they should understand their Excess Profits will be limited to the Roman Year 2010, or New America Year 13. Thereafter, individual Profit will not be allowed; the Excess Wealth we create collectively beyond that necessary to live ac-

cording to an Acceptable Standard should be reinvested in our common Religious, Social, Economic, and Scientific programs.

19 Unbridled Capitalism is based on Deceit, and presumes all Men are Greedy and incapable of Sacrifice for the Greater Good. Wealth is only created by Man's physical and intellectual labor, and Wealth can only be created Cooperatively. One Man's unique Idea can only come to fruition through the efforts of the Community. Hence, Wealth must be shared Equally; to do otherwise is Blasphemy, for the LORD created All Men Equal.

20 Ninety percent of the Workers in Old America are at the mercy of an "economy," "economic forces," and "economic theories" they don't understand, couldn't explain, and which rarely work as predicted by the "experts." Why, then, would Reasonable Men defend that system and not abandon it in favor of Simplicity, Equality, Predictability, and Justice? Why would they support Nebuchadnezzar's Campaign?

21 In this the hour of our greatest Challenge, New Americans should not indulge weaknesses of the Flesh and doubts of the Mind. Together we will be Free, or none will be Free, including our Enemies, so sayeth the LORD to His Prophet, Jeremiah the Second.

29

Laura pretended to stifle a yawn, while Jeremiah used her. Although she had to prostitute herself to keep Steve alive, Laura refused to feign enthusiasm.

"Would it hurt you to show some gratitude?" he asked.

"Hurt me. No, it doesn't hurt me. It might be hurting the baby, however. Sex in the ninth month is never recommended."

"You know I'm careful. But I have needs."

"The baby may remember you beating on him in the womb. I certainly intend to tell him how you beat me up in the alley that day and broke my nose."

"For God's sake, Laura!"

"Using the Lord's name in vain is a sin, Jeremiah. Perhaps you've forgotten that commandment, just like you did the ones about murder and rape."

Jeremiah rolled onto his back, a frustrated look on his face. Laura tried to keep a straight face. This was too easy. He blackmailed his way into her bed and thought she'd be grateful, willing, and passionate. What a moron.

What difference would it make, anyway, if she pretended it was the monster fuck of her life? Jeremiah was absolutely untrustworthy. Laura knew he'd eventually kill Steve, anyway, if he hadn't already. She even doubted he'd let her live, once his son was born. He had to know she'd do everything under the sun to poison the boy's mind against him. It's just as well, Laura concluded. Without Steve, she didn't want to live.

Jeremiah rolled out of bed and pulled on his undershorts. "I know the baby is fine. Dr. Connolly told me."

Dr. Connolly. Laura had berated him, too, when he came to the cabin the day after the nightmare three months ago in the alley behind his office. Each time he visited thereafter, Laura sarcastically and loudly questioned the doctor's credentials, skills, and ethics, until he too could hardly take it anymore. *My mouth is my only remaining weapon,* Laura thought.

"In the morning, we're going to the hospital in Rapid City," Jeremiah said, pulling on a pair of black slacks.

"Why?"

"Your due date is near and March weather here is unpredictable. I don't want to get snowed in."

As always, Laura questioned his real motivations. Was he afraid she'd harm the child at this late date? She wouldn't, not now that the fetus was capable of surviving on its own. This innocent child, a mixture of life forces that had activated an ancient blueprint code, hadn't asked to be.

Laura grew increasingly excited about getting out of the cave and getting it over with. That prospect revived hopes that she and Steve might yet survive, somehow.

"Nature has its own systems of checks and balances," Jeremiah said. "When a new life enters the world, an old one departs."

Laura understood. As usual, he'd had the last word, and once again won their game of one-upmanship.

Laura had a private room on the second-floor maternity wing. The regional medical center was centered around a ten-story tower housing patients. Several wings were devoted to specialty care, including cancer, heart disease, emergency services, an eye institute, and a rehabilitation center.

Laura stared out her window at the real world for hours, enchanted even by the bleak prairie landscape, the howling wind, and the endless sky. One day snow fell slowly for hours and she watched in delight, her hands warmed by a cup of decaffeinated tea.

But Laura didn't quit scheming. "He raped me," she told a nurse with an accent similar to Katrina's. "Would you make a telephone call for me?"

"That would get me killed," the big nurse said. "Just don't give up hope. Everything will work out."

In the late afternoon on March 23, 2000, when Laura could see several signs of spring in the world outside, her water broke and she knew the ordeal was at hand.

Steve feared the worst. A guard he'd never seen before stood in front of his cell. He hadn't seen Laura in four months. Was she giving birth? Had something happened to her? Was it the hour of his execution?

"Where're we going?" Steve asked, as he complied with instructions to back up to the cell door, so the guard could handcuff him.

"You'll see. Please don't make a commotion, Mr. Wallace. It wouldn't be in your best interest, and it won't change anything."

They walked down the hallway past the visitors' room, which was well beyond the limits of Steve's travels all the time he'd been in the jail. At a guard station, Steve's handler passed a written document through the open, bottom portion of a window. The guard behind the glass studied the paper briefly and buzzed them through a heavy, steel door into another corridor.

Magically, they were outside and Steve sucked the cold night air deeply into his lungs as they walked through snow toward an ambulance. His guard opened one of the rear doors, motioned for Steve to turn around, and removed the handcuffs.

"Get inside, Mr. Wallace."

Steve wasn't about to obey now that his hands were free. Only this one guard stood between him and freedom. Piece of cake. But movements inside the ambulance caught his attention and he looked in shock at Katrina Dorfler and a nurse sitting on a bench seat.

"What's going on?" Steve asked, seeing that Katrina was holding a baby wrapped tightly in a blanket.

"This is my son, born two weeks ago," Katrina announced, proudly. "Laura went into labor two hours ago. Her baby will be born tonight."

Steve understood. As Jeremiah had promised, they were taking him to the hospital to witness the final debasement of his wife before his own execution. But he had a few surprises for them. He considered jerking the baby from Katrina's arms. Jeremiah's baby! The perfect hostage. The Prophet wasn't so smart, after all.

"We're going to rescue Laura as soon as she gives birth," Katrina said, freezing Steve in place. "You and her and the baby will be taken by ambulance to Ellsworth Air Force Base, and then you two can go anywhere you want."

"What!"

Katrina nodded, her face glowing with anticipation. "I've been making this plan for many, many months! Get in and I'll tell you about it."

At the hospital, they parked near a west wing rear exit door. The big nurse helped Katrina and the baby from the ambulance.

"Who are you?" Steve asked the guard, who stayed in the van with the driver.

"A friend."

Katrina had the hood of her winter coat drawn tightly around her face as they walked toward the door, which was opened by a man inside the stairwell. Steve, Katrina, and the nurse followed him up a flight of stairs, then down a hallway to a private room. Once inside, the nurse locked the door and Katrina busied herself with the baby, putting it into a bassinet. Then she turned on the television.

Steve soon realized it was closed-circuit television, broadcasting from a delivery room. Laura's delivery room.

"My God!" Steve said, moving as close to the set as he could.

"She's almost ready, I think," Katrina said, visibly excited.

All three watched and paced the floor for the next five hours, as Laura struggled with the contractions, following the orders of the nurses and Dr. Connolly about when to push and when to breathe. At some point, Jeremiah appeared in the delivery room, gowned and masked, but he stayed in the background. *He doesn't even have the decency to hold Laura's hand,* Steve thought, and immediately felt ridiculous, since Jeremiah was the last person on earth he wanted to touch his wife.

Between contractions, Laura had a dreamy look on her face, which caused Steve to think she was the beneficiary of some type of drug, a painkiller or relaxant. Yet when ordered to push, a dogged look came over her face.

Steve couldn't imagine how the birth could happen. It seemed anatomically impossible. But eventually the baby came out of Laura's body—a head with light-colored hair, arms, chest, lower body, and then, suddenly, legs and an umbilical cord. Steve saw a look of disbelief on Laura's face and just a hint of a smile. Steve felt ashamed to be a Peeping Tom. He also was immensely proud of his beloved wife.

"In a few hours, my people will switch the babies," Katrina said. "Then you and Laura and her baby will escape." She showed him a telephone number of a piece of paper. "Memorize this number. When you get settled, call and tell me how I can contact you and Laura in an emergency, if I hear Jeremiah has found out where you are."

Steve had many questions. "How do you hope to get away with this? Do you think you can fool him?" *If you don't, Katrina, you're dead.*

"We will get away with it," she replied, confidently. "I have my own supporters here. I am Walter Dorfler's daughter. Many of the people who helped make New America possible knew my father long before they knew Jeremiah. I command their loyalty."

Suddenly, Steve was happy he and Laura had kept to themselves the likelihood that Walter Dorfler, a founding father of New America, had murdered Jeremiah's first love, Emma Dietze. Otherwise, Jeremiah would have erased

Walter's memory from the minds of New Americans. And he might have killed Katrina.

"As for the baby, Jeremiah will not notice," Katrina declared. "When he discovers Laura is missing, he'll concentrate all his efforts on finding her, and you. He won't pay attention to the baby for days, weeks, maybe months. He knows I'm returning from Germany. It will be convenient for me to take care of Laura's baby." She smiled and winked. "Don't you see?"

It might work, at least temporarily, Steve thought, his emotions soaring. *God works in mysterious ways!*

Early the next morning, Katrina walked down the hallway of the maternity ward as if she'd never been there. She stopped at the nurses' station, announced herself, and asked for directions to Laura Delaney's room. She gratuitously added that Laura had given birth to Jeremiah's child. Not that Laura was the Prophet's wife or loving companion, but just a woman he'd impregnated.

Still, the nurses seemed afraid to speak until a supervisor gave Katrina a room number and pointed in the proper direction. Katrina nodded and smiled at the hefty supervisor with the foreign accent.

As Katrina walked down the hallway, she saw Jeremiah ahead, talking to three other men. He sounded agitated and threatening. She watched him change positions, walking clockwise in a small circle and then reversing his direction.

"What's going on?" Katrina asked, as she approached the men who were standing outside Laura's room.

"What are you doing here?" Jeremiah demanded, startled by her presence. It was half-question, half-accusation.

"I wrote you I was coming today, returning from my visit to Germany," Katrina explained. "Don't you remember? Someone was supposed to meet me at the airport. What's the matter?"

Jeremiah's face had a deep red, almost purplish tint to it, which Katrina recognized it as a sign of undiluted rage.

"I forgot," Jeremiah admitted.

Katrina waited patiently, knowing more questions were forthcoming.

"You talked to Laura all the time before you left. What did she say? Did she have a plan to escape! Who helped her?"

Katrina shook her head, and held out her arms in a gesture of incomprehension. "What are you talking about? Can you at least tell me what happened here?"

Jeremiah pointed at the room, his finger jabbing the air, making repeated exclamation points of anger. "She escaped! Wallace escaped from the prison! They got away together!"

"She hasn't had the baby yet?" Katrina asked.

"Yes, yes, she had the baby! It's in the nursery."

Katrina hurried away in that direction, reminding herself to ask the attending nurse to point out *Laura's baby*. Of course, she picked up her own boy and lovingly kissed him. Such a beautiful and good baby, to have endured so much so early in its life. Two weeks old and already he had flown across an ocean!

A two-week-old baby is not a newborn, Katrina knew, which was one reason she wanted to bundle her son up again and leave, before other nurses she didn't know began asking embarrassing questions.

Katrina wrapped the baby in a blanket so only his face was visible and walked back to where Jeremiah stood. "Let's take the baby and get out of here. I'll take care of him."

Jeremiah looked at Katrina as if she were crazy.

"You wouldn't want someone to kidnap the baby, too, would you?" Katrina responded and was pleased to see the alarm on Jeremiah's face. "Obviously the hospital's security is no good."

Jeremiah nodded his head and Katrina motioned for her driver, who last night had been driving an ambulance.

Later that evening, Jeremiah returned to the cabin in the cave, looking haggard and tired.

"Where have you been?" Katrina asked.

He slumped onto a sofa and she immediately poured him a glass of beer, for which he had a fondness, even though alcoholic beverages were banned in New America.

"What did you find out?"

He drank deeply, the beer's foam creating a temporary mustache on his upper lip. "Nothing! A guard nobody knew walked into the prison. He had a key to Wallace's cell and took him away."

"How could that happen?"

Jeremiah waved a piece of paper at her. "The guard had an authorization signed by me! Unfortunately, I had put the supervisor of guards on notice that I would be coming for Wallace shortly. I had planned to let him watch Laura give birth." Jeremiah crumpled up the paper. "And then kill him!"

"So the guards were not suspicious when someone came for Wallace?"

"No, of course not!" Jeremiah said, standing, pacing the floor like a caged animal. "The stupid bastards! This authorization is a forgery. Someone at the prison had to be part of this conspiracy, that's for sure. I gave the guards a taste of their own medicine tonight!"

Katrina brought another bottle of beer from the kitchen and refilled Jeremiah's glass. "Were any of them lying?" she asked.

"No," he said, disappointed. "Had they known anything, I would have gotten it out of them."

"How did Laura get out of the hospital?"

Jeremiah shook his head in frustration. "More people with more official papers apparently rolled her out on a gurney in the middle of the night, after I'd left. Our observers outside the air base say an ambulance drove through the gate there about an hour after Laura was found missing." He took in a deep breath. "They got away with no trouble at all!"

"Do you think someone at the hospital helped them?"

"We questioned everyone who was on duty last night," Jeremiah replied. "Everyone! From doctors to janitors! They don't remember any strangers being in the hospital."

His eyes narrowed. "But we will question everyone again, tomorrow. A bit more forcefully."

Katrina knew she had to make a phone call to a friend. While describing her lengthy vacation abroad, Katrina would utter a sentence, "Bavaria was lovely, and I spent some time in Innsbruck, too." The message would be understood. Someone should go home.

"At least we have the baby," Katrina said.

Jeremiah frowned. "Where is it?"

"In the nursery, sleeping in the baby bed you selected. Do you want to see him?"

Jeremiah hesitated. "In the morning, perhaps."

"He's very healthy. What will you name him?"

Jeremiah looked perplexed, momentarily. "Walter, I think. After your father."

Katrina beamed, her smile lighting up the room. "I will take care of him, don't you worry. Just as if I were his mother. We will raise him up to be strong, just like you." The words tumbled out of her mouth in an excited rush. "I will do a better job than Laura, anyway. She hated you, and she hated the child. She would have poisoned his mind. You know I won't do that."

He looked at her and reluctantly nodded his agreement.

"You don't need her anymore, Jeremiah. What do you want with a woman who doesn't love you? Who hates you."

His eyes narrowed and Katrina momentarily feared he might take his rage out on her. Then he relaxed and sat down again. "You're right, Katrina. I don't want to ever see Laura again. She can't give birth to my son and then abandon him like he was trash!"

Katrina walked closer to Jeremiah and took the glass from his hand. "You're tired. Let's go to bed. I'll give you a rubdown. I'll tell you about Germany. Mother sends her wishes and wants to know when you'll be coming home."

Jeremiah sighed. "It would be nice to get out of this hellhole."

"Tomorrow, while you're taking care of business, I'll take care of our son." Katrina spoke rapidly, as Jeremiah looked at her suspiciously. "Yes, that's right. From now on,

I'll consider Walter my son. Our son. We will raise him to follow in your footsteps here in New America. Let's never talk again about Laura Delaney."

He let her lead him toward the bedroom. "I appreciate what you're doing for me and the child, Katrina."

"Shush, it's nothing!"

"You're right. We won't talk about Laura again. But they can't do this to me and get away with it. I'll find her and Wallace and kill them! That's a promise to God!"

30

A doctor checked Laura and the baby at Ellsworth Air Force Base, while Steve talked on the phone with Peter Thompson. Laura was immensely relieved when she and the child were given a clean bill of health. She'd survived. They'd survived.

At dawn, they boarded a Gulfstream III executive jet ferrying congressmen and military brass to Luke Air Force Base near Phoenix.

Steve put up the armrests in the middle of a three-across seat and put down blankets to form a makeshift bed for Laura and the baby.

They landed three hours later and took a cab into Phoenix, where they got out at the first hotel they came to. After a few minutes they hailed another cab which took them to an Embassy Suites several miles away. There, Steve called Thompson again, and arranged for bodyguards to be dispatched to their location.

"I've got to get some sleep," Steve said, the moment they stepped into their room.

"Me, too."

They put the baby between them on the king-size bed. He cried and Laura patted and soothed him to no avail. Then she gave him a breast and he was content. Laura watched him suckle for several minutes before collapsing into sleep.

*   *   *

His crying woke both of them. Laura looked
at the radio clock, seeing that it was 3:00 P.M. She groaned,
got up, and took the baby into the living room area of the
suite, so Steve could continue sleeping. Laura was sore,
exhausted, and not certain she should be up. But the thrill
of being free gave her strength.

She let the baby breast-feed while she pulled back the
drapes and peeked out into the courtyard at a swimming
pool, where two men sat in chaise longues, staring in the
direction of their room.

She shut the curtains, certain only that they weren't sun-
bathing in business suits. She hoped they were the promised
bodyguards, but decided to be prepared for the worst.

Laura tiptoed into the bedroom and took a 9-mm hand
gun from the nightstand. Someone at Ellsworth had given
it to Steve, who continued to snore softly.

Laura returned to the front door, cuddling the baby to
her breast and holding the gun in the other hand. She
cracked the door and watched one of the men rise and walk
toward her.

She stuck the gun out the door, causing the man to stop.

"Thompson sent us," he said.

"Good. You got any money?"

"Yeah?"

"I need some diapers and other things. Wait here and I'll
make a list."

Two hours later, when Steve got up, they
talked.

"Are you all right?" he asked. "Any complications from
the birth?"

"Nothing serious," Laura said, breathing a sigh of relief.
"I'm sore and tired. There are some stitches from the epi-
siotomy, but they'll dissolve. What about you?"

"My ribs and insides hurt, and I have a headache that
won't go away."

"You should see a doctor as soon as possible."

"Yeah."

"What about him?" Laura asked, pointing at the newborn boy sleeping on the sofa in a nest Laura had made with blankets.

"What do you want to do?"

Laura thought. "We can put him up for adoption. I suppose Peter could find someone to take him now." *They'll have to find a way to hide his parentage,* Laura thought. *No sane person would knowingly raise Jeremiah's son.*

"It's your call," Steve said.

"Maybe we should give him a name for the time being."

"Why?"

"It's more civilized than calling him 'him.' "

Steve shrugged. "I guess it won't matter. We don't need to tell his adoptive parents about it. He wouldn't get used to the name, would he? And not recognize some other name, later."

"I don't think so. It can't be the name of a friend or relative. They'd be offended forever."

"How about Keith? I don't know anyone name Keith."

"Steve, no! Keith sounds like an accountant."

"Okay, how about Butch. Butch doesn't do books."

They stood beside the sofa and looked at "him." Suddenly, his eyes opened, and Laura thought he looked disoriented. He didn't cry, although he made a sucking, slurping sound. Laura watched his eyes dart from side-to-side, attempting to focus. Could he see them? Did he wonder who they were? *What exactly does a baby think, anyway?*

"He's a pretty good size," Steve said.

Laura grimaced. "Tell me about it. He weighed over eight pounds."

"How about Tiny. There was this big wrestler I knew in college who was called Tiny."

"How about David?" Steve winced, causing Laura to frown. "What's wrong with David?"

"Nothing. Why that name?"

Laura looked sheepishly at Steve. "It was my grandfather's name. My dad's dad. I know, I know. I just broke my rule of not naming him even temporarily after a relative.

But Granddad was a super guy. Maybe it would rub off. know it's stupid."

"David, it is, then."

While Steve showered, the guard returned from his shopping trip. He handed Laura several bags, a purse, and billfold.

"What are these?" she asked.

"Two complete sets of new identification, credit cards and money."

Now we only have to decide where to go, Laura thought

Steve dressed, putting on the new underwear Laura had had the guard buy. Then they examined the new identification.

"We've got to get Peter to somehow switch our various bank accounts and portfolios over to the new names," Laura said. "I guess we should sell the farm."

"So where are we going to live?"

"How about South America?" she suggested. "Some parts of Chile I've visited remind me of Switzerland."

Steve shook his head. "Chile's susceptible to a right wing military takeover at any time, putting in power the kind of people who admire Jeremiah and his politics."

"Okay, what about the real Switzerland?"

Steve shrugged. "It's a possibility. We'd stand out there because of the language and cultural differences, at least initially. It's also too close to Germany, where Jeremiah has friends. What about the Caribbean?"

Laura grimaced. "I'd feel trapped on an island. Boats could drop his men off in the middle of the night."

"There's a downside to almost every location," Steve said. "If we opt for a small town or rural area, we're immediately tagged as newcomers. Everyone will make it their business to know our business. Soon, they'd start guessing about our identities. Plus, we'd be isolated and open to attack from any direction."

Laura picked up on this line of thought. "In a big city we'd have anonymity."

"Crowds provide good cover for assassins," Steve countered.

"We won't really be safe, anywhere," Laura concluded

looking gloomily at Steve. "In that case, let's think about New York."

"You hated New York when you lived there."

"That was then, this is now. Besides, I hate it when everyone expects me to be consistent. I'm a mother now. Hormones are raging throughout my body."

"Rents will be cheaper in New York," Steve observed, wryly, "with everyone moving away from ground zero."

"Jeremiah certainly wouldn't expect us to go there." *Indeed, it seems stupid to move to any of the major East Coast cities,* Laura thought. Jeremiah had threatened several times to destroy these cities with nuclear weapons, since they represented the political and financial heart of the United States, as well as much of the early history and culture of the nation.

But Laura understood Jeremiah's thinking. He liked to bluff, to win ground without actually fighting for it. He wouldn't destroy any part of the United States while he still thought he could rule it all some day.

"It would be an act of faith," Laura explained. "New York stands for everything Jeremiah hates. Its diversity, its complexity. All of which makes his simplistic social solutions impractical."

"It's the center of everything," Steve said. "Finance, culture, the media. An international city, really. We could find something to do there, once this all blows over."

Would it ever really be over? Laura wondered. She collapsed on the bed, planning to sleep the night through, if possible. It was Steve's turn to take care of David.

For several weeks they lived in a New York hotel while Steve evaluated the real estate market in the company of a trusted FBI agent's wife, who also was a realtor. They eventually purchased a penthouse suite on the twentieth floor of a building located in the upper sixties, just off Park Avenue.

The balcony of the spacious, eight-room penthouse became a focus of Laura's life, as she tried to recreate in this small space the outdoor life she'd loved in the northern

Virginia countryside. She lined the balcony with potte plants and flowers; even a miniature maple tree.

Their new home had its pluses and minuses, Steve tol her. The penthouse made attack from the street difficult since there were doormen on duty twenty-four-hours-a-da and security cameras in the lobby. Special pass keys wer needed to take the elevator to any of the building's fou penthouses, which began on the sixteenth floor. The ele vator to their penthouse opened into an entryway monitore by additional cameras.

"The balcony you love is a clear negative," Steve said "Snipers in buildings across the way would have a clea shot at us."

"Then find a solution. I can't stay inside all the time."

"We'll enclose it with bulletproof Plexiglas and instal blinds, so we can block our neighbors' view but still ge the sun."

During their first month in the condo, security expert provided by Thompson installed a host of protective de vices, including additional internal and external security cameras, motion detectors, heat sensors, silent and obtru sive alarms. All doors were reinforced with steel and eve interior doors fitted with locks. They remodeled one bath room into a bunker, with lead-lined walls that couldn't b penetrated by bullets fired from either handguns or assaul rifles.

They had a small arsenal inside the condo, includin handguns of every size and caliber, as well as shotguns an assault rifles. Steve spent countless hours drilling Laura o their operation until she could disassemble and reassembl the weapons with her eyes closed. Twice a week, they prac ticed at a gun range.

Steve said, "We're most vulnerable on the streets."

"We can't stay cooped up here all the time," Laura said

"So we compensate. When we're out, we need to b heavily armed. You take that .38-cal. Colt you like s much, Laura, as well as a knife and stun grenade. I'll alte the storage compartment at the back of the baby carriag so it'll hold a submachine gun." He paused. "There's n way I'm gonna let Jeremiah or his people take us alive again."

Laura nodded. They'd have to protect themselves and not rely solely on bodyguards, such as the traitorous Maria Inglesias.

"We might even consider plastic surgery," Steve said. "But first, let's try some cosmetic disguises—wigs, hats, hair dyes, glasses, contact lenses."

"We should wear loose, oversized clothing," Laura said, "not only to hide our weapons, but our size and shape."

Laura knew it all might not work. Someone could recognize them. One of their guards could be bought. Someone could get close enough to them on the streets to shove a knife between their ribs. But such were the hazards of urban life anyway.

"When we're out, we never take the same route or fall into a routine," Steve said. "We always walk single-file, with me in back. Cross the street every now and then, or duck into a store or hotel. Never order a cab or car service to pick us up in front of this building."

By the end of May, they'd became philosophical about the dangers. Maybe Jeremiah was too busy to be concerned with them, or finally disgusted with her, although she doubted that.

David was a happy, bubbly baby. He recognized both of them and all three pretended to "understand" each other. Even though he was too young to comprehend, Laura often read to David hoping to instill in him a love of learning. More practically, Steve hung a mobile over David's bed and encouraged him to grasp at the various handholds.

One day, while they sat in the back booth of their favorite neighborhood deli, so they could see the entrance and all the other customers, Laura said, "I want to keep him."

Steve looked up from his pastrami sandwich. "I didn't think that was an issue."

"We haven't talked about it, specifically."

"Some things are understood without having to be stated."

"Jesus, here I am in the presence of the Philosopher of Lexington Avenue and didn't even know it!"

Steve reached over to the nearby stroller and tickled David who, used to such distractions, smiled and resumed sucking on a bottle of formula.

"You sure it isn't a problem with you, or won't become one?"

"You mean because of his father?"

"Right."

"You're worried this will eat on my male ego and drive me to drink and other women."

"It's more of an excuse than most men need."

Steve pretended to be hurt. "Male bashing. Will it ever end?"

Laura leaned across the table and grabbed the back of his neck with her hand, pulling Steve close enough to kiss him on the lips. "Although it need not be stated, I love you."

Steve smiled, as he looked at her and the baby. "It's not his fault, or your fault, that Jeremiah is his father. That was beyond your control. The only thing that matters now is how we raise him. You've said that many times. He can be a good person."

Laura looked lovingly at David. "With all the things I read about personality being genetically determined in part, I worry about what kind of person he'll be when he grows up. What kind of personality characteristics made Jeremiah receptive to the idea of ruling the world? Becoming modern-day Adolf Hitler?"

"I don't know, Laura. Raising David will be a classic experiment. We just have to make certain we do our job right. That's all we can do."

31

Jeremiah sat in the great room of a new cabin in another cave. Now that Laura had escaped, he feared she could lead the FBI or federal troops to the cabin where she'd been held. Also, he'd been informed by his state police commander, General Simpson, that several teams of assassins were operating in New America—some of them apparently not under anyone's specific directions. They were just "gunslingers" wanting to make a name for themselves by killing the Prophet.

Jeremiah paid half attention to the television, which was tuned to the New America public television station, WNAP, located in Pierre. Today an exercise in direct democracy was scheduled. New American citizens could log onto a particular Internet web site and assign a percentage allocation of $15 billion in state revenues to various expenditures categories that included: police and public safety, the National Guard, health care and hospitals, education and training, housing and community services, transportation, research and development, welfare and social services, government and judicial administration. And so on.

Jeremiah had approved the exercise as a means of implementing *Second Jeremiah* 5:4, and he wanted to see how it would be received by his followers.

In fact, he could only think about Laura and Steve, as usual, and where they might be. He knew they hadn't returned to the Virginia farm. Never mind, he'd find them eventually.

He couldn't trust anyone—except Katrina. Katrina, forever patient and loyal, had been with him throughout his adult life; waiting, never complaining. *Now she is caring for a child that isn't even her own.* Jeremiah suddenly felt great affection for his cousin and sometimes lover. Before, she was only a convenience. Now he could trust no one else.

Jeremiah called for Katrina to come down from the upstairs nursery so he'd have someone to talk to. He missed the stimulating discussions with Laura, even though she hated him.

"There are so many things to worry about," he said, as Katrina sat beside him. He'd spent the last two months in frenzied activity—trying to locate Laura and Wallace, moving his hideout, reinforcing his army, negotiating with representatives of foreign governments, comforting his people.

"You are a great man, trying to do great things," Katrina replied, holding Walter II, while she fed him a bottle of formula.

"I have reports that a hangar housing one of the B-1s may be under surveillance," Jeremiah said, knowing it wasn't necessary to hide anything from Katrina, who didn't have a deceptive bone in her body. "The Chinese have advised me to strike now, but that would be foolish, especially if the bombers were destroyed before completing their mission. It was never my intent to unleash a nuclear war in the United States anyway. I don't want to destroy the country I one day hope to unite and rule. If I start a war, I'll lose everything. If I threaten a war, I'll win everything."

"It's a brilliant plan, Jeremiah."

"If the November elections in the United States go as planned, I won't need the bombers. I can make a grand gesture and return them, just like I did with the nuclear power plant. By then, the secession amendment will have passed and New America will be a fact. Of course, I'll keep the atomic bombs." He smiled. "There are other ways of delivering them to their targets, if necessary."

"Walter is very healthy and happy," Katrina said, smiling at Jeremiah.

"That's good," Jeremiah replied, indifferently. "What would really help now is if something happened to General Franklin. He's the one after the bombers. I can't kill Thompson now because that would look bad. Besides, he's my lightning rod. You know what's a great idea?"

"What, Jeremiah?"

"Poison. Franklin likes to drink expensive bourbon. What if a special bottle was delivered to his house. Or what if I could get one of our people into a social event at the Pentagon. Someone posing as a bartender. I doubt the general has a taster in his employ."

Jeremiah went to a wall safe, where he dialed in the appropriate numbers, opened the door, and took out a "safe" phone, one that scrambled a conversation through a computer so it couldn't be intercepted. He made several calls, occasionally glancing at Katrina, who fed Walter and whispered to him.

Having finished with his business, Jeremiah sat beside her. "Your stories about Germany got me to thinking, Katrina. Maybe I'll have our friends there purchase a lodge for us, near Garmisch. When things settle down here, it wouldn't hurt for me to disappear again. Let the people run things for a while. It might be a good strategy."

Katrina's face lit up with anticipation. "That would be wonderful, Jeremiah."

Jeremiah recalled a happy memory. "I so loved Nuremberg. The old walled city. Your father's apartment. It was paradise. You remember? There's nothing in America like it."

"No one uses the apartment anymore," Katrina said, hopefully.

"Really?"

Katrina rose and walked toward the bedroom. "Walter needs to be changed and put to bed. I'll be right back. We'll talk some more."

*   *   *

Jeremiah prowled about the main floor of the house, switching the lights off in the kitchen so he could look out into the darkness of the cave. He imagined movements near the far wall. Then he thought he heard a noise in the back of the house. He checked out the downstairs rooms and then walked quietly up the stairs. The door to the nursery was slightly ajar.

Jeremiah peeked through the crack and saw Katrina sitting in a rocking chair, singing softly to the baby in German. Walter, with a German "v" sound. Jeremiah listened, smiling, missing the sounds of his adopted homeland.

He was about to walk away, when he heard Katrina say, "We'll go home soon and see Grandma again, Walter. I promise you. Mommy will take you home."

Her remarks puzzled Jeremiah and revived latent suspicions that had first arose at the hospital, after Laura had escaped. He wasn't surprised she left the baby, but he was surprised by the color of the baby's hair—dark, thick hair, instead of blonde hair, like his and Laura's. Baby Walter had hair like—Katrina's!

Jeremiah shook his head, silently chiding himself. He'd grown truly paranoid as a result of everything going on about him. He'd checked the baby's footprints, taken shortly after birth, against those of the baby in the nursery. The good nurse from Austria had helped him. The footprints matched exactly. The hair color would lighten later, the fat nurse had explained to him. It happened that way with newborns. He'd been too busy to think much about it since then.

Jeremiah pushed open the door to the nursery and saw that he had startled Katrina, who literally jumped out of the rocking chair, pressing Walter tightly to her breast.

She has a strange look on her face, he thought. *Fear and guilt.* "What's wrong?" he asked, suspiciously.

"I was just singing to the baby. I call myself Mommy, even though I'm not. I told you I would treat the child as if it were my own. You said you didn't mind."

The words tumbled out of her mouth too rapidly, he thought, as if she were fabricating an excuse. He inched

oward her. "You said you'd take the baby to see his grand-
mother *again*."

Katrina hurriedly put Walter in his crib. "Did I? It was
a mistake, you know. I meant to say I would be seeing my
mother again. For the baby it will be the first time, of
course." She laughed nervously. "You know me, Jeremiah.
Switching back and forth from the German to the English
and back to the Deutsch, I get the meaning of words confused."

He looked at Katrina as if seeing her for the first time
since she'd returned from Germany. "You've gained
weight, Katrina. Is that why you insist on undressing in the
dark lately?" She suddenly preferred giving him oral sex.
Why?

Katrina lips trembled. "I eat too much while I was in
Germany."

Jeremiah reached out and ripped open her blouse,
grabbed her brassiere and pulled upward, freeing her
breasts. He fondled them analytically. Even though Katrina
tried to back away, he pulled down the elastic waistband
of her pants, so he could see her lower stomach. Stretch
marks. He looked into her eyes, and then he knew.

"You made a fool out of me! And I was too stupid and
too absorbed with everything to see it until now."

"I don't know what you mean," Katrina whimpered, put-
ing her bra back in place, and holding together her torn
blouse. "It's possible for me to nurse. The baby's sucking
starts up the milk production. You're a man. You don't
know about these things."

Jeremiah didn't buy her rationalizations. "This is your
baby! You had this baby in Germany, came back here, allowed Laura to escape with my son, and put your son in
his place!"

Jeremiah watched anger replace fear on Katrina's face as
she stepped boldly toward him and said: "Our son, not my
son! Ours! You are Walter's father. Do you have any doubt
of that?"

He shook his head, trying desperately to control his anger.

"You can do a blood test, you know!"

"You helped them escape, didn't you? Plotted with m
enemies!" *She isn't even sorry,* he thought.

"For once, you're right, Jeremiah. Laura was your en
emy. She hated your guts! If you had kept her in captivity
she would have raised your son to hate you. What do yo
think she would have been telling him all the time you wer
away, leading the nation?"

Jeremiah couldn't control his fists, which clenched an
unclenched. "But I chose her! I told you not to get preg
nant!"

"Big deal! You shouldn't have been fucking me ther
You've never had any sense about women. You chos
Laura when you already had me. The mother of your chil
who will raise him to love and respect you." Katrina bega
to sob violently. "*Why do you treat me like this?* You'
always choosing someone else. Like you did with Emm;
and Laura. My father thought you were a fool! Yes, that'
why he did what he did."

Jeremiah stepped back, stunned by her words. "What d
you mean, 'did what he did'?" He watched Katrina loo
from side-to-side, while wringing her hands.

Jeremiah took a blanket off the top of a cedar chest an
began folding it. "Tell me or I'll smother this baby righ
now."

"No, please! I don't really know what happened.
shouldn't have said anything. I have a big mouth, yo
know."

Jeremiah walked closer to the crib. "Tell me everything.

Katrina confessed, "He said to me when Emma wa
killed, 'I had to do that so Jeremiah could complete hi
mission.' Something like that. It probably meant nothing.

Jeremiah dropped the blanket and a roar erupted fror
his mouth, "No, you lying bitch! No, no, no!" He rushe
Katrina, grabbed her by the throat and propelled her bacl
ward against the log wall, where her head hit with a thuc
He tightened his grip on her windpipe with all his migh
and hoisted her off the floor.

He closed his eyes and moaned as he pinned her again:
the wall. All he could think about was what Walter did
Emma. Katrina struggled violently, making a gurglin

sound, but he only tightened the grip on her throat. She clawed at his hands and her heels beat against the wall. He only relaxed his grip when he felt her body go limp.

Jeremiah let her go, and Katrina fell to the floor. Her head hit hard, causing a loud thump, which woke the baby, who began to cry. Jeremiah put his hands over his ears and retreated from the room, closing the door so he couldn't hear the baby's wailing.

He went downstairs and sat on the sofa in front of the fireplace, trying to collect his thoughts. God, it couldn't be true that Walter had Emma killed! The one woman he'd truly loved, and who loved him back. Emma was everything. Beautiful and determined, her body hard as a rock and as well-tuned as a machine. She had great wealth from her tennis success, but she never lorded that over him. They had both wanted freedom and independence. Emma had wanted to get away from her controlling parents, and coaches, and agents. She'd wanted out of the limelight of her fame. And he'd wanted to get out from under the control of Katrina's father, away from the endless plotting, and travel. They'd planned to live in Palm Beach in a guarded compound. The world could go to hell.

Jeremiah's head began to bob affirmatively. Yes, it probably was true! After Emma was killed, he had felt only numbness and a consuming rage toward the world, with all its injustices. With all its stupid, fucking people! With one stroke, Walter had turned him into an instrument of vengeance; *a swift sword forged in the heat of hatred. That bastard!*

Jeremiah went to the kitchen for a glass of water and gave a businesslike wave to the guard outside on the deck. He walked upstairs to the baby's room, listening at the door. The crying had stopped and an awful stillness prevailed.

He opened the door and stepped into the bedroom, walking on his tiptoes. He knelt beside Katrina, lifted her up, and carried her downstairs. He laid her on the sofa and then saw blood on his shirtsleeve. On the back of Katrina's head was a deep cut.

Jeremiah felt her wrist for a pulse, and put his ear to

Katrina's chest to listen for a heartbeat. But when he looked at Katrina's face, he knew. Her eyes were open, fixed, and dilated.

Jeremiah raised his hands and looked at the ceiling. "Why hast thou forsaken me, Lord? Why!" Like all mortals, his faith had waxed and waned. Once he'd even been a cynic. But his successes implied the Lord's blessing. And he'd heard the Lord's voice, no matter what any of his critics thought. Where else did a man's thoughts come from, if not the Lord of the Universe, who knew all? If it happened, it had to be foreordained and approved by the Lord. Why was he being tested?

Jeremiah climbed back up to the nursery, opened the door quietly, and went to stand beside the crib, staring at his son. His flesh and blood. Somewhere, there was another son; a son stolen away like Joseph, the son of Jacob. Would these brothers be as Jacob and Esau, competing to inherit the promise God made to Abraham and Isaac, and now him, that his descendants would found a nation for "the chosen people." When would his other son return home? Which son would fulfill the prophecy of God, leading New America throughout this new century? Was that the reason for this test? Would it reveal the true inheritor?

32

While David napped, Laura looked for
Steve, thinking they had an hour to themselves. She found
him in the den, sitting in front of the computer.

"I'm right behind you, Steve, so if you're in one of those
sexually explicit chat rooms, you'd better sign off and do
it, instead of typing about it."

When he swiveled his chair around, the grim look on his
face scared Laura. "What's wrong?" she asked.

"Katrina hasn't changed the message on her answering
machine for six weeks."

"Oh, God!" Laura knew that meant something was
wrong.

"What does the FBI say?" she asked. They made the call
from Washington each week so it couldn't be traced to
them.

"They're checking it out."

"Why did they wait six weeks to tell us something was
wrong? Do they know where the answering machine is located?"

"Yeah. It's in a Rapid City apartment occupied by two
doctors who work at the hospital."

"Do they have the apartment under surveillance?
Wouldn't Katrina have to go there to change the message?"

"Yes, and no. Katrina probably calls the machine each
week and uses an electronic code to change the greeting.
It's always been some variation of the fact that she's fine

and so are her family and her friends. I assume that includ us."

"God, do you think he's located us?"

"Not necessarily, although it could mean Jeremiah final figured out what happened." Steve stood and paced abo the room. "Shit, I knew she couldn't pull this off. It w bizarre to begin with."

"She saved our lives."

"And probably paid for it with her own."

"Maybe she just can't get to a phone. Maybe he took h away with him somewhere."

"That's what the FBI is hoping. Why they waited so lor to tell us. Anyway, our friends are going to double t security around here just in case."

That evening, they watched Peter Thompson televised speech accepting the nomination of the America Patriots Party, which held its July nominating conventic in Dallas. It was similar to the "tolerance" speech he given after the Kansas primary and repeated throughout t spring and summer.

Thompson had closed out the primary season by winni more states and more votes than his challengers, althoug the polls indicated a critical percentage of Americans we still undecided about how they would vote in Novembe These "undecideds" would make the difference, Lau knew.

"It was a great speech," Steve said.

"I wish there was some way we could help him," Lau replied.

"I can't think of any."

They continued watching the rest of the political news

President Trainor's supporters in the House of Represe tatives had brought to the floor for debate the constitution amendment providing a process whereby states could s cede from the union.

"The amendment says that states have a right of sece sion, if approved by two-thirds of the voters in a state," t newscaster said. "A seceding state, or group of states, ca petition Congress for commonwealth status, which means the United States and the new nation would cooperate on such matters as trade, foreign policy, and various interstate projects, such as highway construction."

"I still can't believe Congress is seriously considering this amendment," Laura said.

"It's that or deal with Jeremiah's bomber force," Steve replied.

"Trainor's supporters make the amendment sound like the best thing since sliced bread. To hear them tell it, when the United States is fractured into a dozen parts, it'll be a utopia. People will have more direct control of their lives because they are physically closer to their government. What bunk!"

"I love it when politicians twist the meaning of words," Steve said cynically. "One representative said the right of secession would actually enhance diversity and choice."

"How so?"

"People can migrate into new states where the majority of residents share their values."

"Right. We'll have the pro-choicers over here, the right-to-lifers other there. Blacks there, whites here. Protestants on this side of the country, Catholics on the other. Liberals in Massachusetts, conservatives in Texas."

"And every now and then, we can have a good fight between neighbors," Steve said, cynically. "It'll be a wonderful new world order."

In the middle of the night, Laura awoke with a start, drenched in sweat and screaming.

"What's wrong!" Steve asked, bouncing up to a sitting position in bed.

She couldn't reply that Jeremiah had killed Steve in her nightmare and stolen away David. "I was dancing in a huge ballroom," Laura gasped. "Wearing a royal blue strapless gown. Whirling 'round and 'round. *And he was there, watching me.*"

"He'll never hurt you again, Laura."

In the dark kitchen, Laura opened the refrigerator door

and drank directly from a plastic bottle of milk, hoping it would calm her churning stomach. Standing there in the dark, she fought off the urge for a cigarette and concentrated again on the nightmare.

Whirling on a dance floor. Those words kept bouncing around in her mind. Where did they come from? They weren't her words. Suddenly it came to her; *he'd said them.* On the deck of the cave house the day after she'd been kidnapped from the farm. Jeremiah had said those words in despair after she'd threatened to jump off the deck onto the stone floor below, smashing her body and the seed in it. *I chose you! Years ago when I first saw you whirling on a dance floor. A vision of beauty. Why won't you accept me? Steve is dead!*

"Oh, my God!" Laura whispered to herself. The reality was worse than the nightmare. Is that what he actually said? Yes! At the time, Laura hadn't grasped the significance of his statement, largely because she was consumed with the fear that Steve was dead. But Jeremiah's words had stayed in her subconscious and presented themselves in her nightmares.

When and where had Jeremiah stalked her that first time and made a twisted decision that she would be his? *It had to have been sometime when I was dancing unawares in a blue dress.* A blue dress? He hadn't said anything about a blue dress. She'd unconsciously contributed that. It meant the event was real.

Laura tried to reconstruct the dream, but it was elusive and parts dissolved, instead of becoming clearer.

Laura thought of every time she'd been on a dance floor, beginning with the many beauty pageants she'd participated in as a teenager. What about the Miss America contest when she was eighteen? No, she'd played the piano then. Hadn't she once danced on television when she'd been the "weather girl" in Kansas City? As hard as she tried, Laura couldn't pin it down.

In the morning, Laura told Steve everything and they began formulating a plan.

"I'm going to look through all my personal records," aura said. "Bank statements, credit card receipts, travel rochures, my diary."

"Maybe something will jog your memory about where nd when you purchased that blue dress."

"At the same time, I'll review my travel and appearances uring all the time I worked in television. I may have to e the travel vouchers I filed with NBC and UBC."

Steve pointed at the computer. "I'll bet our friends in /ashington can help."

Laura understood. The Pentagon was their Internet serv- e provider. General Franklin's subordinates, including arious computer experts, made certain their account was cure so they could do research and communicate with usted friends and family.

Additionally, they had access to special web sites and p secret information. If Laura needed to get into her travel cords maintained on computers at NBC and UBC, some- ne at the Pentagon could help her do it.

"Here's a suggestion for focusing the search," Steve said. Ordinarily, you'd compare your travel to Jeremiah's and e where the lines intersect."

"I doubt I can get access to his travel records," Laura id, sarcastically.

"No, but what about President Trainor?"

"What!"

"If Thompson and Franklin are right about their suspi- ions, the two of them may have been together several mes, especially in the past, before Jeremiah went public."

"I just don't understand how they could possibly be in is together. What would Trainor have to gain?"

"You remember what Maria Inglesias told you the night eremiah kidnapped you?"

"Yeah?"

"Jeremiah or someone recruited her when she was a poor enager, angry about discrimination. Think about Trainor. e won a Bronze Star for bravery in Vietnam and then ent four months in a military hospital recuperating from is wounds. That had to be a hard time for him, especially uring a very unpopular war."

"That happened to a lot of guys during that time. They didn't all sell out their country."

"Maybe no one made them a good enough offer."

Although skeptical, Laura searched through top secret Pentagon records about President Trainor. In 1978, he rode his war record to a seat in the House of Representatives. In 1982, the governor of Kentucky appointed Trainor to a Senate seat open because the incumbent had died. Died. Laura's suspicions increased. Trainor's career had been enhanced twice by the fortuitous deaths of those a rung above him on the political ladder.

Trainor won election outright to the Senate in 1984 and again six years later. When Bob Carpenter won his party's nomination for president in 1992, the former Oklahoma governor picked Trainor as his running mate, even though both men were from southern states. Conventional wisdom dictated a geographically balanced ticket. What was Trainor's main asset? All the analysts agreed: fund-raising ability.

"Maybe you're right," Laura told Steve. "Jeremiah could be Trainor's money source."

"And Trainor knows the price of reneging on his debt to Jeremiah," Steve said.

"Yeah. Carpenter's fate must have been a powerful reminder."

As Laura searched for an intersection of her travel and that of the president's, the computer cursor bounced line-by-line through newspaper and magazine stories, congressional and White House travel records, secret FBI files, and Pentagon records detailing the use of military aircraft to transport politicians to various meetings, domestic and foreign.

Laura felt her search was going nowhere fast until she discovered Trainor had traveled to the Soviet Union in the late summer of 1991, which was not unusual, given his membership at the time on the Senate Foreign Relations Committee. But Laura remembered being there, too.

An attemped coup had forced the Soviet president, Mikhail Gorbachev, an advocate of democracy and a market economy—referred to in the U.S. as *glasnost* and *perestroika*—to step down temporarily. President Bush dispatched a group of senators to Moscow to monitor the situation.

Then anchor of the NBC morning news in New York, Laura also went to Moscow, in part because she knew Gorbachev from her days as a foreign correspondent. In fact, rumors had sprouted from God-knows-what-source that Gorbachev had been infatuated with her.

As it turned out, Boris Yeltsin, then president of the Russian Republic, headed off the coup and Gorbachev was restored to power, although he and the Soviet Union survived only until Christmas of that year.

Laura and Trainor were both in Moscow from August twentieth until the end of the month. Laura racked her memory, but could only recall interviewing the chairman of the Senate Foreign Relations Committee, a gentleman from Maine. Her main professional effort, naturally, had been to interview Gorbachev, Yeltsin, and the opposition members mounting the coup. She didn't remember dancing.

Laura asked their Pentagon contact to get her copies of film footage taken during that historic event by the television networks and the CIA.

Ten days later, a package delivered to their condo contained a videocassette and an understated note signed by General Franklin and Peter Thompson: "Dear Steve and Laura: You found the needle in the haystack."

They hurriedly opened the package, put the tape in the VCR, and sat raptly in front of the television watching an NBC/CIA composite of events transpiring in Moscow in 1991.

The footage focused on a Kremlin ballroom, where Gorbachev had held a formal dinner and dance, after the coup to oust him had been temporarily defeated. Huge, elaborate chandeliers hung from high ceilings and statuary lined the walls, on which were displayed many famous oil paintings. The marble tiles on the dance floor were etched with scenes from Russian history. Chamber music drew upon eighteenth- and nineteenth-century composers. The overall impact recalled the glory of imperial Russia, Laura thought, rather than the imminent collapse of the Soviet Union.

"Look, there I am dancing with Gorbachev, and then Yeltsin!"

Steve whooped with laughter. "Yeltsin squeezed your ass!"

"He was drunk as a lord," Laura recalled, but the gown held her attention. Now she remembered the Scaasi she'd purchased at a boutique on upper Park Avenue. It was royal blue and strapless. She had whirled, on purpose, to keep Yeltsin off balance and prevent him from groping her again. *Whirling on a dance floor in a blue dress.*

As instructed by a note in the package, Steve used a remote control to slow down certain scenes. Laura opened an envelope containing still photographs blown up from the film.

As Laura viewed the slow-motion film, while sneaking looks at the photographs, she sucked in her breath, nearly forgetting to breathe, until she became light-headed. Three men standing together in the back of the room were the then Senator Trainor, Walter Dorfler—*and Jeremiah*. He was disguised, as usual, and others might not recognize him, but Laura knew the eyes; she'd recognize them anywhere.

"My God, he was stalking me long before he contacted me at UBC!" Laura said, finally, her voice cracking with fear.

"An even bigger question is what the three of them had to do with the collapse of the Soviet Union!" Steve said, shaking his head over the possibilities.

Steve and Laura redoubled their security that night, sleeping in shifts. Sitting in the dark and cradling an assault rifle in her arms, Laura could only think endlessly of the film they'd watched that evening. A film that would be indelibly impressed on her mind forever.

Like most Americans, Steve and Laura were glued to their television set a week later when the National Broadcasting Company aired an exclusive report.

First they showed film footage taken in Moscow nearly a decade ago, using their own archival film. Frozen on the television screen for the audience to see was a still frame of Trainor, Dorfler, and Jeremiah, followed by more recent photographs of all three men. Laura knew Thompson and Franklin were the likely sources of this news tip.

Equally disturbing to the audience, the suave NBC anchorman reported, would be the next photograph flashed on the screen, showing the then Sen. Richard Trainor flanked by Harvey and Boothe Wilkinson. It was taken in the senator's office in 1990, three years before Trainor became vice president.

"We caution our viewers that these photographs and this film footage, by themselves, are not proof that President Trainor has been involved in any wrong-doing," the anchorman said. "For an exclusive interview with the president, we take you now to our White House correspondent, Valerie Caldwell."

The interview took place in the Oval Office, in front of the fireplace. Laura knew Trainor had positioned himself so that wide-angle camera shots would include Charles Willson Peale's portrait of George Washington, father of the nation.

"President Trainor, several photographs and film footage have come to light recently which raise serious questions about you and your relationship with several infamous persons," Caldwell said. "What can you tell us about that?"

Trainor seemed eager to respond. "Well, Valerie, relationship is not the proper word. Let's talk first about the photograph of me with Harvey and Boothe Wilkinson. Harvey Wilkinson was convicted of assassinating Pres. Robert Carpenter, my dear friend and predecessor in this office."

"What were the circumstances of that photograph, Mr. President?"

Laura watched Trainor reflect successive expressions of surprise, helplessness, and disgust. "In 1990, I believe it was, Boothe Wilkinson scheduled an appointment with a case counselor in my Senate office, asking for help concerning a complaint he had pending at the Veterans Administration. This was a standard constituent service performed by my staff when I represented Kentucky in the U.S. Senate. Usually I had no specific knowledge of these meetings, which might number ten or more a day in my Washington office. After this particular meeting, Mr. Wilkinson and his son, Harvey, apparently were brought into my office. I took a few minutes to have my photograph taken with them, as I did whenever possible with every citizen of the great state of Kentucky who visited my Senate office."

"Had you ever met either one of them before?"

Trainor paused thoughtfully. "Not to my knowledge, Valerie, although it's possible they could have been present at one of my campaign events in Kentucky."

"But you didn't know them?" Caldwell persisted.

"Absolutely not! The American public understands that I travel all over this great nation of ours, shaking thousands of hands thrust out to me. Now, if some murderer shows up at one of these events and shakes my hand and a photographer snaps a photograph of us, does that mean I'm an accessory to the murder that guy committed?"

Laura's heart sank as she saw Caldwell, an experienced journalist, nod her agreement. As the camera zoomed in for a close-up of her, the NBC correspondent said, "Unfortunately, we can't ask the Wilkinsons about the circumstance of these photographs. Boothe Wilkinson died of cancer about two years ago, and Harvey Wilkinson was killed in prison under mysterious circumstances."

President Trainor responded immediately, "No one is sadder about their deaths than I, Valerie, because they could have immediately ended this speculation by admitting our paths had crossed only briefly, and innocently, that one time."

Watching from their living room, Steve and Laura groaned collectively. Trainor had adroitly dodged that bullet. Despite his obviously black-dyed hair, the president had an earnest, beseeching demeanor, Laura thought, as if he were desperate for people to believe him.

"What about the television footage shot in Moscow in 1991?" Caldwell continued. "That footage shows you with two individuals identified as Walter Dorfler and the terrorist

Jeremiah. Dorfler, an influential German neo-Nazi, is considered by many to be the mastermind behind the plan to
form New America."

Trainor held out his hands in a helpless gesture. "Again,
Valerie, I was in Moscow at that time as a member of the
Senate Foreign Relations Committee. I was asked to go
there by former President Bush. That's a matter of public
record. Five other U.S. Senators traveled to Moscow, along
with fourteen staff members. We attended the dinner and
ball in the Kremlin, along with Gorbachev and Yeltsin,
among other world leaders. I knew very few people there,
but I did walk around the edge of the crowd, stopping now
and then to introduce myself and chat with those people
who spoke English.

"I don't remember these two characters and I'm not sure,
personally, after reviewing the footage, whether this one
individual is Jeremiah or not, as alleged. The real question,
Valerie, is why someone carefully extracted one or two
frames from the film showing me with these notorious
criminals, if that's who they are. Why not some other senator who was there? Why just me? I don't think the American public will buy this, and I think the experts should
take a close look at this videotape to make certain it's genuine."

"Are you suggesting this film was doctored?" Caldwell
asked, incredulously. "If so, by whom?"

Trainor leaned forward and smiled. "Who would gain
most?"

*The president's political opponents, principally Peter
Thompson. That's what many viewers will conclude,* Laura
thought. In short, all this evidence was circumstantial and
didn't firmly establish Trainor's culpability.

"He did a good job of damage control," Laura said.

"Yeah, but the seeds of suspicion have been planted,"
Steve replied.

33

Their telephone rang a week later, and one of their FBI contacts told Steve to turn on their television. Another important interview was about to be broadcast, this time by the United Broadcasting Corporation.

UBC broke into its regular programming with a news bulletin concerning a medical discovery announced by officials at the Science Center of New America, the giant hospital/research complex located north of Pierre.

"For additional information, we now switch to UBC reporter Julie Burton, reporting live from the Science Center," the announcer said. "Julie, explain to our viewers what this all means."

"Certainly, Martin," Burton replied, as she stood in the lobby of Saint Jeremiah Hospital. Laura remembered the place well from the time Jeremiah had taken her there in restraints for his now-famous "public tour."

"New American scientists have just concluded a news conference here announcing they can control production of an enzyme called human telomerase," Burton said. "For many years it's been known that this enzyme is critical to normal human development during our childhood years, when the body is growing and cells are constantly dividing. But when humans reach maturity, our genetic code shuts down the production of telomerase. If production of this enzyme accidentally resumes during adulthood, it can cause runaway cell division, otherwise known as cancer."

"What exactly is the nature of the discovery?" Martin asked.

"Scientists here have mapped this complex enzyme and discovered the genetic keys for turning it off and on," Burton replied, "which can be done either by the use of new drugs, or gene therapy. This discovery has two applications, Martin. First, if cancer is discovered in an individual; then the production of telomerase can be shut down and the cancer controlled. Second, with very precise doses of drugs containing a newly discovered protein, production of telomerase can be stimulated in amounts that increase the health and functioning of aging cells. Scientists here think that, in time, they can in fact slow down the genetic aging clock and greatly extend the human life span."

"Drugs and procedures to cure cancer and extend life. That indeed would be a historic discovery, Julie," Martin said. "We'll have more on this important development following a commercial break."

"It's nothing but a public relations counteroffensive," Steve said.

"News doesn't have to be true to be news," Laura replied, a chill passing through her body.

Minutes later, the UBC news anchor returned to the airwaves. "We're going back to Julie Burton, who will interview a 'special guest.'"

The camera found the Prophet and Burton sitting in easy chairs situated in front of a blue curtain. Jeremiah wore a conservative black, pin-striped suit. Laura thought Burton's outfit also was significant. The young woman wore a waist-length jacket featuring alternating bands of black material and metallic gold, and a black skirt with a side slit extending to midthigh. Burton's blonde hair was cut shorter than usual, and she exuded excitement.

"Jeremiah, tell our audience about this wonderful discovery," Burton gushed.

"It will save millions of lives each year, and New America will freely share this and all other such discoveries with the people and scientists of the world," Jeremiah said. "We won't attempt to patent this knowledge or profit from its application. It is, rather, the human race's birthright."

"And you predicted this discovery, didn't you?" Burton asked.

Jeremiah responded by quoting from *The Book of Second Jeremiah*, chapter 6:10: " 'Scientists of New America will make several momentous discoveries, including a genetic key that will conquer disease and increase longevity.' "

"I should note that this prophecy was revealed by you in 1995," Burton said.

"Jesus, I can't believe she didn't qualify that statement," Laura said. "It's an endorsement of his claim to be a prophet of God."

The camera focused close-up on Jeremiah, who said, "We plan to send New American scientists and health care workers abroad, at our expense, to instruct and educate their colleagues around the world about this discovery and its application."

"Well, well, New America now has its version of the Peace Corps," Steve said, scornfully.

Laura watched in disgust as Burton slowly crossed her long legs, a move probably intended to hold the attention of a large portion of the male audience.

"Jeremiah, you're aware of the recent controversy implying that you know President Trainor. That possibly the two of you are in league together."

"Disgusting, unsubstantiated innuendo, Ms. Burton. It's one of the reasons many people have moved to New America. They're sick and tired of these endless political games and media sensationalism, where it's impossible to separate the lies and half-truths from reality. I wish people in old America were able to watch our television programs so they'd understand the techniques of direct participatory democracy, which totally eliminates personality factors from the political process."

"Did you meet with Richard Trainor in Moscow in 1991 when he was a U.S. senator?"

Jeremiah shook his head emphatically. "Of course not! That's not even me in that film, but rather someone made up to look like me. You know, Ms. Burton, the FBI and commercial television in old America—including your network, I'm sorry to say—have broadcast so many different photographs that allegedly are me that any discriminating viewer has to be skeptical. I ask your audience to look at me tonight. Am I the person in the film in Moscow? The person whose face you've seen on television, or in the newspaper? I don't think so."

"He's straightened his hair again," Laura said. "And he's wearing dark brown contact lenses."

"So you would agree Walter Dorfler was in Moscow?"

Laura watched Jeremiah frown as if he were uncertain or confused. "Well, again, it looks somewhat like him, based on photographs I've seen of the man. Much has been made of the fact that Walter Dorfler allegedly was my mentor, although the basis for that allegation comes from the FBI, specifically former agent Steve Wallace."

Steve looked at Laura. "Should I demand equal time?"

"Why would the FBI allege this connection?" Burton asked.

"So it will seem I'm a tool of the neo-Nazi movement," Jeremiah replied. "Isn't it convenient that Wallace killed Dorfler in a Quebec hotel before he could be questioned."

"I assume you also deny being Trent Dillman, Dorfler's nephew."

"That's another myth, Miss Burton. Trent Dillman was killed in a skiing accident in Europe in 1980. A death certificate was signed. The dead man's fingerprints exist. The FBI has them. I've offered several times to compare those prints to my own."

"I believe the FBI *denies* having Dillman's fingerprints," Burton said.

Jeremiah looked at the camera, smiled, and shook his head. "There are more unexplained deaths, Ms. Burton. Consider the bombing in Minneapolis. Who did that? The only person to survive was former Atty. Gen. Peter Thompson, now a candidate for president. Does it bother anyone that Thompson also was Steve Wallace's boss at the FBI?"

"What are you saying, Jeremiah?"

"I'm wondering if there's not a conspiracy to call into question my ministry and bring a small group of people to power in the United States."

Laura jumped up from her chair and jabbed a finger at

the television. "How in the hell can the top brass at UBC let this charade continue!"

"Like you said, Laura, truth isn't necessarily part of the definition of news."

"Who are these people you say are conspirators?" Burton asked.

"It's the same group. Peter Thompson, Steve Wallace, Laura Delaney, Gen. Buster Franklin. For example, Laura Delaney invited me to her farm in northern Virginia in 1995. The next thing I know, the place is surrounded by the FBI and the U.S. Army. I'm accused of threatening to detonate an atomic bomb. Yet the public is expected to believe that I somehow escaped this overwhelming force commanded by Peter Thompson, who's declared a hero and appointed attorney general. Delaney and Wallace wrote a book about me, which incidentally is a pack of lies, and they got rich. Meanwhile, I had to go into hiding."

"Jeremiah, when was that the last time you saw Laura Delaney? At her farm in 1995?"

"Of course not. When the people established New America, she came to live with me. People throughout the world saw us together on national television. Laura bore my child before she was kidnapped by Steve Wallace. I don't know where they are now. Except I hope your audience didn't miss the fact that Laura Delaney also was filmed in Moscow in 1991, dancing and flirting shamelessly with Boris Yeltsin. It's rumored, as you know, that Delaney had affairs with several Communist leaders. I think it's obvious she's the source of this film, which may in fact have been doctored to somehow include me."

Suddenly nauseous, Laura went into the bathroom and vomited in the sink. But she could still hear the television in the other room.

"Jeremiah, many Americans are concerned about recent actions of the New American Army in attacking U.S. military installations and seizing weapons and aircraft. How do you explain this?"

"Very simply, Ms. Burton. The Lord told me that New Americans can defend themselves by any means, and I've elayed this for all to read in the form of epistles to my people. Chapter two, verses six and twelve, deal with this pecific topic, in fact. Now, if the Lord's word to me regarding scientific advances is realized, why would anyone doubt his word on other matters?"

"That's a point worth considering," Burton said.

"The New American Army exists only for defensive purposes," Jeremiah continued. "It's only a fraction of the size of the U.S. forces. It's obviously not an army of conquest. Our army seized weapons because we had none, and we wanted to be able to defend ourselves."

"Do you think it was right for them to use chemical weapons in the battle of Kansas City?"

"Ms. Burton, I only claim to be a prophet of God, speaking his words. I am not a leader of the government or military in New America, and I don't always agree with their actions. It's understandable, however, that soldiers about to be killed or captured would resort to desperate measures in an attempt to survive. In fact, the New American Army has been devastated, and is no longer a threat to anyone. We are helpless against the military might of the United States. I must say, however, that I've personally done everything I can to prevent a nuclear holocaust."

"Please explain that statement to our audience."

"I hope everyone remembers that prior to the Minneapolis meeting, I persuaded New American troops to surrender the Lake Anna nuclear power station, so fighting there would not accidentally trigger a nuclear explosion.

"Also, I talked to many New American pilots and begged them not to be involved in any B-1 nuclear attack on the United States. Only God can order destruction of this magnitude. Unfortunately, some of these same pilots took matters into their own hands, largely to prevent annihilation of our army at Kansas City. But we have one selfless man to thank for the fact that this nuclear disaster never occurred. His name was Joe Lambert, and he was the bombardier who sabotaged the attack on Boston."

Burton's mouth hung open. "Do you have evidence of that?"

Laura had returned to her chair in front of the televisio
and she watched Jeremiah hand a videotape to Burton. "Co
incidentally, my meeting with Lambert was recorded," h
said. "And the U.S. Air Force has corroborating evidenc
They recorded conversations between the B-1 crew mem
bers, during which Lambert was accused of not havin
armed the nuclear weapons. But for Joe Lambert's com
mitment to God, and to me, the major East Coast citie
would have been destroyed."

Burton looked into the camera. "This is startling new
which I'm certain UBC will verify. Jeremiah, what do yo
believe the future holds now for you, personally, and fo
New America?"

"What happens to me is of no concern, but I hope Ne
America will not be invaded by troops of the United State
and the many innocent people living here forced to becom
subjects of a government and a society they reject. Such a
invasion would surely generate an extreme response fro
my followers.

"New Americans should be given their freedom, and
appeal to the fair-minded people of the United States t
voice their support of the constitutional amendment Cor
gress is debating. Why shouldn't all people be allowed t
freely choose their form of government and the philosoph
they choose to live? How can a democratic society den
that?"

Burton smiled at the camera. "There you have it, ladie
and gentlemen. An exclusive UBC interview with Jeremia
the Prophet."

In New York, Steve and Laura turned off th

television and sat silently for several minutes.

"I think it's called muddying the water," Steve said, fi
nally. "He made enough allegations to keep conspirac
buffs busy for decades."

"Or at least until the November elections," Laura sai
"Plus, he trashed our reputations for all time."

"Maybe. But I don't intend to let him take control of events."

"What can we do?"

Steve picked up a telephone. "I'm going to call Katrina Dorfler's mother in Germany."

34

Peter Thompson and Gen. Buster Frankli[n]
stepped out of a limousine in front of the Russell Senat[e]
Office Building across from the Capitol. They had an ap[-]
pointment with Sen. Donald Gilmore, the senate majorit[y]
leader and Republican Party candidate for president.

The oldest of the three buildings housing senators re[-]
called an earlier, more formal era, Thompson thought, a[s]
he took in the worn marble floors, elaborate woodwork, an[d]
the high ceilings against which their footsteps echoe[d.]
Everywhere he went now, a phalanx of bodyguards accom[-]
panied Thompson.

Thompson and General Franklin were immediatel[y]
shown into the senator's inner sanctum, a not-so-large pri[-]
vate office notable for a preponderance of gleaming cherr[y]
wood furniture.

"To what do I owe the honor of your presence, gentle[-]
men?" Gilmore asked, coming from behind his desk t[o]
shake hands.

Thompson decided to adopt a light note. "I heard yo[u]
were running for president and I decided to stop by an[d]
wish you well."

"I thought maybe you came to give me advice," Gilmor[e]
said. "No one's been bashful about that."

"Believe me, I understand," Thompson said, sizing u[p]
his opponent. Gilmore looked distinguished and fit, like [a]
senator should. Silver hair, a ruddy, likable face. Thompso[n]

uld imagine the senator singing in a barbershop quartet,
ich was said to be one of Gilmore's favorite pastimes.

"Let's sit over here," Gilmore said, pointing toward a
fa and two high-back, easy chairs.

"I won't beat around the bush," Thompson said, as he
: on the sofa beside General Franklin, who had dressed
a business suit for this meeting. "I'd like you to step
de and throw your support to me."

"Why would I do that, Peter? You only have about ten
ints on me, and it isn't even Labor Day."

"The political landscape is about to change drastically,"
eneral Franklin said, "and Peter is going to be the chief
neficiary."

"What do you mean?"

"My men have located the last of the B-1s. I'm going to
capture or destroy all of them. Soon."

"Under whose orders?"

Thompson smiled tightly. "You can assume it's not our
mmander-in-chief."

"You have a penchant for ignoring the Constitution, Pe-
," Gilmore said, with more good humor than reproach.

"Yes, you even referred to me in a recent speech as being
nstantly bellicose."

"Only after you called me wishy-washy."

"Senator, you know I have the utmost respect for you."

"And I you, sir."

"Jesus, is this love feast about over?" General Franklin
id, pretending to be disgusted. "I might say that many of
ur colleagues on the hill are about to amend the Consti-
ion, Senator, and do it in an entirely legal and constitu-
nal way. But legal ain't always right."

The senator bobbed his great silver head. "Nope, and a
ntal assault ain't always the best tactic, General. You
ght remember, I also was in the corps, although I never
vanced beyond the lowly rank of lieutenant."

"Yes, sir, I'm aware of your service."

Thompson sensed the tension between the two men, but
didn't consider that a bad tactic. The big, blunt-speaking
arine Corps general was playing the role of bad cop, as
y'd agreed.

"I've been a member of the senate for twenty-two years
Gilmore said. "Maybe that's conditioned me to always se
the middle ground. That's where things usually get do
up here. But these are extreme times, and I'm the first
admit my tactics didn't work as well as planned."

"You've run an honorable campaign, Donald," Thom
son said, thinking privately that it was ill-advised from t
beginning.

"I'll tell you why I stayed on the middle ground, gentl
men, and I'll be as bluntly honest as you, General Frankli
I didn't think you'd last, Peter. First, I didn't think you
even get on the ballot everywhere. And if you did, I did
think you'd be able to effectively manage a presidenti
campaign."

Thompson chuckled. "I had the same doubts, Senator.

"I thought you'd stumble and I'd inherit your positio
and supporters," Gilmore said. "You're right, Gener
Franklin, I employed the wrong tactics."

"I apologize, Senator. Peter told me to keep my b
mouth shut during this conversation, but I only know ho
to bull ahead."

Gilmore smiled. "Well, now that we've all retreated
the middle ground, let me say I share your suspicions abo
President Trainor. I believe he's Jeremiah's stooge. And
Julie Burton at UBC isn't in Jeremiah's bed, I'll sing nak
on the Capitol steps."

"Unfortunately, Senator, we only have circumstantial e
idence linking Jeremiah and Trainor. They've both done
good job of damage control. I don't think Trainor can w
the presidential election outright, but he's likely to w
enough votes to throw the election into the house."

"Where a master of logrolling would have a distinct a
vantage," Gilmore said, grinning.

Thompson nodded. "It would be a deal-maker's heave
Senator, and I'd certainly be outclassed by you."

Gilmore nodded, and stared off into the distance. "A
the nation would be polarized and paralyzed for months

"Giving Jeremiah time to come up with more surprises
General Franklin added. "I don't mind admitting I'

rned to respect that demented bastard. He's got more
ves than a belly dancer."

"Even a temporary stalemate might encourage the Chi-
se or other enemies of the United States to make a major
mmitment to Jeremiah," Thompson said.

"Even if I neutralize the B-1s, that doesn't mean he
n't get his hands on other weapons of mass destruction,"
neral Franklin said. "We've got to kill him, or capture
n."

His judgment in the first place, Thompson thought,
tching Gilmore walk to a window overlooking Consti-
ion Avenue. Thompson knew the senator was making
decision.

Gilmore turned around. "I want to do the right thing for
country more than I want to be president, gentlemen.
sides, Peter, it's become obvious to me that you are the
n of the hour. You've done more than anyone else to
ly support for the union. You deserve to be president.
erefore, I'll step aside, but don't think that will solve all
ur problems. I'm the titular head of the Republican Party
ht now, but in no way can I control all its elements."

"I understand, Senator."

"I'll ask my supporters to support you and vote for you
November. Some will, some won't. My name will still
on the ballot. It's too late to take it off. Some within
Republican Party will mount a write-in campaign, prob-
ly for someone else. It's against their religion to give
ay a presidential election to some other political party,
pecially one founded less than a year ago."

"I still believe you can deliver enough votes to put me
er the top," Thompson said.

"Let's hope so, but my support comes with a price tag,
ter."

"I'll do anything for you I can."

"If you win, I want to be appointed secretary of state.
be done in the Senate, anyway. My opponents within
party will strip me of my majority leader post. As sec-
ary of state, I can rehabilitate myself by getting tough
th our enemies abroad."

"I suggest we make a joint announcement, Donald. In

fact, I plan to pledge that half of all cabinet posts, includi
the top spots, go to the Republican Party."

"That'll help. But there's more."

"God, you are a deal maker," General Franklin said, sla
ping his thigh.

"If a vacancy occurs on the Supreme Court, I want yc
to appoint me."

Thompson hesitated only briefly. "All right."

Senator Gilmore shook Peter's hand, then General Fran
lin's. "Let's set an announcement date. How about the a
niversary of Jeremiah's strikes against our milita
installations? September second."

More than a year after Jeremiah's forces ha
overrun Ellsworth Air Force Base, only four of the hijacke
B-1 bombers remained hidden. And Gen. Buster Frankl
now knew their locations.

One had landed in a remote river valley in eastern Mo
tana, and rolled into an abandoned meat-packing plant. Th
other three were similarly hidden in facilities located
Nevada and the upper reaches of the Canadian provinc
of Manitoba and Quebec, respectively.

In the predawn hours of September 10, on an overca:
windy day, General Franklin and a company of U.S. M
rines surrounded the Montana location. He maintained co
stant telephone radio contact with commanders leadi
attacks on the other three locations.

The Montana B-1 had been discovered following a t
from a cattle rancher who had been rudely turned back fro
the location by armed men in a jeep. He'd apparent
brooded on this slight for several weeks before calling t
Pentagon. General Franklin was thankful the rancher hadn
called the White House.

Satellite photographs revealed an unusual number of me
coming and going from a farmhouse located near the fo
mer slaughterhouse. A makeshift runway was visible eve
though Jeremiah's troops kept it covered with dirt and ha

From the cover of a high ridge, General Franklin looke
through binoculars as a squad of marines crept clo

ough to the abandoned building to confirm the bomber's
esence, even though the windows were either blackened
 boarded up.

A Super Stallion transport helicopter swooped down on
e building and disgorged a platoon of heavily armed ma-
nes. The rest of the company had dug in on the ridge,
here they'd set up mortars. Fewer than two dozen New
merican soldiers guarded the B-1. General Franklin knew
e enemy's primary response to discovery and attack was
 quickly get the bomber into the air.

And they almost did. Before General Franklin's marines
uld get inside the meat-packing plant, doors exploded
tward and the B-1 rolled so fast that the mortar crews
uldn't get a bead on it. General Franklin called his "eyes
 the sky" and the B-1 was destroyed by an air-to-ground
issile fired by one of several Marine Corps F-18 fighter
ts lurking above.

The general rode in a jeep down the hill, followed by a
entagon television crew equipped to direct a live trans-
ission to a military satellite, where it could be accessed
y major U.S. television networks. *Neither Julie Burton nor
ny of the other "newsies" will be reporting*, General
ranklin thought. *I'll do this my way.*

With the charred B-1 serving as a poignant background,
e camera followed General Franklin as he approached the
uilding that had served as the B-1's hangar. Wearing full
attle dress, a cigar crammed menacingly in one side of his
outh, the red-headed, three-star general moved like a jug-
ernaut. He conferred briefly with a Marine Corps lieuten-
t and then walked down a line of prisoners, all of whom
tempted to appear stoical, although General Franklin saw
ar and uncertainty in their eyes.

"This man is from China," General Franklin said, di-
cting the cameraman's focus. "And this man is from
outh Africa. Here we have a Syrian and a Vietnamese.
his is the *real* New American Army, folks." The general
oked into the blinking red eye of the television camera.
hroughout the years, he'd cultivated a habit of speaking
s mind. "I'm Gen. Buster Franklin of the U.S. Marine
orps. For all you folks out there in television land, I'm

your entertainment for the day. A lot of you people nee
to pull your heads outta your asses and see what's goin
on in this country!"

The camera followed the general and he stomped bac
toward a helicopter, where he pivoted and said to the cam
era, "After a short hop, we'll be back on the air in an hou
or two, with another news scoop."

Aides kept General Franklin informed abou
developments elsewhere. The other three B-1s were recov
ered intact, although the New American defenders in Ne
vada damaged one bomber extensively with explosive
when it became apparent they couldn't get it off the groun

All the major television networks broadcast the breakin
news from Montana. Reporters swooped down on th
White House and Pentagon, demanding to be told how th
B-1s had been found and who had authorized this militar
action.

General Franklin already knew the Pentagon's prear
ranged response. A spokesman would decline to commer
on a military action in progress, but he'd hand out a pres
release announcing that Air Force Gen. Gordon Avery-
President Trainor's pick to be chairman of the Joint Chief
of Staff—had suddenly retired because of medical prob
lems. He'd been temporarily replaced by a U.S. Navy ad
miral, whom General Franklin counted among his closes
personal friends.

General Franklin also knew the secretary of defens
would be unavailable for comment and would refer all in
quiries about General Avery's resignation and the ongoin
military action to the White House.

During a brief stopover at Ellsworth Air Force Base
General Franklin watched a televised report of Presiden
Trainor's press secretary reading a statement to the Whit
House press corps: "President Trainor previously author
ized the Pentagon to find the hijacked B-1 bombers an
reclaim them, or destroy them. President Trainor compli
ments the Pentagon and Gen. Buster Franklin on its suc

essful completion of this mission." End of statement, no
uestions taken.

General Franklin's televised road

how came back on the air two hours later in the Black
ills south of Deadwood. Another company of his marines
vere in the process of liberating the concentration camp
rst photographed by undercover FBI agent, Ralph Duncan,
who was later killed trying to assassinate Jeremiah.

The action photographed from the general's helicopter
rovided a panoramic view of the military assault on the
amp below, after Marine Corps fighter jets blasted two
AM sites. The camp guards and a detachment of state
olice failed to put up much resistance after that, and the
narines quickly secured the area.

A camera followed General Franklin as he walked to the
amp entrance and lingered near the sturdy steel fence
opped with razor wire. Inside, several thousand men milled
bout uncertainly, talking in a babble of voices that
ounded anxious and hopeful at the same time. Their breath
vas suspended in the cold mountain air.

Only a few lucky prisoners had coats or blankets, Gen-
ral Franklin noted. Many didn't wear shirts, or were bare-
oot, even though the ground was muddy from the constant
nilling about. The stench of the tent-city concentration
amp was awful, as reflected in the screwed-up faces of his
narines.

General Franklin shoved the camp commander toward
ne main gate and harshly ordered him to unlock it. The
ates swung open and a collective shout of joy went up
rom the emaciated prisoners as they surged toward the
pening.

The cigar-chewing general stood to the side of the stam-
ede, now and then reaching out to grab a prisoner by the
rm and ask him, for the benefit of the camera, "What were
ou in here for, son?"

"Drunkenness."

"They said I stole some stuff."

"I didn't do anything, General, except try to go back t Texas."

"I wouldn't work in one of their drug labs."

One prisoner pulled himself up proudly. "I refused t serve in their army."

The general blinked several times. "God bless you, son

The marines loaded the prisoners into trucks headed fc Ellsworth Air Force Base, where the sick and injured woul be treated. Transportation would be arranged to take th worst cases to other military hospitals, General Frankli knew, or take the former New Americans to wherever was they originally called home.

He stepped up to the open end of one of the vehicles an asked those seated inside, "Were there any women in th camp?"

"Yes, sir. They keep some of them in the cabins on th hillside. They were used by the state police and nation guard."

General Franklin moved at a quickstep toward the cabin surrounded by grim-faced, armed marines. They passed th large metal building that served as the camp's motor poc and approached a dozen cabins nearly hidden from vie by surrounding pine and spruce trees.

The marines found about two-dozen women, all of who appeared dazed. Many had bruises and cuts on their fac and arms.

"Goddammit!" General Franklin said, as he turned t face the camera, his face beet red. "I'm in command of brigade of marines that has moved into this area. We wi liberate other camps such as this and investigate allegatio of mass graves located in underground caverns. We wi engage any so-called New American troops or state polic who get in our way. And we'll continue broadcastin throughout the next few days."

He pointed his finger at the camera. "I want you peopl to stay with us. Soldiers aren't supposed to have politic opinions, although that's a bunch of hogwash. I advis President Trainor to order the U.S. Army to immediatel attack what's left of the New America Army located alon the southern border of South Dakota. As a result of a goo

y's work by my marines, Jeremiah's military forces can
longer threaten the United States with nuclear destruc-
on. And if President Trainor doesn't do his job, then I
ope you, the American voters, will kick his ass out of
ffice in the November election! Peter Thompson's the best
an for that job, anyway."

General Franklin started to walk away, but then turned
ack to the camera and gave a thumbs-up sign, saying,
Semper fi."

35

Steve stood on the wooden platform that onc
had been the gallows constructed on the peninsula juttin
into Capitol Lake in Pierre, South Dakota. Here, nearly 1
months ago, Jeremiah had conducted public executions o
"criminals." Today, the ropes were gone, and the trapdoo
shut tight.

Steve looked across the lake at the building that had bee
Hoffman's sniper nest. It was a long shot, he conclude
thinking of his good and brave friend. Steve also looked a
the far fence where he'd stood, waiting his chance. He'
been lucky to survive that day, so why was he back in th
devil's den again?

Steve had accompanied Theresa Dorfler to New Americ
against the vociferous objections of Laura, who was certai
he'd be killed. As a concession to his wife, Steve wore
bulletproof vest.

But things had changed everywhere. General Frankli
and his marines were only a few hours away; indeed, i
response to a call from Steve, the general had moved a
entire regiment to the outskirts of Pierre. As a result, fe
state policemen were in evidence today.

Since the neutralization of his bomber fleet, Jeremiah ha
dropped out of sight and remained conspicuously quie
With the presidential election six weeks away, polls showe
a significant shift toward support of Peter Thompson, no
that Senator Gilmore had withdrawn from the race. Equall

gnificant, Steve knew, President Trainor's negatives were
sing, and support decreasing for the secessionist amend-
lent he'd backed.

Steve's best protection today, however, was being in the
ompany of the woman who'd been married to the man
lany considered to be the godfather of New America: the
eo-Nazi, Walter Dorfler. It wasn't likely that anyone
vould assault his widow, or anyone accompanying her.

Mrs. Dorfler had traveled from Germany to New York
1 response to Steve's telephone call telling her that Katrina
light be in trouble. It wasn't hard to convince her, since
Theresa hadn't heard from her daughter in nearly three
lonths. She first traveled alone to New America and talked
> friends and supporters. When she'd decided to make the
peech, she'd called Steve.

"This is a good place for me to speak?" Theresa asked
teve.

"Once it was a gallows," Steve explained. "Here Jere-
liah hanged several men accused of crimes, including rape
nd murder."

"Then it is an appropriate place."

They'd already visited the offices of WNAP, where
Theresa had requested airtime to address the people. The
tation manager had bent over backward in his effort to
ccommodate her, and hadn't objected when Steve sug-
ested the open-air site.

As workmen placed chairs on the platform, and the tech-
icians set up their lights and cameras, a small crowd began
> form. Steve had made certain notice of Theresa's speech
ade it onto the New America Internet site where public
nnouncements were posted. Even so, he doubted there
vould be nearly a half-million people present, as there had
een the day of the hangings. On the other hand, he and
Theresa couldn't force their attendance. He felt certain there
vould be a large television audience. Given the disappear-
nce of Jeremiah, and an atmosphere of apprehension and
ncertainty, New Americans were searching for under-
tanding and direction.

At five-feet, ten inches, Theresa Dorfer was an impres-
ive figure. She had been a member of postwar West Ger-

many's Olympic track team in 1948, placing fifth in th
world in the javelin throw. Although the seventy-year-ol
dowager now walked with a cane, she projected dignit
confidence, and purpose.

With a signal from the producer, Theresa rose from he
chair and walked to a microphone. She wore a black over
coat over a black dress, and even had on black hose. Bu
she took off the black scarf covering her silver-dyed hai
so those present and the television camera could better se
her face. Her brilliant blue eyes had a fierce and determine
set to them.

She said, in impeccable English, "I came here to find m
daughter, Katrina, and my grandson, Walter the second. H
was born in Munich on March 9th of this year and abou
two weeks later Katrina returned to Rapid City. My frien
here, Steve Wallace, saw her there on the twenty-third. Af
ter that, I heard from Katrina until the end of May. An
I've not heard from her since."

Whatever fears Steve had of being assaulted or shot i
New America had been lessened with Theresa's endorse
ment.

"Katrina may be alive, and if she is watching, I ask he
to contact me and return home with me to Germany. An
if Jeremiah is listening, I ask him to come forward an
explain to me what happened to my daughter."

She knows how to get to the point, Steve thought, glee
fully.

"I have to tell you that I fear the worst about Katrin
and even my grandson. Jeremiah knows what has happene
to them. He's the father of Katrina's child, and he is m
nephew."

The German woman shook her head, and smiled sourly
"Oh, I know what Jeremiah said on American televisio
That he doesn't know my Walter or me. That's not tru
His mother, Frieda, was Walter's sister. Jeremiah's nam
once was Trent Dillman, and he came to live with us i
Germany when he was a teenager. We took care of him
So he owes me an explanation. And if I don't get it soo
I'm going to believe the worst about Jeremiah."

Theresa shifted her weigh and it was obvious to Steve at her hip hurt.

"I want to tell you people in New America a little bit out myself," Theresa continued. "I was fifteen when orld War II ended, and Germany was defeated and nearly stroyed. My father and two of his brothers were officers the German army, and all three of them were killed in ssia. But we had been a wealthy family before the war, d we were better off than most. Even so, I asked my other once, 'what was this war all about?'

"And she told me about national socialism, the Nazis. In e beginning it was the National Socialist German Workers rty. My mother said the party was dedicated to restoring rmany's pride in its culture and rebuilding a war-attered economy. It was about taking care of everyone, t just the rich. It was a movement for the common peo-e. The working people. My mother thought it was a good, ristian movement. In the beginning.

"Now, I'm not a politician, and neither was my mother. e were just sisters and wives and mothers. But even ugh I'm a woman, I'm smart enough to know when a od thing turns bad and ugly. And believe me, when I s a girl, I saw and experienced many bad things. You , Hitler took a good movement and turned it into an evil ng. And in the end, it was the German people who paid price, because they failed to stand up soon enough and eak the truth."

Steve eyed the WNAP producer and members of the mera crew, fearful they'd shut down their equipment. But ile they looked troubled and ill at ease, they continued ming.

"I'm from the old school," Theresa said. "A wife stands hind her husband. For better, for worse. My husband, alter, was a strong man. A talented man. Committed. He d strong beliefs. Some of them I shared, some of them I dn't. That should be everyone's right, even a wife's. eryone has to make up their own mind about what's right d what's wrong."

She sighed, indicating her speech had come to its end.

"I'm going to Rapid City today, and I'll stay there for a

while," Theresa said. "The American army has found ma
bodies in caves, and I have Katrina's dental records w
me. General Franklin has promised me his help. And
know the American army, which has protected our freedo
in Germany for half a century now. They are good me
and I trust them.

"Most people in the world are good, you know. I'm su
that's true of most of you in New America. You don't ne
all this violence and fighting and those awful weapons
destruction. No one wins in that kind of war. What y
sow, you will reap. Read the real Bible. No one should
afraid to go where they want or say what they please.
you have an idea about a better way to live, then that id
is enough. If it is good, it will prevail. If it isn't, the bigg
army in the world won't save it. I learned that a long ti
ago. You should pay attention to me."

Those were her last words. Steve helped the widow De
fler to a black limousine and rode with her toward Raj
City. He had dental records with him, too; dental reco
the CIA and FBI had given him. They could help ident
the remains of Hans Dietrich Hoffman and Ralph Dunc
American heroes, in Steve's mind.

On the night of November 7, 2000, Peter Thom
son attended a victory celebration at the Willard Hotel
downtown Washington, D.C. He'd been elected preside
of the United States. He thought it appropriate that the c
ebration be held in the hotel where Abraham Lincoln fi
stayed when he came to the federal capital, having pledg
to preserve the Union at all costs.

Thompson stood in the middle of the lobby, an examp
of Beaux Arts elegance. As usual, he was surrounded by
shouting, shoving horde of reporters and cameramen, aid
and bodyguards. He pulled his tuxedo jacket into place a
stepped up to a podium bearing the seal of the President
the United States. He didn't mind jumping the gun a bi

"There are many people to thank," he began, "and fo
most among them are Steve Wallace and Laura Delane
Wallace, who unfortunately can't be here tonight. T

tion owes them a debt of gratitude. As it does to Gen.
ister Franklin, a true American patriot." Thompson
inted and smiled at the general, who he thought looked
bit like a modern-day emperor in his evening dress uni-
rm.

"Without the support of Sen. Donald Gilmore, I wouldn't
standing here this evening," Thompson said. "Senator
ilmore's selfless sacrifice has redefined the word 'politi-
an,' and made it in his case a title of respect and honor."

Thompson read from a prepared statement. "Upon taking
e oath of office in January as president of the United
ates, I will declare martial law to exist in several states
the upper Midwest. In my capacity as commander-in-
ief, I will authorize military forces to disarm the rebel
my and arrest all who bore arms against the United States
America. They will be tried for treason.

"Furthermore, I will order the Justice Department to find
d arrest Jeremiah aka Trent Dillman on charges of ter-
rism, murder, treason, kidnapping, and rape. The Justice
epartment will also investigate any and all civil rights
olations alleged to have occurred within the area once
own as New America. A special unit will be established
process complaints.

"Any foreign nation found to have encouraged and aided
med insurrection on American soil will be subject to se-
re consequences."

Thompson hurriedly read the rest of his prepared re-
arks, but he'd already said everything that was important.
e'd won, narrowly, garnering 47 percent of the popular
te, although winning enough electoral votes to be elected
itright.

After he finished speaking, Thompson moved through
e crowd, grasping many outstretched hands and person-
ly thanking key supporters. Forty-five minutes later, he
treated to a private dining table in the Willard Room,
eling physically and mentally exhausted. He felt unchar-
cteristically disheveled and ill at ease. His sister and
other were there to compensate for his bachelorhood,
ong with other family members and close friends. Thomp-
n sat beside General Franklin.

"I liked your speech," General Franklin said. "It was the point."

"Maybe you'll come to the White House and wri speeches for me, Buster," Thompson said, in jest. In trut he couldn't imagine Buster at home anywhere, except tl battlefield, wearing a muddy camouflage uniform, chewir a cigar, and barking orders.

"Maybe. First, I got unfinished business to take care in South Dakota."

"I understand the rebel army has begun to disband."

"Yep. After I had a talk with the senior commander they all decided to go home. Now that was a real shc speech, Peter. The effective sentence was, 'If any of yc bastards are here sixty days from now, I'll hunt you dov and kill you.' "

Thompson laughed softly, having no doubt that eve hardened mercenaries probably had quaked in front of tl no-nonsense Marine Corps general. "Any sightings of Je emiah?"

"Nope. I doubt he's even in the country. On a positi\ note, there's a peaceful revolution going on internally what we once called New America. I think Theresa Do fler's speech helped. Many moderates have emerged in se\ eral communities. Anathoth, for example, north of Pierr They had a community assembly in which every reside pledged allegiance to the United States and promised observe our laws and customs."

But they're not going home, Thompson thought. (rather, their homes are in North and South Dakota. F hoped they'd keep their promise of being good neighbo and citizens.

"It's hard to believe that Trainor still won nearly a qua ter of the popular vote," Thompson said, smiling and wa\ ing across the room at one of his chief fundraisers.

"You can always see the dark side, can't you, Pete Hell, why not. Trainor became a super patriot after Jer miah's bombers were neutralized. It ain't surprising to n that a quarter of the population still thinks the right of sta secession is a wonderful idea. One in four people probab believe Martians are living among us or that the earth is flat. It's the price of democracy."

"I suppose so," Thompson replied. In his heart, he worried that even Jeremiah's failed efforts had torn the social fabric, and that the damage would be there forever.

"Don't worry about Trainor," Franklin said. "I can promise you he'll be the lamest of all lame ducks until you take that oath of office. Otherwise, he might take sick and die."

"Please don't tell me any more, Buster."

"Where's that damn waiter," Franklin asked, holding up his empty glass.

"What can I get you, General?" a waiter asked.

"Jack Daniel's on the rocks."

"Mr. President?"

"Nothing, thank you." Thompson whispered to Franklin. "I can't be seen drinking in public."

"Then being president ain't everything it's cracked up to be, Peter."

"I'll be right back with your drink, General," the waiter said.

36

Following the presidential election in the United States, the following verse was posted on the New America Internet home page:

THE LAMENTATIONS OF
JEREMIAH THE SECOND

1 How forlorn is the Nation that flourished
  amid the tall grasses, full of purpose and hope.
Now, she is as lonely and barren as a recent Widow
  who long ago bid her Children farewell,
and sits, listening to the cold wind howl the time
  and hour of her Death.

2 If you ask how such a thing could occur, look
  to the Vultures and Jackals that circle, for in
their countenance you will recognize many enemies of
  New America, waiting to indulge their Evil
appetites and feed on the Riches they themselves
  could not cultivate nor sustain.

3 The greatest of these Evil creatures is named
  Thompson, known in ancient times as
Nebuchadnezzar, used by God as an instrument to
  express His Displeasure with the Chosen People.

4 But what good is a Prophet who is accorded no Honor
  in his own land! Who spake the LORD's Word,
which was ridiculed, disputed, and debated, not only by
  the Vultures, but by many who chose freely
to take part in this greatest of all God's experiments.

5 Why O LORD choose Me to be thy Messenger, knowing
  I would be abused by so many; that the Two closest
to me would betray me, as Thomas did Christ, stealing my
  trust and stealing the Child who would carry on Thy
Work in the future! What benefits your Plan, O LORD, to
  deny Thy own Words!

6 And the LORD spake to me, chiding me for my Pride;
  reminding me that I, too, am but an Instrument
with a role to play in a Grand Scheme far beyond my
  mortal comprehension. He said to me: Steel is forged
in the fire of Defeat and Purification, so that which
  was strong becomes stronger, and indestructible.

7 The Phoenix that arises from the ashes will be strong
  and pure and will not be smitten in Battle;

nor be as Merciful as before. A lesson has been learned:

He who has a Sword and lays it down because his

adversary has none, is a fool and will suffer

a fool's reward. If ye would slay the Beast, ye

must understand its nature, which knows not Compromise.

8 Remember what I said about Free Will in the book

called Second Jeremiah, sayeth the LORD. Those

who professed Belief but had it not will soon be gone,

slinking away into the night, to join their kind.

Those in the Dakotas know especially that the Wheat

must be separated from the Chaff before it can be

made into Leavened Bread to nourish the Nation.

9 A Remnant will remain, sayeth the LORD, even though

the Nation be scattered to the ends of the earth.

A Nation is an Idea, not a boundary. That which binds New

Americans cannot be broken by time and distance.

It is the Word and it will endure all; out of this Remnant,

a rich tapestry will be woven, I promise you.

10 Those who follow me are Fishers of Men, sayeth the Lord.

Out of the clear waters is pulled the Trout, succulent and

tasty, to adorn the Master's table. But if a greedy household

servant substitutes a Carp for the Trout, the bottom-feeder

will be found unpalatable, full of slime and bones. The Master must fish for Himself, using the right Lure to hook the Trout and hand back the Carp to the Deceiver.

11 New America and the United States are as vessels in God's hand, the former filled with the Wine of Redemption and Promise, the latter with the juice of a bitter, poisonous fruit. Those who choose to drink of the Poison will go mad and die screaming.

12 Ye ask, Jeremiah, why have I forsaken you? Ye of little Faith should read the Prophecy, for not all have come true. When they do, as they must, New America will Rise again and Ye shall bask in the light of My eternal embrace and fulfill the Destiny of Man.

37

In the spring of 2001 David celebrated his firs
birthday and had a rudimentary vocabulary that revolvec
around three words: Mommy, Daddy, and gun.

As soon as David seemed able to comprehend, Laura
warned him about all the guns available in the penthouse
Bad guns, bad guns! She knew they couldn't lock up al
the weapons or fit them with trigger guards, because tha
would not necessarily increase their safety and might actually jeopardize it in the event they needed a weapon—
now!

She and Steve knew Jeremiah could "pop above ground'
at any moment and threaten their safety and lives, as he'c
done so many times in the past. They didn't believe for a
moment he would repent and/or change careers, especially
since God had consoled him, as indicated in the terrorist's
lament.

Although murder was not charged in the deaths of Gen.
Buster Franklin and former President Richard Trainor
Laura knew Jeremiah had somehow killed them. Last fall
General Franklin had contracted a virulent staphylococca
infection that proved resistant to all antibiotics. Shortly after leaving office, Trainor died of carbon monoxide poi-
soning while sitting in a running car parked in a closec
garage. His death was officially ruled a suicide, which
many people thought understandable for one who'd flown
so high and crashed so badly.

Laura knew these deaths were, respectively, a revenge murder and a murder designed to bury the evidence of a conspiracy.

Partly in response to what had happened to General Franklin and former President Trainor, she and Steve reversed an earlier decision and last December began the first of several plastic surgeries designed to significantly alter their facial appearances. When Laura stood in front of a mirror, it increasingly seemed the reflection of someone else.

They also decided to accept President Thompson's offer of a protection detail, financed with private funds made available by the American Patriots. The new guards were drawn from the ranks of former FBI agents and military personnel, and had been subjected to exhaustive background investigations. They were told they were protecting a foreign diplomat and his family, who had been granted political asylum.

"He changes almost every day," Laura said, as she and Steve stood in the doorway of David's bedroom and watched him play with his toys.

"He's a good boy," Steve said.

"I worry about him being so isolated," Laura fretted.

Steve put his arms around Laura, drawing her closer to him. "We could try to make a brother or sister for him."

Laura was stunned. "Are you serious?"

"Sure. The trying alone would be worth the effort."

She laughed nervously. "I just thought that time had passed us by." They were both forty.

"What else have we got to do with our lives, Laura. If we're forever isolated, we might at least have a large-enough family to play baseball."

"That would involve a lot of trying," she teased. "By the time the team was assembled, you'd be too old to swing a bat."

"Never. Besides, what else have we got to do?"

"Nothing, really," Laura conceded. "Okay, I'll give up my birth control pills."

Steve rubbed his hands together. "All right, that's settled. We'll start tonight. Right now, I've got to get to work." He looked at his watch. "Is Melanie coming over?"

"Yes," Laura said. "She should be arriving any time now."

Laura had met Melanie Thurston about three months ago, when they'd bumped into each other at Bloomingdale's. Melanie had a son, Thomas, who was roughly the same age as David. Laura's initial wariness gave way to a desperate need for human companionship, especially with another mother of a toddler. They had so much to talk about.

Later, she'd talked to Steve about the issue of friends. They might be able to do without them, but what about David? Would he become a "boy in a bubble," who grew up lacking social skills? Or did they need to find a way for him to have friends and enjoy a normal life outside the penthouse?

Steve had the Thurstons investigated thoroughly. Although they were by no means an average family, there was not even a hint they might be Jeremiah sympathizers. Randall, Melanie's husband, was employed by a well-known brokerage firm located in the Wall Street area where he was assistant manager of a mutual investment fund. They were both natives of Maine, children of conservative parents, and had attended Ivy League schools—he at Harvard and she at Radcliffe. For the past five years they had lived at a tony address on the upper east side, not far from Steve and Laura's building. Records indicated Thomas was born at Mt. Sinai hospital.

After passing the security investigation, which had taken place unbeknownst to the Thurstons, Melanie began visiting occasionally at Steve and Laura's condominium. To the Thurstons, they were Harry and Erin McCollum—she a housewife, he the head of a consulting firm specializing in security matters. They always begged off on invitations to attend dinner parties at the Thurstons or accompany them to Broadway plays. Even with the plastic surgery, they were still afraid of being identified, especially at public events where photographers and journalists might be present.

＊   ＊   ＊

After Steve left for work, Laura waited patiently for him to telephone and tell her he'd arrived safely at his office, a three-man shop located in the IBM Building, a black, steel-and-glass tower only a few blocks away at fifty-seventh and Madison.

Steve, his secretary and assistant, Phyllis, and another retired FBI agent, Garvin Guckgas, constituted a clearing-house for worldwide information pertaining to Jeremiah, his supporters, and other fascist and terrorist organizations. Laura knew funding for the operation came mainly from the American Patriots. Steve had told her their computer base of information already was the best in the world, even better than the federal government's, if for no other reason than they paid—sometimes handsomely—for important tips and information. They called themselves the Gemini Group, after the zodiac sign signifying ambition, alertness, and intelligence.

Steve's work was self-serving in part, since any scrap of intelligence he and the organization unearthed might help save their lives. Most knowledgeable analysts believed Jeremiah would eventually mount a new campaign. The only questions were when, where, and how? So far, Steve's work hadn't yielded any significant clues.

As soon as the lobby security guard called to announce Melanie's arrival downstairs, Laura hid and locked away the various weapons, which was a breach of her and Steve's security plan, but what else could she do? Besides, Laura increasingly viewed Melanie as a friend. There hadn't even been a hint that Melanie suspected her true identity.

Laura opened the penthouse door to admit Melanie and Thomas. The one-year-old protested his confinement in the stroller, indicating he wanted to play with David, who appeared once he heard the doorbell.

"You're twins today!" Laura said, kneeling in front of Thomas. "You and David have on the same outfit."

"Aren't they darling," Melanie said, referring to the spring "baseball" outfits she and Laura had purchased on a previous shopping trip. They consisted of a red, short-

sleeved top, buttoning down the front, with a breast patc
that read: PLAY BALL! The matching off-white pants had
thin, red vertical stripe.

"People won't be able to tell you apart," Laura said, a
she and Melanie followed the two boys to David's bed
room. Both had been walking only a few months, and thei
steps were herky-jerky.

Laura and Melanie watched protectively from the door
way as the boys began to play. Thomas was not as strong
outgoing or self-confident as David, which secretly please
Laura, although she harbored no ill-feeling toward Thomas
She just wanted David to be better than all other boys a
everything.

"They'll be okay for a minute," Laura said. "Let's go t
the kitchen and get a cup of coffee."

"What a day!" Melanie said. "It's midmorning and I'r
pooped!"

"They take it out of you, that's for certain," Laura said
thinking how great it would be to take care of two or mor
of "them." After Steve went back to work, Laura ha
briefly considered becoming an independent televisio
news show producer, but finally admitted to herself that sh
no longer had the necessary drive and enthusiasm. Beside:
working meant exposing herself, and she wasn't certain sh
could count on her colleagues and friends in the televisio
business to protect her identity.

"Let's get outside today," Melanie suggested suddenly
"Take the strollers and walk to Macy's. They're havin
their spring flower show this week. We can be there befor
noon. Look around, shop, have lunch."

"Great idea," Laura agreed.

While Melanie walked back to David's room, Laur
called a special number, where no amenities were neces
sary. She simply announced her plans. She'd be leaving th
penthouse shortly and walking to Macy's. She knew he
call would result in two armed security men shadowin
them, one in front and one behind, staying in contact wit
each other and command central in a nearby building vi
cellular phones. Other guards would be inside a car tailin
them.

"Here's a present for you guys," Melanie said, taking from her stroller two New York Yankees' caps.

Laura watched as David and Thomas tried on the caps, although she doubted they'd keep them on for long.

It was about fifty blocks to Macy's, which actually was only about two miles from the penthouse. On a lovely warm day in May, Laura and Melanie pushed their strollers side-by-side, with the tops down, so the boys could look at each other and jabber and play some mysterious game with their hands. At a modest pace, it would take them about an hour, Laura calculated, depending on the density of human beings on the sidewalks.

She had shopped carefully for David's stroller, selecting one with rubber wheels, instead of plastic ones, so it would withstand the punishment of long walks on city streets. She'd considered and rejected pneumatic tires, which rolled with less friction, but presented the possibility of flats. Her stroller had a canopy and the seat back could be reclined to a horizontal position, should David want to nap, which he did sometimes on their walks. Also, it had a rear compartment for storing diapers, snacks, an umbrella—and, her .38 Colt and an 18-in., 9-mm Uzi, with a 40-round-capacity magazine.

They walked down Madison Avenue, by the expensive boutiques selling mainly clothing, shoes, furs, jewelry, and antiques. Laura's practiced eye noted the many security guards inside these retail shops—"greeters" who opened the door for customers, while appraising their potential as shoplifters or deadbeats.

Near the south end of Central Park, they turned west a block to get onto Fifth Avenue. Laura loved walking on the Avenue, although it was a security nightmare. She liked the waves of humanity that washed around her and David, especially during the lunch hour, when the noise became a din of voices, shuffling feet, motors, sirens, and horns—incessant car horns of differing tone and pitch. Laura could even tell how irritated drivers were by the length of the horn blast. There were no end of shopping opportunities

and diversions among the buildings and retail establish
ments adorned with readily recognizable trademark names
She and David happily spent entire days here. It symbolize
the melting pot America she loved and had come to cherish
after her incarceration in New America.

They walked by Saint Patrick's Cathedral, its gothi
spires and mission so contrasting to nearby Saks Fifth Av
enue or Rockefeller Center across the street. A beggar nea
the front of the church alternately sang gospel songs and
cursed passers-by who didn't drop coins into his cup.

As they waited for a traffic signal, Melanie said, "Hov
about something to drink." She handed David and Thoma
each a small plastic bottle of apple juice.

At the New York Public Library, they detoured throug
Bryant Park, an oasis of trees and grass in the concret
jungle. Laura saw a diverse group of people whiling awa
time in the park—businessmen in suits on their way to
"power lunch," bicycle messengers taking a break, old mer
sitting on park benches, young lovers reclining on blankets
street musicians and jugglers performing for money, and
drug dealers whispering to possible customers.

A few more blocks south on Sixth Avenue and they wer
opposite the Broadway entrance to Macy's. In the east sec
tion of the sprawling department store, ledges behind and
above the cosmetics and jewelry counters held potted plant
and flowers of all sizes and varieties.

They walked down the aisles, sampling perfumes and
admiring the flowers. Both boys yawned and seemed
sleepy, which was unusual for David, Laura thought. He
ordinarily didn't nap until midafternoon. But the walk and
fresh air must have caught up with him, she concluded
Laura reclined the stroller seat so David could sleep mor
comfortably. She put up the canopy to block out some o
the store noise. Melanie performed the same stroller func
tions for Thomas, as they talked about going to "the Cel
lar," which had rest rooms and a grill, where they could
eat lunch.

Suddenly, a voice behind them boomed, "You, I know
you!"

Laura jerked around to see an elderly, heavyset man

ointing a stubby finger at her. "You're the bitch, Laura
Delaney!"

Laura immediately felt in her jacket pocket for the small-
aliber Derringer, which could be easily concealed in the
alm on her hand. Afraid and shaking, but determined, she
ositioned herself between the man and David's stroller.
he'd rehearsed mentally many times for this moment.

One of Laura's bodyguards got in the man's face and
egan shoving him down an aisle. The man continued to
ell loudly about "the bitch!" and "the betrayal!" and "the
oming apocalypse!"

Laura watched carefully as several store security guards
naterialized, at which time one of Laura's guards showed
is identification. She didn't see the other guard. Maybe he
elt it best to remain an anonymous member of the crowd,
n case there was a second attacker.

Laura glanced into the stroller at David. The commotion
mazingly hadn't awakened him. Laura redirected her at-
ention to the continuing altercation with the man, who
eemed to be quieting down. It occurred to her that now
vas the time to make a quick exit.

It was then Laura became aware that Melanie had dis-
ppeared! Laura grasped the handle of David's stroller and
egan pushing it away from the confrontation. Melanie ob-
iously had been frightened away. Laura wondered how she
ould explain things later. How shocked had Melanie been
o learn Laura's true identity? Was that why she fled? Laura
eared losing a friend, although she feared even worse
aving been identified. Would she have to stay inside now?
Would they have to move?

Laura considered going out the Thirty-Fourth Street exit,
ut there were steps to negotiate there, so she pushed the
troller toward the Broadway exit. She looked over her
houlder and couldn't see the man or her bodyguards any-
nore. Still, she wanted to get far away, fast.

Laura took a cellular phone from her pocket, juggling it
nd the Derringer while still pushing the stroller. She
ressed the speed dial button for Steve's office and told
'hyllis it was an emergency. When Steve got on the line,
he told him to come get her immediately.

Out on the noisy street under the entrance awning, Lau immediately regretted her decision. She should have staye in the store. Had her bodyguards seen her leave? Whe were they? What if others heard the man's accusation Some other ex–New American who might want to do h harm. She made a decision to get David out of the strolle It didn't make any sense, of course, to tie up her hands, abandon the other weapons, but she wanted her baby clo to her, and she wanted to be able to run, if necessary.

She squatted down behind the stroller to take the Co revolver out of the back and put it in one coat pocket. had more firepower than the Derringer. She lifted Dav out of the stroller. He began to cry and Laura pressed h face against his, kissing her son on the cheek. He crie meekly and asked for his mommy in a tiny voice. Bewi dered, Laura held the child at arm's length to look at t face partly hidden by the Yankees' cap. It was the wron voice! It was the wrong face! It was Thomas!

Stunned and panicked, Laura tried to figure out what h: happened? In the confusion had Melanie taken the wron stroller? Laura looked. No, it was David's stroller! Lau backed against the building and looked around wildly the people on the street, convinced they all meant her han She took the revolver from her pocket, so they could s it.

Steve leapt from the car and found Laura sittir on the sidewalk near a concrete pillar, her knees drawn to her chest, her forearms on her knees, her forehead restir on her arms. The child sat between her legs, looki drugged, even stupefied, and crying in a pitiful voice. Stev raised up Laura's head and looked closely at her face, mask of fear and detachment. He'd seen people in shoc before and recognized the symptoms.

"I found this lying on the sidewalk beside her," one the bodyguards said, briefly showing the Colt. Steve looke around and saw the other bodyguard talking to store se curity personnel and a policeman. He wanted to get awa

efore the questioning began, before Laura was detained on
weapons charge.

He picked Laura up and put her in the car, while the
uard carried Thomas. Steve told the driver to go to Lenox
Iill Hospital, although Bellevue was only a few blocks
way on the East River. Steve thought it best that Laura be
ı a private hospital near their home.

Steve hugged Laura and rubbed her hands, which were
:e cold. The driver aggressively wheeled through the
treets, taking the Park Avenue tunnel to Forty-sixth Street,
s Steve dialed several telephone numbers. Soon they
icked up an FBI escort and within twenty minutes they
vere at the hospital, located at Park Avenue and Seventy-
ixth Street.

They diagnosed Laura in the emergency
ɔom as suffering from severe shock trauma. After she was
edated and taken to a private room, Steve felt helpless as
e stared at Laura lying in bed, still as death. He couldn't
elp her anymore and there were other important things to
e done.

Steve walked to a waiting room, where the two body-
uards sat with the boy. A doctor had concluded that Tho-
ıas had been given a sedative. It had worn off, although
ıe boy was still understandably upset and crying.

The cops were long gone, after turning over the case to
ɔcal FBI agents, who'd accompanied them to the hospital.

"Bring him," Steve said, referring to Thomas.

They left the hospital and got into a waiting car. Steve
rdered the driver to the Thurston's address. On the way,
e questioned the guards again.

"I didn't see anyone switch the kids," one said.

"I was trying to get the guy isolated," said the other. "I
idn't see Laura or the Thurston woman leave the store."

At the Thurston's building, Steve showed the doorman
is FBI identification and asked him to find a supervisor.

"Sure, I can let you in that apartment," the supervisor
aid, "but the Thurstons moved out a week ago. Say, isn't
ıat their boy?"

The empty apartment had an ominous quality. Steve s.
Thomas down and the small boy wandered unsteadily abo
his former home, finally lurching into his bedroom, whic
was bereft of furniture, his toys, and clothes. He began ▪
sob loudly, first sitting and then lying on the floor, whe
he sucked his thumb and called plaintively for his mothe

Steve knelt beside the boy and stared at him, thinking c
all the things that undoubtedly had happened to him ov
the past year. Steve picked up Thomas, who was approx
mately David's size, although thinner. Thomas had da
hair, compared to David's curly blond hair.

Thomas clung tightly to Steve, who rubbed his back an
whispered gently to him. The boy's sobs dissolved into
series of long sighs. "There, there, Thomas. I know ho
you feel. Let's go home. I have a place for you to stay."
room that belongs to your stepbrother.

About midnight, Steve again left Laura'
bedside and walked on deserted streets toward the pen
house, where Thomas slept under the watchful eye of ne
guards. Steve no longer trusted the old ones. Although th
limo rolled slowly on the street beside him, Steve no long
feared being identified or attacked. At least not by Jere
miah, who surely wanted them to live; live a nightmare tha
especially for Laura, would be worse than dying.

Get caught reading.

Jake Lloyd reading ENDER'S GAME.

A Message from the
Association of American Publishers